?

"Please. . . . . trace of appeal in his tone; his was a simple statement. And yet Teddie felt inextricably drawn to him.

"Stay here with me, Teddie," he said, lazy, half-hooded eyes piercing her. "Drink brandy with me until the sun comes up over the rise."

"Will you tell me your secrets, Winchester?"

"I might be tempted." The hushed intimacy of his voice flowed through her like warm brandy. Part of her ached to stay with him, to smooth her hands over him, to share the dawn with him, to probe the depths of his secrets, of all the mystery. "You want to run from me. What are you afraid of?"

Like a beast of the night he stalked toward her, forcing her to retreat as he advanced, until the wall pressed against her back and he loomed not a handbreadth away from her.

Teddie struggled for air. "I do not fear you," she whispered, certain that if he moved any nearer she would crumple to the floor. But he did, curving one hand around her neck and the other around her waist.

"Now," he rumbled, drawing her close against him. "Now do you fear me?"

"No," she breathed, unable to tear her eyes from his. "Even now I don't fear you"

"You should."

EMBRACE
the NIGHT

Kit Garland

A DELL BOOK

Published by
Dell Publishing
a division of
Bantam Doubleday Dell Publishing Group, Inc.
1540 Broadway
New York, New York 10036

ISBN: 0-440-22101-3

Printed in the United States of America

Published simultaneously in Canada

October 1996

10 9 8 7 6 5 4 3 2 1

RAD

Mom—
For Kiri and Puccini, Phantom and the
St. Regis, old movies and Jane Austen,
red wine, white linen, rooms with views,
and hydrangeas in full bloom . . .
for all the passions that we share,
this one's for you.

Prologue

It was a perfect night for deserting.

The ship's bell tolled midnight, cleaving through the stillness that blanketed the *Rattlesnake*'s empty decks. Her cannon rested silent. Four furled masts poked into inky, moonless skies. No breeze stirred the air. No other sound rent the night save for the creaking of deck planking as the British man-of-war rode at anchor, waves lapping against her belly, not more than a quarter mile's swim from the shores of Tidewater, Virginia.

The lone watch stood his post, his eyes intent on the horizon for any sign of enemy sail or the outline of a privateer's frigate daring to sneak past them into the open waters of the Atlantic. His watch had been without incident. All had been quiet since twilight had faded.

At the shadowed stern of the ship, a thick hemp rope slipped over the bulwarks, its knotted end whispering a splash as it met with the water. Three shadows shimmied along the length of rope, one close behind the other. Each clung to the hemp as if to a lifeline as they slipped into the water.

"I can do it, Teddie," came Will's hoarse rasp. His baritone tremored with the sudden chill of the water and something more—fear—but Teddie wouldn't allow herself to consider it. They'd come too far, across an entire ocean, and had risked far too much to allow panic to get the better of them at this juncture.

"Of course you can," Teddie whispered, reaching for Will's hand. How many times over the last three months since the night they'd hatched their scheme—the night their father succumbed to pneumonia in the tiny back room of his bookshop—had Teddie gripped her older brother's hand as she did now?

She'd known their success lay not so much in her convincing disguise as a British seaman but in Will's ability to trust her with their fate. Even Will understood that nothing could be worse than hauling coal for a mere pittance for the rest of his life and allowing both him and Teddie to starve because of their country's tyranny. But pride, even Will's stalwart sort, could wane under harsh wartime conditions. Teddie had conquered her own misgivings during the voyage. Will would too. She wouldn't allow otherwise.

Even in the darkness she could feel the intensity of his stare, as vivid purple-blue as her own, as full of fire and life as their father's had once been. But Will's was the stare of a ten-year-old child seeking reassurance just once more.

A ten-year-old child trapped in the behemoth body of a twenty-two-year-old man. A frightened man.

She could feel it in his grip on her fingers. If only this fear would manifest itself in the stamina necessary to carry his sturdy frame through the dark and rolling sea.

Desertion carried a heinous punishment in times of war. Even Will understood that. The *Rattlesnake*'s commander, Rear Admiral Sir Jeremiah Cockburn, had served brilliantly alongside Nelson at Trafalgar and was well known as a military genius. Since they'd set out for America, however, he'd garnered a reputation as the most pernicious and war-struck of the commanders in His Majesty's fleet, a reputation he seemed determined to exploit. Not a week past, after broadsiding an American frigate out of Boston into striking her colors, Cockburn had seized four of the frigate's crew and hung them from the *Rattlesnake*'s yardarm for purported desertion from the British fleet. Later, rumor spread among the *Rattlesnake*'s crew that Cockburn had concocted the allegations simply out of boredom with blockade duty and his paranoia that his own crew needed to be reminded from time to time of their tenuous wartime circumstances, lest they find themselves considering mutiny.

Teddie could still hear the young American sailors' anguished cries of innocence. They'd defended their liberty until the last breaths had been wrung from their necks and the twitches had left their limp bodies. But it had been the satisfied thrust of Cockburn's jaw and the gleam in his eyes as he watched the macabre executions that had ignited the hatred fueling Teddie's determination to see her plan to fruition. The terror roused by the stench of imminent death didn't compare to the bravery inspired by the promise of freedom from such tyranny.

Teddie hadn't allowed herself the luxury of second guesses during the voyage from London. Now was certainly not the time to weaken. Her palms had grown bloodied then callused from hauling rope; her arms were as sun-bronzed and sinewed as those of a young boy, and just as strong. A quarter mile's swim strong, she was certain. Her legs twice as capable.

If only she could believe the same of their companion, Aaron. He was a slight boy of sixteen, spurned by the rest of the crew for his lack of strength and manliness. But he'd found a gentle friend and protector in Will. Despite Teddie's reservations, Will had taken Aaron into his confidence. The boy had then proclaimed himself not only worthy of keeping their plot a secret but also eager to accompany them on their quest for freedom. On hearing this, Teddie had grown uneasy. Will had reacted to her qualms with all the protectiveness of a mother hen. Teddie could no more deny Will one of the few friendships he'd ever found than she could deny him the new life she'd promised him in Virginia and the freedom that would soon be theirs.

"I'll lead," she said, glancing back and forth between the other two, hoping to glean some affirmation from them that all would indeed go as planned. "If you lose sight of me, swim toward the lighthouse. Don't stop. For anything."

With a last squeeze of her brother's fingers, she plunged beneath the waves. Only when she thought her lungs would burst did she surface. The waves, which had looked so gentle from the height of the decks, tossed her about like the hands of some invisible giant. Thankfully, the tide was coming in. She planned to take full advantage of it. Blinking the water from her eyes, she took quick note of the lighthouse, then again plunged beneath the surf. Her arms cleaved against the powerful swells until her lungs burned for relief. Again she surfaced. For several moments she bobbed along with the tide, gulping air into her lungs and staring at the starlit sky overhead. Something slithered past her leg. Clamping her teeth, she strained her ears for some sound of Will, the slicing of his thick arms through the water. She heard only the waves. Over her shoulder loomed the shadow of the *Rattlesnake*, its deck lanterns glowing like twin yellow eyes, watching her.

She dove beneath the surf. Her strokes were sure, and for a rare moment she allowed herself to revel in the promise of freedom that would soon be theirs. This war had driven men to give their lives for liberty every day. She now understood why. Even in her deepest imaginings, on those nights when she'd huddled next to her dying father spooning tepid tea past his pale lips, she couldn't have imagined the heady taste of freedom. It had been her father's dying wish for her and Will. Very soon she would fulfill her promise to him and to Will.

Just as she broke the surface she heard the shout, somewhere behind her. It was Aaron. A moment later came Will's answering cry.

Aaron shouted again, an unmistakable cry for help.

"No—" She gulped a mouthful of salt water. "Don't, Will—"

The blast of the watch's whistle drove like a stake through Teddie's soul. The peals came again and again, rousing the *Rattlesnake*'s crew and bleating out over the water. The boatswain's pipes warbled a call for all hands. The sailing master bawled orders in reply. Moments later a longboat splashed into the bay, its belly full of seamen armed with bayonets, cutlasses, and pistols. Cockburn was no doubt at its helm. In seconds they would descend on Aaron thrashing against the waves.

Swim!

To taste freedom, to feel its promise deep in her soul, only to have it wrenched from her grasp! Frustration burned in her throat, aching for release. "Will! Leave him!"

"I cannot, Teddie!" Will cried out.

With a raw despair she saw Will's broad-shouldered bulk cutting back against the tide toward his friend. Those strokes would have easily carried him to shore had it not been for his loyalty to Aaron.

Tears stung Teddie's eyes and clogged her throat. She heard the splash of the longboat's oars meeting the water, the shouts of the seamen marking them as deserters. Even now the sweep of lantern light illuminated Aaron's flailing arms. In three strokes of their oars they were upon him.

She could still escape, her path cloaked in darkness and the fathomless depths of the bay. The lighthouse beckoned. The rich smell of land wafted over the waves, tempting her just as it had for the past three days they'd ridden at anchor here. She could simply turn and swim to shore.

Will's bobbing head was thrown into relief against the yellow glow of the lantern light. He'd nearly reached his friend when the jutting helm of the longboat blocked his path. His hoarse cries of frustration echoed across the water.

Teddie bit out a cry, knowing Will could never endure this alone. She couldn't abandon him and live with the memory. That was hardly freedom. Better to die alongside him in the name of freedom, just as he would perish alongside the friend he would have saved.

Perhaps there was a certain liberty to be found in that.

Swallowing the last of her tears, Teddie swam from her cover of darkness into the circle of lantern light.

The trio huddled together at the mainmast, their wrists and ankles bound. An ominously silent crew surrounded them, some of their faces twisted with anticipation. Others wore the blank mask that often characterizes dread. So many lanterns had been hung from the masts that the decks seemed bathed in daylight, affording Teddie a clear view of Cockburn's profile as he circled them. His face was marked by impassivity, white-gloved hands clasped behind his back, polished boots clicking with the pompous deliberation of a man who well knew his position as master aboard ship. A position he intended to demonstrate fully. He paused directly before Aaron, his boyishly handsome face creased with a lecherous grin that gleamed as evilly as the gilt-handled sword strapped to his waist.

"Hang this one," he said conversationally, his voice high-pitched, like that of a soprano, but nonetheless commanding.

With a bellow of rage Will heaved himself at the seamen who began to drag Aaron to the ship's yardarm. Four men wrestled Will to the decks. One massive seaman drove his fist repeatedly into Will's belly until his cries for his friend diminished to grunts against the pain. Teddie strained at her bonds, but the hemp only dug deeper into her skin, laying it raw and open to the sting of salt air. Every last expletive she'd learned on this voyage itched to spew in a venomous stream at Cockburn when he gave her brother a smirk then regarded her with the same blithe amusement. She had to bite her tongue to keep it silent. Instinct told her if she stood a chance of saving their lives, venting her fury would not serve her well at this point. Nor would any display of weakness or emotion. She'd come to know enough of Cockburn to realize that he derived perverse pleasure from watching others' agony. She intended to provide him with little amusement.

Aaron's horrified screams pierced the silence shrouding the deck. A low moan came from Will as the seaman landed another punch to his ribs. As expected, Cockburn eyed Teddie closely. She gritted her teeth and reached deep for every last ounce of self-control. Cockburn's lips curved faintly upward, as if he knew she exercised great restraint.

Aaron's dying plea rose up, then was swiftly swallowed by the eerie silence of the night.

Teddie steeled herself against the tears that stung her eyes. Shivers racked her wet body. And still Cockburn watched her.

"I have before me the mastermind of this foiled scheme," Cockburn finally said. "Teddie Lovelace. Such a pretty young boy to decorate our yardarm." Cockburn flicked one gloved finger over the length of ebony hair bound by a cord at the nape of her neck.

Teddie almost recoiled from his touch, yet forced herself to remain outwardly impassive. Will and any number of other seamen tethered their own long hair in the same manner, yet Cockburn seemed to find sudden peculiar fascination with the loosely curling mass laying heavy and slick against Teddie's back. Cockburn's gloved finger brushed over her jaw then rubbed against his thumb. Teddie was overcome with the urge to retch.

"So young," Cockburn said softly. "Hardly more than a boy, but with a man's courage far exceeding that of most on this ship. You are not afraid of death. Nay, I see little fear in your eyes and much challenge, still, bound as you are. Perhaps there is something besides hanging that you will fear more." Cockburn glanced over his shoulder at the men surrounding Will. "Chain that one in irons. And give him the cat-o'-nine until he begs you to stop. But do not kill him, if he is so dimwitted to allow it. Leave him with a few breaths in his lumbering body, then throw him in the hold with the rats and the bilge water to eat at his raw flesh until I instruct otherwise."

Again, Cockburn swung an eagerly expectant eye on Teddie. Spit pooled on her tongue, ready to fling at his face. The thought brought her the only satisfaction she would allow herself at the moment.

"Take this one to my cabin," Cockburn finally ordered two men. He turned around with a sweep of his sword and coattails and strode toward the companionway.

Were Teddie not convinced that Cockburn possessed the most diabolically twisted mind on the seas, she might have felt some surge of relief. But she'd heard him boast on many occasions of his many and varied methods of punishment and had witnessed his looting, burning, and pillaging of the Virginia coast in the best continental military fashion, all to appease his insatiable lust for wartime glory. A man like him would keep his most wicked forms of torture near at heart and hand, in his own cabin. It was, then, with no small amount of apprehension that Teddie found Cockburn's cabin absent of anything devious-looking, save for Cockburn himself.

Finger by finger he tugged his white gloves from his hands, then tossed them atop a pile of nautical charts stacked on a small table, never once taking his eyes from her. With the same deliberation he removed his hat, revealing a thatch of reddish-gold hair that slid over his forehead and gave him a childlike and harmless demeanor. Almost as an afterthought he nodded to the two lingering seamen, who promptly left, closing the cabin door behind them.

The fine hairs on the back of Teddie's neck stood on end. Her gaze fell to Cockburn's sheathed sword. She wondered what the razor-sharp tip would feel like, plunging into her chest. He might well pin her to the cabin wall for exhibition. Odd, though, that Cockburn would suddenly adhere to discretion with an execution, dismissing all witnesses.

He must be planning something truly grim.

With a flick of his hand Cockburn shed his scabbard and sword. Metal clanked as it met with the floor, scraping against Teddie's drawn nerves. A tremor shuddered through her before she could contain it. This prompted an upward curve of Cockburn's lips. He settled one hip against the table, folding his arms across his barrellike chest. He crossed one booted foot over the other, further emphasizing the dramatic tapering of his balloonlike torso, hips, and buttocks to the almost sickly thinness of his legs, as if one part of him didn't quite belong with the other. And none of it, particularly his mind, seemed suitable for so boyishly handsome a face.

Would that a man's countenance could offer her subtle solace. But the stench of death filled her nostrils, her brother's anguished screams her ears. Hatred for this man fired her blood.

"Loyalty is rarely worth the price paid," Cockburn mused. "You would give your life for your brother."

"I would," Teddie replied through stiff lips.

"Then anything short of your life wouldn't be too great a sacrifice."

Something prompted an evasive response, yet Teddie could not deny her heart's dictates. "To keep my brother alive, no."

"I'd rather not kill him, imbecile that he is. In wartime, particularly with such a shortage of English seamen to fight these bloody Americans, a man of your brother's remarkable strength and agility is an asset. Even you, slight though you are, can do the work of a man twice your size. I've watched you, Teddie."

It was then that Teddie had to wonder for the first time on the voyage if Cockburn suspected she was not a boy but a woman, full-grown, twenty years old. Some elusive tone in his voice suddenly seemed more suitable to a man talking to a woman, not a ruthless commander moments from beheading a deserter.

What wickedness was the man up to? Surely he wasn't suggesting that she would not be punished for her crime. Yet she couldn't help but find a glimmer of hope in his words.

His eyes raked over her. All hope plummeted. He knew . . . somehow he'd guessed despite all her efforts to conceal her femininity. She swallowed and kept her gaze level with his.

He shoved himself away from the table and moved toward her. His tongue passed over slackened lips as if he were in anticipation of something. "Yes, I would very much like to keep you alive, Teddie. Perhaps we may come to some agreement that both of us will find satisfactory. A bargain."

He wanted something. Whatever it was she would give it to him if he would just spare her brother.

Slowly, Cockburn circled her. He paused at her back. Teddie stared at the oak-paneled wall opposite, listening to the rasping of his breath, feeling it heat the skin at the back of her neck. Revulsion slithered through her. She'd never hated anyone, or the power he wielded over everything she held dear, more. Prickly hemp dug into her wrists and ankles, a persistent reminder of her complete helplessness.

And then, with both palms and an agonized groan, Cockburn cupped her buttocks.

Teddie jolted. Her scream caught in her throat. Cockburn clamped one hand over her womanhood and thrust his pelvis against her buttocks in a frantic rocking motion. His hand fumbled between her thighs as though seeking something—something Teddie suddenly realized he wasn't going to find. A moment later Cockburn realized it as well.

"Bitch!" He sprang from her as though she'd suddenly burst aflame. He spun her around, shoved her back against the wall, and with one vicious jerk of his hand tore her damp shirt from neck to hem, exposing the stiffly wrapped muslin that flattened her breasts.

He gaped at her, face ashen, eyes bulging. "You're . . . you're . . ." He flexed the hand that had plundered between her thighs, then swiped it against his belly. Scarlet swept to his hairline. "The devil take you, but you're a woman."

"I am." Teddie was certain some humor was to be found in this, given that the revelation caused Cockburn some distress. Whether it was the matter of her deception that plagued him or his intent with her just moments prior, Teddie could only guess. But he suddenly looked at her as though he hadn't any idea what to do with her.

Teddie felt an unexpected surge of satisfaction.

"Good God," he muttered, rubbing a slightly unsteady hand over his brow. "Cover yourself."

"If you would untie me I could."

Cockburn frowned, then muttered something and quickly loosed the ropes binding her hands. He obviously thought an unbound woman far less capable than an unbound, somewhat feminine boy. He even untied the rope at her ankles before moving behind the table, a distance from her.

From a cupboard behind him he produced a bottle half full of amber liquid. Splashing a liberal portion into a tin cup, he gulped the brew, stared at her, then drained what remained. "Loosen your hair, Teddie," he ordered, again filling the cup. He cocked one brow. "Or do you have another name?"

"Theodora," she replied, tugging the leather strap from her hair. She shook the tangled mass until the damp curls fell over her shoulders.

"A woman." Cockburn emptied the cup, then placed it on the table. His lip curled with derision as his gaze swept over her. "You would have made a prettier boy."

Teddie couldn't contain the bite lacing her words or the deliberate arch of her brow. "I was successful nonetheless."

This Cockburn chose not to deny, or perhaps he simply wished to avoid any further reference to his own behavior moments before. "Where were you bound when you thought to escape?"

At the moment she had little reason to lie. Or to test Cockburn's patience. "Virginia."

Cockburn offered a fake smile. "A woman always knows her destination, even more so a brave woman. Men and foolish young boys would set out into unknown territory without any sort of plan. A woman, particularly one saddled with a brother like yours, never would. I think you know someone in Virginia."

"I know several families."

Cockburn gave a patronizing snort. "You should know better than to play any more games with me, Theodora Lovelace. I might not make it a habit to kill women, although I've never met one of your sex as keen on deception as you appear to be. Then again, I've a lusty crew above decks who would use you in ways that would make you beg for death. And there is the matter of your brother, Will. Lie to me and I can add twenty lashes to his punishment, perhaps even hoist him by his thick neck. Remain silent and I will strip that muslin from your breasts and throw you above decks. The truth, my impetuous girl, might serve you well at this point."

What did telling him matter if she could save Will further agony, even his life? Still, the words fell from her lips in a reluctant whisper. "My aunt lives near the York River."

"Her name?"

"Edwina . . . Farrell."

Cockburn's eyes narrowed. "Farrell. I presume she's English like you. Married to an American? Poor woman. This Farrell. Who is he?"

Teddie swallowed. "George Farrell."

Cockburn's lips peeled back over his gums with such perverse pleasure, Teddie felt as though she'd betrayed the uncle she'd never met. "The same George Farrell who is Commander of the American Navy? Ah, but providence is indeed shining upon me this day. But what to do with this piece of luck." Cockburn tapped a finger against his pursed lips, his eyes narrowing to slits. One thick finger stirred the air. "Turn around, Theodora. Slowly."

The slash of the cat-o'-nine crackled through the air. No response echoed from Will. Clenching her teeth, Teddie turned around slowly.

"You've hips as slender as a boy's, Theodora, but I presume you've enough swell in your bosoms to warrant such a tight wrapping. Passably pretty, in a gauche sort of way. I can imagine those American naval men could find something about you to divert their interest from their ships. After all, what is the American navy besides a few fir-built frigates with strips of bunting, manned by sons of bitches and outlaws with a perverse weakness for female flesh?"

"Enough to warrant a sizable British presence in this area," Teddie countered crisply. She was well-aware that Cockburn commanded the entire British Chesapeake Bay operation, one which included three men-of-war.

"We will squash them," Cockburn hissed. His fist jarred against the tabletop, overturning the tin cup and sending charts scattering to the floor. "No upstart power can defy the entrenched majesty of England. These Americans must be swept from the seas. And you, my deceitful and proud Theodora, will aid the English cause. Particularly mine."

"You wish to blackmail me," Teddie ground out, her hatred rising anew.

"I not only wish it, it will be so. You relinquished your freedom for your brother this evening, choosing what you thought was certain death. A most heartwarming sacrifice. A bit of spying for the British can hardly be deemed a sacrifice then, if it spares your brother's life. Surely you cannot hate your mother country so?"

Her eyes misted at first thought of London, of the memory of her father lying motionless among the bedclothes, his gaunt frame barely registering a dip in his bed. They'd all but starved there in that drafty bookshop, driven into squalor by a war that had sucked the life's breath from its people. But what did a man like Cockburn understand of desperation so great one would sacrifice his life to achieve something better? "I hate what war has done to that country and its principles," she said woodenly. "It's no longer mine."

Cockburn snorted. "I trust your loyalty to your brother won't be as fleeting. You strike me as a mildly intelligent female, not likely given to hysterics and emotional flappery. Yet you think yourself too brave by far, and that can cause you to behave with misplaced bravado. Even now, stripped of your secret and with no weapon, you stand before me as openly defiant as any man would dare. I might admire you if I did not think you utterly foolish. However, I feel compelled to warn you that betraying our pact to anyone, particularly to George Farrell, would be most unwise. At the first sign of enemy attack I will have your brother's throat slit. On the other hand, the more useful the information you give me, the easier he will have it.''

"Information," Teddie repeated, knowing the helplessness of her situation, and the irony. Cockburn was asking her to abandon all her principles, to betray the country and the liberty she believed in, for her brother's life. Yet she could do nothing else. And Cockburn knew it.

Bastard. Only now could she fully comprehend a desire for revenge so fierce men would kill to appease it.

Cockburn crossed his arms over his chest and lounged against the table. "You will supply information on American naval maneuverings. I would also enjoy capturing a privateer or two, particularly one heavily laden with American goods bound for some distant port. There is no more stirring sight to our forces than the burning of an enemy ship in full view of land. Especially a privateer. Arrogant bastards, thinking to make fools of us. I'll be damned if they attempt to make a run at Jeremiah Cockburn's blockade!''

"Information like that won't be easy to obtain."

"Bah. You've an obvious flair for duplicity, Theodora. Besides, the circles you will move in as Farrell's niece will provide more than ample opportunity to obtain all sorts of interesting tidbits. You need but exercise a little of those womanly wiles. And the sooner you succeed, the sooner your brother finds himself out of irons, perhaps even with a meal warming his belly. I trust we have a bargain.''

Teddie stared at the porthole and the darkness beyond, acutely aware of each slash of the cat-o'-nine. The price she was being forced to pay was scant compared to Will's. But rather than buying them freedom she was saving them both

from death, guaranteeing their imprisonment. Her throat tightened and rebelled against the words that finally crept out. "Yes,
we have a bargain. But no means."

"Indeed." Cockburn turned to a sea chest, lifted the lid, and
rummaged deep. He held up several pairs of dark trousers,
glanced at her, shook his head, and rummaged some more.
"Ah, this should suffice." He turned, lifting a black cape,
wide-brimmed black hat, and boots. "Before we left London I
coerced a highwayman from his chosen profession and convinced him he had a future at sea. Bastard deserted in Boston."
He tossed the highwayman's items at her. Both reeked of must.
"For our midnight rendezvous upon the shore. A disguise will
serve you better if you come upon an energetic American regiment. As for your meeting with your dear Aunt Edwina—" In
one hand Cockburn lifted a medium-sized bag and what looked
to be a gown of a most revolting shade of orange; he eyed it
warily. "It seems the former captain of this ship had a
penchant for women of dubious good taste. Here, wrap this into
your little bundle there and stow it all in this valise. You can
change once I put you to shore near Hampton. I trust you are
capable of stealing yourself a mount. You managed quite well
on pluck these last months. One horse couldn't possibly stand
in your way, eh?"

She eyed him coolly, clutching the bundle to her belly.

He quirked a brow. "Ah. You regret something. Perhaps
your sentiment for your brother, hmm? Were it not for that you
would have fertile Virginia soil beneath your feet rather than
my cabin floor. Weakness is meant to be exploited, Theodora.
That's a lesson many must learn. I trust it's one you will never
forget."

On that alone, she had to agree with him.

Chapter One

✦

"Winchester! Dammit, cousin, must you forever shove your disregard down everyone's throats?"

Despite the reproachful tones echoing through the foyer in his wake—or perhaps because of them—Miles Winchester didn't break stride as he proceeded two steps at a time up the broad, curved staircase.

"For God's sake, Miles, rumor is bad enough as it is. I've done my best to dispel it. Why, not a moment ago I found myself going on at great lengths to my rather dubious friend McIntire about what a damned congenial fellow you can be. At certain times, of course, albeit fleeting and far between, and if you haven't plunged too deeply into your liquor. My powers of persuasion being what they are, Brett seemed inclined to alter his opinion of you. But then you storm in here as though hounds were at your heels, and up the stairs without a 'by your leave' to our guests. An esteemed lot it is, cousin, even to your jaded eye. And Commander George Farrell among them."

"All the more reason," Miles countered in his typical coarse rumble, his pace up the stairs unabated. "They're your guests. Try another tack if you're hoping for anything remotely resembling congenial. I can't recall a time when I was in the mood for naval hobnobbery."

"Ah. Then I must assume your Wildair won his race today."

At this, Miles paused and regarded his cousin, who stood poised at the foot of the staircase in all his naval finery. Damian Coyle grinned and lifted his nose as if sniffing a stiff salt breeze. To Miles he looked too damned young, too innocently ambitious, and far too caught up in the business he was conducting in the salon. The business of war. Obviously war had gotten the better of his sense. Otherwise Damian would never have dared to admonish the manners of a man most considered rude, intolerably arrogant, and quite possibly out of his mind, then in the next moment grin like a fool, his chest all puffed up with the sort of youthful patriotic fervor he knew Miles detested.

But Damian had not yet realized the inherent folly of youth, inexperience, and patriotic fervor.

Fools, all of them, gathered like fat geese in the salon, chomping on stratagems that in the end wouldn't make a damned bit of difference in the war. After nearly three years of fighting, neither the British nor the Americans had won anything tangible. Countless lives had been lost, and more sure to follow. Looking at Damian, Miles suddenly felt the weight of his thirty-five years like a gravestone on his shoulders.

"See there," Damian observed with a smirk. "You're coming around in spite of yourself. 'Not in the mood' is rather mild for you. A touch gracious. Dare I say it? Bordering on the pleasant, given your nasty views of the war and your generally cantankerous nature. Had Wildair lost the race, and you another precious hundred to our friend Reynolds, I would wager you'd have thrown every last man in uniform from the house in a great thunderation. Even I wouldn't have dared to venture anywhere near you for weeks. As for the servants, even your Jillie would find it prudent to keep herself from your chamber, not to mention your bed—"

Miles worked his quirt between impatient fingers. "What do you want, Damian?"

Damian shrugged. "I need you to settle a small wager. Between me and McIntire."

Miles hooded his eyes.

"Oh, come now, cousin, you needn't look so suspicious. It has nothing to do with the war, though now that I think about it I do believe there's a Brit involved. On our side, though I don't suppose that matters much to a man who has loyalties to no one but himself, eh?" Damian lifted a cocky brow, obviously feeling his oats this evening. "It will take but a moment of your time, just long enough for a draught or two of rum, and then you can retreat to your cave and sulk as long as you wish. I will ask nothing more of you for at least a millennium.''

"So long as you win."

Damian grinned and seemed to grow an inch in his shiny black boots. "I always win."

So damned young. Oozing bravado. Damian truly believed himself invincible. Miles might as well have been looking at himself just eight years before. Just like Miles then, Damian had no idea what this war could do to him. Too caught up in the feel of the uniform on his back and the warmth that uniform inspired in his female companions. He obviously hadn't learned a thing living beneath the same roof with Miles for the past eight years, forced to face the living dead each day. The day Madison had declared war on England Damian had bounded off to enlist, believing like most that his youth and exuberance would keep him alive, at the very least safe from the ominous fate that had befallen Miles. Perhaps, like the rest of the geese, Damian simply assumed that Miles had never recovered from his father's sudden, horrific death in Tripoli's harbor those eight years ago. After all, Miles had been on the same boat with his father when it had happened.

Miles had left them all to their rumor and conjecture over the reasons, never considering offering an explanation for his moods or his behavior. He'd long since numbed himself to the reasons why part of a man dies, just as he'd tried to forget the worst of it. The stuff of nightmares. The unimaginable. Visions that tortured him only when he was most vulnerable, in those brief moments when he allowed himself to succumb to sleep despite the nocturnal specters that awaited him. They knew nothing of all that. And they never would.

Because then they would realize that Miles had indeed lost part of his sanity out on the Tripolitan desert. His soul he'd left in Tripoli's harbor the moment the sloop's magazine blew and all thirteen of his crew members, his father among them, were blown into tiny bits of flesh that had seemed to rain endlessly from the sky.

"Miles."

The quirt slapped against his thigh as he jarred from his thoughts.

"I don't suppose I need to warn you, cousin, that Farrell's determined as hell to change your mind about captaining the *Leviathan* again. Your rather obvious aversion to the war hasn't dissuaded him thus far. But one can hardly blame the man for trying to get the swiftest privateers under his command. As commander of our fleet he simply wants the best striking power to be had on the seas. Who better than the most brilliant captain to survive the Barbary Wars, the son of the greatest man to ever sail under the American flag? He plans to sway you one day."

"It won't be today. Where did you get the rum?"

"Smuggled in from the West Indies, I presume. I found it in a very deep and dark corner of the cellar." Damian lifted a mildly suspicious brow. "Jillie knew precisely where to find it. Odd, that. One might think she was dipping into the brew nightly."

Miles turned on his heel and descended the stairs. "One drink and a settling of your wager. Nothing more. I've hogsheads to fill early tomorrow."

Damian gave a smug smile. "I knew I'd hit upon it soon enough. Every man has at least one weakness."

"Don't count on it."

"A love of fine Jamaican rum can hardly be viewed as an abysmal character flaw, cousin, not that you have any. It certainly wouldn't be a weakness for women." He fell into step beside Miles and threw wide the salon's double doors, pausing briefly to add, "One day you will have to let me in on your secret with the fairer sex."

"Get me a drink, Damian."

"See there. You're disagreeable as hell, and damned if I know why. But it's your indifference that intrigues me most. I can only wonder how you manage it, given our dire state of war. But I'll admit to a bit of envy over it. You've a scarred face that should inspire terror in the most stout-hearted of women, yet they all quiver and fan their overheated bosoms the moment your boots tread upon the same carpet as theirs. And you don't even have a fortune in your coffers or a uniform on your back. I'd be inclined to think they were all terrified of you, were it not for one rather determined and very eligible young widow, Mrs. Lydia Lawrence.'' Damian paused, obviously expecting a reaction that never came.

Miles turned his back on his cousin, poured himself a draught of rum from a crystal decanter, then drained half the glass. ''You've got two minutes. I wouldn't waste it talking about women.''

''Ah, but I must. The wager depends on it. Now, where did she go?''

Damian craned his neck to peer around the room clustered with uniformed gentlemen and a scattering of women. Talk was hushed. Even the lighting was covertly dim, a testament to the gravity of the current situation with England. That such a gathering was taking place at all hinted at the delicacy of the discussions and the imminence of the British threat riding at anchor not a half mile off the coast. One sweep of his eyes around the room assured Miles that the who's who of American naval commanders were all in attendance, plotting strategy and maneuverings and discussing the current position of British ships.

He drained his glass and poured another.

''Women resemble ships, Miles.''

''Is that what you brought me here to discuss?''

''Perhaps it's the only way I can think of to capture and hold your attention. Not so long ago you were one of this country's finest sea captains. Your mistress was the sea, your boots never without the rolling decks of the *Leviathan* beneath them.'' Damian smiled despite Miles's hooded indifference, then indicated a stout, white-haired woman maneuvering around a crimson velvet settee. ''Consider, if you will, cousin, the triple-decker man-of-war plowing along under a heavy press of sail with a ponderous grace not unlike that of yon overstuffed dowager sweeping through our grand salon. The Edwina Farrell, wife of our esteemed commander. Ah, level your glass upon the northeast horizon, Miles. A frigate, the Lydia Lawrence, fresh out of dry dock and eager to catch the wind in her full, thrusting sails. Notice the lush blond wood, the fully fashioned bow and stern to bear the stoutest riding of waves. How she aches for a master's firm hand to guide her wheel.'' Damian cleared his throat, gave Miles a lascivious grin, then swung his gaze back to the room. ''But it's the sloop I'm looking for, the darkly elegant sloop. The wager involves her. Ah, blast it, Brett's gotten her to heave to in the far corner. Perhaps not. Looks to me like he's the one ready to strike his colors. Took but one of her well-aimed broadsides, I'd wager. The man will be on bended knee by night's end, dammit.''

Miles finished his drink and reached for the decanter, giving the room and its occupants his back. In another minute, if instinct served, Commander George Farrell would descend on him with all the force of a damned flotilla. Just one more drink and then he'd leave. If only the rum didn't taste so sweet and warm. If only it didn't make all this just a bit more bearable. He scarcely registered his cousin's next words.

''She's Edwina Farrell's niece, Miles. Theodora Lovelace.''

The sudden breathless reverence in Damian's voice drew Miles's brutal regard. His gaze followed Damian's to the far-thest corner of the room, where young, darkly handsome Captain Brett McIntire stood with head bent low to the woman beside him. Miles narrowed his eyes on her profile. She stood just inches below McIntire, her face thrown into luminous relief by the gentle hues of the firelight. She was tall for a sloop. A sleek, elegant beauty, to be sure. But Miles regarded her dispassionately, as he would a piece of horseflesh for sale. Indeed, he found himself comparing her to the long-limbed filly he'd considered buying that very afternoon. Even the lush fall of her midnight black mane and the swell of her breasts thrusting at McIntire brought to mind the image of the spirited filly. His eye lingered on her more obvious charms only a mo-ment, drawn instead to the almost imperceptible arch of one black brow and the faint upward tip of her lips. Charming, certainly beautiful, but unremarkable to Miles were it not for the flat, fathomless depths of her eyes. Miles had never seen such a look on a woman—on many a man, yes, and most of them enemies. She wasn't the least bit coy. No, her bearing was that of a woman mercilessly intent on something. The warm-blooded filly became the sloop once more, slipping covertly through a sea tangled with lumbering craft unsuspecting of the cannon in her hold.

"Stay away from her," Miles said, tipping his glass to his lips, in that one instant dismissing Theodora Lovelace.

"You're a bit late for dire warnings, cousin. You see, I've determined to make her my wife."

Miles didn't temper his scoff. "Then you're in good company with the rest of these fools. A pity for all of you that she'll do the choosing."

Damian seemed to square his shoulders. "Precisely my point in making the wager. Who, Miles, will she choose? The over-zealous McIntire, or me, perhaps?"

Miles raised his glass to his lips. The liquor spilled a welcoming fire down his throat. Over the rim of his glass his eyes again found the luminous profile. She was smiling up at McIntire, a gentle curving of her lips that hinted at whimsy, but to Miles's jaded eye betrayed far more. McIntire, however, flushed clear to his hairline and stared like a salivating pup. "She will choose whoever gives her what she wants," he muttered.

"Blast it, but I wonder if McIntire's hit upon it. What do you think by the looks of it, Miles?"

"You've neither the fortune nor the rank, Damian. And neither does McIntire. Don't look so damned baffled. You betray your inexperience." Miles paused, his eye drawn inexplicably as Theodora Lovelace laid one gloved hand on Brett McIntire's sleeve. The delicate movement, so natural when combined with the upward tipping of her lashes, proved as potent as a salvo launched by any ship of the line. McIntire looked at the ready to lay down his very life for the girl. The duplicitous Miss Theodora Lovelace obviously knew the inherent power of understatement. And the significance of good lighting. With the firelight dancing on her flushed cheeks and the plump swells of her bosom, she was at that moment the object of many a man's desire. Miles, however, had had more than enough. "She wants what every woman wants. Money, position, and to ruin a man's life—and not necessarily in that order. Be thankful that she's set her sights on fatter prey.''

''Meaning?''

Miles set his empty glass on the sideboard, feeling the effects of the rum on his already short temper. His tone held a good deal of bite. ''Meaning that she won't content herself with a mere captain.''

Damian scowled and glanced around the room. ''So who the devil does she want? A lieutenant? Harrigan's married. Eagan's old enough to be her grandfather—'' Damian blinked and paled considerably. ''God help us, Miles, you can't possibly think that exquisite young woman is after an old lecher like Josiah Eagan?''

''Does it matter? Pity the man, Damian, whoever he is. But for Christ's sake, don't envy him. Now let me pass.''

Damian shifted his shoulders, effectively blocking Miles's path to the door. The younger man gave a sheepish smile that made Miles suddenly itch to throttle him. ''One more moment, cousin. I find myself inclined to disagree with you.''

''The inclination has overcome you of late.''

''Perhaps, but not without good reason. To my eye Miss Lovelace seems quite intent on young McIntire. Therein lies my hope.''

''And your folly. Theodora Lovelace is very much aware of the attention she is commanding, from you and every other man witless enough to think her an innocent. As her luck would have it, you've provided her a roomful of them. Now move aside.''

''God, but you're a cynical man, Miles. Look at her. She's a dove.''

''I know what I see when I look at her, Damian. Now get the hell out of my way.''

Damian remained rooted to his spot, a circumstance that brought the color to both men's collars. Damian cocked a belligerent brow. ''Can you deny she's beautiful?''

Miles hardened his stare. ''I'd take her to bed. Just as I'd take Lydia Lawrence to bed. And that, cousin, would be the beginning and the end of it.''

"So certain, are you?"

Miles raised a brow. "Of my ability to escape a woman's wiles? Absolutely."

"I think you're afraid of women."

The quirt slapped against Miles's rock-hard thigh. "Don't push me, Damian."

"Someone should. You've become a heartless old bastard, or at least you'd like us all to think you are. I often wonder why I bother with you."

"My thoughts precisely. Now get the hell out of my path."

Damian was astute enough to comply this time, even offering his dour cousin a mocking half-bow as they brushed shoulders. Miles had just gripped the door handle when he was stopped, cold, by the sound of Farrell's voice. But the commander hadn't addressed Miles. He was talking to another captain just at Miles's back.

"Damned if I can understand it," Farrell was saying. "But the Night Hawk was spotted by one of our regiments late last evening at Lighthouse Point."

"Lighthouse Point? Odd. Isn't Cockburn's fleet anchored in the bay just off the point?"

"My thoughts exactly."

"Surely you're not suggesting—"

"That the mysterious Night Hawk is spying for Jeremiah Cockburn?" Farrell snorted. "That remains to be seen. But I'll be damned if I don't find out who our elusive night rider is. And if he's spying for that British bastard, God help him."

Abruptly, Miles released the door handle and turned as if to speak again to Damian. It was at that most inopportune moment that Lydia Lawrence insinuated herself between Miles and Commander George Farrell and his companion. She must have fairly flown across the room, judging by the color in her cheeks and all the breathless heaving of her plump white bosom. Typically, Miles would have found a woman in Lydia's current state of mind and dress holding a certain mild appeal. Unlike the understated and therefore more dangerous Theodora Lovelace, Lydia wore her desires and her motives like her clothing, with an audacity a man would be hard-pressed to ignore. Particularly when those desires were focused with such lack of reserve on him.

At the moment, however, Miles was of singular purpose, and the blond, voluptuous, and determined Lydia Lawrence wasn't it. Gallantry, odd as it might be for Miles, could prove the best course.

"You're not trying to escape, are you?" Lydia purred, her small Cupid's bow mouth curling around the words. She slanted her eyes at him, one long fingernail brushing the air over the scar cleaving Miles's face from cheekbone to the deep cleft in his chin. Despite the oppressive evening heat she seemed unable to suppress a shiver. "Need I remind you that my year of mourning has just passed, Miles?"

"You needn't." With deliberate leisure, Miles hooded his eyes on the extravagant display of womanly charms surging from the deep scoop of her bodice. Her gown was of the deepest-crimson taffeta, immodestly cut and adorned, as if specifically designed for young widows eager to shed their mourning weeds. Young widows perhaps intent on acquiring another doddering, obscenely wealthy husband to see into the grave. Or, as in Lydia's case this evening, a lover with far more savage appetites.

A faint heaviness settled in his loins.

Miles wrapped his fingers over hers around her empty glass and watched her eyes dilate a fraction. "Let me get you another." He moved to the sideboard just as Damian joined in on Farrell's conversation. Miles presented the trio his back, for all outward purposes seemingly unaware of their conversation.

"Did you say the Night Hawk?" Damian asked. "I heard he outmaneuvered an entire regiment last evening, then vanished into the woods without a trace. A remarkably clever fellow."

Miles splashed rum into two glasses, taking keen note of the reverence in Damian's voice. It was a common enough tone whenever the locals spoke of the Night Hawk, and they'd been talking a great deal about him for the past fifteen months.

"Clever, indeed," Farrell replied. "Or too damned lucky. They'd surrounded him, just off Lighthouse Point."

"What the devil was he doing at the bay? Thought the fellow

kept to the shores of the James, and further south, toward Albemarle.''

"After last night some of the men would prefer to think he's a ghost, Commander," Damian said. "His black horse proved himself capable of speeds in excess of our military's finest. The horsemanship he displayed put our men to shame, not to mention his prowess with a sword—"

Sword? Miles's head snapped up and he found himself scowling at the Reynolds portrait of his grandfather Maximilian on the wall above the sideboard. The big, brash, red-haired gentleman's stare offered Miles a certain mocking disdain at the moment.

"One soldier even bears the mark of his expert shot."

The decanter in Miles's hand slid ominously against the lead crystal glass.

"He shot one of our men?" Damian gasped. "In the dark?"

"Shot his pistol from his hand," Farrell replied. "The soldier was rather quick to mention that a full moon had risen at that point. Regardless, I believe there's ample cause for concern. This is the second time in as many weeks that the Night Hawk has been spotted near the point, precisely when Cockburn's fleet has been at anchor just off the coast there. Too damned coincidental to suit me."

"You don't mean to suggest our Night Hawk has turned traitor on us, sir?" Damian asked, his tone dipping noticeably. "Why, down near Albemarle he's regarded as a hero right out of folklore, down to his black cape and mask. We'd all assumed he was simply engaged in smuggling with a local privateer, a rather innocent crime compared to spying, sir."

"Dammit, Coyle, there is no such thing as an innocent crime," Farrell growled. "But I'll admit even I turned my head to the mysterious Night Hawk for quite some time. And, by God, that may be precisely what he wanted us to do. Perhaps his intent all along has been far more sinister than we ever imagined, having nothing to do with privateering. With Cockburn sitting in the Chesapeake with his sixty guns, it would be suicidal for a privateer to attempt to break through there. We must assume, therefore, that his business at the point involves something altogether different. He is, I believe, a serious threat to our war effort, and we must act accordingly. A few merchantmen escaping port concerns me far less than that butcher Cockburn being privy to our maneuverings.''

Miles's scowl deepened.

''He could be a Federalist,'' Damian snapped with his typical swift ire, particularly when the war effort was at risk. ''Some fellow from the north, determined to sabotage us in the war. Don't those New Englanders yet realize that fighting these English bastards is a matter of our young republic's existence, our subsistence, our very being? We must oppose the lawless seizing of our vessels and the impressment of our sailors onto English ships, as a proud young man must fight to prevent being bullied.''

''Remember, Coyle, the Federalists are businessmen first, patriots second,'' Farrell replied grimly. ''Their concerns lie with the goods rotting at their wharves and those piling up in their warehouses. So long as the war continues, the blockade stands. And no American goods will leave our ports.''

''The English don't care if they starve themselves in the process.''

''Quite right,'' Farrell said. ''As long as their navy reigns on the seas, they don't give a damn if their people eat.''

''The Night Hawk could well be one of the Federalists, sir, eager to end the war by whatever means necessary, even treason. What the devil are we to do about him?''

''Catch him, of course.''

''And then, assuming that we can somehow?''

''We'll make him wish Cockburn had caught him.''

Something warm slid over Miles's belly, then hooked in the banded waist of his riding breeches. ''Did you have to sail to Jamaica to get the rum, Miles?'' the sultry female voice crooned.

Miles curved Lydia's eager fingers around her glass before they could venture any lower. ''I may have to before the night is out.''

Her breath whispered hot against his neck, left bare by the

open collar of his linen shirt. "You smell of horseflesh, Miles. And leather. And heat."

Miles regarded the empty decanter. "It seems we're running low. How thirsty are you?"

"Insatiably. Have you a cure for me, Miles?"

Lydia Lawrence was obviously not a woman dissuaded by a man's notorious, disagreeable, and generally black reputation. Or his dour mood. Perhaps because she was after one thing this evening, and the more unconventional, the better. Were he not unduly distracted at the moment Miles might have been inclined to oblige the lady without much hesitation. After all, she seemed of the temperament to content herself with a simple, calculated slating of base desires. She would ask nothing more of him, knowing that he had nothing more to give a woman. Because Lydia was not looking for a husband this evening. She wanted, quite desperately, a man to tame her.

Unfortunately for both of them, Miles had something he had to do at the moment. But it wouldn't take long.

"Are you staying the night?" he asked without looking at her.

He felt her quiver beside him, heard the sharp intake of her breath. If he touched her, he expected, she would quite possibly burst into flame. "Why, yes," she breathed. "I believe I will be enjoying your hospitality until morning, Miles, as will most of the guests. It's quite dangerous during wartime to travel any distance after dark . . . and Miramer is so isolated out here on the river, so far from civilization. There's no telling what could happen in such a place. It fires one's imagination."

Particularly a young widow's. Old Lawrence must not have been much use to her for quite some time before he finally died. But she'd known that when she'd married him, no doubt finding consolation in the fortune and the plantation that ultimately became entirely hers. A woman of means, completely without need, except for a hunger that required immediate— and no doubt frequent—attention. Her plantation was relatively close. Close enough. Indeed, Miles found himself, for the first time in years, envisioning a mutually beneficial arrangement with a woman. So long as he didn't have to lay any trust in her.

He slanted her a hooded look and watched her lower lip tremble like a plump cherry waiting to be plucked. "You'll find the accommodations most to your liking in the east wing. Use the rear stairs. Third door on the right."

Without waiting for her reply he turned and left the room. Before the door closed behind him Lydia Lawrence was banished from his mind in favor of a problem requiring his more immediate attention.

The stables were set back some distance from the main house, at the end of a path fringed with dense honeysuckle. The evening air hung thick with the sweet aroma, but Miles barely took notice, his boots moving with haste along the cobblestones. He pushed open the stable door, grunted a curt greeting to the dense shadow that was his prized stallion, Wildair, and moved quickly along the row of stalls to the small closed room located at the back of the stable.

Beneath the shove of his hand the door thudded against the wall opposite. The rangy black man didn't glance up from his work. His hands moved in a seasoned, unhurried rhythm, polishing tack. On the floor beside him a bridle made of the finest leather gleamed in the soft glow of a dim lantern.

"Evenin'," the black man said without looking up, even when Miles slammed the door closed.

"Farrell's men spotted the Night Hawk at Lighthouse Point last night, Simon."

Simon's hands stilled. "I thought the Night Hawk didn' ride las' night."

"He didn't. We've an impostor, Simon."

Simon glanced up sharply, his heavy-lidded eyes glowing. "What you gonna do?"

Miles felt the skin of his cheeks draw tight against the grim upward slash of his lips. "I'm going to catch him. Before Farrell's men do, and before he can lay complete waste to my reputation and my plans. Now listen closely, Simon. I have a plan."

Teddie stifled another yawn behind gloved fingers and swallowed a hiccup. Lifting misting eyes and a wan smile to her

Aunt Edwina seated opposite her, she glanced for the tenth time in as many minutes at the mantel clock. Her heart fell. Just past nine. None of the other guests had yet to display any inclination to retire. She didn't dare be the first. Not that someone could even begin to suspect the reason for her fatigue, that it had anything remotely to do with a late night rendezvous at Lighthouse Point that had required every last ounce of her horsemanship and weaponry skill . . . but one couldn't be too careful. Particularly when Aunt Edwina was looking at her with more than her usual amount of effusive maternal concern. As Teddie's luck would have it, her aunt had chosen to alleviate her worries by plying Teddie with cup upon cup of warm, rum-laced tea.

"Medicinal, my dear," her aunt had reassured her, going so far as to add a dash of rum to her own steaming cup despite the beads of perspiration dotting her upper lip.

The room had grown unbearably stuffy, the air hanging thick with cigar smoke. Teddie blinked and nodded vaguely to the handsome young captain at her side. An energetic young man, of her brother's age, she guessed, perhaps a few years older. Her heart twisted around itself and she had to lower her eyes to her hands clenched in her lap. Last night Cockburn had propped Will in the longboat they'd rowed to shore to meet her. In the hazy moonlight her brother had looked pale, eerily so, his cheeks sunken. He'd spoken to her, his voice raw from misuse, his words not his own and sounding as if rehearsed countless times. But he was alive. The information she'd fed Cockburn would keep him that way: All American ships were otherwise occupied far north, in the St. Lawrence. Cockburn had seemed pleased.

She thought no further than that. If she did, she wouldn't be able to look into the eyes of these kind young American naval captains and smile as though betraying them and their cause was furthest from her thoughts.

"My dear girl." Aunt Edwina's touch was gentle upon her hand. Beneath an elegant sweep of snow-white hair, her eyes were rheumy from her overindulgence in spiked tea. "Forgive me, Theodora, but perhaps you could accompany me to my room. I'm afraid I must retire, rather prematurely.'' One gloved hand stirred the air over her flushed cheeks. "The heat—''

Teddie could barely temper the relief flooding her features. They made their gracious apologies to their host, the charming Damian Coyle, and exited the room at a pace accommodating Edwina.

"The devil take the other one,'' Aunt Edwina muttered, smothering a hiccup with a sweep of her lace handkerchief, then leaning heavily on Teddie's arm.

"The other one?''

Aunt Edwina's heavily powdered face, so typically uplifted in pleasant regard, drooped dramatically with her scowl. "The cousin. Winchester. A decidedly nasty fellow. Foul-tempered and evil looking. Cares only for his''—her ponderous bosom jerked with another hiccup—"horses and nothing for his country. Why George even bothers with him I haven't a notion. But you know men. Their ability to forgive knows no bounds when brilliant seamanship is at stake. And a war. George has come under the mistaken notion that he can win the blackguard over and get him at the wheel of a ship, as if such a man would be an asset to any navy. I say leave him to his demons. But George hasn't listened to me in years. No, this way, Theodora. I have it in the strictest confidence from that handsome young Coyle that the shortest route to our rooms is via the rear stairs. In the east wing.''

Teddie guided her aunt around a corner and down a wide, deeply shadowed hall that led to the rear of the behemoth plantation house. She felt the probe of the older woman's stare as they passed beneath the dimly lit wall sconces.

"A fine young man Coyle,'' Edwina mused. "His eyes seem in a perpetual state of mirth. Did you notice?''

For a brief moment Teddie pondered the loss of her youth, that carefree sublime sort of existence that might have allowed her to notice such things in a man. Her heart might have even quickened a pace when his eyes met hers. She imagined that a young woman could well have enjoyed herself this evening, despite the deeply felt presence of the war hovering over all. But thoughts like these, though fleeting, were heinously indulgent, because at that moment Will lay chained in irons in the bilge-filled bowels of the *Rattlesnake,* his life at the mercy of a demon British commander.

"He appears quite taken with you," Aunt Edwina continued as they reached a set of wide stairs.

"You must have been atrociously bored, Aunt Edwina, allowing your imagination to run so far afield."

"The devil I did. A pity that I must point out the obvious to you, my dear. Good heavens, but these steps are steep."

They reached the second floor, Edwina marking this with a great huff. "I believe my room is the second on the left. Yours is one further, next to mine. An accommodating fellow, that Coyle."

"Do you need any assistance?" Teddie asked as they paused outside of Edwina's room. "I can wake Maggie for you."

Edwina sighed, abandoning for the moment her quest to stir Teddie's interest in Damian Coyle. "Thank you, but no, my dear, leave the poor girl to her sleep. We've a full day of it tomorrow. Indeed, I will take to the chaise in a great relief. But something tells me I won't find peaceful slumber this evening."

Despite her fatigue Teddie was thinking very much the same. "It's all this talk of war."

"Good heavens, no! I would never let war talk keep me from getting my sleep. It's the rum. Gives me outrageous indigestion." Edwina kissed the air beside each of Teddie's cheeks, her words a comforting murmur close to Teddie's ear. "The time for mourning your dear father has long since passed. You can enjoy yourself now that you're here, you know. He would have wished it. Indeed, he would have instructed you to abandon all your melancholy with that hideous orange excuse for a gown you were wearing the morning you arrived upon my doorstep. Now good night, my dear."

Teddie stared at her aunt's door long after it closed. Of their own accord her fingers found the delicate gold bracelet at her wrist, the bracelet her father had given her not a week before he died. It had been her mother's, he'd told her, given to her by him on their wedding day.

Teddie's finger moved over the fragile gold links. He could have easily sold it for precious food and coal. Surely his life had been worth more than a memento.

She could have sold it just as well instead of risking her life and Will's on some far-flung scheme to escape the poverty and the inevitable horrors of their life in war-ravaged London. And she hadn't.

But Aunt Edwina knew nothing of all this. To her understanding Teddie had crossed the Atlantic alone. She knew nothing of Will, of Cockburn's blackmail scheme, of Teddie's donning of a local legend's disguise to make her weekly midnight rendezvous with Cockburn. And she wouldn't until Teddie devised a plan to free Will. Until then she couldn't risk his life by confiding in anyone, no matter how desperately she might wish it.

Turning to seek her room, she felt the bracelet slip from her wrist and fall to the floor. Sweeping her skirts aside, she scanned the carpeted floor, an impossible task if there ever was one, given the inept lighting. She turned around several times, her eyes straining in the semidarkness. Exasperated, she sank to her knees and swept her palms back and forth over the floor. She turned again, repeating the motion of her hands. There . . . her fingertips brushed the delicate chain.

Tucking the precious bracelet deep into her palm, she rose and moved to the closed chamber door just down the hall. With deliberate care, she turned the handle and pushed the door open. No sense in rousing Maggie, Edwina's maid. Teddie had offered to share a room with the girl, knowing the chaise would provide more comfort than whatever might be found in the servants' wing.

No fire dwindled in the hearth. No welcoming candle burned. No pale moonlight penetrated the heavily draped windows. Not even Maggie's soft breathing cleaved the unearthly silence of this chamber.

Then she would indeed sleep well, Teddie thought, slipping out of her shoes as her fingers moved over the row of buttons at the back of her gown. The pale taffeta met the floor with a gentle rustle, followed seconds later by her chemise and her stockings. With a tug of her fingers, her hair tumbled down her back in a soft whisper against her bare skin.

The heavy August heat bade her to forgo her thin cambric night rail, and she gave momentary thought to throwing a window wide despite the risk in waking Maggie. Even in such sweltering heat some wayward breeze could surely be found, abundantly laced with the scent of honeysuckle. Since she'd come to Virginia she'd found sleep many a night with a warm, fragrant breeze wafting over her.

Even in the darkness the bed seemed to loom, its shadow bulky, rather enormous for guest accommodations. Her groping hands found the high edge of the mattress and the crisp fold of a sheet. She smoothed her palm over the cool cotton. A groan of drowsy satisfaction parted her lips as she lifted the sheet and slipped beneath.

The sheet billowed once, then drifted slowly over her bare skin, emitting some elusive, slightly peculiar scent. Whatever it was, it prompted her to snuggle deep against the pillows and leave the sheet at her hips.

Sleeping without clothes was one thing given the night's oppressive heat. But some attempt at modesty for Maggie's sake was certainly warranted, and she drew the sheet to her chin. The bed felt divine, the cotton like a whisper of heaven against her skin. She felt, for the first time in her life, just the least bit wanton.

Just before she sank into a dreamless slumber she made a mental note to thank Damian Coyle first thing in the morning for such wondrous accommodations. With the rum warming her blood, she doubted anything could wake her until morning.

Chapter Two

A clock somewhere in the house chimed once when Miles finally climbed the rear stairs to the east wing. His boots barely registered a whisper as they moved over the fine Aubusson carpets his grandfather had brought with him after escaping from England on the day he was to die for crimes against the crown. Flame-haired Maximilian Winchester had been a man of impeccable taste, and unmatched daring. Along with the carpets he'd brought with him the King of England's mistress, Mira, the woman he'd seduced from the king's bed and had nearly given his life for. Apparently, he'd also been a man of fierce appetites. They'd founded Miramer Plantation, built this sprawling house, and filled it with ten children, all of whom, including Miles's father, lay buried in the cemetery on a rise just north of the plantation. His mother lay there as well, alongside the graves of Miles's seven sisters and brothers.

Cursed or blessed, Miles was all that remained of Maximilian Winchester's legacy, sole heir to a dynasty. In his hands alone lay Miramer's future, and certain failure loomed if he were to abide by the blockade and allow his tobacco to rot in the fields unsold, something he knew his grandfather would never have allowed. After all, several generations of Winchesters had reverted to breaking laws they didn't particularly like. Perhaps this explained Miles's blithe forsaking of principles that men were fighting to the death every day to uphold. Some would indeed consider covert negotiations with the enemy during wartime treasonous. But if a simple bribe of a few British sea captains got Miles's ship to the Indies and back safely and filled Miramer's coffers until the next harvest, he would be a damned fool not to take advantage of the opportunity. That his neighboring plantation owners hadn't availed themselves of the same opportunities out of some misplaced sense of patriotism certainly was little reason for self-recrimination. Miles could think of no better time for having loyalties to no one but himself. And he'd be damned if he'd allow some plucky impostor to threaten his carefully laid plans, and Miramer's future. He'd been spared in Tripoli for some reason, dammit.

Besides, his grandfather wouldn't have stood for it either.

He entered his bedchamber, finding the hearth cold but the room far too stuffy for sleep. Not that he and that particular state were in any way friends. But the wash of a cool breeze over his skin oftentimes eased the onslaught of memory deep in the night, memory so vivid his skin fired as if bitten by a desert sun. He moved past the bed to the heavily draped windows and drew the velvet wide. Frothy moonlight spilled through the etched panes. Miles doused his candle and pushed several windows wide, allowing passage to the faint stirring of air that would have to suffice for a breeze this night. Even now, so late in the evening, his linen shirt clung to his damp skin as he shrugged out of it. He lingered at the windows, filling his lungs with the lush scents of late summer: the honeysuckle, the tobacco plants, the smoke from a cookfire somewhere in the slaves' quarters. In the distance fields of flowering tobacco swayed like a gently rolling sea, and beyond that the James River sparkled like a fine diamond in the moonlight.

A memory stirred, one so faint Miles scarcely recognized it for what it was. A childhood memory, no doubt. No pain sliced through him. Just a warmth too fleeting. He remembered so very little of his childhood.

Turning from the windows, he lifted his glass to his lips with one hand, with the other loosing his riding breeches. He should have brought the bottle of rum up with him. Long after he drained his glass the taste lingered on his tongue, the fire simmered in his blood. He wanted more.

He sat on the edge of his bed, drew off his boots, then stood and shed his breeches. Perhaps he should consider summoning Jillie with the rum. She'd proven herself more than amenable to his moods and most accommodating. But even Jillie wouldn't appease his restlessness tonight. Nor would the rum, for that matter.

He stretched out on the bed, the sheets like a cooling salve on his heated skin. Moonlit patterns played on the ceiling overhead. In the distance a hawk cried out his lonely wail, cleaving the stillness of the night. And then, out of the darkness, directly at Miles's side, came a woman's unmistakable sigh.

Miles lay still, musing on this. It couldn't be Jillie. She never entered his chamber or his bed before he told her to. He searched his rum-dulled memory. Ah, the hungry widow. Lydia Lawrence. He'd all but forgotten his invitation. She obviously hadn't. Judging by her deep, even breathing, she'd been awaiting him for some time.

In the darkness she was but a deeper shadow, a smooth curve of white-blue sheet against a backdrop of moonlit skies. Miles rolled to his side, suddenly acutely aware of the fragrant heat she emanated. This roused no memory. Odd, but he thought he would have remembered the faint lilac scent of her, simply because of the way his body immediately responded to it and instinctively drew nearer until he felt the play of her breath on his throat. His hand claimed the warm curve of her waist, slid over her hip, and pressed her sheet-swathed loins to his.

The sleeping widow stirred like a sleek cat from slumber, arching up against him so winsomely that Miles felt desire flame through him with an urgency that jarred him. His body turned to stone, rigid, unyielding, yet as alive and pulsating with need as that of a young man inexperienced in the ways of love.

With something very close to chagrin he felt heat sweep from his neck to his forehead. Damn, but he'd been without a woman for far too long. Even Jillie, despite her far-reaching talents, had never once stirred so immediate, so startling a response in him. Yet despite this the widow's breathing had resumed its deep, even meter. She still slept.

Perhaps she required further rousing. Lowering his mouth to hers, he tasted her lips, finding them warm, petal soft. Even in her sleep they parted beneath a nudge of his tongue, allowing him easy passage to the honeyed recesses of her mouth. She tasted faintly of rum, of slumber, of breathless innocence on the verge of discovery. . . .

What the hell had prompted such a thought? Widows, especially women of Lydia Lawrence's bold inclinations, were pleasingly accomplished in the art of lovemaking, the only kind of women Miles would consider taking to his bed on those rare occasions when the mood struck. Surely she knew this. No virgin, no matter the inherent nature of her allure, brought a man surcease without exacting a dear price from him.

True. But innocence was proving unusually intoxicating at the moment. Ah. His lips twitched faintly upward. Of course. This must be some sort of female ruse designed to enflame him to limits unknown. At the moment he could think of nothing better than a slumbering, sheet-swathed, lilac-scented temptress to rouse whatever gentleness he could muster, even while his body went up in flames to have her. Miles was rather certain he'd never before considered taking such care with a woman. No occasion had yet required it.

He found the change oddly refreshing.

Christ, but she was a supremely clever widow. Why the hell hadn't he sensed this in her long before tonight? In all truth his interest in her this evening had been born more of whim than of need. Prior to this he couldn't recall taking more than a moment's notice of her.

Again, the elusive lilac scent beckoned. He buried his face in the luxurious cloud of her hair and made a mental note to heed whim more often. An arrangement with her could prove immensely, albeit unexpectedly, satisfying.

He would indulge her ruse, for a short time. Then the game would be his.

His fingers curved around her jaw, feeling the delicate bone structure beneath the silken skin. He caressed the length of her neck, his mind blossoming with the image of a magnificent curve of luminous ivory. He might have reached to the bedside lamp, some part of him needing to see her in the soft golden light, but she seemed to turn her head away from his, as if seeking escape. With one finger beneath her chin he tilted her lips again to his.

"No," he rumbled softly in the darkness, as he might have with a virgin bride. He filled his hand with the curve of her sheet-swathed hip and again brought her pelvis full against his. The startling evidence of his arousal should wake her, he thought wickedly, nuzzling her temple, then the downy sweep of her cheek, to the tilted corner of her mouth.

"Yield to me," he murmured huskily, his desires raging.

A breathless sigh escaped her lips. Miles could wait no longer. A gentle manner was one thing. Not taking his fill of heaven while the moment was right was quite another. After all, no Winchester had ever squandered opportunity before, much less allowed a woman to make the rules in his bed.

With one sweep of his hand the sheet billowed to the foot of the bed. He heard her soft outcry and rewarded her by crushing his mouth over hers. She seemed to stiffen, and in that single moment he suffered his first and only doubt. But then he drew her full against him and his world exploded with savage, sensual pleasure.

Against his sinewed bulk she was lush, pliant, as delicately curved as he was harshly chiseled. Every inch of her seemed as if precisely made to fit his hands, her mouth his mouth. Her every movement was guileless response, her every breath, every touch sweet heaven upon his fevered skin. He plunged deeper into the abyss. Only once before had he experienced this sort of mindless passion. So intoxicating was it, he'd become a slave first to the woman, then to the drug she gave him. And though he'd conquered his obsession with both, hardly a moment passed when he was with a woman that the air didn't seem laced with a nauseating pungent opium haze, and his mind dulled and fogged with the memories.

But tonight only moonlight dared trespass in this chamber, only lilac danced on the warm breeze, and memory remained mercifully at bay. And Miles felt as if his soul had been freed of its bonds, to need—yes, he needed this woman—with a ferocity that staggered him. With every kiss he took her breath deep into his lungs, then breathed new life into her. But he wanted more, so much more. In her he would be reborn.

He pulled her beneath him, aware only of his raw, consuming need to find surcease deep within her. The fingers gripping her head possessed little tenderness, his kisses only a savage hunger as he nudged her thighs apart. Again she cried out against his mouth, then arched up against him, her full young breasts a sweet, torturous undulation. He would explode if he didn't take her now . . . he must . . .

There was no turning back now, even for the iron-willed.

The barrier caught him dimly unawares. She went entirely rigid beneath him, as though she'd suddenly plunged into frigid waters. No, this couldn't be . . . surely she wasn't . . .

It was a ruse. Just a ruse. He'd had enough women to know the depths of their guile when it served them.

"Open for me, love," he rasped against her parted lips, one hand lifting her hips into his. His bulk afforded her little choice as he adjusted himself, then eased deeper against the barrier, despite the distant clamoring in his mind. There was no turning back . . . he couldn't possibly deny himself of her now.

The barrier gave way. "Sweet Jesus—" He felt the flow of warmth, an exquisite tightness gripping him, and immediately he withdrew, bracing himself over her, his body rigid with unspent desires, his mind refusing to acknowledge the undeniable. Moonlight reflected in the twin fathomless pools of her eyes and danced like blue fire in her hair.

Her lips trembled with her whispered plea. "P-Please d-don't—"

The room momentarily spun around him. "You're not Lydia."

The bedchamber door thwacked open. Lamplight flooded the room and then, before Miles could suitably roar with his fury, with the abominable injustice of it all, a piercing shriek shook the rafters. The source of this extraordinary high pitch hoisted her lamp and swept to the side of the bed in a flurry of pink silk robes and a startling abundance of blond hair.

"You bastard!" Lydia Lawrence hissed through bared teeth. "I suppose I came a few minutes too soon, eh?" Her eyes raked over him with murderous intent. He gave her little opportunity to ogle or indulge her whim, bounding from the bed and clamping his hand over her mouth before she decided shrieking would serve her best at the moment. She obviously cared very little if she roused the entire household, a circumstance he'd rather not consider.

"Calm yourself, Lydia," he muttered, experiencing some difficulty restraining her thrashing arms and legs. "There's been an obvious misunderstanding."

Lydia thrashed anew, her ire unassuaged by anything he could possibly say. And then, with the fury of a rabid canine, she bit his hand. Miles exploded with a scathing curse and Lydia wriggled free.

At that precise moment Commander George Farrell, wearing nothing but a nightshirt, sprang through the doorway with his pistol leveled squarely at Miles. At his heels fluttered his wife, who gave Lydia Lawrence a dismissive glance, then, at first sight of Miles in all his unabashed naked splendor, promptly flung a hand over her eyes.

"Good grief, George, the man's entirely without his clothes. Do put down that ghastly pistol. He's no murderer."

Farrell's regard remained suitably grim even when Miles snatched up his breeches from a nearby wing chair and hastily donned them. "Perhaps you'd rather I shoot him, Edwina," Farrell muttered, the pistol never once wavering from Miles's bare chest. "The blackguard has your niece in his bed."

"Theodora!" All color drained from Edwina Farrell's face as she slowly lowered her hand from her eyes. "Oh, my dear, no—" Her gaze softened considerably as it probed the shadowy recesses of the bed, on whose sheets Miles was certain lay the startling evidence of his most recent misdeed.

"Ha!" Lydia Lawrence glanced between Miles and Farrell, her lips twisting with perverse pleasure. "It seems your schemes have run amok, Miles. You sacrifice a night with me for the virgin charms of Farrell's niece, and not only are you left rather noticeably unsatisfied, from what I could tell a moment ago, but soundly trapped in the yoke as well." She arched a brow, giving a satisfied sigh. "I do believe I feel avenged. Goodnight all." And with that she swept from the room in a wave of heady jasmine.

Miles returned Farrell's chilling stare and felt the bottom fall out of his life. No words existed in any combination to exonerate him, of this he was grimly certain. His guilt in the matter was unquestionable, the evidence irrefutable. It mattered very little that he'd thought the young woman someone else. Only a fool and a coward would attempt to defend himself against the obvious, particularly with a pistol aimed at his chest.

He turned, his dispassionate gaze settling on Theodora Lovelace. Swathed in sheets, with her ebony hair tumbling in glorious disarray over her shoulders, she looked far too young and ingenuous to have masterminded any sort of scheme to entrap him. Gone was the sleek, elegant sloop with the sly purpose, cunningly picking her way through a sea tangled with unsuspecting craft. In its place a pale, glassy-eyed, unduly ravaged young innocent, who still bore the mark of his unleashed passion on her swollen lips. Her silence spoke far more eloquently than any display of hysterics. Her eyes remained downcast, as if avoiding his and her aunt's. But he could detect no traces of guilt there. Or victory, for that matter, though she had indeed won this battle. Looking at her, not a soul in the world would label her the perpetrator. Miles, however, knew better.

Of its own accord his gaze lowered to the luminous swells of her breasts, rising and falling above the sweep of sheet. In the dim lamplight her skin gleamed like the finest porcelain, just as he'd imagined when he'd touched her. She'd felt like silk against him in that solitary haven of darkness.

He watched her slender fingers twist into the sheets, then found his gaze riveted on the splash of crimson marring the pristine white expanse, just beyond the reach of her fingertips. His teeth clicked together.

"Oh, my dear child," Edwina Farrell barely whispered. "Why did it have to be Winchester?"

Theodora Lovelace glanced up sharply, her violet eyes widening the merest fraction when they met her aunt's. Miles was certain her full lower lip quivered before she caught it with her teeth. The rosy splashes of color high on her cheeks seemed to fade instantly. Her fingers gripped the sheets with a sudden white-knuckled intensity. Hell, he could almost believe she hadn't any idea who she'd chosen to entrap this evening, so utterly devastated did she seem by her aunt's revelation.

Not for the first time, he had to wonder at her motives.

"Aunt Edwina, please listen to me—" Her voice drifted over Miles like a mellow summer breeze, husky, low-pitched, slightly hoarse, a soothing balm to the insistent pounding in his head. He found himself wishing she'd meet his gaze. Perhaps then the seductress would betray herself. As it was, he was having one hell of a time keeping an apology from springing to his lips.

"Oh, my dear," her aunt breathed with acute resignation. "I'm rather afraid you took the matter entirely out of my hands and your own when you disposed of your dress and chemise on these lovely carpets. George, good heavens, put the pistol away and think. Surely we've another course in the matter besides—"

"He'll marry her," Farrell growled.

Miles's head snapped around. "The hell I will. There's been a mistake."

"Indeed, sir," Edwina trilled. "And the mistake was wholly yours!"

"Madam, I know my own bedchamber."

"And I know my niece, you black-hearted scoundrel," Edwina shrieked in a pitch known only to hysterical females. "How dare you suggest your only fault in the matter lies simply in your retiring to your bed for the night!"

Miles worked a muscle in his jaw against the throbbing at his temples. "Indeed, madam, if it were only that simple."

Edwina Farrell blinked furiously and again tested the reach of her soprano. "Shoot him, George, and be done with it. I can barely stand the sight of him. You ravaged an innocent young woman, Miles Winchester, a tender, fresh young dove who knows nothing of your rutting ways, of your insatiable lust for—"

"Enough." Miles swiped an impatient hand through his hair. "The deed has been done."

"On that alone, sir, we can all regretfully agree," Edwina spat.

Miles addressed George Farrell squarely. "I will take full responsibility for preserving Miss Lovelace's reputation."

"Ha!" Edwina Farrell huffed. "I'm afraid your scorned mistress might make that a bit difficult for you. By morning the entire household will be abuzz with the news."

"I'll take care of Lydia," Miles said, again addressing his remarks to Farrell. "As for Miss Lovelace, I've the means to provide her a generous settlement to forget the entire matter."

"You fiend!" Edwina shrieked anew, surging against her husband's restraining arm with the look of the devil in her eyes. "No amount of money could possibly restore the physical damage you've done to this girl, much less wipe her mind free of the wretched memory! My niece, sir, shall not be bought!"

Miles arched a brow. "Many a ruined young woman has found unexpected comfort in remuneration, Mrs. Farrell. I find nothing tawdry in such an arrangement."

"Spoken like a true scoundrel," Edwina hissed. "George, do something besides point that pistol."

Farrell's stare remained cold beneath shaggy white brows, his commanding air not the least diminished by his lack of uniform. "Your father was the bravest, most honorable man I've ever known, Winchester, as well as a lifelong friend. Not a day passes that I don't remember and miss him. I am being generous when I say you do his memory a heinous disservice. For that reason alone, I can't idly abide it. But as my niece is involved, I believe I hold utmost sway in the matter. Either you marry my niece or I will press you into naval service under my command, captaining a frigate."

"George!"

"Silence, woman."

Like any dutiful wife, Edwina Farrell ignored her husband. "You're all but bargaining with the lout. Surely you've lost your mind."

To Miles's eye, Farrell's deeply lined visage betrayed no madness, simply a calm determination. What Farrell hadn't bothered to mention, of which he was undoubtedly certain Miles was aware, was that as the highest-ranking official in the area during wartime, Farrell could indeed sentence Miles to any punishment he desired. At the moment Miles would have vastly preferred pistols at dawn to marriage. But of course the clever Farrell hadn't offered him that alternative. He'd chosen something far more devious with which to negotiate.

Miles couldn't shake the feeling that Farrell somehow tested him. His eyes narrowed on the older man. A glint of satisfaction shone deep in those dark eyes, as if Farrell knew damned well that he was offering Miles no real alternative here, rather that he was forcing Miles to admit his deepest failing, his one unpardonable weakness, that which he could never conquer.

Trapped. The bonds were different than they'd been eight years before in Tripoli, but the rage tasted just as bitter. Miles could only hope his revenge would be sweet, and everlasting.

"*No!* George, dear God, you cannot sentence our lovely Theodora to hell with this man! Why punish *her* when the fault was surely his? I say shoot the rogue where he stands! I simply cannot allow this—"

Nor could Teddie. Not for another moment. Gripping the sheet tightly around her, she slid from the bed onto unsteady legs. Her movement silenced her aunt and drew Miles Winchester's unwelcome, black-eyed regard. He turned toward her and she instinctively drew back, repulsed by the mere thought of his hand extending to help her. She lifted her eyes for the first time to his with a stony look of warning. A jolt seemed to pass entirely through her.

He was, without question, the most ominous-looking man she'd ever seen, certainly not at all resembling the classically beautiful dream lover in whose arms she'd thought she slumbered just moments ago. Had she but imagined the scarred length of cheek, the sardonic twist of his lips, had her mind conjured such cold, lifeless black eyes beneath a sinister slash of brows, she would have thought herself caught in a nightmare's talons. And she would never have surrendered to it. But the tender brush of his lips on hers, the smoothly seductive rumble of his voice, even the comforting magnificence of his body against hers had lured her inexplicably deeper into the haven of her dream with the promise of passion, warmth . . . love. . . .

But this man knew nothing of these. Caught up in her dream she'd no doubt imagined the tenderness, the thrill of desires first roused—until the pain. The pain had been all too real, seizing her from her moon-dappled dream, thrusting her back into cold, grim reality.

It had been no dream. She'd given her virginity to a stranger, and with a startling lack of self-restraint or hesitation. Indeed, she'd responded to him as if somehow, unknowingly, she'd been awaiting him and that moment all her life, eager, ripe, completely his to take for his own.

Color flooded into her cheeks with such dispatch that she had to avert her eyes from his, before those glittering black pools registered the slightest response. Or the merest glint of satisfaction. No doubt even now, with his neck caught soundly in a noose, he savored the ease of his conquest as he would a fine liqueur, lingeringly, smugly, all but smacking his lips with deeply felt bravado. And wanting her to know he did.

Then again, a man didn't simply acquire such insolence or confidence in his abilities without the benefit of a good deal of experience. Perhaps, in all truth, the ease of his conquest wasn't the least bit remarkable for him. Indeed, there might have been nothing extraordinary about it. Or her. After all, he'd obviously mistaken her for another woman, a woman he fully expected to be in his bed awaiting him. *That* sort of man possessed an ease of conquest no doubt enjoyed by very few other men.

She slanted her eyes up at him, meeting the full measure of his cool, fathomless regard. No satisfaction lurked there. No glimmer of smugness. Just lifeless pits of inky black. She could have been staring into pitch.

The hairs on the back of her neck stood on end.

"No," she said, inching her chin up another notch, the better to meet his gaze directly. He stood a good six inches taller than she, perhaps more. The extravagant breadth of his bare shoulders and well-muscled arms no doubt only compounded the feeling that he could, at his whim, squash her. Or perhaps the memory of being pressed deep into the feather ticking was still too fresh. His flesh had burned every inch of hers. Even now his heated male scent filled her nostrils. . . .

Again, a flush heated her cheeks. Why the devil had she no power of will, no self-control with this man? She—a woman who had stood toe to toe with Cockburn, successfully betraying no emotion, no weakness, for the sake of her brother's life— was now reduced to the sort of furious blushing common only to tongue-tied, dumbstruck ninnies? Preposterous. Miles Winchester, she decided, had humiliated her enough for one evening.

"No," she repeated, drawing herself up as though she were swathed in royal robes, not a simple white bed sheet. "I believe I'd prefer a settlement." The subtle arch of her brow was met with an ominous narrowing of those black eyes. "And do be magnanimous, Mr. Winchester. The deed, as you so mildly put it, was not so grand and glorious as I'd thought it would surely be. I believe I would be most remiss if I did not expect you to make further amends for my . . . disappointment." The air between them suddenly sizzled with a heat so palpable, Teddie felt the burn deep in her womb. The shadow over Winchester's face deepened, leaving Teddie with the disturbing feeling that he was the hunter, she his prey, and somehow she'd already been caught.

"Theodora!" Aunt Edwina gasped. "How can you speak so . . . so *casually*! And of *settlements*! I've never heard of such a thing. Taking money from a man who just ruined you, bargaining for more because he . . . because you didn't . . . why, it's unthinkable!"

Miles Winchester's lips thinned over a slash of feral white teeth, his eyes never leaving Teddie's. "I believe the lady and I could come to an agreement."

For some reason his tone—hushed, almost intimate—set Teddie's pulse leaping in her veins and she drew back a step, clutching the sheet tighter around her. Suddenly she needed air, a cold slap of air to clear her head, to awaken her from this blasted spell. Even now her aunt's voice sounded as if from a great distance.

"Whatever can you be thinking, Theodora? You've just suffered great loss at his hands. He ruined you."

Indeed, sniveling might serve her at this point, at least to rouse sympathy. But Teddie had never sniveled in her life, and she wasn't about to let Miles Winchester drive her to it. Particularly when they both knew she'd been an eager, albeit naive, participant in the deed. It mattered very little that she'd mistakenly chosen his bedchamber for the night. Teddie could have fled at any time and she'd chosen not to.

Until the last moments he'd given her ample reason to stay in that bed, in his arms, beneath him.

Then again, many young women had been reduced to tears out of shame. A pity, but even for her aunt's sake she couldn't summon them. She simply wished to be done with this business, while exacting some sort of recompense. She rather doubted an apology would be forthcoming. Indeed, at the moment she preferred to place great distance between herself and Winchester. He made her disturbingly aware of herself, acutely self-conscious for the first time in her life. She didn't like it in the least. Besides, she wasn't about to allow a hastily arranged marriage to interfere with her business with Cockburn and saving Will.

"George, talk to her."

Teddie squared her shoulders. "Talk all you wish, Uncle George, but I will marry only when I fall in love. And I'm certain that I could never love him. Now, if you would excuse me . . ." Retrieving her clothes and slippers from the floor, she breezed past all with head held high. She got as far as the door when her path was suddenly blocked by a wild-eyed Damian Coyle. Bracing himself in the doorjamb, he took complete notice of her from head to toe in one blink, flushed a raging scarlet clear to his sleep-mussed hairline, then erupted with a curse.

"Damn you, Winchester!" he roared, charging past her and into the room with fists clenched in the flowing folds of his emerald silk dressing gown. "Damn your rutting hide to hell!"

Winchester deftly sidestepped Damian's first wild swing, catching his cousin's fist in his wider, open palm. His eyes spat black fire, his words hissing from between his teeth. "The lady requires no champion, Damian. I don't think you want to do this."

Damian surged against his cousin's seemingly immovable bulk, his voice quivering with fury. "You knew, you bastard, you told me to forget about her, to pity the man who had her. And all the while you planned to take her for your own. Isn't it enough that your very existence besmirches the Winchester name? Having one woman in your bed isn't enough, is it? Must you defile sweet young virgins, with no other intent but to slay your lust and ruin them for any other man? What kind of devil's spawn are you?"

Winchester's stare remained bleak and unforgiving. "You know nothing of the circumstances, Damian. Save yourself some embarrassment and go to bed."

"The hell I will." Again, Damian threw a punch that Winchester caught well before it met its mark. "I could kill you for this, Miles. Or by God I'll die trying. Dawn tomorrow, cousin. In the far north pasture. Choose your weapon."

"Don't do this, Damian," Winchester rumbled.

"Choose your weapon, coward."

Winchester turned to stone. But Teddie wasn't about to let his arrogance and Damian's bullheaded gallantry rule the matter. She'd seen enough of the havoc wreaked by this war to harbor much trust in men's judgment, particularly when they believed their bloody honor at stake. She'd watched men die for much less. Besides, for some inexplicable reason she was certain the noble Damian stood little chance of besting his cousin, in any arena. She certainly wasn't going to allow anyone to risk their life for something that was in any way her fault.

"Thank you, Captain Coyle," she said, drawing both men's sudden regard and her aunt's wide-eyed stare. "But I'm afraid getting yourself killed would prove nothing."

"By God, your honor must be avenged!" Damian cried with such fervor that Teddie's heart fell. He thumped his fist over his chest. "And I, Miss Lovelace, shall be that champion."

"Dammit, Coyle, you've a ship and crew awaiting you in

Baltimore. Don't be foolish—'' Farrell began, but Damian would hear nothing more.

Shoving against Winchester, he withdrew a step, wiping a hand over his mouth as though his words left a bitter taste. "Dawn tomorrow, Miles. Or I shall run you through while you sleep." He turned, took one step, then spun toward his cousin, his fist arcing upward from behind the shield of his dressing gown.

The unexpected blow smashed into Winchester's jaw, snapping his head back with the force. But for that, his body barely registered the impact, his feet unmoving, spread wide on the thick crimson carpet. Teddie braced herself for the inevitable when his fists balled against his thighs. She felt the urgency in her aunt's trembling grip on her upper arm. Even George Farrell seemed to stiffen in anticipation . . . of something that never came.

Whether this was credit to Winchester's self-control Teddie didn't wish to consider, but his fists remained at his sides. "Would that we could call ourselves even now, cousin," he growled, his heavy black brows descending over his eyes. "I will indeed meet you at dawn tomorrow. Now, get out. All of you. Get the hell out."

Chapter Three

The low-hanging mantle of fog had barely lightened a shade when Teddie stepped from a door at the side of the main house and hurried along a cobbled path to Miramer's stables. Her footsteps echoed in the silence, and she might have thought herself trapped in a gray, honeysuckle-laced cocoon were it not for the vivid memory of the glorious sweep of grass she knew extended from this path in three directions until it met with the lush banks of the James River.

Early last evening, just as the sun settled low in the west, she'd ventured from the overheated confines of the house and had wandered this very path, drawn there by her aunt's vivid descriptions of Miramer's much-touted beauty, which was due in large part to its location at a sharp bend in the James River. From this vantage the river seemed to surround the house entirely on three sides, nestling it like a rare jewel. Indeed, the impressive columned portico extending from the front to both sides of the house seemed designed to afford the most spectacular views of the river and surrounding countryside. Teddie wondered how many British warships had sailed past the magnificent plantation, with cannon at the ready. From any of the windows, she imagined, those ships would seem to loom out there, the menace amidst the splendor.

The other source of much gossip regarding Miramer among Aunt Edwina's circle of friends was its stables. With the exception of the esteemed Reynolds's holdings, the Winchesters had apparently long been known for the most prized horseflesh in the region. They had also acquired a reputation as notorious gamblers, particularly with regard to racing their horses. According to Aunt Edwina, the rivalry between the Winchesters and the Reynolds had recently grown rather heated, a circumstance that was sure to provide vast entertainment for the locals in the form of races for some time to come. A bit of a gambler herself, with her own passion for horses, Aunt Edwina had promised Teddie they would be regular attendees at such events, if only to offer Jules Reynolds support. It was from Reynolds that George Farrell had purchased a sleek black Arabian filly named Cleo for his wife several years before. And Teddie had good reason to trust in Reynolds's eye for prime horseflesh: On Teddie's latest midnight rendezvous with Cockburn, Cleo had proven herself more than adept at evading American regiments, well-mounted themselves, and had weathered the hell-bent flight across the moonlit countryside without displaying the least sign of distress afterward.

At the moment, however, Teddie hoped for Damian Coyle's sake that the Winchester stables would provide comparable offerings.

She found precisely what she was looking for in one of the first stalls. A stallion, black as pitch and over sixteen hands at least, with the look of Lucifer in his eyes, greeted her as she quietly entered the stable.

"Perfect," she murmured, her gaze moving appreciatively over the steed's well-muscled chest and flanks, sure testaments to his speed and endurance. The north pasture, she'd learned, was at least two miles from the main house. And dawn was fast upon them.

Quickly she moved the length of the barn, her eye taking keen notice of the dozen or more horses stabled here. She paused at a back room, finding it empty save for a cot, a small stove, and neatly hung rows of tack. Retrieving a bridle and quirt from one hook, she returned to the black's stall.

"There's a fine boy," she crooned in a lilting singsong sure to calm even the most temperamental of mounts. His ears pricked, nostrils flaring to catch her scent. "You are obligingly unattended, sweet," she purred, musing on her luck. Slowly she pushed against the wood and slipped within, one hand extending beneath his mouth. Warmth fanned over her palm and fingers as he blew.

"Such a handsome fellow," she murmured, ever watchful of

his ears. They remained pricked, yet he'd not made any moves to encourage her further. "There's a good lad," she whispered, edging her hand from beneath his mouth to the subtly flaring muzzle. She laid her palm flat against his warmth. Immediately he dipped his head, as if guiding her hand up the length of his nose and between his ears. Teddie smiled and dug into the pocket of her dress, withdrawing two lumps of sugar, which she pressed beneath his mouth.

"I've need of you, boy," she whispered with a pat to his thick neck. With ease she slipped the bit into his mouth and drew the bridle over his ears, all the while crooning softly. He followed her from the stall and into the early morning murk.

"Your master has you well-trained," Teddie mused. Grabbing a handful of black mane, she hoisted herself astride his broad back and gripped the reins as he danced lightly. She smoothed her dress as best she could over her bare legs. As it was, the pale yellow cotton rode just above her knee, displaying sleek muscled calves unknown to most of the ladies she knew. "Now which way is north, I wonder—"

"Hey! You there! Stop, I says!"

Teddie glanced sharply around. From the side of the barn a tall, gangly black man emerged, one fist waving at her, the other hoisting his suspenders up over his shoulder.

"Not nobody rides Wildair 'cept the massa hisself!" he shouted, punctuating this with another wave of his fist. "Not nobody. Not even Simon!"

Wildair pranced, taking the bit fully into his mouth, eager to be off. Teddie felt the untested power beneath her and wrapped the reins twice around her wrists before gripping them tight in both hands. Perhaps this mount would be a match to her Cleo. She cocked a brow at the man. "And where is the master?"

The man stared at her, moving slowly nearer, his step infused with wariness. "You can' ride in no fog. Too dangerous, even for da massa, 'specially on Wildair. Git down now, missy, 'fore you hurt yo'sef, 'fore the Massa Miles sees you on his best horse and shoots you."

She barely touched the reins and Wildair responded, dancing several paces back along the path. "Where is the master?" she repeated, entirely indifferent to the man's warnings. She'd ridden blindly through the darkest of nights, over countryside unknown to her, on a most spirited mare. The fog didn't scare her. Neither did the thought of Miles Winchester's wrath. She doubted very much that even he would shoot her. She narrowed her eyes on the man. "Is he not at the house?"

Had she not watched him so closely she might have missed it. But no, his head inclined almost imperceptibly to the right. In a direction she knew was away from the house, and undoubtedly to the north. Unable to resist a smile, she reined Wildair about.

"Dammit, where you goin', missy?" the man roared.

"To save them all, of course!" Teddie shouted over her shoulder, digging her slippered heels into Wildair's flanks and relaxing her hold on the reins. Instantly Wildair plunged into a full gallop. The unexpected force all but yanked Teddie's arms from their sockets. Her chest smashed into his pumping neck, driving all the breath from her lungs. She struggled to retain her seat, feeling the bite of the leather straps as the reins dug into her hands. Immediately the fog swallowed them, and she fought against the reins. Yet Wildair only lengthened his stride, bearing into the ground with an alarming ferocity.

Teddie battled the first stirrings of panic. Tears blurred her vision. Wind-whipped mane stung her cheeks, and she buried her face in Wildair's neck. Flames seemed to lap at the muscles bunched in her arms, in her thighs gripped about his back. She couldn't hold on much longer, her strength no match for Wildair's.

Through a blur of tears she detected the faint outline of trees amidst the fog. It seemed to be lifting, at least enough to allow her to somehow guide him, if he'd allow her. Beneath Wildair's hooves came the unmistakable thud of hard-packed dirt. She gripped the reins with renewed faith. The horse had chosen a path, perhaps one that led to the north pasture.

And then she was certain. Wildair knew precisely where he was taking her. He was going to his master. A well-trained mount indeed. If only she could hold on for the ride.

Her arms had gone almost entirely numb when Wildair finally slowed his pace. Teddie raised her head, realizing with some chagrin that she'd endured the ride with eyes closed. The fog had lifted considerably upon this soft rise some distance from the river. It was well past dawn. She was too late.

"No—" The plea barely escaped her lips.

A gunshot rang out above the roaring in her ears. "No—" Before Wildair could come to a stop she slipped from his back. Instantly her legs buckled beneath her and she fell to her knees on the damp grass. "No—" The fog seemed to swallow her scream. "Don't—please—" She struggled to her feet, her eyes probing the gloom. And then she saw him running toward her out of the mist, impossibly tall, his white shirt sleeves billowing, his scarred face twisted and unforgiving. In his hand he gripped a smoking pistol.

He caught her in his arms just as her legs gave way. She stared into a face as bleak and barren as death. "You killed him, Winchester," she choked, her fingers digging into his forearms.

"He lives," came his harsh reply.

"But I heard the shot—"

"I would never kill anyone over a woman. Even you." His lips relaxed faintly, but there was no mirth in this. "Can you stand?"

His words were a soft rumble in his chest, his English accent laced seductively with a liquid, soft slur. His eyes seemed to burn into hers. And Teddie was gripped by a powerful urge to flee. "Yes, I can stand," she managed, though she wasn't the least bit certain she could. But she'd do just about anything to get his hands from around her waist, to put distance between them. She averted her gaze, reveling for the moment in the feel of the strength returning to her limbs.

"You stole my horse." His breath fanned hot against her forehead.

She stared at his black boots, then again lifted her eyes to his lest he think her the least bit apologetic. "I had no choice. I overslept." She would have turned away from him then, but he caught both her hands in his much larger ones. His thumbs moved over the welts left by the reins.

"You're lucky to be alive," he said, his tone brusque. Yet something in the way his thumbs moved over her skin roused memory best left buried deep.

A flush swept over Teddie's cheeks. Again she attempted to turn away, but he held her fast, turning her palms up. At once her fingers curled into her palms, shielding the calluses where there should have been lily-white softness.

"Miss Lovelace!" Damian Coyle emerged from the fog, his voice heavy with concern. "My God, Miles, she was up on Wildair. It's a wonder she wasn't killed!"

"She could be hung," Winchester rumbled. "She stole my horse."

"Thank heavens he didn't shoot you, Captain Coyle," Teddie said, tugging her hands from Winchester's. Ignoring him, she faced Damian, summoning a tone that typically brooked little resistance from her brother, or her father, for that matter. "And you're not going to get the opportunity to shoot him either, Captain Coyle, not over some misbegotten sense of justice."

Coyle flushed crimson. "Hardly misbegotten, my dear Miss Lovelace. We Virginians are known for our deep sense of honor." Coyle slanted Winchester a cool look. "*Some* of us, that is. I, for one, will not allow your chastity to go unavenged or your reputation to remain besmirched because of some tawdry monetary settlement."

There simply was no arguing with a man bent on gallantry. She'd only begun to realize that last evening after they'd left Winchester's chamber and Damian Coyle had offered her little chance to talk sense into him. His commander, Uncle George, had achieved the same lack of success. All had retired to their bedchambers amidst a great banging of doors.

This morning the situation was no less explosive. Perhaps more so. Indeed, Captain Coyle's fingers gripped his pistol with white-knuckled intensity, as though he could barely wait to return to that field to put a lead ball into Winchester's heart. If Teddie didn't intervene and offer some alternative this was sure to happen, and at least one life would be needlessly sacrificed to the code duello. Over the last three months she had witnessed enough bloodshed to last her a lifetime. And something about Damian Coyle—an unwavering nobility of purpose—reminded her of her brother. Perhaps this explained the protectiveness she felt toward a man she barely knew. "A settlement will not suffice?" she asked him, her brows knit.

Coyle's classically handsome features hardened. "If anything, the idea only gives me more cause to shoot my cousin for even suggesting such a thing. You are in Virginia now, Miss Lovelace. We are not *all* barbarians. Now, if you would, cousin, return to the field of honor. I believe the turn is now mine."

Seizing on a sudden, somewhat irrational thought, Teddie gripped Coyle's sleeve and blurted, "If I marry your cousin, Captain Coyle, would you then lay down your pistols, with a most heartfelt promise to put the matter aside?"

With a start Coyle blinked at her, clearly aghast. "My dear Miss Lovelace," he slowly said. "Are you quite certain . . . that is, my cousin would never agree—" He paused, swallowing deeply and casting Winchester a befuddled look. "I—I suppose we would have little choice then but to consider the deed avenged."

"Fine," Teddie said crisply. "Consider it done then."

"But there are others who would . . . that is—" Damian blinked furiously, clearly taken aback by the audacity of her suggestion. "You've more than one choice here. I, for one, am not above . . . that is . . . my dear Miss Lovelace—"

"Do call me Teddie, Captain Coyle. I much prefer it." With a brisk shake of the dew from her hem, she turned to Winchester, drawn rather than repelled by the ferocity of his stare. Never had she allowed a man or circumstances to intimidate her. She wasn't about to start. Still, her fingers twisted deeper into the folds of her gown when his gaze seemed to probe the very depths of her thoughts. "Surely we can come to some type of marriage arrangement that would be agreeable to both of us."

Miles could recall few occasions when he'd been stunned clear to his boots. And by a woman, never. Deceived, yes, once, but only once. Yet in less than a day the impetuous Theodora had caught him unawares at least thrice over, beginning with their disturbing and unconsummated encounter in his bed last night, the effects of which no doubt accounted for a great deal of his surliness this morning. Yet even under the influence of tightly strung nerves and an uncharacteristic desire to crawl out of his skin, compounded by the insistent throb in his swollen jaw, Miles had aimed his pistol into the sky instead of putting a ball into Damian's leg. Not that his young cousin wasn't deserving of it, so blindly awash was he in noble self-sacrifice. He'd also punched Miles in the jaw and had called him a coward, more than ample reason for any gentleman worthy of the name to take up his pistol with due outrage.

Miles could have killed his proud cousin. He'd chosen not to out of some damned inconvenient surge of conscience. Inconvenient, indeed, knowing that he stood squarely in Damian's sights, just moments from the white-hot impact of a shot that was sure to come. And Damian would have shot him. Of this neither harbored a doubt. Apparently Theodora Lovelace harbored the same convictions.

Teddie. In some suitably unconventional way the nickname fit, far more than Theodora. *Teddie.* He wanted to feel it rolling off his own tongue. On hers it had sounded as fresh as the fields after a welcome rain.

From just at his back Wildair snorted. Damian was staring at him. So was Teddie. He'd never known a woman to possess such intensity of purpose or eyes of such extraordinary hue, an icy, impenetrable blue-violet. In his bedchamber, by the glow of the lamp, they'd shone a hauntingly deep purple, half-hooded by a thick fringe of black lashes. The look of a woman impassioned. . . .

Miles set his teeth. He would, of course, refuse her. Marriage? A preposterous notion, even if he had to take a lead ball instead to prove the depths of his aversion to the idea. He would allow no woman to trap him.

Yet something betrayed her outward display of sublime confidence. Certainly not her bearing, which remained as bold and forthright as any man's. Something . . . His gaze narrowed on her lips, that full, winsome curve of rosy pink. He detected the faintest quiver there, an anxious quiver. She certainly didn't fear him, peculiar as he found that. No, the lady was not as entirely confident as she appeared.

An irrational, perplexing desire to call her bluff suddenly came over him. Amazing, as he abhorred women's natural inclination for trickery. He'd certainly never before considered playing along for the sheer intrigue of it. Particularly with the stakes so high. Acting on a moment's impulse now could saddle him with a wife for a lifetime.

She blinked up at him, an extraordinary blend of innocence and guile, audacity and complete helplessness. To the casual eye she seemed to have laid it all in his hands. But she'd done so anticipating his response. She was gambling all, knowing he'd refuse her. And if he did, what then?

Miles shifted his gaze to Damian. His cousin's fervor to plunge a ball through his heart was exceeded perhaps only by his noble desire to protect Teddie. If ever Damian had chosen a cause that needed no championing, the capricious Teddie had to be it. But though some might be inclined to underestimate his cousin's will, Miles never had. For that reason he could almost sense the turn of his cousin's thoughts, could almost feel his anticipation building to a frenzied pitch as he awaited Miles's response. Indeed, even to Damian, glory on a field of honor paled when compared to the idea of marriage to a beautiful but tragic young woman who would think herself eternally saved from ruin.

They both wanted him to refuse.

His gaze met and held his cousin's. "Put your pistol away, Damian, you've no further use of it. Miss Lovelace"—Miles gave his best attempt at a gallant incline of his head—"at your convenience, we may wed." With a certain satisfaction he watched the color drain from her rosy cheeks. Her full lips parted, no doubt with surprise, and Miles knew a sudden fierce desire to feel her mouth beneath his. He couldn't have kept his hands from her if he'd tried, wrapping his fingers around her upper arm, feeling the supple strength in the slender limb. A mere flexing of his biceps drew her nearer, bringing her glittering eyes up to his. "You wouldn't care to change your mind?'' he purred, all too aware that a fire leapt to life in his blood the moment he touched her.

She stiffened against him, a mask of indifference suddenly sweeping over her features. ''Once I make up my mind, Winchester, I never change it.''

His eyes hooded. ''You just might.''

''Good God, Miles,'' Damian sputtered, his plans duly squashed. ''You've quite lost your mind. This is extraordinary even for you.''

Miles arched a brow at his cousin. ''Indeed, Damian. Why choose a lifetime of penance when I could have taken my punishment swiftly on that field and been done with it?'' His gaze again found the rosy fullness of her mouth, just inches below his. ''Indeed,'' he muttered, ''Most men would consider me without a bit of sense. But then again, most already do.'' It was with a certain disturbing reluctance that he released her. His tone sank quickly into its typical harshness as he motioned to his bay tethered beneath a nearby oak. ''Take Miss Lovelace back to the house on Zeus, Damian. Inform Commander Farrell that I will meet with him in the salon in an hour. I've hogsheads to fill.'' Grasping Wildair's reins, he slanted Damian a glance. ''Would you give me a leg up?''

''I'd rather shoot you, cousin,'' Damian replied, nevertheless assisting Miles onto Wildair's back.

Theodora Lovelace turned her face into the first rays of sunlight that penetrated the fog, her eyes on some distant rise, her thoughts just as far away. Miles felt soundly dismissed. Standing there in the lifting mists, her unbound hair a cascade of ebony in the warm hues of dawn, she commanded an air of such serene strength that Miles found himself momentarily captivated. Indeed, her peculiar allure went far deeper than her physical beauty, though looking at her any man would be hardpressed to ignore her more obvious attributes, especially any man who'd held her naked and splendid in his arms just the night before.

It struck him then, as he tore his eyes from her and dug his heels into Wildair's flanks with far more fervor than he would have liked to display: His agreeing to her marriage scheme had far less to do with honor than it did with all those haunting images of her. And as Wildair lunged deep into his magnificent stride and the wind struck tears into Miles's eyes, he considered the disturbing probability that he was marrying her for one reason alone: so that no other man, Damian in particular, could ever have her.

A Rembrandt Peale hung over the mantel. A Reynolds between the windows. From the ceiling hung a magnificent crystal chandelier, its center of deep blue Bristol glass, its gallery of gilt dripping with enormous teardrop crystals. From the windows the grounds spread out in great sun-dappled stretches of grass, broken only by sudden profusions of boxwood and honeysuckle clustered beneath the widespread limbs of a dogwood. A faint midmorning breeze stirred the delicate lengths of exquisite lace at the windows, flooding the room with the scent of roses in full bloom. At the sideboard, heavy lead-crystal decanters awaited anyone's pleasure, and above that loomed a portrait of a most striking and fierce red-haired gentleman.

A Joshua Reynolds, to Teddie's well-trained eye. She almost wished her father had not devoted himself so fervently to her education, else she couldn't possibly have comprehended the splendor of the Winchester salon, indeed, of the entire mansion. Perhaps then she might have perched upon the very edge of an exquisite Hipplewaite armchair awaiting his lordship cloaked in naïveté and not the slightest bit intimidated by the majesty surrounding her. Indeed, had Will instead been blessed with the sharp mind and thirst for knowledge, her father would have undoubtedly poured all the bookshop's profits into a private education for him, leaving Teddie to the typical womanly pursuits of cooking, mending, and housekeeping. Instead, Will's permanent dull wit coupled with his extraordinary size and strength relegated him to a life shoveling coal, while Teddie grew into womanhood as educated as any of her male contemporaries, nurturing dreams better suited to those ambitious young men. Not surprisingly, with that ambition and knowledge came an idealistic and opinionated view of the world. And an unwavering confidence in her abilities to meet any task head-on.

Save for cooking and mending, of which she knew frightfully little.

How then had she managed to maneuver herself into such a quandary? Education and ambition obviously had little to do with controlling one's innermost passionate self.

Winchester should have refused her proposal. Indeed, since she'd possessed such an obvious lack of sense in blurting out such a ludicrous suggestion—driven to this, of course, by the cousins' eagerness to put their pistols to use—then he certainly should have had enough sense to refuse her. Why the devil hadn't he?

The mantel clock ticked like a death knell. Her eyes followed Uncle George as he paced for what seemed the hundredth time across the length of the room in front of the hearth. His bootheels clicked on the polished floorboards, echoing with a certain impatience. Teddie could well imagine that her Aunt Edwina wore her own path in the carpets of her bedchamber as she waited in self-imposed exile one floor above them.

Her uncle paused, snapped open his gold pocket watch, and growled something under his breath. Stuffing the watch into the pocket of his deep blue naval jacket, he resumed his pacing, brows caterpillared as though he deeply contemplated the grave state of the nation. And from her chair in the corner Teddie watched, feeling like a child called to task over something that at the moment seemed rather insignificant compared to the horrors of war.

She heard Winchester's footsteps just moments before the salon's double doors burst open. As though swept before some great wind he didn't pause upon entering, not even to close the doors behind him. Nor did he bother to glance up from the parchment he held in one hand to give a hint of notice to the room's two other occupants. Only briefly did he lift his head as he moved to the sideboard, presenting both Teddie and Uncle George with the magnificence of his back as he filled a glass from a decanter of clear liquid. Lifting the glass, he paused, again studying the parchment.

The mantel clock ticked five times. Teddie glanced at her uncle. He'd stopped midstride. The color rising from his starched collar did not bode well.

Winchester muttered something, drained the glass in one gulp, then turned around abruptly, his gaze meeting with Uncle George. "Ah. Of course, Farrell."

Could that possibly be a softening of those austere features, perhaps Winchester's best efforts at an apology? He was, after all, twenty minutes late, and looked remarkably like a man distracted by something else entirely, a man consumed with his work, all at the expense of the American naval commander, no less. With his black hair windblown, his face bronzed and flushed with his rigors, and his shirt sleeves rolled above his elbows, Winchester looked every inch the successful planter hard at work. His towering height and formidable bulk further enhanced his aura of prosperity, as did the sumptuous trappings. Still, for the briefest moment Teddie was certain she glimpsed a softening in his eyes, a humanizing. At this distance, however, with the sun streaming into the room with such glorious abandon that the white of Winchester's shirt all but blinded her, Teddie couldn't be certain of what she saw. Slowly, she rose from her chair and stepped into her own pool of sunlight. Immediately, Winchester's gaze swung to her. And she realized her eyes had indeed deceived her. The chill remained like a shroud over his features. Little wonder her heart had fluttered in her breast like a frightened sparrow when he'd entered the room.

"Odd that your work should occupy you so, Winchester," her uncle said slowly, as if his words were carefully chosen. He resumed his pacing, pausing only when he stood nose to nose with Winchester. "Considering that we are under full blockade. You've no intention of running that blockade with a ship you've got secreted somewhere, of course."

Winchester arched one brow, his stare unwavering. "Why, that would be illegal, sir."

"Quite." Still, her uncle seemed somehow not entirely satisfied with Winchester's response. "I wasn't aware there's sufficient demand from Richmond for all the produce out of this region.''

''There isn't. I ship upriver what I think I can sell in Richmond. As for the rest, the war can't last forever.''

''Damned inconvenient for you, isn't it, Winchester?''

''Sir?'' His tone oozed respect, his face remained impassive, and yet he exuded a palpably rebellious air, his very existence defiant.

''The war, damn you,'' Farrell suddenly growled. ''You see it as nothing but an inconvenience.'' He leaned closer until his chest all but touched Winchester's. His voice dipped ominously low. ''What the hell happened to you in Tripoli?''

Winchester's lips barely moved. ''I've been to hell and back. I've no intention of returning.''

A chill suddenly chased through the sun-warmed, rose-scented air, startling Teddie. Winchester turned, refilled his glass, then drained it, exhaling with such satisfaction that Teddie's mouth watered. The play of the muscles along the length of his throat caught her eye until she became aware that she'd commanded his regard. ''Would you care for some water, Miss Lovelace?'' he asked.

She blinked at him, soundly caught, it would seem, in her ogling and her surprise. For some reason she thought he'd imbibed something far more potent. ''No. I—''

Again, he dismissed her with a mere shifting of his eyes.

''I didn't ask you here to discuss my tobacco crop, Commander.''

Uncle George clasped his gloved hands imperiously behind his back, casting Teddie a sideways glance from beneath the bushy overhang of his brows. ''I was rather hoping you were, Winchester. Not that I wasn't pleased to find Captain Coyle looking sound this morning, all limbs intact. One of you obviously had sense enough not to carry out that damned duel.''

''I believe I owe Miss Lovelace for that, sir, in the form of an untimed interruption.''

To her dismay Teddie blushed furiously as both men gave her their unwavering regard. Of the two, her uncle's stormy glower held far more comfort. She lifted her chin a notch and said,

"Uncle George, I could hardly let them go out into that fog and kill themselves over an indiscretion that was . . ." She swallowed, battling an urge to avert her eyes in shame. But she couldn't, knowing Winchester expected her to. ". . . that was . . . my fault . . . partly, that is." There. She'd admitted it, though saying it seemed to make the fact altogether too horrible to contemplate, especially when her partner in indiscretion watched her with an intensity that made her want to squirm.

Her uncle's scowl deepened. "I see."

Again she swallowed, clasping her hands before her like a docile young maiden on her way to the gallows. "I've agreed to marry Wi-''—her eyes shifted—"him."

Her uncle glanced sharply at Winchester, no doubt registering with some surprise the younger man's curt nod of affirmation.

"I've several barks to get upriver to Richmond by week's end, Commander," Winchester said, glancing at the missive in his hand. "And several days' business there. The wedding can take place shortly thereafter, at your convenience, of course."

Farrell snorted. "Dammit, man, nothing about this is convenient. There's a war going on, in case you'd forgotten. Sir Jeremiah Cockburn, the butcher of the British navy, sits in the bay as we speak, in a man-of-war fitted with over sixty guns. On a whim he could sail his whole damned flotilla up the James and blast you and all of your tobacco from here to Charleston.

"I have to be in Washington as soon as possible to confer with the President and the governors regarding this matter and getting some ships down here. It seems our entire fleet save for one sloop at Baltimore is otherwise engaged under Oliver Perry between Lake Erie and the St. Lawrence in an effort to intercept supplies for British troops in Canada. In other words, until I can get a damned fleet built or order a squadron south, which could take the better part of two weeks, we are powerless to stop this monster should he tire of blockade duty and decide to raid the whole of Virginia. He's already demonstrated his prowess at that. There's little telling when the notion might again strike him. So, no, the idea of a wedding, much less of delivering my wife's niece here for the rest of her sorry life, is not at the moment particularly convenient, or comforting, for that matter. And I don't give a damn whether she was willing or not''—he gave Teddie a dire look of warning—''though I'd rather your aunt not be privy to that, young lady. Let's hope the distraction of planning a wedding will more than compensate for her distress over this, which, I might add, is entirely justifiable. The woman wept the entire night through.''

Winchester's eyes flickered once over Teddie as though she were nothing more than horseflesh in need of hay and a mucked stall. Teddie gripped her violet-sprigged cream muslin skirts and felt her fury ignite.

''Your niece will be exceedingly well-tended,'' Winchester said in a businesslike tone.

''She damned well better be,'' Farrell growled with such ferocity even Winchester's attention piqued. ''You've got my word that I'll make certain of it.'' His bleak smile never quite reached his deep-set eyes. ''I'll wager you never thought you'd give me even more reason to be the thorn in your side, eh, Winchester? I could be a congenial in-law, however. Just say the word and I'll put you at the wheel of a frigate with fifty guns and twice as many men. We could use you and your ship, man, desperately.''

Winchester simply stared at Farrell, his stoic silence in the face of her uncle's desperation striking a forbidding chill in Teddie. What could possibly account for his stunning lack of regard for his country, his very liberty? Was the man without soul or conscience, his concern only for the sale of his tobacco crop?

Her uncle snarled a curse, though his eyes never once wavered from Winchester. ''Come along, Theodora. We leave for Timberneck Manor within the hour.''

Teddie vacated the splash of sunlight, moving beside her uncle with eyes fixed forward. She realized after several moments that she stared at the open vee of Winchester's shirt, her eye drawn by the contrast of white linen against the bronze beneath. His skin beneath its black furring seemed to glisten, beckoning not her eyes but her hand to smooth over that expanse.

He was, without question, despicable, a cold, calculating cynic. The man she was to marry in less than two weeks. A chill gripped her soul like shackles. She was trapped. And she'd no one to blame but herself.

"You'll be hearing from me once the wedding date is set," her uncle promised.

"I look forward to it, sir."

"The hell you do." Then, like a true gentleman, her uncle inclined his head at Winchester, offered Teddie his arm, and led her from the room.

They'd nearly reached the front staircase when Teddie glanced at her uncle and found him not scowling, as she'd expected. Instead, a glimmer of a smile tipped the corners of his mouth. She nearly missed the first step. "Uncle George, you do realize you're smiling."

"I am?" He took her elbow as they proceeded up the curved staircase. "Indeed, maybe Winchester's not entirely lost."

"Lost, sir?"

Her uncle looked thoughtful. "In wartime men witness gruesome things, Theodora. They may suffer unspeakable torture, particularly if they're captured by the enemy. They may experience terrible loss and may wonder why the hell they've been spared when their closest friends were not. Some men find a way to live with these memories and get on with their lives. Others, like Winchester, never fully recover.

"No one knows precisely what happened to him in Algeria. At first we believed he'd perished with his fellow commandos, his father included, when their ship's entire magazine blew in Tripoli's harbor. We thought no man could have survived such a blast. But six months later Winchester wandered into one of our camps in the middle of the desert, at least twenty miles from Tripoli. He'd obviously been imprisoned by the Dey of Algiers. Somehow he escaped and walked that twenty miles of desert. But he's never spoken about those six months of captivity. I doubt he ever will. So, my dear, when a man like Miles Winchester could refuse something—like a forced marriage—

and he doesn't, for no obvious reason, I find that curious. I also find hope in that."

"I wish I could. Then again, I'm marrying him."

"Take heart. You're a woman of high character, Theodora. Your letters to your aunt over the years bespoke as much. She found great solace in those missives when I was away at sea."

Teddie stared at the crimson-carpeted stairs, her tone laced with irony. "Women of high character don't often find themselves in these situations."

"They do more often than you'd think. You don't hear of men running off to fields and killing each other daily, do you? In Virginia far more weddings than duels come of indiscretions." They paused at the top of the stairs, her uncle giving her hand a comforting pat. "I could be wrong, and God knows your aunt doesn't believe I possess an ounce of intuition, but this marriage might prove far more effective in freeing Winchester of his demons than any threats I could possibly make."

"I'm quite sure I don't know what you mean."

"All's the better," he replied, his eyes twinkling with such warmth that Teddie felt the pain of her betrayal of this noble man deep in the pit of her soul. The pain only deepened when he added, "Leave the particulars to me, my dear. And don't fret. Your indiscretion could even prove beneficial to the American navy. Now, we must hurry. I leave for Washington this afternoon."

They moved down the hall, Teddie worrying her lower lip as her thoughts invariably strayed to the war. And Will. "Is Virginia truly as vulnerable to attack as you suggested?"

"From Jeremiah Cockburn?" Farrell snorted. "Absolutely. I think the only deterrent to him at the moment is his belief that our militia numbers in excess of three thousand. The truth is that less than three hundred responded to our call to arms, and the majority of them are marching to Washington. If Cockburn were to learn the truth before I can amass some kind of fleet against him, he could quite possibly decide to press inland."

"And more innocent lives would be lost," Teddie murmured, her thoughts on her brother, chained in the *Rattle-*

snake's hold. "Once the fleet arrives do you plan to attack Cockburn?"

Farrell's face shadowed with grave concern. "He has larger ships with more guns, but we've got heavier guns and, I believe, surprise on our side. And with smaller, swifter ships this sort of covert attack can be vastly successful. For now, however, I'd be content with establishing a presence near the bay should he tire of blockade duty. But enough of this. Even women of exceedingly high character and intelligence shouldn't trouble themselves with the machinations of war. Dreadful stuff, your aunt says. Come along. You've wedding preparations to occupy your thoughts."

Teddie murmured her assent, and as the morning waned into a flurry of afternoon activity, Miles Winchester was as far from her thoughts as he could be. Thankfully, the man would be in Richmond for the better part of two weeks, incapable of disrupting her. She would need all her wits about her if she was to succeed in her charade as the Night Hawk. Indeed, she could only wonder how she was to keep her brother alive and Cockburn pacified without betraying her uncle's plans and threatening the liberty of the people she'd come to love.

Chapter Four

Teddie pulled Cleo to a stop in a dense thicket and dismounted. Murmuring reassurances to the horse, she crouched behind the tangle of brush and peered out at the fathomless pitch of the bay. Not twenty feet away she could hear the tide washing over the sand. Its rhythm was almost comforting in the deepest hours of night, when darkness seemed its most menacing.

Even here along the shore, no breeze stirred the blanket of August heat. Teddie blew at a wayward curl that clung to her forehead, and adjusted her wide-brimmed black hat further back on her head. Perspiration wove a slow path down her back and into the banded waist of her black breeches. These, like her long black cape, were of a heavy wool, as cumbersome as the knee-high black boots she wore and all smelling of an unlikely mix of bilge water and stale rum. It mattered little what ne'er-do-well highwayman had claimed the garments before her, only that Cockburn had seen fit to supply her with a pistol and a cutlass as well, which had necessitated his sneered reminder that attempting to use these weapons against a longboat full of his men would be tantamount to suicide.

Her eyes strained in the darkness for the telltale outline of the ship. Where the devil was the *Rattlesnake*? She couldn't possibly risk signaling yet. Considering her near-disastrous encounter with the American regiment at Lighthouse Point just two nights before, she'd decided tonight to ride some distance north of the point, choosing as the rendezvous spot a shallow curve of shore fringed with dense thicket. From here her lantern signal should be visible even if the *Rattlesnake* rode at anchor off the point, precisely where Cockburn had said the ship would be at midnight.

If only she could be certain. She hadn't encountered any

regiments yet, hostile or otherwise. Once she signaled and the longboat came ashore, her chances of being discovered rose considerably. She harbored scant desire to test her prowess with a pistol again. As it was, she'd been lucky to escape the regiment. Her luck was certain to run out at some point.

Several minutes later the moon emerged from behind the clouds, bathing the bay in a silver-blue brilliance. Teddie scanned the horizon from north to south. There, not an eighth of a mile out from the jut of shore known as Lighthouse Point, loomed the unmistakable shadow of the man-of-war. Teddie fumbled in her pocket, struck flint to steel, and lit the lantern. She stepped from the thicket, lifted the lantern, and swung it in a slow arc. Not thirty seconds later a light aboard ship motioned in response.

Dousing the lamp, Teddie crouched again into the thicket and waited, her eyes on the *Rattlesnake*, her ears straining for any sound that she'd been seen by someone other than the *Rattlesnake*'s watch. Only the gentle wash of waves meeting shore reached her ears. After several minutes the shadow of a longboat eased away from the larger vessel and approached shore, its oars registering a whisper of sound as they met with the water. Teddie tested Cleo's tether, then slipped from the thicket, drawing the brim of her hat lower over her eyes. With cape billowing in her wake she clambered down a gently sloped dune that spilled onto the shoreline. Her heart thumped in her breast as the longboat pulled ashore and she immediately recognized from among the handful of seamen her brother's stalwart, broad-shouldered silhouette at the stern of the boat.

"Will!" she cried, stumbling in the sand. She ran into the surf, heedless of the water seeping into her boots. "Will—" Choking on a breath, she pulled herself into the longboat and threw her arms around him. "You're warm," she choked out against his shoulder, her voice cracking when her fingertips met with the raised welts that still crisscrossed his back. Thick scabs marked some. Others oozed as if the flesh had only recently been laid open to the salt air. "Thank God, you're alive—"

"I'm fine, Teddie," he replied, his voice sounding tired, as though he was sapped of life. "Don't cry, Teddie."

"I never cry," she whispered, blinking back her tears by sheer force of will. "Are they feeding you?"

"Some." He swallowed deeply, his breathing coming in shallow rasps as though his ribs ached with every breath. "Enough to haul rope and mend sail. Not enough to escape."

Teddie gripped his bare shoulders and stared into his eyes. "Don't try to escape, Will. Even if you think you have the strength. Promise me you won't. They would kill you."

A sadness swept over his handsome features. His Adam's apple worked in the thickness of his throat. "Don't make me promise that, Teddie. Please don't."

Teddie thought her heart would burst from her chest with the injustice of it. Denied the ability to succeed mentally, Will had always taken great pride in his extraordinary strength and agility. Asking him to deny himself use of his physical gifts was like asking him to sacrifice what remained of his self-respect. It might be asking too much of him, but if his life hung in the balance she could do nothing else.

"You must promise me. Whisper it to me, Will. They won't hear you or think you're weak. It takes a man of great strength to know when not to fight. Papa taught you that, remember? Now please, promise me."

Will blinked rapidly, his mouth twisting with frustration, the muscles popping in his arms and chest as he strained at his bonds. "I can't promise that, Teddie," he rasped. "These men hurt me. They send you away and you come back looking so sad." His eyes shone in the moonlight. "Th-they killed my friend. They cut him down and fed his body to the sharks."

Her fingers trembled upon his cheek, the words catching in her throat. She ached to apologize for everything, for even thinking they could succeed in their scheme. Alone in London, penniless and hungry, she'd thought nothing could be worse. But to watch Will suffer like this, powerless to help him . . .

She mentally shook herself. Wallowing in despair certainly never helped anybody. Will must maintain his faith in her, and she must remain, for his sake, outwardly strong. "Dear Will," she murmured, "I'm going to make it right. All of it. Believe me. And one day you will sail as a free man aboard a ship—"

"Enough!" Cockburn's command sliced through the air like the crack of a cat-o'-nine.

Gritting her teeth, Teddie glanced over her shoulder. Moonlight flashed off the brass buttons of Cockburn's coat and glittered in his eyes. He motioned his head to shore and offered a white-gloved hand to assist her. Resisting the urge to slap his hand aside, Teddie nevertheless ignored it and slipped over the side of the longboat into thigh-high surf.

"I'll be back," she said to Will. "I promise."

"Don't go with him, Teddie."

"I must."

Cockburn awaited her some distance from the longboat.

"You don't want them to hear us," Teddie couldn't resist goading, with a glance at the longboat. "The less informed they are, the easier to manipulate. I wonder if their confidence in you would waver if they knew you conspired with a woman."

"Cheeky tonight, eh?" Cockburn sneered. "You must have something worth telling me."

Teddie set her jaw. "Allow my brother to bathe."

Cockburn merely arched an expectant brow.

"Some of his wounds still fester. He needs tending."

Cockburn folded his arms over his chest, the movement stirring a clank from his sword. "So many demands, Theodora. My interest is duly piqued."

"The Americans have mounted a militia, anticipating your attack in Virginia." She kept her stare even, as though she revealed nothing but the truth. "Their numbers are in excess of three thousand."

"Indeed." He paused, and Teddie tensed, anticipating the worst. "I suspected as much," he finally said. "Tell me more, particularly of naval maneuverings."

George Farrell's image bloomed in Teddie's mind, his brow knit with grim determination. No doubt Farrell hated Cockburn almost as much as Teddie did. "Their entire fleet is occupied near the St. Lawrence. They believe they don't need to spare a ship with so strong a militia in these parts. They believe three thousand men sufficient deterrent.''

''Only a fool would mount an attack against such numbers.'' Cockburn snorted a curse and swiped a hand through the air. ''What the devil good is a war at sea with nobody to fight? I tell you, *I* should have been sent to protect Canada, or better yet, to defend English shores against the French, not left here to rot in this heat. Blockade duty grows tedious and my men lazy from inactivity. Perhaps you have news of the privateers.''

''The American captains speak mostly of the Night Hawk operating somewhere south, across the Elizabeth near Albemarle,'' she said, this no half-truth. ''They suspect he may be in league with a privateer.''

Cockburn's eyes narrowed. ''Near the Elizabeth. We've one frigate patrolling in the Albemarle Sound, and Captain Osgood's ship is stationed near the mouth of the Elizabeth and the James, ready to capture any cargo being transferred south to Albemarle. No privateer would dare it. Still . . .'' His thumb brushed thoughtfully over the hilt of his sword. ''This Night Hawk bears watching. Find out all you can about him. Doomed is the man who attempts to run Jeremiah Cockburn's blockade! We've successfully intimidated all the others, eh?'' His pomposity was palpable.

Teddie refused to feed his arrogance. ''They talk of no one else but the Night Hawk.''

''A daring fellow,'' Cockburn mused. ''Or foolish. But that remains to be seen. Indeed, this Night Hawk might prove adequate diversion for me, for a time. Perhaps then the Virginia militia will grow restless with inaction as well, and Farrell will send a good number north to Washington, thinking I have no intention of taking Virginia. Advise me at once if this occurs, Teddie.''

''Allow my brother to bathe, and see to his back,'' she replied through gritted teeth.

Cockburn shrugged and pulled his tricornered hat lower over his eyes. ''I'll do what I can, Teddie, but I cannot allow insubordination to go unpunished, can I?''

''The man is in irons,'' she hissed, her gloved fingers brushing over the pistol tucked into the back of her waist. "He doesn't know how to be factious."

"Perhaps. But he gets a look in his eyes, Teddie. And God knows he possesses the strength of five men. I must keep all that in check or I risk losing control of my entire ship. An example must be set, particularly of a prisoner."

Teddie's fingers curved around the pistol, her rage igniting. "Then choose another, not Will."

"You know," Cockburn continued, in the same blithe tone, "I cannot help but marvel at how such a dullard came to be the brother of so clever a wench." In a flash he caught her hand and wrenched it behind her back just as her fingers wrapped around the pistol. Forcing her up against him, he bared his teeth in a feral grin. His breath was stale and rank upon her face. "Do not try to outsmart me. I will know if you lie. And I will hang your brother from the yardarm with zeal and leave him there until the crows have gotten their fill of him. Do I make myself clear?"

Teddie merely hardened her stare, refusing to give an inch.

Finally, he thrust her from him, smoothing one hand over the front of his uniform as if to sweep all traces of her from the cloth. "Bloody impertinent wench," he spat. "A pity more men aren't like you. If you live to see the day, you will make some man vastly aggrieved that he ever took you to wife. We will meet two weeks hence at midnight at this location. Should you require contact before then, simply signal. We'll be in these waters. And do be sure to have something of value for me." With a tip of his tricorne, Cockburn swept past her and returned to the longboat.

She watched until the craft had safely reached the *Rattle-snake*, then returned to the thicket. Untethering Cleo, she mounted and drew the pistol from the back of her waistband. It weighed potently in her hand. Again she strained her ears for some sound of an approaching regiment, but she heard nothing above the muted rush of waves. Perhaps their lantern signals had gone undetected. Yet when she urged Cleo from the thicket and the moon again disappeared behind the clouds, plunging everything into darkness, apprehension swept over her.

"Relax," she chided herself. "An American regiment would not shoot the Night Hawk on sight. They believe him an ally. . . ." Unless they'd seen her on that beach and suspected the legendary Night Hawk of conspiring with Cockburn. Then, at the very least, they would attempt to capture her and turn her treasonous hide over to George Farrell. They would never believe that they'd nabbed themselves an impostor.

A lump wedged in her throat. That twinkle-eyed gentleman could turn as brutally vengeful as Cockburn if he suspected he'd been deceived. On more than one occasion Teddie had paid witness to the full measure of his anger from behind closed doors at Timberneck. Nothing his officers could say on those occasions ever appeased him. His rage thundered like a tempest long after they'd left with scarlet faces averted. If she was captured, Teddie knew that nothing would convince her uncle of her reasons for betraying him if he believed he had proof otherwise. Will would surely be lost then.

She had good reason to be cautious. Unfortunately, good reason oftentimes allowed an imagination to run far afield. Ordinary sounds seemed magnified. The night had never seemed so dark, the air so still.

Blast, but she'd never been faint of heart or given to wild imaginings. Drawing herself up in her saddle, she guided Cleo through the tangle of brush that led to the dirt path. This path, which edged the coastline, was flanked on both sides by steep dunes and stretched south to Lighthouse Point and beyond. To reach Timberneck Manor she intended to veer west off the path just north of the point into dense woods, avoiding open fields and well-traveled roads. From that direction she would approach the rear of her aunt's manor house and the stable at Timberneck under the cover of trees. She had little doubt that her movements there would go undetected. If only the path south to the point weren't so open, so vulnerable.

Cleo suddenly bobbed her head and stopped short, her ears pricking forward. Teddie's mouth went dry. Her eyes probed the darkness. Her ears strained for some sound. Seconds later an owl hooted from a nearby tree, yet Cleo's ears remained pricked forward.

"There, girl," Teddie murmured, her breath exhaling in a slow hiss. "I'm making you nervous, aren't I?" Cleo responded to the gentle squeezing of her thighs and picked her way through the tangled brush at a pace that would have made escape impossible. Had it not been for the thorny bushes lurking in this brush, Teddie would have given the mare her head and raced for Timberneck Manor without once looking back. And she would, once they reached the open path.

Still, just before Cleo stepped from the cover of brush and climbed the dune onto the path, Teddie tugged back on the reins. The night remained peaceful, the air still.

Urging Cleo up the shallow dune, she immediately reined her left then tugged back sharply on the leather. Not ten paces farther along the path, squarely facing her, stood the massive silhouette of a lone horse and rider.

The fine hairs on the back of Teddie's neck stood on end. Inside her leather gloves, her palms dampened. Her pulse thundered in her ears as Cleo nickered and danced sideways on the path. Neither horse nor rider moved.

He'd come as stealthily as the night.

Suddenly, moonlight spilled over the apparition. Indeed, Teddie would have preferred that he was a ghost; this man was too large, too powerful-looking to offer any solace. He was cloaked in a voluminous black cape and low-slung hat, both of which shadowed his features completely. To Teddie's eye his mount looked as immense and darkly foreboding as he, perhaps because he stood so quiet and still, as if at his master's silent command. Even the agile and spirited Cleo might have difficulty escaping such a mighty steed if his rider intended to give chase, which he most certainly would. Wouldn't he?

If he were going to kill her he would have done so by now. The gloved hand resting on his thigh looked devoid of any weapon. Strange as it seemed, Teddie was certain that no matter how fearsome he might appear, this man meant her no harm. Yet.

A shout shattered the stillness, some distance over Teddie's shoulder. Before she could spin around another shout rang out in reply, this one perilously close, not more than a tenth of a mile farther up a sharp curve in the path. The unmistakable thud of hoofbeats meeting with tamped dirt proved more than enough to dig Teddie's heels into Cleo's flanks. Of the two, Teddie feared capture by an American regiment far more than an encounter with a mysterious caped stranger. Besides, she suspected he might flee as well.

Just as Cleo sprinted past him, he whirled his mount and charged after her. In less than three strides the mighty black's powerful forelegs pulled even with Cleo's sleek haunches, both horses thundering at breakneck speed down the path. Through a blur of wind-whipped tears, Teddie glanced over her shoulder. With his cape flapping against the wind her mysterious companion looked like some massive bird of prey . . . a hawk, descended out of the night.

Teddie's heart slammed into her ribs. No. Not the Night Hawk. She hadn't anticipated this when she'd donned this disguise. She'd thought his activities would keep him much farther south. How could he have known where she would meet Cockburn? No, her charade could not be up—not yet—not with Will still chained aboard the *Rattlesnake*. Not with so much left to do.

Desperately, she leaned over Cleo's pumping neck, urging the mare even faster with coaxing murmurs. The filly gamely responded, lengthening her stride and pulling ahead of the other horse, but only for a moment. This time the stallion pulled alongside her with startling ease. Indeed, while Cleo's ears were pinned back in full flight, the stallion's remained peaked, his head arched and high, his reins taut, as though his master had yet to give him his head.

Teddie choked back her fear. Somehow she would escape him. She would not allow herself to be caught and humiliated in her charade. An American regiment might spare her. But would this man?

A pistol's report rang out not a moment before something whizzed over Teddie's head. She bit her lips to keep from crying out and pressed her cheek close against Cleo's neck. Just a quarter mile farther south she could see the lighthouse tower, its windows dark, unwelcoming of British ships. Just a little farther now, around a sharp curve. Then she could veer from the open path, taking full advantage of the cover of bramble, brush, and dense woods that blanketed the countryside the entire five miles farther to Timberneck Manor. In that tangle of trees Cleo had proven herself adept at escaping the regiment's more cumbersome mounts. Yet she imagined the immense stallion easily trampling anything that dared to block his path, even the thickest, tallest trees. How the devil could she escape him or his rider?

The curve loomed just ahead, but the stallion remained beside her, blocking her path into the concealing brush. With a mounting desperation Teddie leaned into the curve, and the stallion drifted slightly behind her. With a recklessness that surprised even her, Teddie suddenly reined Cleo sharply right, directly into the stallion's path. His rider growled a curse and hauled back on his reins. Cleo surged past the rearing stallion and down the steep embankment. The mare stumbled almost to her knees, ripping the reins from Teddie's hands, then plunged into the brush.

It took all of Teddie's horsemanship to keep her seat as the wild-eyed mare zigzagged through the snarl of trees. Behind her she heard the thunder of at least a dozen horses' hooves crescendo, then fade to the south. Another pistol shot crackled through the air, echoing through the trees. The regiment had followed the Night Hawk, and he, for whatever reason, had chosen not to follow her. Still, when she finally retrieved the reins, Teddie didn't temper the mare's flight through the woods. Nor did she make any attempt to slow Cleo when the mare plunged headlong into a shallow stream that wove south to an area bordering the Timberneck properties. For more than two miles she kept the mare to the water, guarding against any likelihood that she would be followed and their path to her aunt's house tracked.

Even after she'd cooled Cleo and bedded her down in the stable at Timberneck Manor, Teddie's heart still raced. And when she'd climbed the trellis of Virginia creeper and slipped through the open window into her bedchamber at the rear of the sprawling manor house, safe at last, something told her as she looked out over the moon-splashed countryside that she hadn't seen the last of the mysterious Night Hawk.

"Damn!" With a growl Miles dismounted and handed Wildair's reins to Simon. Sweeping his cape from his shoulders, he scowled at his bloodied left arm, then strode toward the back of the stable. "Damn, damn, damn," he muttered as he tugged off his leather gloves and carelessly tossed them atop a battered sea chest that had belonged to his father. The fine worsted wool cloak and broad-brimmed hat followed. He bit back a wince as white-hot pain shot through his arm, then snarled, "Damn!"

"Suh?" Simon stood at his back, appropriately undaunted by Miles's mood and his bloodied shirt. Or perhaps simply used to the unusual. After all, he had been under a Winchester's employ the majority of his fifty-odd years, ever since Miles's grandfather Maximilian had purchased Simon and his mother at a slave auction in Charleston. Very little surprised Simon anymore. He'd witnessed much in his lifetime.

Turning, Miles worked open the buttons of his linen shirt. "He's been adequately cooled," he said, his scowl flickering over Wildair and inevitably softening. The stallion had exceeded Miles's every expectation this evening. "Just unsaddle him for me, if you would. I'll rub him down."

"Not wit' that arm, you ain't. You need me to git the whiskey?"

With a brisk shake of his head Miles shrugged out of his shirt and tossed it atop the sea chest. "I didn't take a bullet, Simon." His fingers probed the bloodied gash through the fleshy outer curve of his upper arm. Another inch to the right and he might have been left without use of his arm entirely, had the bullet shattered bone and not merely grazed him.

"Yo' plan done worked good, uh huh."

Miles glanced sharply at Simon, scowling anew at the man's overt sarcasm. A scathing rebuttal sprang to his tongue, but the overseer had turned around and was leading Wildair back to his stall.

"Know your place, Simon," Miles finally barked after him, then glanced around the small room for bandages.

A distinct "hmmph" came from the direction of Wildair's stall.

"I'll have you know that my plan was working," Miles felt compelled to add, his scowl deepening when he bent to rummage through a cupboard stuffed with all sorts of odds and ends. "Just as I suspected, our impostor chose the inlet just north of the point for his rendezvous. I saw it all, Simon. Unfortunately, so did Farrell's men. Damned reckless fool. I would have had him too, had that regiment not shown up. Where the hell are the bandages?"

From the doorway Simon regarded him with marked disdain. Then, with a shake of his head, he muttered something about "other damned fools" before producing the bandages from the back corner of the cupboard, precisely where Miles had been rummaging. He handed them to Miles. "They shoot him too?"

Miles slammed the cupboard shut and set his jaw. His fingers tightened around the roll of bandages. "No, dammit, because at that point they were only firing warning shots over our heads."

"They shot you."

"Because they couldn't catch me. And they would have shot him too, dammit, but he'd escaped by then."

Simon's brows arched high. "Escaped? My, my, an' you let him."

"Of course I let him!" Miles thundered. A grim half-smile creased his face. "I *purposely* did not follow him, or Farrell's men would have as well. I'm not about to let them catch him before I do. Besides, his mare couldn't have outrun that regiment on open road as I did. He obviously suspected the same and took cover in the woods."

Simon folded his arms over his chest, one corner of his wide mouth twitching upward. "His mare."

Miles began wrapping his injured arm with vigor. "Listen to me, Simon, I don't give a damn if he's riding a three-legged mule. This impostor is doing more to sabotage my plans to ship out my tobacco than the entire British presence off this coast.

Farrell's regiments are swarming up and down the coast this evening, and I can tell you they're not looking for British ships. They're looking for me, thinking I'm some damned spy. The English captains have a price. But this impostor—'' Miles paused in his wrapping, his brows diving over the bridge of his nose. "He's got Farrell's men shooting at me, dammit. They think their old ally the Night Hawk is suddenly spying for Cockburn. Simon, they don't realize there are two of us, that the man they're after is an impostor. That I'm not guilty of anything—''

" 'Cept smugglin', privateerin', an' bribery.''

Miles hardened his stare. "The navy wouldn't hang a man for that, Simon.''

"They'd make sure you didn' do it no more.''

"And I'm not about to give them that opportunity. I'm going to find out who the hell our impostor is and what he's doing for Cockburn. And then perhaps I'll turn him over to Farrell to be hung . . . if I don't find it necessary to kill him first.''

"You gotta catch him 'fore you kill him.''

Miles's laugh was short and brittle. "I'll catch him.''

"You said that two nights ago when you come up wit' yo' plan.''

Miles stared hard at the other man. "You find amusement in this, Simon?''

Simon shrugged and settled his rangy limbs in a low chair by the stove. He took up a rag and a bridle and began polishing the leather. Without glancing up from his work he said, "I say it's 'bout time you met yo' match.''

"The hell I have.''

Simon chuckled his typical smooth, mellow singsong. "He's tauntin' you.''

Miles scoffed and finished securing the bandage at his arm. "He doesn't know what the hell he's doing. He looks young. His build seems slight, like that of a youth. I tell you, on luck alone he's played his charade this far. But his luck is about to run dry.''

Simon glanced up, his gaze oddly probing. "I ain't seen you so angry in a lon' time. This have anythin' to do wit' yo'

weddin' to that little missy what stole yo' Wildair?'' Without
waiting for his reply Simon dissolved into the same lumbering
chuckles, replete with a slow shaking of his head. "I says
they's both tauntin' you. An' you don' like it. Not one bit.
Look at you. Standin' there wit' yo' hands on yo' hips, you
look jest like yo' gran'pappy use to. 'Cept he had all that wil'
red hair an' he was even bigger'n you. But Mira—she weren't
'fraid o' him, uh uh. She weren't 'fraid o' nobody. Like that
missy. She ain't 'fraid o' you or yo' Wildair. An' you don' like
it. You's much happier when they's all 'fraid o' you. Uh huh.''

Miles listened to his teeth grind for several moments, knowing there was little to be gained from arguing with Simon,
particularly when the man seemed to be enjoying himself so
immensely and at his expense. Shoving a hand through his
unruly hair, he muttered, "I'm going to bed."

"You wan' me to send up Jillie?" Simon's eyes swung up at
him.

Miles met the other man's stare, knowing full well where
this was leading. Simon had asked the same question for the
last two nights. Tonight he would receive the same reply. They
both knew it. "Not tonight, Simon."

"You's awful tired lately," Simon mused, his whole body
moving with the slow, circular motions of his hands on the
leather, his tone rousing its typical defensiveness in Miles.
"You's never been this tired. Uh uh. Not since I known you.
Jillie's gonna start to wonderin' if you got yo'self another
woman. Mmm hmm."

Miles glowered at the other man and planted his hands on his
hips. "She won't wonder for long, not with you around. You
seem to know damned near everything tonight, Simon."

"I know what I see. An' you ain't tired."

"Is that so? I did, after all, just outrun an entire regiment, an
exceedingly well-mounted regiment, I might add. And I spent
my entire day loading hogsheads onto barks for the trip upriver
to Richmond tomorrow. Any man would be tired. I need sleep,
Simon. I need to be alone."

Simon slowly shook his head, his gaze never wavering from
his work. "You ain't alone in that bed an' you know it. That

missy's there wit' you, all the time, in yo' mind. An' you can' git her out. 'Til you do, you ain't gonna be callin' fo' Jillie no mo'. Uh uh.''

Miles bit back his denial, his mind refusing to acknowledge what Simon suggested. He, suddenly incapable of putting a woman from his mind? Preposterous. Unthinkable. True, he'd felt little need for the blond, sloe-eyed Jillie since that fateful night he'd found Teddie in his bed. He'd simply preferred solitude, even to Jillie's far-reaching talents. As for the haunting lilac scent that still seemed to cling to his sheets, even after they'd been washed and aired: a wayward breeze. Nothing more. The fact that the lilac trees surrounding Miramer hadn't bloomed in over four months didn't dissuade him from this theory. He was not a man obsessed. The woman might have robbed him of sense once. And somehow, with the aid of her confounded womanly wiles, she'd gotten him to agree to this marriage. But he'd be damned if she'd invaded his mind.

"Is that so?" He planted his hands on his hips. "I'll have you know all this damned arguing has me feeling energized, Simon. Now that I think about it, send Jillie up." Giving Simon a satisfied smirk, he turned and strode up the length of a stall, tossing over his shoulder, "And tell her to bring the rum."

Chapter Five

"Would you just look at this exquisite needlework, Theodora! My mother quite obviously sewed herself silly *for months* before she wed my father." Aunt Edwina held up an embroidered napkin of the sheerest, starchiest white linen imaginable to the spray of late afternoon sunlight shining through the windows of Timberneck Manor's front parlor. Edwina sighed. "Simply exquisite. And I've tablecloths to match in the same imported French linen, surely as fine as what you'll find in any musty bureau at Miramer." She punctuated this with a deliciously smug look and placed the napkin in Teddie's hand as though she thought the linen might dissolve to dust at the slightest mishandling. Edwina had obviously never put any of the lovely linen to its intended use. Teddie could well imagine her aunt's reaction if the exquisite embroidery were to somehow find its way onto Miramer's dining table or, worse, crushed in the hand of some careless dinner guest.

Exerting the same care, Teddie placed the weightless napkin atop the smallest of the piles of linen surrounding her on the settee. The stack at her feet had reached her knees. Those beside her threatened to topple if she dared move. "Exquisite," Teddie murmured, brushing her thumb over the dainty stitches. At the moment she was finding it difficult to think she'd descended from a long line of vastly talented and patient women who'd been capable of sitting for hours working a tiny needle through sheer fabric, then, when finished, wrapping all of it in muslin and storing it away in a deep trunk with little intention of ever using, much less seeing, it again until they bequeathed it all to their daughter or niece years later. Teddie considered herself far too impatient for such intricate work, her need for accomplishment far too immediate to allow her to consider hiding her work away, even to preserve it.

With a certain dismay Teddie watched her aunt's torso disappear once more into the enormous trunk just as Maggie waddled into the parlor beneath the weight of heaping armfuls of colorful gowns. Precisely how much linen and clothing did a woman require to get herself properly married, especially to a man like Winchester? There was certainly nothing proper about the man, or the circumstances of their wedding, for that matter. Her aunt, however, despite her initial angst, had somehow managed to look beyond the ticklish matter of the bridegroom's ominous reputation and had since launched herself out of despair and into a flurry of preparations, among these the bequeathing of her entire trousseau to Teddie. Teddie could hardly refuse, especially when the dusty trunk had been recovered from the attic and opened. Aunt Edwina's soft gray eyes had misted with fond memory and with regret at never having borne a child of her own.

As the oldest of the two sisters, Edwina had pursued the gay, independent life so common to daughters of successful London merchants. Without the smothering yoke of convention to dictate her behavior, she'd scorned marriage proposals in favor of traveling to the continent and America, unchaperoned, very much a product of the nouveau riche. Much of the details of her unconventional life remained a mystery to Teddie, save for the snippets Edwina had revealed in her letters and the occasional tidbits Teddie had wormed out of her father. For some reason Teddie was relatively certain Edwina had known several men in her life, quite well. But she claimed never to have given her heart to any man until she met rakish American Captain George Farrell at the ripe age of thirty. They'd wed within a month of their meeting, a recklessly romantic end to an intensely passionate courtship. In contrast her sister, Eugenia, Teddie's mother, had embraced marriage and motherhood as fervently and as hastily as Edwina had avoided it. Unlike Edwina she'd been blessed with two children, only to die, much too young, after giving birth to a child that didn't survive the night. Two sisters, two entirely different lives, and yet both had sacrificed dearly for their love.

Teddie worked loose the top few buttons of her cotton gown, laying her neck open to the slightest stirring of the air. The afternoon heat was oppressive. Surrounded by heaps of pristine white linen, gowns in every imaginable shade, and the incessant chatter necessary to planning any successful wedding, Teddie might have found it difficult to imagine their country was at war. But it was there, hovering over her like a cloud despite the sun-dappled brilliance of the day. It permeated her every thought, every action, and only emphasized how utterly ridiculous and out of place a wedding was in such troubled times.

"Life, my dear, must go on," her aunt had chided, clearly taken aback by Teddie's reluctance to indulge. "Men's games of war are certainly no reason to deny oneself a lavish wedding and lovely wardrobe, particularly when a great deal of consolation is in order."

If Teddie were to require consoling over her circumstances, she certainly wasn't going to start throwing open armoires in a desperate search of a new gown to pacify her. But she wasn't about to tell Aunt Edwina that. The woman wallowed blissfully in excess, her powdered cheeks flushed with excitement, her tongue churning out a delightful discourse on the necessity of an abundance of flowers at a wedding.

Teddie left her to her glory. After all, with Uncle George only today returning from his two-week sojourn to Washington, Edwina would have been beside herself without a wedding to plan during his absence.

The thunder of approaching hoofbeats swung all three women's heads to the front windows. "That must be Uncle George," Teddie said, just as Maggie deposited the heap of gowns on a chair beside her.

Edwina shook her head, then rose and attempted to maneuver her way through the tangle of linen and clothing piled all around the room. "George never rides as though the fires of Hades are at his heels. It's someone else." She reached the windows, hesitated enough to pale considerably, then offered

Teddie a tremulous smile. "Why, good heavens, it's Winchester."

Teddie's heart slammed into her ribs and her mouth went instantly dry. "What the devil could he want?" Edwina blinked so furiously, so guiltily, Teddie almost leapt from the settee. "Aunt Edwina?"

"Why, Theodora, I can only venture to say . . ." Edwina raised innocent brows. "But I suppose if I were to guess, which I probably shouldn't, I would say his visit has something to do with the letter."

Teddie set her teeth. "What letter?"

Edwina waved a dismissing hand. "It's not quite a letter. . . ." Again she blinked, her fine brows knitting. "Rather more like a contract."

Teddie's stomach seemed to sink. "Composed by whom?"

"Why, George, of course, with a bit of my help. Your uncle orates magnificently, Theodora, but he can scarcely compose a sentence when he gets pen in hand. He expected to be here when Winchester arrived to—that is, we anticipated Winchester would wish to discuss it. I wonder what could have possibly kept George."

Teddie gnashed her teeth. "It's a marriage contract, isn't it?"

The entire house shook beneath the sudden banging on the front door. An ashen-faced Maggie froze in her tracks until Edwina nodded slowly, as though she were sending the servant, albeit reluctantly, to her doom. Maggie scurried off, closing the door behind her.

Teddie surged to her feet, sending linen tumbling to the floor. "You both know he won't abide by it, Aunt Edwina, no matter what it says. He will refuse to sign it. He does not suffer humiliation well."

"No man does, Theodora. For that very reason he will sign it. Of that your uncle is certain. You must trust us, my dear. We would do nothing to jeopardize your happiness or your safety."

Teddie grabbed fistfuls of cotton skirting, unable to argue with this. She'd been welcomed at Timberneck Manor with open, loving arms, embraced so wholly into their fold that her heart wrenched at the thought of leaving them so soon. "This is nothing short of humiliating," she finally said, her anger simmering. "I should have been told, long before the invitations were sent." At a sudden thought she narrowed her eyes on her aunt, who promptly occupied herself with an invisible speck of lint on her sleeve. "But, of course, the contract was intentionally drawn up and delivered *after* the invitations were sent, wasn't it, Aunt Edwina?"

Edwina summoned an appropriately helpless look. "George handled that, my dear. You know men, always neglecting the details."

Teddie folded her arms over her chest and watched her aunt reposition herself on the edge of a chair as though she sought the perfect spot to do battle with the enemy. "Hardly a detail, Aunt Edwina. Perhaps a little added insurance that I won't cancel the wedding and risk embarrassing you with all of your friends, hmm?"

"You must admit, my dear, you've the kindest of hearts."

Teddie's breath released in a low hiss. "Winchester will assume I was party to it."

"All's the better if he does," Edwina sniffed, smoothing her skirts around her with swift slaps of her hands. "Think of it as a business arrangement, nothing more. Once you hear of the terms you will be grateful, my dear."

"Winchester won't be told what to do. And neither will I."

Aunt Edwina looked up, blinked, and gave Teddie one of her confoundedly opaque smiles. "Indeed. I suppose one could easily wonder why we would even attempt to try."

The staccato of his bootheels registered on the hall floor an instant before the parlor door slammed open. In that instant, Teddie experienced her first desire to flee, to melt into the floorboards, to disappear on the next shallow breeze. Not that she feared Winchester. Hardly. But control over her life—something she valued greatly and had struggled to retain—had again been wrested from her. And without knowledge of the contract's contents she was at a distinct disadvantage to regain that control. Particularly with a man like Winchester.

She lifted her eyes to his and felt a jar deep in her soul. The fires of Hades had indeed left their mark on him. He seemed as if born of some raging tempest, a savage sent to plunder the pristine tranquillity of their sun-splashed, linen-draped parlor. His presence was suddenly overwhelming, momentarily sapping the breath from Teddie's lungs and the strength from her limbs. He loomed larger than life, with his raven's hair windblown, his shirt and breeches dusty, his face flushed with an obvious effort to control himself. Beneath the white linen, his chest heaved, drawing the cloth taut with each breath. His eyes blazed. His fists clenched and unclenched against rock-hard thighs, crushing the letter he held. He'd spread his black boots wide as though bracing himself for battle.

And from the depths of Teddie's consciousness roused the memory of all that hot, vibrant sinew pressed against her own flesh.

Miles watched the color climb high into Teddie's cheeks. Christ, but he'd never met a more impudent woman. She apparently felt no compulsion to conceal her guilt in the matter. From her there would be no appropriate averting of flaming cheeks. No fluttering nervously about. No fleeing the room with a murmured apology. Just the same stubborn jut of her chin, a prim lift of her nose, and a forthright stare that momentarily shook him to his boots. For a fleeting moment he felt more than the slightest bit foolish to have burst in on them, on all their—

He took it all in with one sweep of his eyes around the room. The heaps of clothing and linen. The aunt, looking appropriately scandalized, as though she hadn't any notion why he'd come in such a hurry, straight from the fields and looking like it. The servant girl simply gaped at him, unable to utter more than a squeak since he'd stormed into the house. And his duplicitous bride stood there, surrounded by a wide fortress of white linen, looking like a pale yellow rose about to burst into bloom. She'd cloaked herself in so cool and regal an air, he imagined the slender length of her spine would feel rigid beneath his fingertips. But that silken skin would simmer with the same heat that colored her eyes a deep, passionate purple.

He crushed the letter tight in his fist and forced his gaze to

Edwina Farrell. Before he could summon a tone more appropriate to tranquil, sun-splashed parlors, Edwina Farrell rose elegantly from her chair. "Good heavens, Mr. Winchester, you look in desperate need of something to drink. Maggie, dear, do get Mr. Winchester something to drink." Edwina Farrell blinked up at him from beneath an expertly coiffed sweep of white hair. "What would you like, Mr. Winchester?"

Miles gnashed his teeth. Nothing was as frustrating to an angry man as a roomful of women who didn't seem to realize he was angry. "Nothing," he growled with what he thought was a good deal of impatience. "Is the commander here?"

"It's no bother really," Edwina fluttered, astoundingly impervious to his impatience. "Maggie, get us all some lemonade. And some tea cakes. Theodora? It's too blasted hot for tea, don't you think?"

"Indeed, lemonade would be better." She barely murmured the reply, but Miles detected an arrogance lacing her tone, as though she knew precisely what game they played with him. Damned women.

"Would you care to sit?" Edwina Farrell indicated an armchair that a man of his size would never find comfortable. The whole scene smacked of a carefully orchestrated plot to frustrate him and take the wind entirely out of his argument. Indeed, the longer he stood there, the more foolish they intended to make him feel. Well, he wouldn't have any of it, dammit.

"Is your husband in residence, Mrs. Farrell?"

Edwina Farrell began to fluster about, plucking tiny piles of linen from chairs and tables and placing it all in an enormous trunk set before the hearth. "Who, George?" She turned to him and paused, her brows puckered. In her hands she held what to his eye looked like a filmy pair of women's white silk stockings, replete with dainty white silk garters. When she spoke her hands gestured, a typical habit of hers, but the motions only seemed to bring the feminine undergarments more strikingly into focus for Miles. In fact he was experiencing difficulty not imagining those stockings on a lissome pair of legs. Indeed, he remembered them as exceedingly well-shaped, extravagant in length, particularly the thighs, precisely where those garters would ride.

"Mr. Winchester? Did you say something?"

Miles nearly shouted with his frustration. "Your husband, Mrs. Farrell—"

"Ah! Our lemonade! On that table over there, Maggie. I'm afraid there's little room elsewhere." Edwina breezed past him, trailing silk stockings in her wake. Though the fabric brushed like a whisper against his bare forearm when she passed, Miles's skin pulsed as though branded by flame. He turned around, teeth set, only to find a tall glass of lemonade pressed into his hand.

"Drink up!" Edwina Farrell chimed, again blowing past him with stockings fluttering in her uplifted hand. "Ooh, Theodora, look at these. Made in Paris of the finest—"

Teddie snatched the stockings and garters from her aunt's hand and crushed them against her stomach. "Aunt Edwina, Mr.—that is, Winchester—"

"Oh." Edwina Farrell stopped in her tracks and again blinked at Miles as though she'd forgotten he was there. "I suppose you're not interested in Theodora's trousseau, Mr. Winchester."

"Not at the moment," Miles rumbled, the promise lurking in his words not lost on his future bride. With a certain primal satisfaction he watched her enormous eyes dilate a fraction and her full bosom swell with her agitated breaths. Indeed, he felt oddly victorious, as though he'd worn down the first impenetrable lines of an enemy's defense. But nothing about her suggested defeat. Perhaps because she'd again managed to distract him from his purpose. Damn. "Mrs. Farrell," he ground out, "I must speak with your husband."

Settling once more in her chair, Edwina Farrell gave him an apologetic smile, the first and last he expected to ever receive from her. "Why, George isn't here. I expect him quite soon. Perhaps you would care to wait."

"Thank you, but no, I've had quite enough." He tipped the glass of lemonade to his lips and drained it, all but smacking his lips as he handed the empty glass to Maggie with a murmur of thanks.

"Perhaps I can be of assistance," Edwina Farrell offered.

Miles shook his head, his gaze settling dispassionately on his bride. "I believe Miss Lovelace can. Perhaps a stroll through Timberneck's gardens."

Edwina leapt from her chair. "I cannot allow—"

Oddly enough, the force of Miles's stare finally silenced her. "I've done all the harm I can do to your niece, Mrs. Farrell. A chaperone at this point would be rather ineffectual, don't you agree?" Miles turned abruptly and held a hand to the door. "Miss Lovelace, if you please?"

"But—"

To Miles's surprise Teddie glanced at her flustered aunt, murmured something, then, lifting her skirts, extricated herself from the maze of linen and clothing with such grace that not one piece of cloth even fluttered as she passed. There was a singular elegance to her movements that reminded Miles again of a long-stemmed rose. But as she passed and the scent of lilacs in full bloom washed over him, the immediacy of his physical response proved beyond doubt that this lovely rose possessed dangerous thorns. Thorns that could probe dangerously deep if he ever allowed them to again.

As he followed her from the parlor through a side door that opened onto the veranda, he grimly reminded himself that, in his experience a woman's allure, however mysterious, began and ended in bed. Knowing this he would have anticipated feeling a distinct weariness at engaging any female in a garden conversation, especially one that involved the particulars of a legal document. Indeed, whatever idle chatter she would provide would only frustrate him further regarding the matter, wouldn't it? She certainly couldn't clarify the issues. Hadn't he just paid witness to the female capacity for muddling matters?

And yet, as he quickened his step to hold the door wide for her and received barely a slant of her eyes in acknowledgment, he felt no weariness. In fact he'd never felt more vigorously alive, strangely so. Of course, rage had been known to get a man's blood thumping in his veins, and God knew being dictated the terms of his marriage might be enough to get any man energized. Yes, that was it. He was angry, he decided as he sauntered along behind Miss Theodora Lovelace across the veranda and out into a broad expanse of manicured lawn toward a grove of trees. Damned angry, he reminded himself when the sunlight seemed to strike blue fire in her loosely coiled hair. Angry enough to spit, he reiterated when she stopped suddenly beneath the most fragrant honeysuckle tree he could imagine and spun around with eyes flashing a most incredible shade of violet.

He'd never met a more vibrant woman. And he was possessed with a desire that was as irrefutable as it was disturbing.

Only then did the contract burn in his fist with renewed urgency.

"Have you a problem, Winchester?"

He moved nearer, possessed by a need to tower over her, to fully impress his fury upon her, to penetrate that cool veneer. He waved the contract skyward, and she looked not the least bit daunted. "You know damned well what brought me here," he rumbled.

"I've an idea."

"Though the damned thing doesn't require your signature— only mine—you obviously agreed to it. All of it."

"And why shouldn't I?" She blinked up at him, her face like that of an angel, framed by a halo of wind-tossed curls. "It's in my best interests."

"Your best interests," he muttered, shoving a hand through his hair. "No Winchester has ever been contractually bound in a marriage, dammit."

"Ah. I see."

He narrowed his eyes on her, wondering if she did indeed see anything. "I won't be told how to conduct myself," he said slowly.

Her finely arched brows knitted, as though the logic of it were plain to see by all except him. "Then don't sign it, though I'm afraid my uncle would then make quite certain that you enlist, quite speedily."

"That appears to be his intent. Have you considered, Miss

Lovelace, that you're a pawn in his game of war? That he's simply using you as a vehicle to get me back on a ship?''

She shrugged. ''If he is then he's simply taking advantage of the opportunity that was laid rather indelicately in his lap. My uncle had nothing to do with what transpired in your bed, Winchester.'' She turned then, and Miles moved with her, settling into stride beside her. He watched her closely for some hint that memory haunted her. She betrayed nothing as she moved slowly through the grove of trees. Indeed, any other woman might have embraced her role as the victim in this, carefully exploiting the situation to her advantage. Not her. ''Are there specific points that upset you, Winchester, or simply the idea of being told what to do?''

''I'm not upset.''

''Ah.'' She clasped her hands behind her back and seemed momentarily preoccupied with the sweeping branches overhead. ''Women become upset. Men bang doors, stomp about, ride their animals into the ground, and shoot at each other in the fog. Tell me why you didn't kill your cousin.''

''I—'' He paused, frowned, then found himself peering up into the branches along with her, distinctly uncomfortable with the turn of conversation. ''Damian is hardly yet a man. Doesn't know a damned thing about life.''

''Unlike you.''

He glanced sharply at her, but she still peered overhead, exposing the slender length of her neck clear to the base of her throat, where three tiny pearl buttons gapped open. She looked so vulnerable, possessed of such a childlike innocence, Miles found it almost impossible to believe that such a creature could burrow under his skin so easily. ''Sometimes I feel like I've lived three lifetimes,'' he muttered, scowling at nothing in particular in the distance. ''It doesn't matter. Damian will get himself killed on his own. And there will be nothing chivalrous about it. I only postponed the inevitable.''

''I see.'' She quickened her pace, her distraction overhead suddenly forgotten. He got the feeling she knew precisely where she was going. ''You were saying . . .'' She glanced at him, her stride lengthening as though naturally adjusting to his much longer one. He'd never walked along with a woman so effortlessly before in his life. "Regarding the contract, Winchester. Perhaps you should take it item by item."

"Fine." Miles thwacked open the crumpled contract and squinted at Farrell's bold scrawl. "Good enough. There's this business of your happiness. Too damned ambiguous. An impossible task if there ever was one. I've never known a happy woman in my life, which is great cause for concern considering that half my plantation is in the balance should you decide to become the least bit unhappy."

"Ah. Which half?"

He arched a brow, his tone sharpening. "You mean you don't know? Surely you had something in mind when you composed the damned thing."

She seemed to consider this, her full lips pursing. "I suppose the house. It's quite lovely. The gardens as well. It reminds me of a grand English manor house set high upon a hilltop belonging to some very important duke."

"It should. Supposedly my grandmother would settle for nothing less. The natural eminence of the terrain along the banks of the James provided the most desirable homesite. As for the house, my grandfather built it himself, of bricks fired on the plantation."

She was watching him again, closely. "I see. You've indeed holdings enough for at least a dukedom, I would think."

He gave a short, brittle laugh. "Land is more plentiful here than in England. I suppose if you're used to the relatively small estates there, you might easily misinterpret the significance of owning substantial acreage. To survive, a planter has to have large holdings to provide new fields demanded by tobacco, not to mention the timberland necessary to build the barks to transport it and the sheds to dry and house the leaves." His gaze swept over the horizon. "Hell, I still don't have enough acreage. Tobacco wears out land and men before their time. Sometimes I think my future lies elsewhere."

"Not at Miramer?"

Her voice gently coaxed, even the resisting and the unsuspecting. "Always at Miramer."

"Then that wouldn't be quite fair, now, would it? After all, if I took the house where would you live?"

His scowl descended with startling dispatch and he swung on her, his ire reignited, perhaps even more so because of his momentary lapse. "On my damned boat. Under your uncle's command."

"Oh, of course. But you've made it perfectly clear you want that even less than you want a wife. One indiscretion—" Her eyes slanted quickly up at him, then just as quickly averted. "Which is not to assume that you haven't engaged in others, no doubt with far greater success. Which makes it all the more vexing, I suppose, that our little indiscretion could sentence us both to a lifetime of misery. We might deserve something, but I doubt it's that. Don't you agree?"

"Yes," he heard himself say, entirely certain that he hadn't the vaguest idea what she meant. Only that he was fairly sure she would approach the marriage as diplomatically as a woman could be expected to approach any type of punishment. His eyes met hers. "Miss Lovelace, it would make matters much less difficult if you could say precisely what you require for some measure of happiness."

Her eyes seemed to glaze over, as suddenly as a shadow darkened her features. "Peace," she said, half to herself, as though she'd forgotten that he was at her side, feeling atrociously out of place for some reason.

From any other woman he would have expected a different answer entirely, some endless gush of all the clothes and jewels and shoes necessary for any woman to even consider being the least bit happy, all neatly tied up with a vow to show her off in all her finery at all the appropriately highbrow functions attended by all the proper people. Any other woman would have mentioned children and just as quickly nannies and governesses to care for those children. Any other woman would have demanded an entire wing for herself and even hinted at the possibility of discreetly taking a lover should the notion strike.

Miles could provide all this, and more. But peace? Hell, he'd given up on finding that long ago. He sure as hell couldn't help someone else find it.

He didn't know what to say. Apparently, she didn't await his answer, or perhaps she realized she was asking too much of him. Without even glancing at him she lifted her skirts and began to run down a gentle slope that swept into an open field scattered with wildflowers. At the base of the field several horses grazed in a fenced pasture, and further north beyond that, over a shallow valley of woods, lay the sparkling blue waters of the York River.

Miles paused just as he emerged from the grove of trees, his eyes following her as she ran toward the pasture, her blue-black curls tumbling down her back. Who the hell was this woman-child? One moment she epitomized serene elegance and cool detachment. The next she flitted from thought to thought, "ah-ing" as though she were wise well beyond her years, and frolicking among the wildflowers like a young girl who'd been denied such pleasure until now.

He listened to his boots swish through the tall grass, following the path she'd laid. Here the wind swept off the bay across the fields, carrying the earthy scents roused by the heat of the sun. Miles filled his lungs with it. He felt the sun slap at his forehead, the wind billow in his shirt sleeves. There was something simple and elemental about it all, far removed from the hassle of his daily life that allowed little time for enjoyment of much else but the meeting of daily quotients of hogsheads filled and tonnage harvested. He couldn't help but be affected by it.

By the time he reached her she'd climbed onto the fence and was feeding what looked to be several of her aunt's tea cakes to an exceptional black mare and several bay companions.

"Your uncle has an eye for fine horseflesh," he said, leaning his forearms on the fence and giving her his full regard.

"They're beauties, especially Cleo," she murmured in reply just as the black mare shoved her tapered nose against her skirts. Thinking she would fall from her perch, Miles caught her arm, unconsciously drawing her nearer. Their eyes met just as their shoulders brushed, and the winsome smile that flirted with her lips instantly faded. Again the shadow descended over her features, and she stiffened as though she anticipated being struck.

The thought brought his brows low. Yet he didn't release her. A sudden breeze tossed a wayward curl against his chest laid bare by his open shirt. She smelled sweeter than an entire meadow of wildflowers. "Do you think you could be happy at Miramer, Miss Lovelace?" he asked softly. "Or has your uncle set me to an impossible task?"

There was no guile in her response. "I could certainly try."

"So will I." His fingers relaxed on her arm as she dug again into her pockets and offered still more tea cakes to the horses. "I assure you that you will want for nothing. Simply let me know if anything is not to your liking." Again he glanced at the contract. "As for the next point, regarding allowing your aunt and Farrell free rein to come and go as often as they please—" She glanced at him, the subtle glitter of amusement in her eyes not lost on him.

His frown deepened. "I suppose they'll have to satisfy themselves somehow that you are indeed blushing with contentment. So long as they don't interfere with the smooth running of the plantation."

"My aunt is discreet, Winchester."

"Miles," he said before he could catch himself. Why the hell should it matter what she called him? Her slight frown only added to his chagrin. He scowled at the contract. "As for the final point, I assume you're in agreement."

"Should I be otherwise?"

He glanced sharply at her, again taken aback by her response. "No." He forced a shrug through his broad shoulders, feeling the slightest bit self-conscious and, yes, dammit, uncomfortable discussing it. Damned Farrell. "Absolutely not. I assumed the matter was fully understood, requiring no specific stating in a contract. The term, particularly, surprised me."

"Ah. The term."

He watched her play with the horses, aware of a frustrating need to capture her full attention. "Why just a year? Is it not universally understood at the outset of most marriages of convenience that they will endure for lifetimes? Why stipulate the need to maintain separate beds for one year only?''

She seemed to freeze, her wide gaze slowly lifting to his. He might have thought she was taken aback herself were he not convinced she'd contributed a great deal to composing the thing. No doubt her perpetual happiness in the marriage and his remaining unimpressed on to one of Farrell's ships depended on his adhering to this particular clause. Not that he had anything to the contrary in mind. In fact, this part of the contract, term or not, suited him just fine. He had absolutely no intention of sharing a bed with Miss Theodora Lovelace ever again. No woman would bring him to his knees with that kind of mindless passion twice in one lifetime. Indeed, if a man was to find himself in these circumstances, a marriage in name only—at least with this particular woman—was precisely what he should want.

''I suppose there's an implied assumption that one of us might wish to change our minds at some point after that year.'' She blinked up at him with the same unnerving forthrightness that seemed to tangle his tongue.

He lifted his brows. ''Which, of course is—''

''—silly—''

''—Quite.''

They both turned away to look at the horses.

''There is no mention of children,'' he finally continued, scowling again at nothing in particular. ''I assume you don't desire children for happiness.''

''Do you?''

He paused, then answered truthfully, ''I don't suppose I've thought about it. My life has never lent itself to that sort of responsibility.''

''I suppose one's needs for happiness change over time. Perhaps one day we may decide we . . . We could—that is, only after a year has passed, of course—''

''Yes. I suppose we could then—''

''Only for that purpose, of course.''

''Of course.''

''If we agreed I suppose we could try—''

"Yes, we could try."

"Once or—"

"Perhaps twice, depending on our success."

"Yes, of course. It doesn't just—"

"No, it doesn't. It might take a bit of trying. The frequency may also depend on how many children we want. If any."

"True. We might never want any."

"Quite true."

A hawk circled high overhead, capturing both their attention for several moments.

"But if we had one," she finally said, "I suppose I would want another. One child would be so terribly lonely without a sister—or brother—" Obviously lost in her thoughts, for a long moment she stroked Cleo's nose. It was then that Miles realized he wanted to know so much more about this woman than she would ever tell him. Intuition dictated that she revealed only what she chose to reveal. Nothing more. What secrets could so young and innocent a woman harbor? A lost love, perhaps? What else could it be? The thought struck him suddenly, disturbingly. Could she have left some young fellow behind in England, tragically torn from him because of the war? A young, proud and noble man who would have laid down his life to give her everything she deserved—

A curse rumbled through his chest, bringing her wide eyes up to his. Too much damned sunshine, flowers, and talk of children were muddling his thinking, softening him, by God, filling his mind with thoughts better suited to romantic fiction. His fingers curled tightly around the fence, his deeply clefted chin jutting forward with manly Winchester pride. A tic took up residence in his jaw. As if some English greenhorn could provide her with more comfort than he! He'd all but agreed to sign a damned contract guaranteeing her happiness, hadn't he? He'd even engaged in conversation about children, as dumbfounding as that seemed at the moment. He would give her the legacy of his name. Her children's veins would flow with Winchester blood. Indeed, for a woman who had fallen into the wrong bed and handed him her virginity, she could hardly justify complaining about her circumstances or the sacrifices he intended to make to accommodate her. Hell, a softening of manner toward her and any lost loves she might mourn was hardly appropriate when she held Miramer's future in her dainty hands.

And yet, impressing the magnitude of her good fortune on her with a great deal of shouting and stomping about didn't seem the proper course for him to take. Indeed, a gentler hand steering her slowly to this conclusion might prove far more successful and just might erase the clouds from her violet eyes.

Perhaps she might even smile again.

The trouble was, Miles had never taken time or care with any woman, particularly when the reward was nothing more than her effortless smile. He found the prospect more daunting than keeping a field of tobacco free of hornworms for an entire season. No doubt Farrell had composed the contract with this clearly in mind.

Damned tests everywhere he turned. If Farrell intended to make him feel trapped he'd done it, by God, and his instrument was the winsome, oddly accommodating, and thus perplexing Miss Lovelace.

He turned, but she'd left him there to his thoughts and was already halfway across the field of wildflowers.

"Damned woman," he muttered, starting after her, knowing he'd lingered amidst the sun and the wildflowers too long already, knowing too that he still had a good half day's work left to accomplish. And mounds of paperwork to wade through.

After that, when the household settled quiet for the night, he would again take to the coastal roads in search of his elusive impostor. Perhaps until dawn.

And yet despite all this he'd been content to linger for quite some time among the sunshine and wildflowers. Odd, but as he strode through the field alone he grew increasingly aware that the day suddenly seemed to have lost its ability to enchant and distract him from his duties. He briefly considered that Miss Lovelace might have something to do with this. After all, he'd found her not the least bit dull. Captivating, actually.

He didn't see her again once she disappeared from his sight into the grove of trees. Returning to the house, he scrawled his name at the bottom of the contract, left it with the servant girl, and bid an astonished Edwina Farrell a curt good day.

He departed Timberneck Manor thoroughly convinced that he could have done nothing else.

Chapter Six

The wedding was to take place at noon. As if in reminder of the indelicate circumstances that had necessitated the event, Mother Nature rose to the occasion with a dazzling display of early morning violence. Overnight the heat never abated, and at dawn the air seemed to build and crackle in anticipation as great billowing purple-black clouds galloped in from the west. Electricity shot from a sky gone dark as night. Thunder shook the land, rattled china in cupboards, and threw everyone from their beds at an indecently early hour. Rain poured to the ground. Wind pummeled the house. Standing at the window of her bedchamber with her cotton wrapper slung over her shoulders, Teddie decided there was nothing promising in it whatsoever.

An hour later the sun emerged and began to slowly bake the rain-soaked earth. Steam rose in great abundance and seeped into the house, a circumstance augmented by Aunt Edwina ordering every window thrown wide to catch any vagrant breezes. None were to be had.

The heat only swelled.

A half hour before she was to descend into the front parlor and become Miles Winchester's bride, Teddie stood in the center of her sweltering bedchamber in nothing but sheer silk stockings, garters, and a parchment-thin white linen chemise. Maggie fluttered around, poking at Teddie's hair and every now and then dribbling rice powder onto her shoulders to give them the expected luminescence. A futile task in such heat, though Maggie seemed determined to give it a good try. The young servant alternately giggled and babbled as though this were suddenly the happiest day of Teddie's life.

Teddie stared from a lace-draped window out over the grove

of mulberry trees to where the river waters sparkled, her thoughts on the man-of-war riding at anchor somewhere out on the bay. She had to bite her lips to keep from shrugging off Maggie's ministrations and tending to herself alone. The ability to simply stand still and allow others to see to one's every possible need had to be the result of centuries of impeccable breeding. It made Teddie, who was of decidedly muddled blood, distinctly uncomfortable. Not that she wasn't painfully aware that her aunt's house was grand, her bedchamber a sumptuous study in pale pink, the food bountiful, her trousseau exquisite, and the piles of clothing and accessories filling her trunks enough for five women. Teddie had never dreamed of anything like it and she was deeply grateful to her aunt. But she would have done without any of it to have Will be free. Enjoying herself for even a moment—be it in conversation with her aunt over dinner, appreciating the feel of French silk stockings and transparent linen on her skin, or bathing in a tub scented with lilac oils—seemed blasphemous and flooded Teddie with guilt.

That guilt-ridden part of her viewed her impending marriage as just desserts, a bit of penance to pay for falling so neatly into luxury while Will awoke in irons each morning not knowing whether or not it was his last. Marriage to Winchester was scant price to pay considering that Will faced Cockburn each day.

At just after midnight the night before, Teddie had met the admiral's longboat. She'd kept the meeting frustratingly brief, knowing she only tempted being discovered the longer she lingered there on the moon-splashed shores. After assuring herself of Will's health she'd presented Cockburn with a few choice bits of news she'd managed to overhear her uncle discussing with several of his militia captains, about the Night Hawk and his covert maneuverings near the mouth of the Elizabeth River. Conjecture had it he was refitting a privateer somewhere south of the James. She'd overheard more, of course, regarding declining morale among the militiamen, who were apparently growing tired of chasing caped riders in the night with little success. They were also becoming increasingly apprehensive that Cockburn might bombard the ineptly guarded Fort McHenry and sweep inland. Farrell hadn't alleviated their concerns when he'd told them it would be weeks before he could put a fleet to sea against Cockburn, if then. Shipbuilding took time, and Farrell had yet to convince Madison that the three heavily armed frigates being constructed near Baltimore would serve the Americans far better in the Chesapeake than they would north in the St. Lawrence chasing British supply vessels. If Madison didn't come around in his thinking, nothing but several hundred militiamen would stand in Cockburn's path if he decided to attack Virginia.

Teddie hadn't mentioned any of that distressing news to Cockburn, knowing he might well attack simply because he knew the Americans feared it. He'd seemed well-satisfied with the news of the Night Hawk. As long as was practicable, satiating his thirst for more immediate confrontation seemed the obvious course. Better to occupy him with news of the Night Hawk refitting a privateer with the intent of making a run at the blockade than to focus his energies on the militia or the American navy. At least then she didn't feel as though she betrayed anyone.

She'd made no mention to Cockburn of her impending marriage or what effect her change in circumstances might have on her ability to provide him with useful information. Not that she hadn't pondered this, well into many sleepless nights. But Teddie had not been raised to doubt her abilities. A woman did not acquire a fine education without achieving the confidence and self-reliance that inevitably went along with it. She believed herself capable, regardless of her circumstances. If not for this she might have succumbed to despair when her father died, leaving them with nothing. She might indeed begin to think that Will would never be free of Cockburn and that they were both pawns in Cockburn's game, to be as easily disposed of as poor Aaron had been when Cockburn had little use for the weak boy save for setting an example to his crew.

Usefulness was the key to both of them staying alive. Intuition told her that Cockburn valued Will's strength and agility far too much at the moment to kill him on a whim, so long as

Teddie continued to supply Cockburn with information. Once she was at Miramer she would find a way to continue doing this. She'd managed to elude both the Night Hawk and any stray regiments last evening, hadn't she? Escaping Winchester's baronial mansion undetected would prove far simpler.

"He's here," Aunt Edwina breathed with obvious relief as she surged into the bedchamber in a swish of pale blue taffeta.

"Of course, he's here," Teddie said, her tone a touch crisp. "For the rest of his life the man is bound by contract."

"Ah, yes. Quite right. You are thankful for our foresight, my dear, regardless of our less than forthright methods?"

Teddie pursed her lips and gave her aunt a gently reproachful glare. "I suppose that's as close as you'll ever come to admitting you behaved underhandedly. I would have preferred knowing about it before he arrived with it."

Aunt Edwina fixed her attentions on resuscitating the wilting lace at her wrists. "Perhaps you object to something in the contract?"

Something in her aunt's blithe tone brought a quiver to Teddie's brows. "Should I?"

Aunt Edwina stared at her a moment, then lifted one shoulder in an elegant shrug. "No, indeed. Your happiness is all but guaranteed, I would think. Yes, we quite thought of everything. I must say I expected Winchester to object rather stridently regarding—" Her aunt's voice broke off with an expectant lilt.

Their eyes met and Teddie felt a greater heat radiate from her cheeks. Quickly, she lowered her eyes and plucked at a loose thread. "Oh, that."

"It's for your protection, dear. I couldn't sleep knowing I'd delivered my Eugenia's sweet Theodora back into that blackguard's . . . into his . . . for him to . . . You understand, of course."

"Entirely."

"I suppose Winchester understands as well. He did sign it, after all."

"I believe he relishes the alternative even less."

Aunt Edwina looked thoughtful. "Indeed. I must say he's made of stern stuff." She shrugged off Teddie's curious glance.

"But with a man like Winchester one can never be quite certain that anything will hold him, contracts, obligations, or otherwise." Drawing one limp wrist to her forehead, Edwina said, "The devil take us all, but it's too bloody hot for a wedding. A good thing that George saw fit to arm himself against the likelihood that the groom might suffer a sudden change of heart. He's posted a few of his men at the exits."

Teddie arched a fine black brow. "Has he mounted a regiment to stand guard at the manor's gates as well?"

Aunt Edwina blinked several times, then drew a gloved index finger to her lips. "Why, I hadn't thought of that."

Teddie all but hung her head in her hand, prevented, of course, by Maggie's strict instructions to avoid excessive head movement lest her intricate coiffure fail to survive such a rigorous test. "Good grief, Aunt Edwina."

"Don't fret, dear, the guests won't suspect a thing. The weaponry will be well-concealed."

"That contract was all the weaponry required."

"As I said, with Winchester one can't be too careful."

"He would never flee. He might be many things, but he's not a coward. And he will honor that contract."

"You sound so very certain, dear. You barely know the man."

Teddie considered this a moment. "True, but I know he would never leave Miramer. I believe it's all he has."

"Indeed. A pity I cannot share your confidence at the moment, perhaps because I have invested a small fortune and my entire reputation in this wedding. In wartime you might expect people to be less discriminating in their pleasures. But the Virginia plantation set is even more particular than the landed gentry in London, no matter that we are at war. I learned very quickly after arriving here that these Virginians' convivial natures, like their extravagant hospitality, is rooted in the social isolation of our plantations. Good food, good drink, good company, and good conversation are cultivated as arts here and practiced with great flair. An event like this can be nothing short of a grand success. I certainly will not provide Winchester with the opportunity to ruin it for anyone, dear. Some of the guests might even decide not to spend the night. Theodora, nothing is as essential or as greatly valued as a relief to the loneliness and monotony of living so far from one's nearest neighbor as overnight visitors. Here, take this. I need a chair.''

Teddie frowned at the porcelain bowl full of ice chunks her aunt placed in her hand. ''Where did you get this?''

Aunt Edwina dissolved into an overstuffed chair placed before the open window, snapped open a lace fan, and began to flap at her bosom. ''Your uncle hires a veritable army of men in the heart of winter to haul great chunks of ice from the river to our cellar. It doesn't quite melt until October. I'll have you know I fetched it from the cellar myself. I must say hefting a sharp instrument against a block of ice would do us all a bit of good every now and then. Put it on your wrists, Theodora. It will cool you and calm your nerves before you put on the dress. He looks most ominous this morning.''

''Winchester always looks ominous.'' Teddie applied the ice to one wrist, then slid it up the inside of her forearm just as Winchester's very ominous image loomed in her mind. Delightful shivers danced up her arm. Her breath caught in her chest. Again she slowly slid the ice down her arm. Nothing but a warm trickle of water remained when she reached her wrist. She reached for another small chunk. There was something sinfully delicious in the feel of ice melting on heated skin.

This time she drew the ice over her shoulder and up the curved side of her neck. Heavenly . . . and just a bit wicked. She was tempted to surrender to it. Her lips parted with a sigh and her eyes swept closed.

Again Winchester's image bloomed vivid, fierce. And yet with the wind ruffling his hair and a riotous field of wildflowers surrounding him, he'd seemed a great deal more human. Disturbingly so. When he'd looked into her eyes, seeking the recipe for her happiness, she'd even detected a brief hint of vulnerability in him. An odd thought, given that the man was elementally male in every sense of the word and that he made her feel primally, deeply, and elementally female.

The sliver of ice slipped from her fingers and plunged down the valley between her breasts. Her eyes snapped open and she spun around before her Aunt Edwina or Maggie could achieve an eyeful. With a certain dread she lowered her eyes and felt her cheeks flame. The peaks of her breasts distended almost painfully against the filmy linen, suddenly achingly sensitive to each whisper of the cloth against her skin as she moved.

"I should dress," she said, her voice suddenly husky. And yet she almost feared the simple movements required to don a dress. With each stirring of air her breasts felt more swollen and heavy, and a peculiar ache had settled low between her thighs. What the devil was wrong with her? "The heat . . ." she murmured.

"Of course, dear," Aunt Edwina said, rising from her chair and laying warm, comforting hands on Teddie's upper arms. "We're all growing restless with this heat. Maggie, if you would, please. I don't trust myself with all those buttons. Besides, my fingers are shaking at the mere thought of what this heat is doing to the icing on the cake. I suppose as hostess I should go watch it all melt and slide away into wretched nothingness. Ah, a better thought. I'll have George fetch more wine. A fine Virginia vintage. Forgive me, dear, but there isn't a drop of champagne to be had since the blockade. Wine should do. And lots of it. Indeed, I think we should take our drinks in the gardens, where the guests can best avail themselves of picturesque prospects and salubrious breezes. Perhaps then no one will notice the cake." A rustle of skirts brought her to Teddie's side. Gently, with one finger beneath Teddie's chin, she lifted Teddie's eyes to hers. "Why, you look frightened, dear. Just like your mother did on the day she became your father's wife. Oh, my dear . . ." With a sigh Aunt Edwina drew Teddie into a cushy, rose-scented embrace. "I'm sorry to say, but it's the woman who can make a marriage work, Theodora. With your kind of quiet strength I think you could make a success of it with a man like Winchester. Think of it as a business partnership. That always helps when things seem most bleak."

A business partnership. Teddie clung to her aunt's words. Indeed, with her mind for figures she could contribute substantially to the operation of the plantation. Besides, she would need something to occupy her mind or she might go mad over her inability to free Will and herself from Cockburn's clutches.

Her first smile of the day softened her lips as she stood stiffly and allowed Maggie to work her way down an endless row of silk-covered buttons. If she was to find herself in such indelicate circumstances with a man like Winchester, a business partnership was precisely what she should want from a marriage.

Miles's first thought upon seeing his bride struck him unawares. *Take the commission under Farrell's command.* At least the demons then would be familiar to him, the ghosts, the descent into madness almost comforting in their certainty compared to the surge of uneasiness and ineptitude that swept over him like a chilling ocean surf when Theodora Lovelace appeared at the entrance to the parlor.

Swathed in a sea of shimmering ivory silk, splashed by a ray of sunlight, she achieved a level of feline confidence extraordinary even for her. She captured every eye, held it, seduced it, and refused to release it, all with a guileless ease that startled even a cynic like Miles. Though he might have wished it, there was no cunning in the tilt of her full lips, no telling sparkle in her eyes of the game handily won, no boastful jut in the extravagant fullness of her bosom. Her beauty required no such drama to enhance it. Perhaps somehow, in her naïveté, she realized this.

She was, therefore, far more dangerous than any cunning, crafty, wily, manipulating female Miles had ever had the misfortune of encountering. Or bedding. Much less marrying.

Finding oneself ensnared by a scheming woman was one thing and certainly justified a great deal of annoyance. A woman like that could be held, to a certain degree, accountable. A woman like that could be dismissed out of hand simply for possessing such tendencies. A woman like that would then be rather easy to find oneself married to, particularly in a house of Miramer's size. If he so desired, Miles could arrange to move about without seeing that sort of wife for months.

Yet as much as it would have suited Miles to believe otherwise, Theodora Lovelace was not that sort of woman. She was quite simply like no other woman —or man, for that matter— he'd ever known. He'd faced countless enemies during his years on the seas, a twisted, diabolical, and bloodthirsty lot. But none of them had ever so handily maneuvered him into so distinctly uncomfortable a situation. At the moment he would have preferred the storm-swept decks of the *Leviathan* and the spray of salty seas on his face to the confines of this over-stuffed, airless parlor where his nostrils twitched at the smoke billowing from a gilded, wax-dripping chandelier directly over-head. He would have gladly faced the maniacal leers of a le-gion of pistol-waving desperadoes intent on ravaging his ship and cutting him down rather than subject himself to the smug, sardonic scrutiny of every bloated plantation owner within a twenty-mile radius, men who had made little secret of their contempt for him and who had no doubt come here to feed it to him. They must fair squirm in their finery with satisfaction at seeing him so neatly bagged. That a woman had accomplished what their government could not only sweetened their victory. Besides, it was commonly known that Miles Winchester's aver-sion to the war was exceeded only by his disinclination for marriage. Their smiles might have spread a tad less wide had he refused the marriage and signed on under Farrell to defend their fair shores.

Again the thought struck him with an unexpected force and an almost instantaneous self-contempt. Christ. That he would allow a woman to affect him so deeply, especially after Tripoli, after the traitoress Manal, was beyond comprehension. He had to remind himself as he watched Teddie move toward him that Manal had also been an innocent when he'd met her. She'd shed that encumbrance with a startling dispatch. Just as Teddie had. He could only wonder if his new bride, like the deflowered Manal, would just as handily turn traitor.

His gaze locked with Farrell's when the stalwart commander delivered Teddie's hand into his. Miles gave a brief, suitably polite incline of his head, which was met with a narrowing of Farrell's eyes, no doubt in warning. Miles had half a mind to tell the venerable commander that all the artillery in his entire

American navy lacked even a hint of the power of the young beauty sacrificed into the bonds of marriage.

He drew her fingers deep into his hand, sensing the trembling in her. But he saw no fear in her eyes as they finally lifted and met his. Her ivory-skinned luminescence was not born of an intolerance for heat or a too-tight dress, but of some inner source, something far too mysterious to be so easily explained. She would not crumple beside him, of this he was certain.

He watched her eyes lower, her lashes sweeping to her cheeks in that brief moment that she took notice of his formal attire. He wondered if she could appreciate the level of discomfort he was subjecting himself to solely for the sake of her happiness. The heat that she seemed so impervious to was proving all but intolerable to him at the moment. His body temperature seemed to have risen dramatically since she swept into the room like the first breath of spring. His cravat suddenly clutched at his throat. His finely woven gabardine breeches and topcoat seemed to trap all the heat within, making him feel as though he were on the verge of combusting. His circumstances did not improve when his gaze followed the curve of her neckline where it swept low to expose the lush, uppermost swells of her bosom. Her skin glowed with a pearly, dewy luminescence that made his fingers itch to touch her.

Abruptly, he turned to face the minister poised in front of the hearth, knowing simply by the startled look on the man's pallid face that he was failing miserably at keeping his agitation concealed. With half an ear he listened as the minister launched himself into the ceremony, his gaze drawn to the portrait of George Farrell hanging above the mantel. For some reason this younger version of the commander reminded Miles of his own father as he remembered him at his most glorious, out there in Tripoli's harbor. They'd all been so certain that their plan would work, Miles most of all.

He closed his eyes, shoving memory aside, but it snuck up and enveloped him like a snake. His bride spoke, her husky tones like a balm to his soul. If she could imagine in all her innocence the demons that tortured him, the madness that had trapped him, she would flee this room, the marriage yoke, and fervently embrace any other punishment. She was so lovely to behold in her wedding finery, her serenity in the face of her doom only compounding the injustice of it.

He found himself staring into violet pools gone wide with expectancy, as though she knew he gave serious thought to saving her for some young man she'd left behind in London, sparing her of himself and an inevitably empty, cold marriage.

"Sir?" The minister's drone barely penetrated Miles's consciousness.

Her rosy lips parted with her whisper. "Winchester?"

And behind him came Damian's growled "Cousin. Put the damned ring on her finger or I shall do it myself."

No. For all his sudden nobility of purpose to save this fresh young beauty, Miles knew with certainty that he didn't want Damian stepping in to do it. A fleeting image took shape of his cousin as the eager bridegroom, stripping his bride of her ivory silk, of white silk stockings and lace garters drifting to the floor of Damian's bedchamber at Miramer, and Miles in his study below, listening.

He definitely didn't want that.

The simple gold band slid easily over her finger, as easily as the words spilled from Miles's tongue, forever joining him to this woman. The minister swiftly concluded, then lifted colorless brows at Miles, obviously expecting something. Looking down at his bride, Miles grew aware of the expectant hush that seemed to swell around him, as though every last eye was trained on him, awaiting satisfaction. Like hell he'd give that to them. He'd had enough of serving himself up for their fickle enjoyment.

His eyes briefly met with Teddie's, hooded, then lowered to her mouth. How fitting that she should summon a blush at such a time, her eyes lowering, her manner pious and demure. A rose that was his for the taking.

How humbly she seemed to have accepted her fate. Then again, she could well be bracing herself against the fumbling kiss of an ardent bridegroom.

Someone coughed. The moment had passed. Her eyes swept to his. Relief mingled there with all that innocence. Relief. He knew a sudden disconcertion. Hell, she could barely temper her joy at his declining to kiss her. Indeed, she fair bounced with it as she placed her hand on his arm and swung her thoroughly disarming smile away from him toward the guests. He half expected a collective sigh to pass through the crowd at such radiance.

The bride, it seemed, was happy. Why then did he feel as though he'd been soundly left out of the fun?

A moment later she drifted off beneath the swooping wing of her aunt and a gaggle of overdressed females. Someone muttered something about the ladies retiring for several hours until luncheon. Closeted in a parlor of cigar-belching, war-addled plantation owners, none of whom cared the least for him, Miles would have preferred twenty lashes to this bit of news. He slid one finger into his starched white collar and pondered how best to appease his sudden thirst for rum.

"Congratulations, cousin," Damian said with a tinge of sarcasm as he drew himself up to his full height, from which vantage he no doubt thought it best to attempt to lambaste his cousin. "You may now look forward to making the poor girl miserable for the rest of her life." Without awaiting Miles's reply Damian turned on his heel and briskly made for a group of young American officers gathered near the door.

Farrell strode past, paused, gave Miles a satisfied grunt and a glower, then moved on. Miles set his teeth and determined to find the rum on his own. A hand on his arm stopped him just before he reached the open double doors leading into the foyer where the fluttering ladies had encircled the bride, all but trapping her there.

"You can't leave just yet, old boy. That would surely spoil all the fun for the rest of us." At Miles's hard glance, Jules Reynolds's lopsided grin deepened the weathered creases around his eyes but did nothing to diminish the man's audacious good looks. Just as Miles's brooding, almost sinister darkness buoyed his notoriety in the Tidewater region, Reynolds's golden-haired, blue-eyed, Adonislike mien never failed to propel his reputation as a consummate philanderer in a land where playboys—particularly of the handsome, unmarried variety—were few. Here the aristocracy worked, married, and produced housefuls of heirs. The plantations required it of their owners. Reynolds, undoubtedly the more wealthy of the lot, nevertheless exuded the air of a man intent on nothing but a singular pursuit of leisure. And pleasure. Even the manner in which his white cravat lay plump and carelessly fluffed at his throat attested to the man's flouting of convention.

It was rare when Miles could meet another man's gaze at eye level or when the breadth of his shoulders and the strength in his arms was so evenly matched by that same man's. Even Reynolds's horsemanship tested the very limits of Miles's same abilities, as did his quick wit and sharp tongue. In every arena save one, fate and circumstance seemed to have pitted them against one another.

Were it not for the ivory-handled cane Reynolds gripped and braced solidly against the floorboards, Miles suspected Reynolds would have challenged him to a footrace long ago to prove himself the more fleet of foot. But a man did not pursue pleasure without inevitably straying where he should not. In Reynolds's case this had been into the bed of the wife of his own fleet commander several years before, when that fleet commander returned unexpectedly early from Tripoli. Instead of killing Reynolds, which was certainly justified given the apparent ease of Reynolds's conquest, the fleet commander instead chose to impart a life sentence on the swaggering sea captain, regardless of the toll it took on his own fleet. The two met over pistols. With a merciless precision the commander plunged his shot into Reynolds's right thigh, shattering the bone and leaving him, at least as far as the American navy was concerned, a useless cripple, permanently unable to captain a ship. He had no choice but to abandon his roguish life at sea for the staid confines of the plantation.

Rumor had it that the commander's wife, a lush blonde some twenty years younger than the commander, fled for Reynolds's plantation, Mount Airy. After a year of seclusion Reynolds suddenly reappeared and with his typical bravado scoffed at the rumors. Oddly enough, the commander's wife hadn't been seen or heard from since. As for the commander, he'd taken an early pension and moved to Washington to embroil himself in politics.

For all this, Reynolds seemed none the worse for wear and had since amassed a stunning array of jewel-studded canes to complement his vast wardrobe. His passion for the sea had found surcease in horse breeding and racing, which he accomplished despite his physical limitations. His passion for women endured unabated. He had often confided to Miles that his injury and the circumstances surrounding his acquiring it only fueled female interest.

Theirs was an uneasy camaraderie, fueled by common interests and abilities and a mutual contempt for the war and its more fervent players, but nevertheless forever guarded by their fiercely competitive natures. Besides, Miles didn't quite trust Reynolds.

He found every last one of these suspicions flaring to life when Reynolds's eyes flickered over Miles's shoulder toward the women still gathered in the foyer. Miles immediately recognized the slight drooping of Reynolds's lids for what it was: a pure, unabashed feasting complete with a subtle flaring of his nostrils.

Miles didn't even pause to consider his words or the acerbic bite in his tone. "Watch yourself, Reynolds. A man could feel a great compulsion to kill you for even finding you in the same room with his wife, much less looking at her."

Reynolds's gaze shifted to Miles. A disarming grin curved his mouth. "Even I'm not that good, loath as I am to admit it. But I must say"—his leonine head inclined toward the foyer and his gaze inevitably followed—"it makes the heat a bit more bearable. Where the hell did you find her?"

The rumble of appreciation in his tone made Miles acutely aware of his distinct dislike for the man at the moment. He glanced over his shoulder, through a sea of pastel frocks and some rather alarming backsides. There was no mistaking Teddie's willowy silhouette. He realized they could all have been swathed in sheets and he could have just as easily spotted her among the group. Particularly from the rear. Unconsciously, it seemed, he'd committed that part of her to memory.

Though the manner in which the ivory silk seemed to cling to her hips filled him with a primal satisfaction, he could have done without any reminder of the lush proportions of her body at the moment. She bent to receive a bouquet of flowers from a young child. The movement pulled the silk taut over the narrowness of her waist and around the curves of her buttocks, offering up a lavish visual feast for any warm-blooded male with even the slightest bit of imagination. Abruptly, Miles turned back to Reynolds and purposely into the other man's line of vision. He forced a cool smile to his lips, finding his grin deepening in direct proportion to the descent of Reynolds's brows over his aquiline nose.

"We made our acquaintance not three weeks ago," Miles said, his pleasure multiplying twofold when a liveried servant pressed a crystal flute into his hand. The wine spilled in a cool torrent down his throat.

Reynolds cocked a brow. "Impetuous."

"Understandably."

"Quite so." Reynolds considered his own wine a moment. "The rumors paint a vastly different picture, of course."

"They always do."

In contrast to Miles's voracious consumption of the wine, Reynolds sipped slowly, lingeringly, as though he savored far more than the fruity essence of the brew. "One never knows what to believe about you. As one who has never been the least surprised by even the most depraved of the rumors—and might I add there have been several quite choice accounts of your time spent in the desert, something about you and several talented Tripolitan concubines belonging to the Dey of Algiers—" Reynolds paused, as usual awaiting a response that Miles refused to provide. Reynolds's impeccably tailored burgundy waistcoat barely registered the shrug of his shoulders. "It doesn't help matters that you're so damnably closemouthed about it all. Perhaps that's why nothing would surprise me about you. Indeed, until I arrived I even believed that you had agreed to a sudden marriage of convenience. How you managed to find yourself in such a quandary, knowing you as I do, escapes me at the moment, though that isn't what troubles me.

My puzzlement is not born of my inability to *believe* that these circumstances occurred. Indeed, having seen the young lady I can in all honesty say that I can fully comprehend your inability to exercise due restraint if given the least opportunity. Even I would have neglected caution at the risk of being discovered. If given the choice I believe I, too, would have chosen the yoke over the relative freedom of another lead ball in the thigh.''

"On this alone it seems we can find no argument.''

"On the contrary, old boy. The gossip rang true for me until I saw your young bride enter this parlor. I was then convinced that the rumors were merely fluff. Indeed, what man in his right mind would take such a woman to wife with the vow to keep himself from her? I wouldn't expect it even of you. I'd wager you've enough demons to battle without inflicting that kind of torture on yourself.''

Reynolds arched a brow, his gaze probing deep despite the nonchalance lacing his words like carefully applied spice. Miles drained his glass and leveled Reynolds with a hard glare. "Your concern is touching. Not the least bit self-serving, eh?''

"Never.''

"Simply curious, are you?''

"As a friend. I never gossip. You know that.''

"Ah.''

"You can hardly blame me for wondering, old boy. The thought of that woman being free to discreetly take her pleasures elsewhere cannot help but stir the imagination.''

Miles listened to his teeth click. "Especially yours.''

Reynolds feigned a deeply affronted look. "Don't look so damned self-righteous. I've never pursued a woman, married or not, who was otherwise satisfyingly engaged.'' His wicked smile lit fires deep in his eyes. "I like my women accommodating and eager. I've spent the better part of the last decade spotting them. You know the look a woman gets when she's been ignored and left to rot on the vine. As time passes she denies her need and occupies her mind with other pursuits. She attempts to ignore these feelings and begins clothing herself in virginal white and all sorts of lace and frills in a vain effort to appear unaffected. But inevitably the hunger builds inside her until even the most virtuous and restrained young thing can scarcely contain it. Her body is no longer her own. The merest breeze touching her soft skin rouses her passions. She trembles with it, aches with it, and is ultimately consumed by it like kindling by flame. She has no choice but to find surcease, else she'll go mad. Some poor man must help her. It might as well be me.''

"You haven't a philanthropic bone in your body."

Reynolds's chuckle oozed bravado. "I know of several women in that foyer who might be inclined to disagree with you."

Miles's smile was cool. "Then you won't lack for distraction this afternoon. Juggling them all must require deftness and a great deal of concentration, particularly with their husbands lurking. You'll have time for little else."

"Normally that would only sweeten the inevitable victory for me, were there only one. However, two mistresses who know nothing of each other is a sure recipe for disaster and a great deal of screeching and hair-pulling. Of course, I could always use a bit of distraction from all that." Reynolds jerked his head at the uniformed men gathered near. Miles wondered if the sudden hardening of his features betrayed his still-burning passion for the life at sea denied him or if Reynolds simply shared Miles's contempt for the war-addled. A moment later Reynolds grinned roguishly. "Odd, but I suddenly feel quite overcome with a need for something that does not cling and whine like a demanding mistress who feels as though she's not being paid the proper homage. No woman takes kindly to being ignored, no matter the circumstances. They take even less kindly to being duped. At the moment I'm not in the mood to deal with all that, particularly from those two women out there." Reynolds's chest expanded as though he drew in great gulps of air. "I need something fresh."

"Try a walk through the gardens," Miles suggested. "Edwina Farrell's roses are supposedly without compare. She keeps them in a private walled garden to one side of the house. No one would find you there."

"I just might do that. One never knows where one might find

the rare perfect rose." Reynolds inclined his head and leaned both hands on his pearl-handled cane, his fair brow furrowing. "You're rather testy today, old boy. A bit dour even for you. Not reconsidering our most recent wager, perhaps?"

Neither had ever backed away from even the most reckless wagers or challenges on the race course. Miles gave a swift shake of his head. "The wager stands. My two Bulle Rock mares if your Valiant wins at Devil's Field on Saturday. Your Godolphin stallion if he loses." It was an extravagant wager, a guaranteed calamitous loss to at least one of them. To the winner, three horses descended of the most highly valued bloodlines in all of Virginia and England and the prospect of breeding them, the rewards of which, in future winnings alone, were outrageous. Both men knew it. So did the rest of Tidewater. For this reason both believed the rumor that onlookers from miles around intended to witness the race. "Don't smile yet," Miles said, his lips curving with less than subtle confidence. "Wildair has beaten Valiant twice before at that distance."

"Precisely my point. You've scant reason to look so glum. Whereas I—" Reynolds fiddled with the crisp ruffle spilling from his cuff and over one hand. A diamond glittered on his little finger. "I've countless reasons to bemoan another day. And yet I sense a certain spring in my stride of a sudden, as though I sense an anticipation building of some great event. But I can hardly expect you to understand." Reynolds slapped Miles heartily on the shoulder. He seemed to catch himself just before he was to amble off. "So sorry, but I can't quite set from my mind the vision of your bride standing with you before that minister. How considerate of you to refrain from indulging in the celebratory kiss. Then again, lack of restraint in one's own bedchamber is one thing. In the young lady's parlor full of guests quite another, eh? Why tempt oneself? Ah, I see the female imbroglio has just disbanded, and two familiar ladies seem to be glancing about with a certain recognizable distress. If you would be so kind, old boy, as to direct me along the quickest path to the rose garden. No sense in courting disaster if I can avoid it."

Miles was glad to do it. As he watched Reynolds escape

undetected from a side door with an agility uncommon to most men, he was aware of a burgeoning hope that the man would lose himself among the roses for the rest of the day, at least until Miles had squired Teddie from the premises, which he intended to do at the first opportunity. The compulsion to do this, of course, had more to do with the work awaiting him than any ridiculous need to keep Teddie away from Reynolds.

Indeed, what could possibly happen?

He snuffed the thought. At the moment he preferred to direct himself to preventing opportunity from arising. He scanned the foyer, his gaze settling on a billowy blonde of lavish proportions, well known to be the wife of the gray-haired lieutenant speaking with Damian. He noted the manner in which she lingered unobtrusively to one side of the foyer, and yet an expectancy lit her eyes as they flitted about above the flapping edge of her fan. Though her husband stood well within her sights he was apparently not whom she sought. Not five feet from her a willowy redhead, seemingly engaged in conversation with an elderly woman, displayed the same agitated flapping of her fan and covert glancing about, all the while affixing a pleasant smile on her face as though she listened attentively to her companion.

With a sudden, wicked thought, Miles set aside his empty flute and moved toward the blonde. It was with a certain disconcertion that he watched her amber eyes flicker over him, away, and back again, then widen with obvious distress the moment she realized she was his destination. He doubted Reynolds's handsome golden countenance had ever stirred such a blatantly terrified response in a woman. Ironic that women had far more to fear from the slyly charming Reynolds than they did from Miles, as scarred and ominous as he might appear.

Still, bearing such a reputation was damned annoying at times. He paused, inclined his head, and softened his mouth into a curve. Her eyes fixed on his scar and widened. "Mrs. Edwards, I believe you would enjoy Edwina Farrell's rose garden." At her look of profound confusion, which was understandable considering Miles had never spoken to the woman, he lowered his voice and deepened his gaze. "I believe there you will find what you're looking for."

She blinked up at him, flapped her fan over her voluminous bosom, then erupted with a furious blush. Hastily, she averted her eyes. "Indeed, I feel in great need of air. If you would direct me, sir."

Which he did, ever so gallantly. He lingered there precisely three minutes, then approached the redhead, moments later directing her along the same path toward the private, walled rose garden.

If all went as planned Reynolds would find himself occupied for a better part of the afternoon. With a smile that seemed to emanate from somewhere deep inside him, Miles turned and headed back into the parlor.

Chapter Seven

At precisely two o'clock Edwina rang for the guests to assemble at her dining table, where all enjoyed a sumptuous dinner that would have done honor to any nobleman's house in England. From her vantage at the foot of the table Edwina beamed and made good on her promise to keep the wine flowing freely. The guests accommodated and consumed an amount in direct proportion to the burgeoning heat.

Seated between Winchester and Damian on one side of the table, Teddie raised her glass when Damian lurched to his feet and proposed the fourth toast of the afternoon.

"To Virginia," he bellowed above the swell of conversation. His cheeks were flushed, his hair slightly tousled. But for all his youthful exuberance his voice rang with a noble vibrato that struck a deep sadness into Teddie's heart. He hoisted his glass higher. "To Virginia. May our land remain free, our men honest, and our women fruitful."

Teddie swung her gaze to Winchester and found him staring at her with such intensity that she flushed and stuck her nose in her glass. That all in attendance seemed to be watching their exchanges with perverse curiosity only heightened her discomfort. Or perhaps it was the images inspired by Damian's choice of words.

Gulping her wine, she tried not to notice that Winchester's own wineglass remained untouched in favor of the glass of amber liquid he clenched in one massive fist. He'd retained his typically stoic demeanor since the ceremony, yet to Teddie he seemed all the more conspicuous for it the further the meal progressed and the more animated the conversation became. If he meant to impress his displeasure at being there upon all who were present, Teddie doubted very much that he succeeded.

All around him the room swelled with gaiety. The thirty-odd guests drank heartily, ate with gusto, and engaged in quick-witted exchanges. But though Winchester remained palpably removed from it all, Teddie grew uncomfortably aware that his bearing was much like a grizzly bear guarding his den. This struck her as odd even for him. For some reason it made her want to squirm in her seat. Better that she think him simply impatient to be done with the farce. He was staring at her merely in anticipation of her weary nod that she was eager to depart. Yes, that was it. At the moment she relished far less the idea of returning to Miramer alone with him than she did lingering in the sweltering confines of her aunt's dining room. She wasn't ready to abandon the comforting haven just yet. Let Winchester simmer and stare. She'd never succumbed to intimidation before in her life.

She found herself caught up in the festivities. Not that Damian Coyle would have allowed otherwise. Impervious to his cousin's grim regard—or perhaps for that very reason—and buoyed by at least a half dozen glasses of wine, Damian regaled Teddie with tales of his childhood along the Tidewater shores. But quite suddenly his features blackened and his voice grew hoarse and impassioned.

"Do not bear the Winchester name with even the least disregard for its venerable history, Teddie," Damian said, a chilled bitterness invading his tone. "Your husband had eight uncles who lived to adulthood. One aunt, my mother, God rest her soul. She lived long enough to bury them all at Miramer. You'll know the spot well one day." His drooped eyes angled briefly toward his cousin. "Miles can be found there some nights, pondering his own damned mortality, I suppose. Guilt is inevitable when all your brothers and sisters met their deaths in childhood and you, for reasons that elude us all, were spared."

"That's enough, Damian," came Winchester's rumble, so full of ominous undertones Teddie felt the fine hairs on the back of her neck stand on end. She laid her fingertips on Damian's sleeve, hoping to direct his thoughts elsewhere.

He seemed unaware of her. With obvious disgust he grunted and toyed with the stem of his wineglass. "Violets bloom profusely on that hill from March to September. My mother used to say this was because of all the tears shed there for the Winchester children taken too early in their lives. The uncles were all young. None married, save for Miles's father. They fought alongside him in the revolution, brilliantly, of course. They all possessed that damnable instinct for heroism and bravery in the face of the most insurmountable odds. To the last they met noble deaths on their fields of battle.''

With a heavy heart Teddie watched Damian drain his glass and motion for another. ''Do not envy them their deaths, Damian,'' she said so softly she wondered if Winchester could possibly overhear her. Something told her he heard every word even above the din of conversation swelling around them.

Damian's jaw set into resolute lines. ''I may not bear the venerable Winchester name, but my blood is the same as that spilled on those fields and my pride just as uncompromising. Make no mistake. I will uphold the Winchester legacy and carry that honor with me into battle as bravely and nobly as my uncles did.''

A chill crept into Teddie's bones. She clenched her hands together in her lap to keep from wresting Damian's from his wineglass. ''There is no heroism in dying before your time. Only tragedy. Defending one's country and one's liberty is noble and good. Courting death for the sake of upholding a family legacy of misfortune is quite another, and not altogether wise.''

''Wise?'' Damian's harsh laugh cut like a blade through Teddie. She nearly recoiled when he lifted haunted eyes to his cousin and his mouth twisted as he spat the words. ''My dear Mrs. Winchester, no man will suffer in silence the ruination of his family name by anyone. Particularly by a contemptible, arrogant bastard drowning in self-hate.''

''Damian, please—'' Teddie whispered, aware that she was trembling, that something terrible was about to happen on her wedding day at her aunt's lovely table, and she was powerless to stop it. How the devil had this happened? ''Take me outside at once, Damian,'' she demanded, laying her hand on his arm and pushing her chair back from the table.

He shrugged off her hand, his voice rising an octave with his vehemence. Inevitably, several guests took notice. "How he mocks us all sitting here. Content to fill his belly and count his money. Content to allow other men to die defending *his* lands and *his* liberty!"

Teddie sat stiff as an ancient oak, anticipating a brutal response from Winchester with her next breath. "He will not allow you to bait him," she whispered. "Stop before you—"

"Before I what?" Damian sneered, tossing aside his lace-trimmed napkin. His chair legs scraped against the floorboards as he shoved back from the table. The room grew instantly still. "I can make no bigger fool of myself than he already does. Indeed, we're fools, all of us, to allow this to continue. His very existence mocks us all. He should be imprisoned and left to rot! He should have been castrated for what he did to you in his bed, not presented with a lifetime of opportunities to despoil you again and again, to fill your belly with his demon's seed—"

Teddie leapt to her feet. Beside her she felt Winchester surge from his chair. Without thinking she spun toward him and found her palms resting on his chest. Beneath a crisp plane of white linen shirt the heat of him leapt into her skin. A raw energy seeped out of him as though his frame couldn't contain it another moment. How could she possibly exert any influence over him if she couldn't control Damian Coyle?

She lifted her eyes to his and felt the breath leave her lungs. The devil himself would have been humbled by the ferocity of his gaze. Silence crackled around them.

"Don't," she simply said. She sank her teeth in her trembling lower lip when his eyes fixed on her mouth.

"Even I won't suffer some things in silence," he murmured, the softness in his tone only emphasizing his barely contained rage. "No man will speak of my wife like that and get away with it."

A strange bubbling filled Teddie's belly. "But I've already forgiven him."

His cold eyes probed deeply into hers. "Have you forgiven me?"

She felt a jar somewhere deep in her soul, a rousing of something fierce and foreign there, completely unexpected. Her fingers curled into her palms and she dropped her hands from his chest. She lowered her eyes, her confusion burgeoning.

Behind her Damian crowed, "Do let's finish what we took up in that field of honor, cousin. I don't believe I was afforded an opportunity to take my shot. If I remember correctly you hid behind your wife's skirts then as well."

Winchester moved so quickly, Teddie barely felt the floor beneath her low-heeled shoes as he snuck one arm around her waist and whisked her behind him. With some confusion she turned and levered herself against the hand still resting on the curve of her waist. Rising on tiptoes, she attempted to peer over his shoulder. The click of a pistol hammer instantly chilled the blood in her veins.

Damian sat with booted feet spread wide and a pistol leveled at Miles's chest. At that range, with so broad a target, even a man addled by too much wine couldn't possibly miss his shot. A moment of stunned silence passed, then a chorus of shrieks arose from the women guests. At the head of the table Uncle George surged from his chair, one hand immediately reaching for his sheathed sword. Several uniformed young men did the same, but all froze when Miles lifted a hand.

A strange, lopsided grin drifted over Damian's face. "Scared yet, cousin?" The pistol waved over the assemblage. "They are. They sit there fish-mouthed knowing that one word, one slight movement could be impetus enough to squeeze my finger against this trigger. Or perhaps they're simply eager for me to finish it for them, eh? There isn't a person here who wouldn't thank me for killing you. Your new bride perhaps most of all."

"Put down the pistol," Miles said calmly, his manner so unflappable Teddie couldn't help but achieve comfort from it. "Just put it down and we can go home to Miramer."

"Home?" Damian snorted. "I'm going to sea, cousin, as are all my fellow countrymen. Sailing out of Baltimore to free our land from tyranny. I, for one, cannot count in mere money the slavery of our impressed seamen, the decay of our national spirit! This is worth fighting for! Our freedom! Without it life is not worth living. The imminent threat to our liberty unites us all, and yet you dare to stand apart from us. Before you draw your last breath, cousin, tell us all why you scorn your heritage and your country. Tell us, dammit! Or by God I'll commit the unpardonable, such does my hatred for you consume me at this moment. Tell us!''

Damian's last words were bit off in a startled cry as the pistol was smacked from his hand. Miles caught the pistol beneath one boot as it spun across the floorboards.

''A timely entrance, Reynolds,'' Miles said, addressing the tall, golden-haired gentleman who seemed to have materialized from air behind Damian's chair.

The gentleman grinned, displaying a startling flash of white teeth against his sun-bronzed skin. Eyes the color of pale azure glittered with amusement. ''I have yet to be accused of bad timing, old boy. Glad we could be of service.'' He hoisted a stunning pearl-handled cane with such dexterity that Teddie found it easy to believe he had indeed wielded it against Damian's pistol with great effect. The pressure of one impeccably attired forearm over Damian's chest was all that was required to keep the younger man restrained. That, and a good deal of embarrassment, Teddie surmised, judging by the color climbing from Damian's high collar and his sudden inability to look anyone in the eye. The wind had fled his sails with remarkable dispatch. He'd obviously been taken unawares by this Reynolds fellow. They all had, so stealthily had he moved.

''Carry on, all!'' Reynolds boomed with such an enigmatic smile the guests couldn't help but comply, perhaps believing this sort of thing commonplace at Miramer. Reynolds's commanding presence and brilliant disarming of the situation no doubt bolstered their confidence that the matter was now well in hand. Aunt Edwina yodeled for more wine and demanded that all weaponry be returned to its proper place.

Teddie didn't realize that she gripped one hand tightly against her belly until Winchester quite unexpectedly took her hand and clamped it beneath his on his sleeve. All breath again seemed to leave her lungs when he drew her close to his side. A disturbing possessiveness marked his movements, a possessiveness Teddie suspected had a great deal to do with Reynolds. Oddly enough, given her chilled apprehension just moments ago, a certain coy satisfaction warmed her. Or perhaps it was simply the warmth that invaded her whenever Winchester loomed near.

"And here I'd thought you'd left," Winchester said to Reynolds.

"Not before I met the bride." Reynolds's compelling stare settled on Teddie and deepened. "I've been rather unexpectedly detained in your aunt's rose garden, Mrs. Winchester. Forgive me my late arrival to dinner."

"You are forgiven, sir." Teddie couldn't contain the smile curving her lips. To what extent this sprang from the combative camaraderie she sensed between Reynolds and Winchester, she couldn't have guessed. Perhaps she was simply surrendering to Reynolds's outrageous charm and wicked good looks. She doubted any warm-blooded woman could have resisted, even on her wedding day.

Reynolds inclined his head and dropped his voice to a purr. "Jules, dear lady. All my friends call me Jules." Azure eyes slanted at Winchester. "Save for your husband here. Then again, I'm never quite certain where I stand with him. I don't suppose any of us are. Neither friend nor foe, I'd wager."

"You saved my husband's life," Teddie replied, aware of the huskiness invading her voice, which typically betrayed that her heart was in some way entangled. With Winchester? The devil take her but she was imagining things. She simply had not wished the man dead. Any man. This time her smile seemed to crack her face. "I consider you a dear friend, Jules."

"See there, old boy? I told you I'm a damned likable fellow. I must make it a point to come calling at Miramar very soon indeed."

"I insist," Teddie chirped, some part of her plumply satisfied that Winchester's chest expanded against her side with a palpable agitation. "You are a true hero, Jules," she added sweetly.

Reynolds beamed.

"He wasn't going to kill me," Winchester growled. "In

another moment he would have handed me the damned pistol. He's never been able to stomach liquor.''

Reynolds arched a dark golden brow at Teddie. "See there? This is the thanks I get for saving his life and keeping this pup here from getting himself jailed.'' Reynolds slapped a meaty hand on Damian's shoulder, rousing yet another flush from the younger man, who slumped further into his chair. With a look of complete bafflement Reynolds added, "I suppose the old boy will now accuse me of somehow orchestrating the entire scene to afford myself the best opportunity at heroism, all to win your heart, my dear lady.''

"The thought had crossed my mind," Winchester replied, his gaze hooding on Teddie. "I'll have the footman get your things.''

The look in his eyes brooked little resistance. As did the heated pressure of his hand over hers. His commanding demeanor somehow sapped her of all will to resist him. He displayed not the least embarrassment over the scene, just a blithe acceptance. It seemed Winchester would argue with no man, no matter the bait. A chill crept up her spine at the thought of his stubbornly taking a lead ball to fully play his hand.

"The devil you're taking her from me just yet," Reynolds protested, duly affronted. He lifted a brow, one ear cocking. "Ah, listen there, old boy. Your bride's aunt has gracefully met this near calamity head on with a brisk sweeping of the guests into her grand salon, where a small ensemble sets bows to strings in a lovely minuet as we speak. Don't tell me you can't hear those delightful strains. Surely you're not going to deny your bride the prospect of a turn around the floor on her wedding day?''

Winchester seemed to set his teeth, but his gaze never wavered from Teddie's. "I don't dance.''

"What a shame, old boy. I don't suppose it comes as much of a surprise that I manage the minuets quite well.''

"I'm not the least surprised, Reynolds. You sit a horse better than any man I know.'' A black brow arched over fathomless pools of darkness, betraying any trace of indulgence Teddie might have thought she heard in his voice. "My dear, the choice is yours, of course."

Teddie glanced at Reynolds, aware that Winchester watched her like a hawk. "My husband wants me to be happy, Jules."

"Indeed, a happy woman makes life worth living. A wonder the old boy realizes it. But realizing it and accomplishing it are two altogether different prospects. I sincerely doubt he has considered that. Ah. Another minuet. Shall we, dear lady?"

Teddie stared at Reynolds's proffered arm and wondered how she'd ever maneuvered herself into such an enviable situation, smack between two men. Two entirely different men, each fiercely compelling in his own manner. Some women she'd known would have killed to be her at the moment.

"Perhaps another time," she replied with a genuine smile. "You're most charming, Jules. Do come to Miramer soon."

Lifting her skirts with one hand, she tugged on the other, somewhat surprised when Winchester relinquished it. With chin lifted, she paused to squeeze Damian's shoulder, then breezed past a stunned-looking Jules Reynolds. Into the foyer she swept and toward the curved staircase, making it to the second step when Winchester's voice stilled her feet.

"Teddie."

She turned slightly and felt her stomach flip-flop the moment her gaze alighted upon him, poised just below her at the foot of the stairs, one hand curved around the banister. What the devil was causing this inner distress? If she were the sort of woman prone to romantics, she might have understood it. The resonant echo of his deep voice would then have been enough to crumple her legs beneath her. He'd never called her by her first name before. There was something uncomfortably intimate about it. And of course it helped little that he looked so coolly dashing in his finery, a virtual magnet for every eye. A woman could fair swoon at the sight of him.

Still, to Teddie's keen, decidedly unromantic eye his manner somehow defied convention, as though by simply donning such garb he mocked them all. His face never seemed to lose its cloak of cool disdain, his voice its sarcasm. The whitening of the scar cleaving his cheek only enhanced his arrogant demeanor.

Sensing all this, she should have been finding it difficult to like the man, much less care whether he get himself shot. She should have been finding it easy to believe the worst of him. She should have been devoid of all this flip-flopping in her belly. She wondered then why she wasn't, which didn't sit at all well with her. If anything Teddie took great pride in knowing herself, understanding her thoughts, rationalizing her yearnings. The idea that she suddenly made little sense to herself alarmed her. And when Winchester's eyes hooded on the uppermost curves of her breasts, she realized she would have preferred remaining imprisoned on Cockburn's boat. At least there she understood the enemy.

Instinctively, she lifted a hand to her chest in some vain effort to cover herself. From Winchester's vantage one step below her, she must have seemed as though she offered her more visible charms up to him in a blatant visual feast. The immodest cut of the dress—her aunt's idea, of course—didn't help matters. Her cool fingertips trembled at the edge of ivory silk where it met with the plunge of décolletage. Dark fires lit his eyes. His stare remained uncompromising, trapping her, making retreat impossible. Her body responded beyond her will, suffusing with a heat that weakened her limbs and drew the peaks of her breasts taut against silk.

And part of her reveled in it. Riotously. Joyously. For one reckless moment.

She gripped the banister and clamped her teeth together. "I will be but a moment," she managed, her voice sounding breathless, as though the exchange had left her incapable of speech. Impossible.

His gaze finally lifted to hers. A tic seemed to have taken up residence in his jaw. "Take your time."

"Did you require something?"

"I'm curious." One corner of his mouth curved slightly upward, lending him an immediate and disarming congeniality that Teddie found more disturbing than his most ferocious scowls. The lyrical strains of violins drifting over them only heightened her discomfort. "I believe you're the first woman, married or otherwise, to refuse Reynolds anything. He's staring out the dining room window, looking rather mystified."

"And you wish to enlighten him?"

"He's not the sort to think himself unattractive to any female."

"Understandably. He's quite magnificent." She met the subtle arch of his brow with one of her own. "I would be less than truthful and a fool to say otherwise, Winchester. We both know it. Are you perhaps testing me?"

He suddenly seemed to draw up another inch in height. The scowl descended over his brows. "Testing you? Hell, no. The thought never occurred to me. I'm simply curious, dammit. Women find Reynolds hard to refuse, that's all."

Teddie felt a great compulsion to press her advantage. "You envy him this."

He glared at her. "Christ." Shoving a hand through his hair, he swung his scowl in the general direction of the dining room, then seemed to think better of stomping away. He glowered up at her. "You want to know the truth of it, woman? I wouldn't have cared a whit if you kept the man company for the remainder of the afternoon on that dance floor."

"I see."

"The hell you do. Why are women always seeing things that aren't there?"

"Ah. You've obviously experienced trouble with women before."

Again his brows dove over his nose. The tic in his jaw became more pronounced. "My experiences with women prior to meeting you—no matter how far-reaching—in no way prepared me for you, wife."

Teddie felt an unexpected smile curve her lips. "Thank you, Winchester."

Her reply only seemed to frustrate him further. "You're a baffling woman."

"Because I refused Jules?" Her laugh bubbled up effortlessly. "Winchester, there is no great mystery here. I refused him because I cannot dance."

He stared at her. "You can't dance?"

"Precisely. I never learned. You might as well know it right from the start, but I'm frightfully inept at the female graces. Dancing and piano playing being the very least of my shortcomings. I sincerely hope you weren't anticipating long, lazy afternoons gathered around the pianoforte listening to me lift my voice in song, because I can't sing either. Can you?"

He hesitated a moment. "There hasn't been music at Miramer since my mother died. I was only ten at the time. I don't remember ever singing. Besides, I haven't the time for that sort of thing."

"I'm sorry, Winchester." She caught herself, her voice dropping. "No, you don't want that, do you? Perhaps Jules can shake the rafters with his deep vibrato." She couldn't resist slanting her eyes at him.

"I'm certain if you wish he could teach you to play the pianoforte. The man's abilities to pursue leisure are boundless."

"We could all use a bit of that every now and then."

Winchester's gaze seemed to deepen, and she tensed, completely certain that if given the briefest opportunity he could strip away any fortress she'd ever thought to erect around herself. True, her comment might seem odd given that she'd been wallowing in excess luxury and idle time since she'd arrived on her aunt's doorstep less than a month prior. No matter his powers of perception, even Winchester couldn't guess that she'd had no respite or relief from her torment and from the prison she'd made of her life and Will's.

As she stood there, in that long moment, for some reason she became possessed of the unthinkable. Something in Winchester's manner, something elemental about him touched some lost and lonely part of her soul, which suddenly ached to unburden itself of her deception. Perhaps this man would understand.

She bit her lips hard, mentally shaking herself. The man need only shake his best topcoat free of dust and take a comb to his hair to render her for the first time in her life helpless and unable to bear a burden alone? Preposterous! That she would even consider taking such a risk! True, Winchester cut so dashing a figure one could easily believe him capable of great heroic feats. And her pulse seemed to frolic whenever he passed near. To her knowledge, however, disturbing good looks and the ability to set pulses racing had never qualified any man to be a champion. Had she any sense she'd realize he was the very last person she should consider engaging to help her. Winchester cared for no one but himself. She knew this. Then why the devil was she finding it so difficult to remember at the moment? Perhaps because reason had never stood a chance against the dictates of her instincts before. But remaining determined and self-confident in spite of reason was one thing. Foolishness was quite another.

At the moment nothing was more foolish than to remain staring into Winchester's eyes. God only knew what she could imagine in those inky depths. Worse still, she could unwittingly betray far more than she wished.

"I must go," she blurted, averting her face. Truly, she must flee him or she would surely lose part of herself on those stairs. Stricken with alarm and confusion, she lifted her skirts, turned to take to the stairs, then froze when his fingers wrapped around her wrist.

"Wait."

Surely she imagined the hint of appeal in his voice. Winchester would never feel compelled to appeal to anyone, least of all to her. Damned romantic delusion. She'd obviously fallen victim to the notion of a wedding, to the heady scent of roses and jasmine, to the heat and the wine and the music. All had conspired to drive sense from her. Winchester was still the same callous, black-hearted scoundrel. And she the spy for Cockburn. Their marriage was a sham. And Will was still a prisoner. Her becoming a bride hadn't changed any of it.

She didn't turn back, even when she yanked her hand from his and rushed up the stairs in a rustle of ivory silk. She didn't need to. He watched her until she disappeared around the banister and into the second-floor hall.

* * *

With a feeling of complete ineptitude, Miles swung around and did momentary battle with an overpowering urge to climb those stairs after her and shake the truth out of her. Something had upset her, quite suddenly. Not that he was unfamiliar with a female's tendency for upset. Some women he'd known had spent their entire lives in upheaval and had enjoyed every minute of it. He just hadn't believed Teddie susceptible without damned good reason. And hell if he knew what that could possibly be.

He stretched his neck out of his tight collar and felt his scowl settle into place. Damned woman had him feeling like a greenhorn. Inept. A touch bumbling. And completely mystified.

The hell he was. With a grand and determined stride he headed for the dining room, his scowl deepening when the strains of a waltz drifted to him on a breeze fragrant with the lush scents of summer. Damned music and wine. Damned clinging ivory silk. And damn her guileless laughter. So effortless. So bewitching. He'd allowed it to addle him. Just as he'd allowed Reynolds to get under his skin, and hell if he knew why. In all the years Miles had known him, through all the wagers won, the races lost, the pitting of each against the other, Reynolds had never proven more the thorn in Miles's side than he had this afternoon.

Miles, then, wasn't the least surprised at the bite in his tone when he found Reynolds assisting Damian from his chair.

"Leave him," Miles growled, drawing Reynolds's keen perusal. "Let him walk on his own."

Reynolds offered a cajoling grin. "Haven't we embarrassed him enough for one afternoon? The least we can do is help him to your carriage."

"The fault is his alone," Miles replied crisply. "He should know better than to overindulge in spirits."

"The occasion overwhelms us all, old boy. No harm done."

Miles grunted, then slanted an unforgiving glare at his cousin. "If I have to tie him to the saddle with a chamber pot balanced on his knees, he'll ride alongside me the entire trip to Miramer. My wi— that is, Theodora will have solitary privilege of the coach.'' Ignoring Reynolds's obvious "Ah," Miles stepped in front of Reynolds, twisted one hand into Damian's lapel, and hoisted his cousin to his feet.

His glower softened in spite of himself when Damian lifted watery, red-rimmed eyes and slurred, "Forgive me, cousin. I am duly ashamed. I—"

"Enough." Swiping one hand over the front of Damian's rumpled blue uniform, Miles abruptly turned him to face the door. "Concentrate on walking."

Damian teetered like a man bracing himself on the deck of a storm-swept ship. "The wine overcame my good sense. It—"

Despite his prior dictates, Miles caught Damian's arm and assisted him along toward the door. "I understand, Damian."

"How can you, cousin? You, the man with no vulnerabilities. Whereas I—I have no control over this weakness. I am imprisoned by it. I honestly believe I might have killed you, Miles."

"No, you wouldn't have."

"So certain, were you, of Reynolds's arrival?"

"He surprised us both. No, Damian, a man gets a certain look in his eye just before he kills."

"You're suggesting that I am incapable of committing the final act, that my eyes somehow betray me?"

"Yes, that's precisely what I'm suggesting."

"You insult me, cousin."

Miles gave a caustic grunt. "I would think you'd find comfort in that."

"Comfort? To a soldier? And a Winchester? You cut me to the quick. But you do indeed, as always, inspire me."

Miles drew up short as they entered the foyer. "To do what?"

Damian's rheumy eyes met his. "Why, to learn to kill, of course. If I am to die young and tragically I'd surely wish to take a few of those British bastards with me."

Miles tightened his grip on Damian's sleeve, even as the younger man attempted to shrug it off. "If you somehow manage to survive that day, how do you intend to live with the blood of those men on your hands?"

Damian paused, leaning heavily against Miles's shoulder. "Why, just as you do, cousin, appropriately tortured and tormented. And thus, perhaps, even more of an enigma than my forefathers. Either way I will do the Winchester name justice."

Miles bit off his next words, his hand falling uselessly to his side when Damian shrugged him off and wove toward the front door, where a liveried footman held the door wide.

"Good God, old boy, you look positively paternal."

Miles didn't even glance at Reynolds, though his words struck an oddly uncomfortable chord in him. "You've so perfected a silent tread, Reynolds, I'm beginning to think you haven't any need for that cane."

Reynolds's deep laugh echoed around them. "Next you'll be suggesting I'm that Night Hawk fellow everyone's been talking about."

Miles shot Reynolds a quick look. "Ah, a confession."

Reynolds's grin oozed wickedness and promises sure to be kept. "You won't be getting rid of me that easily. Although a man need only own a black horse to be considered suspect these days." Reynolds arched a brow that Miles returned with a cool stare. "We Americans don't take too kindly to the notion of a spy lurking in our midst."

"You count yourself among them, I take it."

Reynolds gave him an odd look. "And you don't? Our very liberty is at stake here. Ah, but you've heard all that from the war hawks. Perhaps you think in more immediate terms. Your cousin's life, perhaps?"

"He's determined to get himself killed. The war simply provides him a vehicle." His tone brooked little argument, though Reynolds seemed oddly satisfied with his reply. He directed himself to a more pressing matter, one that had kept him from sleep for the past several nights with no success. Either the impostor hadn't dared to venture out since their encounter two weeks prior, or he'd grown wings. "Have they caught this Night Hawk fellow yet?"

Reynolds shook his head. "I don't hear much, of course. Indeed, I spent the better part of my afternoon attempting to extricate myself from Edwina Farrell's rose garden. No naval fellows to be had in there. Just their wives. I don't suppose you had anything to do with all that?''

Miles kept his smile cool. ''What possible reason . . . ?''

''Of course. I must say the strategic maneuverings I displayed in that garden would be the envy of the American navy. But to your question, I believe I overheard one fellow mention that the Night Hawk was spotted just after midnight last evening some distance south of the point.''

Miles set his jaw. He'd missed him. Somehow. Dammit, he'd scoured the area surrounding the point until long after midnight. He'd watched the man-of-war as she rode at anchor for any telltale signals. He'd seen none. The rendezvous must have been swift. Too swift. And the impostor's escape as soundless as the rising of the moon over the horizon.

''Of course, he managed to escape before the regiment reached the shore,'' Reynolds added. ''A slippery fellow, quite obviously. I don't envy anyone the task of watching a good five miles of shoreline for some phantom rider of the night to make an appearance. An impossible task at best. They might never catch him.''

No, they wouldn't. But Miles would. And when he did he'd congratulate him on a game cunningly conceived and skillfully played, then he'd exact his payment for being taken for an inept fool. The price rose with each passing day.

''Devil's Field. Next Saturday.'' With that clipped reminder to Reynolds, Miles took brisk leave of the foyer and the house to await the momentary arrival of his bride. Beneath a merciless late-afternoon sun he paced the curved front drive while Damian dozed in his saddle. By the time Teddie appeared some thirty minutes later with enough baggage in tow for ten women, what little patience Miles had been born with had been soundly tested and thoroughly trounced. Another fifteen minutes of teary good-byes only exacerbated matters, as did the time required to come to the momentous decision that the mare Cleo would go along with Teddie to Miramer as a gift from the Farrells.

With curt formality Miles handed his bride into the carriage emblazoned with the Winchester crest, tested Cleo's tether at the rear of the coach, then mounted Zeus and set his heels to the stallion's flanks. Were he of a different temperament he would have shared the confines of the carriage with Teddie. Somehow the air around her seemed fresher. But he wasn't about to subject himself to any more tests today.

He'd been made to play the incompetent fool one time too many to suit him. He needed accomplishment, and a great deal of it. The physical kind would suit, even if that meant taking to a ripe field to cut tobacco. Better still, he could fill and stack thousand-pound hogsheads. Or ready a fresh field for planting. After the morning's rains the soil would be damp, rich, and loamy, ideal for planting.

He intended to fill his ship's belly with fine tobacco and make ready to sail within the month. The war hadn't stopped him. And neither would a wife or an impostor.

Chapter Eight

From a tall window at the front of Miramer's secluded west wing, Teddie watched the sun set, with her arms folded and brow furrowed. Not that nature wasn't providing a dazzling enough display for her pleasure. If anything, the sun's magnificent golden descent only compounded her restlessness.

Restless when she should be content as a kitten in cream. All had gone smoothly. She and all her baggage were cozily ensconced in what had to be the grandest of all plantation homes in Virginia, in a bedchamber the size of a London city block, in her own private wing, miles from anyone else in the house, particularly Winchester. She hadn't seen *him* since he delivered her into the coach with his typical brusque demeanor. Even Damian had disappeared into one of Miramer's twelve bedchambers, no doubt to sleep off his wine and his embarrassment before his sojourn into wartime glory tomorrow.

She should be satisfied that she'd been left entirely to herself. Why the devil wasn't she?

She shifted her gaze across the horizon, uncertain what it was she was looking for. The vantage afforded her an unimpeded view of Miramer's mile-long private drive, which extended north from the black iron gateway in the brick wall that enclosed the manor house, past the tobacco fields, several large sheds, and the workers' quarters, to the public road. Fields of tobacco swept endlessly in either direction from the drive, the plants' trumpet-shaped flower tops swaying in the breeze. In one field male workers moved among the tall plants, swinging long, curved blades against some of the flower tops. Others stacked the cut leaves in large piles on scaffolds, while others transported the scaffolds across the fields to the sheds. In an adjoining field, where the plants hadn't grown as high, one young Negro boy wielding a long stick scurried a flock of fat-bellied turkeys through the plants. For what purpose Teddie couldn't imagine, particularly when the birds were allowed to nip leisurely at the stalks. In yet another field bare-chested Negro men steered plows through the black soil. Others worked the ground with hand hoes, rendering the soil soft and fluffy. Children scurried behind them, readying the soil into flattopped hills and these hills into arrow-straight rows.

Watching all this and having accomplished nothing save for changing her dress—this with the unwelcome assistance of a silent, doe-eyed young Negro girl—Teddie realized how utterly vacuous the role of mistress of this plantation was. Unless she did something about it. Uselessness was not something she wished to experience.

Isolated and useless. Little wonder she felt so restless.

Just as she turned from the window her eye was caught by one particular Negro man working a plow through the near field just beyond the front wall. Something about him roused her fascination, something in the way he moved behind the plodding workhorse, maneuvering the heavy plow with an ease and confidence unmatched by the other men. She pressed her fingertips against the windowpane, riveted by the play of his arm and shoulder muscles beneath glistening, light-mahogany skin. His hands were huge, his wrists thick, his fingers long and curving around the plow handles. Her breath fogged the glass and she rubbed a spot clear. He'd turned the plow, presenting her with the magnificence of his back, which tapered dramatically to his waist, and the high, well-muscled flanks of his buttocks snugly encased in black knee breeches. Her eyes narrowed on the faded crisscross scars marring his back, the telltale imprint of abuse by a whip. Those scars would never heal. For some reason she didn't believe Winchester would stoop to such methods.

Thigh muscles bunched and rippled as he planted one boot in the soil and dug the plow deep. He paused, shoving one forearm over his brow, then tugging off the white kerchief that covered his head. A certain uneasiness swept over her as he swiped his face with the kerchief, a familiarity of motion, as familiar as the smooth blue-black undulation of his hair falling halfway down his neck. Then he turned, affording her the first glimpse of his face.

She swallowed past a throat gone bone-dry.

Winchester.

He spoke to a nearby worker, an immense man with an ambling gait, then pointed toward the children forming the hills. The two shared a moment's exchange. Winchester nodded and then, quite unexpectedly, he grinned, a wide, easy, affable grin that set fires dancing in his eyes even at this distance.

Teddie leaned heavily against the window, her fingertips pressing into the glass, a languid heat spreading low through her belly. With lips parted she watched him as he swiveled around to view his work, the movement bringing his bare chest full against the golden rays of the sun. The skin beneath its black furring glowed like molten bronze. The devil take her, but she remembered the heat of that chest flattening her breasts, the play of shoulder muscles beneath her hesitant fingertips, the heady sensation of potent male surging against her trembling body. A hollow ache welled up inside her, a longing so deep and elemental she nearly cried out.

"Is there anything you'll be needing, ma'am?"

Teddie spun around, then all but flattened herself against the windows. A woman in a servant's gray muslin stood just at her back, her appearance all the more startling for the stealth with which she had entered the room. Then again, Teddie was certain a mounted regiment could have thundered through her chamber a moment ago and she wouldn't have noticed.

"N-no—"she stammered, struggling with a burgeoning feeling that she had been caught in some devious act.

The woman's gray eyes angled to the window and riveted on something below. "He works in the fields today. Most white planters wouldn't be found in a tobacco field, doing work meant for the inferior slaves."

Teddie glanced sharply at her, biting off the chilly rebuttal that sprang to her tongue, because something else in the woman's voice struck Teddie as odd. A clipped, possessive tone. Teddie battled a growing uneasiness as she stared at the woman. She was no more than a hand shorter than Teddie, several years older, and compactly made, her shoulders narrow, her arms and torso as trim as a young girl's and ideally suited to the severely tailored gown she wore, save for the noticeable swell of her bosom, which seemed to test the seams in her bodice with each breath she drew. The hair primly pinned beneath her white cap was the color of flaxen, her skin unearthly pale, her full pale-pink lips the only splash of color on her. As with most servants, her face revealed little emotion and her bearing was suitably austere, hardly justifying Teddie's apprehension. Then what had caused it?

Teddie glanced at the window, her eye immediately drawn to Winchester. He was bending the plow to the earth again with great strides, his buttocks pumping rhythmically as he moved. Hastily, she turned away and found her gaze locked with the woman's. There was no denying it this time. Challenge lurked in those deep-set gray eyes.

This woman and Winchester had been lovers. No doubt they still were.

Teddie took an invisible blow to her midsection. If she betrayed herself the woman gave no hint that she'd noticed. Deeply unsettled and not sure why, Teddie moved to her dressing table, her fingertips brushing over an array of neatly arranged gilded hair brushes and combs, aware that the woman lingered at the windows. "You are . . . ?"

"My name is Jillie, ma'am. I am Miles Winchester's woman servant."

Having come into adulthood without the benefit of servants, Teddie hadn't any idea what duties Jillie's position required of her, though she couldn't recall encountering Jillie on the evening that Damian had hosted them all for dinner, which suggested that Jillie was not a menial downstairs servant. Her impeccable gown and smooth white hands were not those of a scullery maid or cook. If she was indeed Winchester's upstairs servant, what purpose, save for those self-serving, did she have for seeking Teddie in the west wing? Unless she'd come to issue claim. If so, she'd accomplished that the moment she laid her eyes on Winchester.

Standing there with a delicate crystal perfume flacon clutched in her hand, Teddie had to remind herself that she truly did not care with whom Winchester chose to satiate his lust. Little wonder he had agreed to the contract. His life as he'd known it, down to his liaison with Jillie, would go on as it had before he'd married her. It was as if she did not exist.

Two separate lives. Purely a business arrangement. She had Will to think about.

Then why was she suddenly possessed with a violent loathing for a woman she'd just met?

The crystal flacon scraped against the marble-topped dressing table, drawing Jillie's stiff regard. Without once glancing from the mirror Teddie tugged the pins from her hair, allowing it to fall freely to her waist. She threaded her fingers through the heavy curls, then plaited the mass into one braid, aware that Jillie watched her closely. Moving to a gilt-edged armoire, Teddie threw the doors wide, reached within, then tossed a well-worn blue serge onto the bed.

"You are going out, ma'am?"

"I'm going riding."

"I shall inform the kitchen staff at once."

Teddie glanced up from unhooking her gown. "I don't care who you inform. I wish to ride alone. The kitchen staff need not accompany me."

Jillie arched one brow, her lips pursing with a trace of agitation. Good. Teddie intended to agitate the woman as much as possible.

"I was thinking of dinner, ma'am. Mi—that is, your husband takes his dinner precisely at eight o'clock in the formal dining room."

"Then he and Damian will have to dine without me this evening."

"Captain Coyle intends to take his meal in his chambers."

"Then my husband will enjoy his meal without unwanted interruption."

"He need not. I will join him."

Teddie's fingers fumbled over one hook, but she kept her eyes to her task and her tongue in check. She'd never found it prudent to take the bait. Besides, she cared not one whit who shared Winchester's table. Or his bed for that matter. She had far more pressing concerns to occupy her, the least of which was familiarizing herself with the plantation grounds and establishing straightaway that she intended to come and go as she pleased, no matter Winchester's rigid schedules. Tomorrow she would make her presence clearly felt to all the inhabitants of this vast plantation. Perhaps then her role here would present itself.

She freed the last of the hooks. "You may go now, Jillie." But when she glanced up she found that the servant had departed the room as soundlessly as she'd entered.

With a freshly wrapped cigar in one hand and a brandy snifter cradled in the other, Miles leaned back in the enormous gilt-edged marble tub his grandfather Maximilian had stolen from a Turkish pasha visiting King George at his palace in London over fifty years ago. Inhaling deeply of his thin cheroot, Miles watched darkness creep beyond his bedchamber windows and briefly contemplated how the merchant sea captain had managed to escape the palace with his prize. The tale had it that the pasha had been soundly enamored of the king's mistress Mira and in the course of lavishing his attentions on her had presented her with the tub. That the roguish Maximilian had snuck the tub and the renowned beauty Mira from beneath the noses of both the King of England and an enormously wealthy and much-enamored pasha spoke volumes of the legendary Winchester's charm and daring. And of Mira's reckless devotion to him. Had they been caught in their duplicity the king wouldn't have hesitated to deal out swift, brutal punishments.

The pashaw must have been an obscenely large man, the tub of a length and width to easily accommodate both Miles and the water necessary to cover him clear to his neck. He stretched his legs, leaned his head back against the edge, and allowed his eyes to droop. His muscles ached from overuse, his skin stretched taut, overbaked by the sun. He'd filled his belly with wine, boiled beef, and potatoes. A welcome weariness weighted his limbs. So why the hell did he feel so restless?

He stared at the ceiling. The house lay silent as a tomb. Odd, but tonight the hollowness seemed unusually palpable. He wondered if the west wing seemed as desolate. His mother had occupied that wing at one time and had decorated it to her taste in pale pastels, overstuffing each of the bedrooms with goose-down bedding, French linen, and tulle lavishly draped over the bedposts, scorning the heavy velvet drapery and upholstery so common in the more masculine east wing. Any woman would find comfort there. So why was he concerned that his new bride might find disfavor with any of it?

The brandy spread a low warmth through his belly. But instead of inducing its typical languor, the liquor stirred his thoughts this evening. Dangerous thoughts. Carnal thoughts. Thoughts of Teddie in those feminine trappings, beneath the same roof, immersed in a lilac-scented bath, watching the same twilight skies. A new bride would surround herself in sheer white linen and cambric, lacy chemises, and French silk. Only these would touch her skin.

A jolt of white-hot desire flooded his senses and drowned reason. He closed his eyes, surrendering to the memories, reliving the feel of her lush young body arching eagerly against his. Remembering the luxurious texture of her skin beneath his callused palms, the gossamer soft cloud of her hair, the exquisite perfection of her breasts. The blissful torture he'd found between her silken thighs for one blinding moment. The depths of control he'd exercised to withdraw still astounded him, given the savage depths of his desire. This was the root of his fascination for her, of course, the reason the memories refused to be vanquished and put to rest. If a man could conquer the memories of Tripoli, the memories of a few minutes' interlude in his bed should prove easy to erase, even if his desire had been left unassuaged. But they weren't. And tonight he hadn't the will to fight them.

He drained his glass and drew deeply on his cheroot. The fires leapt in his blood, the memories raging now more vividly, refusing to be tamed. He'd once been a man of insatiable passions, as driven by lustful fancy as Jules Reynolds. He'd been convinced that Tripoli had forever scarred him, physically and mentally, his experiences there enough to destroy desire in the most lust-driven of men. It seemed he'd been wrong.

Palms smoothed over his shoulders with a familiar touch, but prompted little response save for an urge to escape. As usual she'd crept silently into his chamber. He leaned forward in the tub—an obviously evasive movement—and her hands trailed down his back, lingering, kneading the muscles. He sensed her hesitation and made ample use of it. Rising out of the water, he stepped from the tub and grabbed his towel from a nearby chair, well aware that his manhood stood painfully full and heavy, an unmistakable testament to the nature of his thoughts moments before. They both knew he typically required significantly more than a simple touch of her hands to become so blatantly aroused. They both also knew her ministrations had found little reward for many weeks, most particularly just two nights past. She was a brave woman to have ventured into his chamber this evening, given all this. His guarded, impenetrable mood at dinner should have proven sufficient deterrent.

Jillie sucked in a swift breath, her eyes limpid and fixed rather pointedly on his erection. "Miles—" she breathed. For a woman who had perfected a fathomless expression even in the face of complete household disasters, tonight she wore her desires obviously. Her hair hung in loose waves over her narrow shoulders, its color that of smooth alabaster in the dim candlelight. Her high-necked muslin gown lay unbuttoned to midchest, offering him unimpeded view of the thin cambric beneath and the swell of bosom ineptly contained within. Her fingers toyed with those parted buttons, and one hand reached for him as he briskly rubbed the towel over his chest then slung it over his neck. "Let me, Miles."

"You needn't."

"I want to."

He caught her hand in his and gently squeezed, his gaze arresting hers. "Not tonight, Jillie."

"Yes, tonight," she softly beseeched, her fingers working the remaining buttons of her gown free. She drew his hand beneath the parted muslin, filling his palm with the weight of one breast. "Tonight you need me, my lord. I am warm and in great need. Let me cure what ails you."

With an unusual urgency she stepped near and drew his head to hers, offering her mouth up to his, pressing her body close for his pleasure. For all that he wished it wasn't so, she left him utterly cold. Bedding her this evening would be physically impossible. Miles stiffened a moment before their lips met. "I'm sorry, Jillie."

He might have slapped her. An icy chill descended over her features and her gaze flickered low once more, registering his dwindling response with a tightening of her mouth. She dropped her hands to her sides. "As you wish, my lord."

Casting off the towel, he snatched up a midnight-blue silk dressing gown and knotted it loosely at his waist. He had no desire to explain himself. He never had, to any woman, particularly one who had understood from the onset of their relationship eight years ago that he was not a typical man with typical desires. Over the years she'd gracefully faced every version of chilled response, even rejection countless times, and had required no explanation. Tonight, however, her simmering discontent was as unusual as her unconcealed ardor had been just moments before.

He dismissed it as easily as he dismissed her, with only a trace of guilt. The door closed behind her with uncommon force, plunging him into silence once again. For a moment he stared from the windows into the darkness, well aware that the glass reflected the bed looming at his back. Only a fool would pursue memory precisely where it haunted him most. For the past several nights he had not dreamed of the horrors of imprisonment or the hells of ridding himself of his need for opium. Instead, the feel of the sheets against his skin felt like a woman's silken limbs, their rustling like the breathless sighs of an innocent on the brink of discovery. Scooping up his brandy snifter and a candle, he strode from the room, intent on finding solace somewhere in the cavernous depths of the lonely house.

With a plate balanced in one hand and a glass of wine in the other, Teddie entered through a side door at one end of the wide hall that bisected the manor house, nudging the heavy door closed with her hip. With growing curiosity she proceeded down the hall dimly lit by wall sconces, pausing to peer into the few rooms whose doors stood ajar. A music room with tall windows facing the river stood silent and dark, moonlight setting the lone piano aglow with eerie blue light. She passed several small sitting rooms, all sparsely furnished and unwelcoming, then another four closed doors. Without a candle to light her way her explorations were severely limited. Besides, she was anxious to shed her riding clothes and don something more suitable to enduring the blanketing heat. Even now, with the top buttons of her blue serge open to any breezes, her skin shone with a fine sheen.

Still, she paused at one door that stood slightly ajar, perhaps because a single taper set the walls aglow with warm golden light. Easing the door open, she discovered that the glow was emitted from the floor-to-ceiling shelves of exquisitely bound books. She required no further invitation.

The smell of the room struck her first, the familiar musty smell that permeated a room that housed many books. Her father's bookshop had smelled like this room: warm, welcoming, bidding her to shed her troubles at the door and immerse herself in its folds. But this room was also laced with a pleasant blend of beeswax, tobacco, and an elusive spicy scent that for some reason brought an extra thud to her heart and cast aside the last of her reservations that she might be trespassing.

Her slippered feet sank into the plush crimson carpet, prompting her to kick off her shoes and wriggle her toes deep into the soft depths as she took a sip of her wine. The room wasn't overly large or the least pretentious, despite the sumptuous trappings. A certain disorder reigned here beneath the luxury, a rarity from all she'd seen of Miramer's cold, unwelcoming rooms on this floor. Like the detached kitchen building she'd just left, this room was well-used, lived in, again reminding her of the bookshop. An enormous, exquisitely carved mahogany desk occupied the space before the velvet-draped windows, its surface and the floor around it littered with stacks of correspondence. To one side ledgers lay open atop one another. Beside them stood an inkwell, blotter, stand, and an array of quills. Next to that, within hand's reach of the tall chair behind the desk, sat a half-filled decanter of brandy, several long cheroots, and the candle. Beyond the bowed windows to the south swept the moon-splashed lawns. The sun must flood the room from midmorning to late afternoon with warmth. Little wonder the chair behind the desk faced the windows, as though it anxiously awaited the morning.

Setting her heaping plate on a vacant corner of the desk, she nibbled on a piece of cheese, sipped her wine, and scanned the bookshelves. As she moved closer her toe nudged a stack of books piled on the floor, some left open with pages earmarked. Closer inspection revealed these to be books on medicine and law, their pages well-worn, the margins filled with scrawled notes. Bending closer, she noted that the passages bearing the most notes were those on pregnancy and childbearing. She glanced up, her interest drawn to a section of shelving to one side of the hearth. Rising, she traced her fingertips over the extravagant and unusual gilded bindings of the long row of books, unable to decipher titles from the odd markings. Curious, she set her wine aside and drew one book from the shelf. Flipping open the cover, she was assailed by a fleeting pungent scent that twitched at her nose. She scanned the pages with a deepening frown.

"It's Arabic."

Spinning around, she clutched the book to her chest and felt the blood drain from her limbs when her eyes met Winchester's. He slouched low in the chair behind the desk, a brandy snifter cradled in one palm, and the look of the devil firing his eyes.

"They're from the Dey of Tunis himself, Bey Hamouda," he continued, his voice resonating low like distant thunder, yet silky smooth as though tempered by a great deal of warm brandy. This alone rooted Teddie to her spot.

"Hamouda was typically an ungrateful, brutish, shaggy beast," he went on, strangely uncaring, it seemed, that he had caught her trespassing. "Like many of his fellow Barbary rulers he would sit for days on his fat rump on a low bench

covered with a cushion of embroidered velvet, with his hind
legs gathered up like a bear. From that spot, and with nothing
more than nods and harmless grins, he received countless con-
suls general offering up sizable fortunes in exchange for peace,
and he commanded seven kings of Europe, two republics, and
the American continent to pay tribute to him with a naval force
barely equal to two line-of-battle ships.'' His jaw hardened, his
voice dipping so low Teddie had to strain to hear him. "I hated
the bastard. But before I left the Mediterranean he summoned
me to his palace in Tunis and presented me with the complete
volumes of the Koran and its teachings, to thank me for humiliating his rival from Tripoli, Dey Yusef Karamanli, the Dey of
Algiers.'' He barely moved, but his silk gown rippled in the
soft candlelight, the garment of a fabric and color Teddie
would never have associated with Winchester. Yet somehow it
seemed to accentuate his brooding masculinity, perhaps because it drew Teddie's eye where it typically wouldn't stray. It
occurred to her that what lay beneath the silk could only enhance whatever garments he chose, be they silk or the coarsest
muslin.

A breath-halting expanse of his chest lay bare, the rise and
fall of the burnished skin almost mesmerizing in its sculpted
magnificence. Smooth dark fur blanketed him from the ridge of
his belly clear to the thick column of his throat, and lower,
where the loosely knotted silk belt rode low, frighteningly low,
its tasseled end riding between his parted thighs.

Teddie felt her throat close up entirely. The gown draped
provocatively over his thighs, leaving a startling length of his
well-muscled legs bare, its folds barely shadowing what lay
between his parted legs. If one were of the inclination to look
close enough, one might become uncomfortably aware of the
precise shape and size of his . . .

Teddie shuddered with humiliation. Not because she'd been
caught trespassing in what was undoubtedly Winchester's private domain. Because she knew beyond a doubt that he wore
nothing beneath his silk. Gripping the book with white-knuckled intensity, she tried to ignore the flurry of activity in the
lower reaches of her belly. Winchester offered little help, his

manner ominously focused on her. That he spoke so tonelessly of a time and place that had remained a complete mystery to everyone only heightened Teddie's certainty that if he chose he could suck her into the depths of his hellish memories right along with him. Shivers quivered along her spine.

"Careful," he rumbled, his gaze warming her breasts. "Those volumes are damned near priceless." His lids drooped yet his gaze didn't falter from her quivering bosom when he drank deeply from his snifter.

Unable to bear his scrutiny, Teddie attempted to replace the book on the shelf. But whether fate or trembling hands were to blame, the priceless volume slipped from her fingers and fell open, facedown on the carpet. Deeply chagrined, she bent to retrieve it, but her entire body went rigid as stone when two large feet braced wide on either side of the book. She couldn't swallow. She could barely breathe. He'd made no sound when he'd moved, just as he'd made no sound when she'd entered the room. Had he wished it, she might never have known he occupied that tall chair by the windows.

Praying that she didn't commit the unpardonable and glance up, she snatched the book and jerked to her feet. She would have turned away, but his fingers twined around her upper arm, as though he anticipated her flight. She stared at the book clenched to her belly and wondered if he could hear the thumping of her heart. He stood so close she could feel his deep breathing, so unlike her own short, rapid gasps. The warmth of his breath stirred the tendrils on her forehead and seemed to bathe her in a brandied heat. A raw energy flowed out of him this evening, wrapping like invisible bonds around her, pulling her gaze up to his.

The floor tilted beneath her stockinged feet. Her breath escaped in a long, torturous sigh, a potent reminder that she'd yet to make a sound. Warm fingers moved down the length of her upper arm in a slow, gentle caress, cupping her elbow. The whisper of air separating the upward curve of her bosom from the thrust of his chest evaporated beneath the gentle pressure of his hand on her elbow.

Teddie felt as though she were being swallowed by a fire-breathing dragon. For a fraction of a moment her eyes flew wide and panic gripped her when she saw the dragon there, in the blackest depths of his eyes, and some unrecognizable, thoroughly wanton part of her responded. She turned to the shelves so abruptly, one sharp elbow jammed into Winchester's ribs.

"I-I'm sorry," she stammered, attempting to shove the book into the shelf.

"Let me," he said, his voice so close to her ear she froze, fearing any movement whatsoever. His hand engulfed hers and slowly guided the book into the shelf. His fingers were warm, exceedingly long and tapered, like those of a well-bred Englishman. But no English gentleman's hands bore such scars, the most pronounced a half inch in width and extending from the tip of his index finger to his wrist in a jagged band of shiny white flesh. Swallowing, Teddie snuck her hand close and struggled to draw a clean breath into her compressed lungs.

"I was accused of thievery," he murmured, as though reading her thoughts. "They would have taken my hand if I'd let them. A gracious host, the Dey of Algiers."

"I'm sorry," she said, again thinking of the brutal scars marking his back. He'd endured many forms of torture there.

"Don't be. I was guilty of the crime."

Her gaze lifted to his.

"This surprises you?" The unforgiving slash of his mouth seemed to soften slightly. "When a man is imprisoned for months in a hole with the dead and dying, thrown bits of goat cheese and water to eat from the floor like a dog, there is no such thing as compromising his scruples to survive. He will do anything. I've watched decorated admirals and men who've ruled nations lick their food from the floors they share with rats. I've watched them fall to their knees and weep for their lives. I've watched them steal and kill to survive. And I've watched them die."

"Little wonder memory haunts you."

He arched a cool brow. "Is that what you've been told? That I've fallen victim to memory?"

"People will always find ways to explain what they don't understand. Natural curiosity, I suppose."

"And what of you, wife?"

Teddie moved away from him, bracing herself against the desktop, battling the quivering in her limbs. *Wife.* Surely she'd imagined the huskiness in his voice when he'd spoken the word. It was a simple title. Her role. Not an endearment, though her heart had suddenly skipped a beat. A man so deeply tortured one moment didn't epitomize masculine sensuality the next. Did he? A man renowned for his lofty, callous self-interest and lack of loyalty didn't willingly take to the fields and labor alongside his own slaves with an affable ease. A man rumor had depicted as all but dead inside didn't seek the knowledge to bring babies into the world. Or did he? Her gaze drifted over the stacks of correspondence scattered over the desktop, the turmoil amidst the cool veneer. The same myriad opposing forces working in Winchester were much more difficult to grasp, much less to understand. How did one go about reconciling it all into one man?

His voice swirled around her, sensual, strangely compelling. "You strike me as one of the more curious of your sex. Rare indeed is the woman who would forgo a meal to snoop around a plantation."

"One doesn't snoop while bounding about on a horse."

"A clever woman could."

One corner of her lips curved upward and she traced one fingernail over the edge of the desk. "Ah. You think me clever, at least."

"Indeed, at the very least."

Warmth flooded her cheeks, but he seemed not to notice the effect his words had on her. Moving into her line of vision, thankfully behind the desk, he fixed his attention on refilling his glass, and Teddie watched her finger trace back and forth along the desk edge. "And what did you discover?" he asked at length. "You were gone for over three hours."

So he'd noticed. Ignoring the fluttering in her belly, Teddie brought her chin up and swallowed deeply, aware that the reflex brought his gaze to the parted buttons at her throat. She curled her fingers around the edge of the desk to keep them from flying to her neck. "I found the rear of the house more welcoming of visitors than the front. I also discovered that like in England the sheep keep your lawns neatly cropped and the turkeys keep your fields free of green worm—"

"Hornworm."

Teddie suppressed a shudder. "A true misnomer."

One corner of his mouth twitched upward, a devilish glitter lighting his eyes. Teddie had seen that same look on Will whenever he was up to great mischief. The idea jolted her. Preposterous. There was nothing fun-loving or mischievous about this man. And yet . . .

"Imagine spending entire days in a field infested with them," Winchester said slowly, as if savoring each word, each image. "Your hands in constant search of them, knowing they will devour half the crop before you can find even half of them."

Teddie gulped, knowing the color had left her cheeks, knowing Winchester delighted in her response like a young boy would when teasing a girl he'd taken a fancy to. Shoving up her chin, she squared her shoulders and replied, "I suppose I would set fire to the fields and set off on another course."

He watched her closely, all mischief vanishing. "Like what?"

She thought a moment, her gaze flickering over his shoulder toward the river, where the waters flowed swiftly, powerfully. "I'd build a mill along one of the streams that cut through your properties. I'd dam the stream to create a millpond, and from the lush timber along the river I'd build the mill with a great wheel to endure the current and drive the millstones. I'd grow wheat and perhaps corn for the livestock. Indeed, I would become a miller. The soil here is certainly rich enough." She paused, aware that her cheeks felt suddenly hot and that Winchester was staring at her with a peculiar intensity. She dropped her gaze and fiddled with the edge of the desk. Surely she'd imagined the appreciation in his eyes.

"You think like some very wealthy men I know further up the river. They did precisely that when hornworm took their crops. This was before some lucky bastard accidentally loosed some turkeys in his tobacco field and singlehandedly saved tobacco from hornworm. The turkeys, he discovered, are particularly dexterous at finding them, eating them up voraciously, and prefer them to every other food. They keep the fields more clear of hornworm than all the slaves I've got could, were they employed solely for that end.''

''The man should be canonized.''

Winchester grunted. ''He's found what some would say is unjust rewards. His discovery led many to believe he possessed the ability to govern. He is now in Washington, a formidable member of Madison's cabinet, I believe.''

His sarcasm was not lost on Teddie. ''A quirk of fate,'' she said.

''It can change men's lives overnight.'' Their gazes met, held, as though they both remembered the moment fate had conspired against them in Winchester's bed. Silence swelled.

Teddie looked away and sought a light tone. ''I discovered that in order to do a proper job of snooping around the perimeter of your lands I would require at least three days. However, I found your slaves obliging with directions and easy with their smiles. They seem well cared for and oddly content with their lot.''

''You thought I beat them, eh?''

''I've heard such things exist here in America.''

''We may be barbarians, but we're not stupid. With the Brits promising them freedom in exchange for information, I'd have few slaves to call my own if I treated them poorly. To my way of thinking, chattel slavery never got the fields harvested and the hogsheads filled. Wise is the planter who never forgets the legal personality of the Negro. Without this he has no rights to personal security, property, marriage, or even parenthood. Besides, it's good business. But before you start thinking I'm noble consider that some of us have been known to beat our wives if they don't obey us.'' Over the rim of his glass his gaze remained unflinching. ''You look dubious. Could it be my reputation is not as dastardly as I'd thought? Or are you as fearless as you appear?''

''Which would you prefer?'' she challenged.

He lowered his glass, his eyes glittering as he braced one

hand on the desk and leaned perilously near. "Without question I prefer a fearless woman. You are truly an anomaly, wife."

"As are you, Winchester."

"You will not bore me," he said softly.

"You sound surprised."

"I am. You're a constant reminder that I've still much to learn about females." For a breathless moment, he stared at her mouth until she nervously sank her teeth into her lower lip. The effect was not as she had anticipated or intended. His gaze deepened.

Teddie shoved away from the desk.

"Don't." He might as well have lunged across the desk and clamped his hands around her wrists, so compelling was his command. "Please. Don't leave yet." There was no trace of appeal in his tone, and none of the terseness common to commands. His was a simple statement, revealing little emotion. And yet Teddie felt inextricably drawn to him, to do his bidding, as though he exercised a mysterious power over her she couldn't understand or deny.

He settled one hip against the desk, and the silk molded the powerful curve of his buttock and thigh. Bicep rippled beneath silk as he lifted the glass to his lips. Teddie swallowed with him, her lips burning as if she tasted the fiery liquor.

"Stay here with me, Teddie," he rumbled, lazy, half-hooded eyes piercing her. "Drink brandy with me until the sun comes up over the rise."

"Will you tell me your secrets, Winchester?"

"I might be tempted." The hushed intimacy of his voice flowed through her like warm brandy. Part of her ached to stay with him, to smooth her hands over him, to share the dawn with him, to probe the depths of his secrets, of all the mystery. "You want to run from me. What are you afraid of?"

She forced her fingers from gripping at her skirts. "I do not fear you."

"Indeed, I'm contract bound. What's to fear?"

"That's not the reason." She took a step back when he rose from the desk, set his snifter aside, and moved around the desk.

Dark fires flared in his eyes and shimmered in the rippling midnight-blue silk. "Imagine for a moment that no contract stands between us." Like a beast of the night he stalked toward her, forcing her to retreat as he advanced, until the wall pressed against her back and he loomed not a handbreadth away from her. "Imagine, Theodora . . ." His voice was a soft purr, his eyes reflecting nothing as they lowered to her lips, then dipped to the parted buttons at her throat. "Would you fear me then?"

Teddie struggled for air. "No," she whispered truthfully, certain that if he moved any nearer she would crumple to the floor. But he did, curving one hand around her neck and the other around her waist as though he anticipated her legs might dissolve beneath her.

"Now," he rumbled, drawing her close against him so that she couldn't help but feel the undeniable maleness of him. "Now do you fear me?"

"No," she breathed, unable to tear her eyes from his. She pressed her palms against his chest, almost surprised to feel the rapid beating of his heart beneath the silk. "Even now I don't fear you."

"You should." The warning was unmistakable. As was the promise. "You are woman enough to tempt any man from a vow. Even if it means a sentence to hell. You were correct, my lovely Theodora," he breathed huskily. "Memory haunts me. The memory of you beneath me. . . ."

She shuddered, closing her eyes against the images as he traced his thumb over her jawline. The gentle pressure of his hand at her back molded her closer against him until she felt as though she'd been swallowed by his heat. She was drowning in it, lost in the heady, wondrous sensations he evoked with whispered words and the achingly gentle touch of his fingers.

"You remember," he murmured, his voice deep with satisfaction. He tilted her lips to his with a nudge beneath her chin. A growl rumbled through his broad chest. "Your lips tasted like sweet, ripe cherries that night."

Her eyes swept closed. "Please don't . . ." And yet despite her plea her fingers dug into his shoulders.

"I wouldn't be able to stop with one kiss," he whispered

against her lips. "I would need to have all of you. Every last sweet inch of you."

She quivered, suspended in awakening desires, her lips aching for his, her young body as though starved, needing release from the pressure building low in her belly and pooling between her thighs. Had she tried, she couldn't have concealed her response.

"Go to bed, Theodora," he rasped, his eyes boring into hers with a sudden chilling intensity. "You will find no surcease with me. Only torment. Go." He released her so abruptly, she almost stumbled against the wall. Yanking the door wide, he swept past her with a cold, brutal look, then turned and moved to his chair behind the desk. At once he riveted his attention on the pages strewn before him. As easily as he'd donned his silk robe, he'd drawn his cloak of cool calculation around him again.

Teddie shoved herself away from the wall and stalked to the desk, her fury and frustration over her inability to contain her response to him bringing a tremor to her voice. "You allowed me to glimpse the man within the monster this evening," she said. "Why?"

He didn't glance up. "An obvious mistake, and an unwitting one. I don't need your pity."

"You won't be getting it, I assure you. Any compassion I might have felt for you was utterly wasted."

He glanced up sharply. "Because I won't make love to you?"

Teddie flushed crimson to the roots of her hair. "I-I was speaking of friendship."

One black brow arched dubiously. "Between you and me?"

Teddie set her teeth and resisted the urge to fidget beneath his unwavering regard. "Ridiculous, isn't it, that anyone would wish to be friends with you."

"Quite."

"A business partnership is vastly more suitable."

"I quite agree."

"Good. Meet me here at eleven tomorrow morning and I will outline my role in the partnership."

"Make it ten."

"Ten it is." With a swift incline of her head she turned and took three steps, when his voice stopped her.

"I don't care whether people like me, Teddie. I never have."

Glancing over her shoulder, she replied, "Then you will die a sad and lonely man, Winchester. And all your efforts with this plantation will have been for nothing." She swept out of the room then, before the haunted look in his eyes made her do otherwise.

Chapter Nine

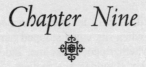

"If you don' mind my sayin', in this light you look like you ain't slep' in a month."

Squinting against the midmorning sun, Miles shot Simon a look that had been known to daunt the most stalwart of men. Most recently he had applied it to the hard-bitten lot he'd put to work refitting and loading the *Leviathan* for her upcoming voyage. Miles had dredged up the motley crew from notorious sailors' boarding houses along the Virginia and Albemarle waterfront. Some were ruffians, others criminals, no doubt with more than a sprinkling of deserters among them, but all were adventurers hoping for quick and easy fortune. Upon close inspection they resembled a leather-skinned, shifty-eyed, murderous lot of pirates. But they were fearless to a man. Miles had promised to make them all rich once they reached the West Indies. This no doubt saw them through the delays and the tedium, of which there had been much.

Yet despite these setbacks, they'd never questioned his word or second-guessed his plans. With them his reputation still managed to carry formidable weight. Simon, however, much to Miles's chagrin, seemed impervious to his employer's notoriety and black moods. He returned Miles's scowl with a lazy grin, then fell into step beside him.

As was their daily midmorning habit, they moved through the slaves' quarters tending to the sick and seeing to the handful of women who were heavy with child. This role fell to every plantation owner, as the nearest doctor lived close to Richmond, far too great a distance to expect a man to travel for every need. Over the years Miles had delivered babies, sewn up fingers slashed by the knives used to cut tobacco leaves, set splints to broken limbs, and even served as magistrate to marry his slaves.

"You ain' gonna be worth nothin' come Saturday," Simon pressed.

"I feel fine," Miles muttered, quickening his pace as he turned on a path that cut through two fields of waist-high plants and led to the main house. "Wildair would win that race with you in the saddle."

Simon grunted, then spat into the dirt. "Maybe yer jest gettin' old. You know, yer walkin' kinda stiff like. 'Course comes a time when some things jest stop workin' on a man."

Pointedly ignoring Simon and his innuendo, Miles paused to inspect the leaves of one plant. As he'd expected, a clammy moisture covered the broad, heavy leaves, indicating the field lay ripe and ready for cutting. "Watch yourself, Simon. I could order you into this field to cut for the day."

Simon's grin spread wide and easy over his face. "I's jest talkin' 'bout what I see."

Again Miles set off toward the house. "You talk too much. Go tend to Wildair. See that he's kept clear of Cleo. Now that he's caught that mare's scent no paddock will hold him if he sets his mind on her."

"Mmm hmm. That's how it always is. But I done thought o' that already." Simon stretched his gangly legs to keep stride with Miles. "I s'pose Jillie gonna be bangin' pots in the kitchen from now on an' sendin' the scullery maids all cryin' to their mamas like she done this mornin'. 'Course that was after Miss Teddie come 'n set a spell in the kitchen, jest like she was one o' the servants. 'Course she don' look like no servant. She's a lady, fresh 'n young as a spring flower. Ate enough fo' two men, she did, like somethin' plumb wore her out last night. I 'spect that's when Jillie started her bangin' and hollerin'."

"I'm not responsible for Jillie's moods," Miles muttered, certain that he indeed was in this case. He'd never thought Jillie possessed of a temper or a jealous streak. "Jillie's been the only female in the house for over eight years. Women tend to be proprietary about that sort of thing. That must account for a great deal of her mood.''

Simon grunted. "I's jest tellin' you what I seen. Miss Teddie was up 'fore you were.''

Miles felt his spine stiffen. He'd risen at dawn after a fitful night of battling dreams and losing. An overindulgence in rum seemed the likely culprit, though his encounter with Teddie in his study had only plunged him further into a foul mood and the need for more rum. His head had pounded until he'd completed his tour of the fields. "What the hell was she doing up and about at that hour?''

"Tendin' to her mare an' pickin' flowers in great bunches. I found her down at the warehouse by the river.''

Miles glanced sharply at Simon. "What was she doing there?''

"Askin' questions. Countin' hogsheads. Talkin'.''

Miles set his teeth. "Christ. What did you tell her?''

"She asked a lot o' questions. I don' recollect everythin' I said. She's a damn fine-lookin' woman.''

"You're not offering me much reassurance, Simon. She's as clever as she is beautiful. It wouldn't take her long to figure out that all that tobacco isn't going upriver to Richmond, but somewhere else entirely.''

"I didn' tell her nothin',," Simon crowed, puffing his chest and nodding vigorously. "Though it was hard, her bein' so damned purty. Jest showed her 'round.''

"That might have been enough." Miles withdrew a gold watch from the pocket of his breeches, snapped it open, and snarled, "Past ten. I'm late. God knows what the woman will discover if she starts snooping in the ledgers. Damn, but I hadn't considered this.''

"What you so worried 'bout?''

"Dammit, Simon, she's not . . . normal. *Normal* women lie abed until noon, drink chocolate and eat macaroons until two, and finally descend the stairs bathed and dressed in time for late-afternoon supper." He punctuated this by shoving one finger skyward and lengthening his stride. "*Normal* women occupy themselves with womanly pursuits, things that involve needles and tiny bits of cloth. *Normal* women sing songs, play silly parlor games, gossip with their friends, and generally fade into the background of a man's life, over time becoming nothing more than a passing nuisance, one he can banish to another wing without thought. If a man has to find himself saddled with a wife, he should make damned certain that she's normal, Simon. Particularly if he intends to keep his secrets or his privacy. No man needs a snoopy, wily, clever, overly energetic wife poking her turned-up nose into his business.''

"You know it musta been the light back there. You look younger an' yo' movin' like you got fire at yo' heels.''

"Dammit, Simon, Theodora Lovelace has nothing to do with putting spring in my stride or making me feel any younger. The woman is nothing but a damned thorn in my side.'' Miles tried to ignore the strident tones creeping into his voice. Freeing his mind of the image of Teddie gazing up at him, with eyes a mesmerizing shade of purple and lips moist and full, was proving as difficult this morning as it had throughout the night.

"You could tell her what yo' doin' down in Albemarle.''

Miles stopped in his tracks and glowered mightily at Simon. "The hell I will. Women are by nature a sly, duplicitous lot, Simon, completely incapable of exercising good judgment. Their tongues wag at the most inopportune times, all the more fervently when they think they've a secret they must keep. Hell, a woman can barely sit still if she's got a secret. It doesn't matter if men's lives are in the balance. Their itching little tongues know no better. Do you honestly believe that I would entrust a woman, much less one I barely know, with Miramer's future?'' His harsh laugh cut through the air like the swipe of a blade. "And God help us all if she chose to spill it all out for her busybody aunt. I'd be thrown into service under Farrell before the next sunrise, and Miramer would become yet another victim of the damned war. I'm not about to risk it.''

Simon folded his arms over his chest, his head inclined thoughtfully. "So what you gonna do?''

"I'm going to find her a job, Simon. Hell, several jobs, all of which will keep her little fingers busy and her mind occupied.''

He paused, considering this. "And keep her where I want her, which is well away from the river warehouses."

"Sounds to me like yo' gonna have to keep both eyes on her, from mornin' to night."

"Then so be it. It's scant price to pay."

These words echoed in his mind with a certain ironic foreboding when he entered his study several moments later and found her balanced precariously on a stool he knew had two loose legs, straining on tiptoe to reach the uppermost shelf just beyond her fingertips. The sight of her snooping around in his domain did not strike the expected annoyance in him. In fact, to his astonishment, given his concerns not moments before, he found nothing about her the least bit unpleasant or irritating. Rather alluring, in all truth, a balm to the soul, and looking like a buttercup in a simple pale-yellow gown that made his hands at once itch to span her narrow waist. With her arm stretched high and her back arched slightly, her breasts thrust from the gentle sweep of her ribs, firm, high, and extravagantly full. His narrowed gaze followed the sinuous curve of her back to the lush upward curve of her buttocks, where the beribboned end of her single thick braid swung hypnotically, to and fro.

He was instantly made aware of the cataclysmic effect she had on his senses. He could remember no other woman ever holding such power over his desire. This, of course, called for a swift and sure bolstering of his defenses. During the night he'd come to the grim realization that Farrell, being an astute and abominably clever man, had seized upon opportunity and intended to test the very limits of Miles's character and resolve by dangling before him the lush and sensual Teddie like ripe fruit just beyond the reach of a starving man. That Teddie quite possibly could be unaware of her uncle's intent mattered little. She was a pawn, and pawns were meant to be used in games.

A game. His lips curved in anticipation. A man didn't survive twenty days alone in the desert without honing granite-hard physical and mental capabilities. He'd risen above the most grueling of tests as a prisoner of the dey. Knowing this was his test, resisting a woman—any woman—should prove pitifully easy.

"Damn," she muttered, her fingers trembling just a hair-breadth from grasping the bottom edge of one book wedged tight between two others.

He narrowed his eyes on the volume she sought: *Tactical and Strategic Naval Wartime Maneuverings-Catching the Enemy Unawares.* He'd read the book himself, many times, especially when he'd been sent to the Mediterranean to thwart the Barbary pirates. The title didn't promise hours of light reading. An odd choice for a woman, given that his shelves contained every imaginable classic, including volumes of romantic poetry his mother had collected.

It seemed he'd taken an oddity to wife. No woman in his experience had ever displayed the least interest in naval maneuverings. Why should she? Of course, a woman who hadn't any interest in typical female pursuits would display the same tendencies in her choice of reading, wouldn't she?

The hem of her gown lifted as she stretched high on one foot. She wore no underskirts, no shift, and no French silk stockings. Her leg was startlingly, beguilingly bare, an unexpected splash of firmly muscled female flank. And on her feet she wore no dainty slippers. His peculiar wife had somehow found herself what looked to be navy-issue laced ankle boots. Undoubtedly these were better than flimsy slippers for riding and snooping around the acreage of a plantation.

The paradox of those practical boots on such lissome legs was not lost on Miles. And somehow the idea of it roused his senses like no aphrodisiac known to the lascivious rulers on the Barbary Coast.

His breath wheezed from the heavy compression in his chest. She suddenly jerked and attempted to look over her shoulder, a feat made impossible when one leg of the stool collapsed beneath her. For an instant she seemed suspended in midair.

"Miles!" she shrieked, but he'd already sprung across the carpet, catching her around the waist with one arm just as the stool crashed to the floor.

"It's all right," he said, wrapping both arms around her waist, suddenly aware that his face was crushed against her bosom. At once he shifted her lower, which only made matters worse as this brought her flush against him from thigh to breast. She felt like his own private heaven, exquisitely formed to mold against him. She smelled of flowers, of summer-fresh meadows, of morning sunlight, of crushed lilac bouquets. In his arms she was like gossamer. "You can let go of my hair now," he ground out, his pain having nothing to do with the ten fingers gripping his hair by the roots.

"I'm sorry," she said quickly, her voice shaky. Her fingers released their hold on his hair and braced against his shoulders. He couldn't tell if she was clinging to him or pushing him away. "I—You can put me down now," she said.

"Of course." God knew what possessed him to seek any more torture at that point, but he lowered her as though he wanted nothing more than to memorize every curve and hollow as it passed over his rigid length. She was staring at the open neck of his shirt, refusing to meet his gaze. The instant her feet touched the carpet, she twisted away and bent to the broken stool.

"Leave it," he said.

"I'm sorry."

"Quit apologizing."

"I'm sorry, I didn't realize—" She glanced up at him and bit her lip. "I did it again, didn't I?"

A man could lose himself in those violet eyes, could forget everything except that he was a man and she a woman. He reached up, nudged her book from the shelf, and handed it to her. "Here."

She took it, glanced at the title, then handed it back to him, her eyes lifting to the shelves. "Good heavens, what would I do with this? I wanted the book to the right of this one."

He hesitated, certain that she had been reaching for this particular book. No other.

Her lips parted with a smile. Something inside him melted like butter over a low fire. "That one there," she said.

Glancing up at the shelf, he nudged a slim volume from the shelf. "The book of sonnets."

"Yes. The sonnets." She plucked the book from his hands,

glanced at the cover, then offered him another smile. "Yes, this is the one. Thank you."

Something struck him as odd. Perhaps the sudden eagerness of her smiles. Not that he didn't find himself suitably charmed and hungry for more, but he innately sensed that beneath her congenial, gracious manner she concealed something. He hadn't a notion what that could possibly be and what a book on naval tactics might have to do with it. He placed the naval book on his desk, aware that beneath the sweep of thick lashes her eyes followed the book. His chest swelled with suspicion, yet he forced a lightness to his tone.

"You're looking for something to do, I presume," he said, indicating the book she held against her bosom.

A shrug drifted through her shoulders. "I need something appropriate to read beneath one of those enormous boxwoods that shade the stream at the north pasture."

"I know the place."

Her brows quivered. "You go there often?"

He suddenly felt as though he'd trespassed where he shouldn't have, into a splendid little spot that was hers and hers alone, regardless that it was his property. "Rarely," he hedged.

Her face brightened. "It's quite perfect, shady and cool, nestled like a little valley between the rises. One could feel very much alone there."

This struck him. He understood the reasons he sought a solitary haven. But why would this innocent young woman? Most women loathed being alone.

He directed his attention to stacking papers on his desk. So she enjoyed peace and solitude. What the hell was so odd about that? And why was he finding everything about her so damned intriguing, particularly the lush scent of her this morning, as though she were a bursting summer bouquet? At this rate, he'd get nothing accomplished, much less ensure that she'd have little time to wile away beneath a shady boxwood or to wander about the plantation.

"I'm sure you noticed that I'm accumulating a great deal of paper around me."

"Men hate correspondence."

He glanced sharply at her.

She lifted her brows, eyes wide, innocent, betraying the surety of her observation. "They despise it. Too much cordiality and all that, not to mention the need for good penmanship. . . ." She glanced at the desk, one brow arching at Miles's scrawled notes.

Miles resisted the urge to snatch the paper from beneath her prim little nose, feeling very much like a pupil called to task before his teacher. He'd never been a patient man, and his careless scrawl bore this out. But he'd never felt the least compulsion to apologize for it, by God. And he wasn't about to start.

"Like you, I suppose, my father much preferred the particulars of managing the business," she continued, lifting her eyes to his once again. "He divested himself of tending to correspondence and the ledgers and bookkeeping."

"So he drowned in paper."

"Of course he didn't. I did all of it for him."

He felt soundly set in his place. He should have known. A woman of keen intellect *participated*. He warmed to the subject immediately, intensely curious about her life in England. "Your father was a merchant?"

Her chin jutted up a good two inches and her eyes flashed proud defiance. "No, he was decidedly working class and fiercely ambitious. He owned a bookshop in the heart of London. A small enterprise, nestled on a narrow, dark alley, but he was immensely successful for a time, particularly with the scholars and deep-thinkers."

"He expanded his operations?"

"No. He sent me to school."

He must have betrayed his shock, because her chin seemed to inch up another notch and color bloomed in her cheeks. "It was a private institution," she added quickly, "under the direction of one of my father's patrons. Of course, no girls were allowed, but my father and this patron came to an understanding. They were very close friends. Both rather progressive thinkers."

"Obviously. How did you manage it?"

"I dressed as a boy, of course, and traveled every day from London to the school. I couldn't possibly *live* with the other students, could I?"

Miles did his best to keep his eyes from straying to the swell of her breasts. At the moment he found it difficult to imagine this woman had ever been a child, her chest flat and shapeless, her flaring hips narrow.

She didn't wait for his reply. "I don't believe the other students ever guessed, and I was there for many years, until long after I—that is, the difference quite suddenly became more difficult to conceal." Abruptly, her eyes skittered away and she flushed red from her hairline clear to her high, lace-trimmed collar.

Womanhood must have burst upon her with the suddenness of a summer storm. Yet while her female contemporaries had fretted over which gowns did proper justice to their blossoming charms, young Theodora had no doubt cursed her fate and tightly bound herself, denying her femininity to achieve an education.

An overwhelming compulsion to gather her into his arms took hold of him. Curving his fingers around the edge of the desk, he banished the thought. "You could have been a highly paid governess. Yet you chose to work alongside your father as any son would have."

"He needed me," she said simply.

"You had no brothers to help with the business?"

"One." She moved to the windows, her gaze far in the distance where the river waters were visible over a gentle rise. "He worked in the coal yards. That suited him best, though he would have loved the sea. He has some sort of mental deficiency. The doctors all agree that this resulted from a difficult birth."

Watching her, Miles grew certain her brother's mental infirmities were not the cause of the veil of sadness that had drifted over her features. "He's still in England?"

She hesitated, lifting one hand to the windowpane. "He is with the English." Her melancholy was so subtle, so carefully veiled, Miles suddenly realized he'd misread it when he first glimpsed her in his salon almost three weeks ago and believed her glacial, aloof manner betrayed a scheming, fickle heart. Then he couldn't possibly have imagined the vivid sparkle that gave luminous depth and life to her eyes or the natural grace and innocence in her manner that no scheming woman could ever imitate. If he had, he might have known her cool manner was the aberration. But he had been too eager to label and shelf her along with all the other beautiful and thus deceitful women he'd known. With this one woman it seemed he'd been grievously mistaken.

He stared at her luminous profile and grimly wondered which of them harbored more secrets. At the moment he'd bet the finest bloodlines his stable had to offer that she did. A sudden surge of curiosity, an intense yearning to know, to grasp, hold, and fully understand this woman swept over him like a billowing wave of heat, catching him unawares. Perhaps even more disturbing was his intense need to lift the veil and banish her melancholy. The reasons for it, oddly enough, could wait. For now. No man, no matter how determined or curious, could unveil Theodora Lovelace in one morning. He wondered if a lifetime would afford him the opportunity.

"It seems you're perfectly suited for what I have in mind," he said, his tone purposely businesslike. This achieved its desired response as she glanced sharply at him, her eyes brightening with interest sparked.

Something about her brother had greatly distressed her. . . . A brother, not a lover as he had suspected?

Filing this away he swept a hand to the desk. "Could you possibly make some sense of all this? I realize it's an enormous undertaking. . . ." He lifted a letter, then another, glancing at them. "Correspondence mostly, several invitations to weddings of people I don't know, that sort of thing, all requiring responses. You know, things that demand effusive cordiality and exquisite penmanship."

"Of which you have neither, I presume."

He arched a brow at her. "Something tells me you keep these in your vast arsenal of talents, Theodora."

Her smile lit stars in her eyes and sent a shaft of desire

piercing through Miles. "I believe I could wield my talents against this mountain of paper with smashing results, Winchester. And what of these?" She laid her hands atop the stack of ledgers. "My father proclaimed me possessing of superior logic and mathematics capabilities. I'd be happy to demonstrate them for you. I'd wager your ledgers haven't balanced in months."

Masculine indignation roused to life, bringing his brows together over his nose. "It hasn't been all that long."

"Ha! Just as I suspected." She all but smacked her lips with satisfaction. "My father's books were all but indecipherable when he dropped them in my lap. In less than two months they even balanced. I must say nothing is half so rewarding as putting something in order, Winchester. Making it work. Can I do the same for you?"

He almost said yes. She was too damned sweet and tempting, her smile so guileless and charming, her confidence so refreshing, for a moment he considered laying it all in her lap, just as her father had. He didn't doubt that she could burrow a clean, logical path through a ledger hopelessly tangled and indecipherable. But in the process she would realize that the crop going upriver to Richmond accounted for only a fraction of his yield. One or two trips to the river warehouse, an inventory of the fields and all the activity there, and she would be irrevocably intrigued. Undoubtedly suspicious. She might even guess that he was nearly three-quarters complete in loading the *Leviathan* for her trip to the West Indies. She was, after all, far too clever for a woman.

"No," he said, his tone brusque before he caught himself and forced a smile. "Leave those for now. I'd rather you see first to the correspondence. And then, if you would, bring some sort of order to the bookshelves, grouping subjects together, perhaps alphabetically by author."

She stared at him, as though she suspected he did indeed grasp at diversion. "You want me to reorganize your bookshelves before I see to the ledgers?"

"Yes."

She scanned the walls of shelves surrounding them. "That could take months."

"If you'd rather not—"

"No," she said quickly, with palpable conviction. "I'd much prefer that to supervising the kitchen staff. I believe I would be more hindrance than help there . . . not that I didn't find it a marvelously cheery place, divinely nestled well back of the house. It's full of luscious aromas, very homey and welcoming compared to—that is—" She seemed to catch herself, then bit her lip and shifted her gaze to a far corner.

He stared at her. "The house displeases you."

Her eyes flew to his. "I didn't say that."

"You prefer the kitchen."

"I do. The place bursts with activity . . . with life. You can feel the vitality of the place. The open windows welcome the sun and the breezes. I've been there only a few times, of course, but even then kittens and puppies scampered underfoot. Children ran about, grabbing big handfuls of things they shouldn't and upsetting the cooks."

His chest grew strangely tight. "You wish to have children."

She blinked at him, her mouth opening and closing three times before she sputtered, "Th-that's—I didn't say that."

"You want kittens and puppies scampering about the house?"

"A few would be quite nice. Except for this room, the house seems very big and very empty. Rather sad, as if ghosts wander the halls at night."

He'd never thought of his home in those terms, though at times the ghosts had seemed palpable to him. He awaited a displeasure and resistance to her idea that never came to him. "What else would you like, Theodora?"

"I'd like to open all these closed and locked doors. Is there some reason for keeping half the house closed up like this?"

He shrugged. "I haven't been in some rooms for years. I haven't a need for that much space, and we entertain so rarely. Jillie prefers that the rooms left unused be kept closed up." A deepening of her stare prompted him to add, "For cleaning purposes, I suppose. But as mistress of Miramer you have access to every inch of the house and grounds."

"Good. Then I would like to throw the windows wide so that the breeze can waft through the house. I want to put fresh flowers in every room. And I will order that everyone take lemonade and tea on the eastern veranda at precisely four o'clock each afternoon, when that side of the house is cool and shady."

"Everyone."

"Servants and slaves alike." Her eyes slanted up at him. "Even you, Winchester."

"I've never drunk tea in my life, at four in the afternoon or otherwise."

"Then you don't know what you're missing."

"Obviously."

Their eyes met and held for several long moments of absolute silence. Her forthright manner didn't challenge him to deny her anything. She didn't look like a woman who had asked for much. In all truth, she hadn't. But with most women the idea of giving in to any of their wishes, no matter how insignificant, usually galled a man and went straight to the roots of his pride and his innate need to rule his home. With Theodora, however, he doubted whether he could deny her anything at that moment.

A warmth settled near his heart. "Fine," he said.

Her eyes widened. "Fine? To all of it?"

He shrugged, puzzled by his desire to grin as though he'd emerged victorious, not her. Her charm had deeply affected him, it seemed, prompting a teasing tone to his voice. "Yes, to all of it. Would you like a new bonnet, as well, while I'm in the mood? Perhaps several new gowns, silk slippers—"

She went instantly still. "You don't care for my clothes."

Without thinking he swung around the desk and took two steps toward her. "No, that's not—" He reached for her hand, then caught himself, chagrin drawing him up stiff as an old hickory tree. He clamped his hands to his taut thighs, feeling like a complete fool and trying his damnedest not to show it. "Your clothes—what I've seen of them—are fine. I . . . ." He swallowed, wondering why he couldn't seem to ever do the right thing with this woman, wondering, too, why he so desperately wanted to. "I was teasing you, Theodora. I meant no insult."

"Oh." She pursed her lips thoughtfully, her eyes lowered. "You're not the teasing sort."

"No, I don't suppose I am." He considered this as he watched her fiddle with the tassels binding the ledgers. Would she enjoy teasing and play of that sort? He supposed she would. He couldn't remember the last time he'd felt the least like engaging in anything lighthearted.

She stood so close, if he wished he could reach out and press those fiddling hands between his, he could slip one arm around her waist and draw her close against him. With some surprise he realized that his need for her at the moment had far less to do with base, physical lust than with something far deeper, something that emanated from the lonely, hollow depths of his soul, where he'd kept many doors and windows tightly sealed for years.

He didn't understand it. When she lifted her luminous face and her eyes met his, he preferred that he didn't.

"Teddie—" His fingers brushed over hers on the ledger. But she didn't pull her hand away, and he wrapped his fingers around hers. "Listen, I—"

"There you are, cousin," Damian suddenly crowed from the open door. "I was just leaving for Baltimore and—why, will you look at this."

There was something very telling in Theodora's swift snatching of her hand from his, something strangely satisfying in the way she held her fingertips to her lips, something remarkably enchanting in the rosy hues flooding her cheeks. She seemed, to Miles's profound amazement and certain satisfaction, quite incapable of words for what had to be the first time in her life.

Feeling as though his puffing chest would burst through his linen shirt, Miles swung a broad smile on his cousin. "Ah. All ready to chase glory, I see."

Damian stared at him, mouth slightly sagging. "You don't look yourself today, Miles," he finally said. "Not at all."

"Thank you, Damian. Oddly enough, I don't feel quite the usual today either. I'll walk you out."

"What?"

Miles swung around the desk and advanced on his cousin, well aware that the younger man retreated several paces into the hall as though he were being stalked by a temperamental tiger. "I want to see you out. You know, leave you with some profound words of wisdom to take with you into battle."

"Have you been drinking, Miles?"

Miles scowled, feeling the levity seeping swiftly out of him. "Dammit, I just want to see you out. Wish you well."

"Wish me well," Damian repeated, his stare deeply suspicious. Thoughtfully, he fingered his chin with a white-gloved finger. Suddenly his face lit up and he pointed one finger skyward. "I've got it. You want to make certain that I do indeed leave. That's it. Can't abide the thought of me beneath the same roof with Teddie, eh, Miles? Or are you afraid that I'll shoot you in your sleep?"

Miles slid his teeth together, hooded his glare on Damian, and said nothing.

"Ah, but you're not afraid of anything, are you, cousin?" Damian smoothed a hand over the front of his brass-buttoned uniform, one reddish-gold brow arching. "Odd for a man who has nothing but enemies. It's only a matter of time before you give someone all the reason he needs to do you in."

"Good day, Damian. And may you do your heritage proud on the battlefield." With a curt incline of his head Miles brushed past his cousin and headed down the hall toward the side door. His strides were long and sure, his head held proud and high, his manner unflappably stoic and confident, befitting a planter with much to get done and too little time in which to do it. But the echo of Damian's words cut through him with the force of a fine blade and lingered with him throughout the remainder of the day.

Chapter Ten

The barks slipped soundlessly through the waters of the James River, their path lit sporadically by a moon content to dally behind the clouds. Beneath the weight of the thousand-pound hogsheads strung like fat sheep across the canoes, the cumbersome vessels rode perilously low in the water, all but intractable even in the best of conditions.

"Fast to port," Miles ordered from his post at the foremost bow of the string of barks. Behind him Simon and three of his strongest, most trustworthy slaves set their oars as he did against the current on the starboard side of the interlinked vessels. The barks pitched left, narrowly escaping the shallows near the southern banks.

"Easy," Miles muttered, his eyes straining in the darkness for the telltale brush and low-hanging tree branches that fringed the shoreline. He depended entirely on his oar to judge the depth of the water beneath their bellies and to maintain the surety of their course, one purposely chosen to hug the shoreline and offer the greatest concealment. The slightest misjudgment of depth, given the unwieldy nature of their vessel and its weighty cargo, could plow them disastrously into a river bottom of three-foot muck. The vision of loosing half the hogsheads into the river in order to free the barks set Miles's jaw with determination and tightened his gloved fingers on his oar. Nudging his wide-brimmed black hat further back on his head, he leaned low over the bow of his vessel, his eyes probing the pitch. Behind him, his cloak ballooned and snapped as the barks gathered speed.

"Easy, boys," he said. "If instinct serves, we should be right . . . about . . . there. Aha."

Not more than fifty feet ahead, precisely where the James

and Elizabeth Rivers met, a lantern flashed, its light so dim he would have missed it had he not been watching for it. "Set your oars fast," he ordered, hefting his own dim lantern in reply. The barks gradually slowed against the current, allowing Miles to steer them toward the lamplight.

As planned, the longboat had been wedged tight against a fallen tree jutting from the water about twenty yards from shore, affording the approaching barks a dock of sorts without the hazards of the shallows.

Beneath Miles's firm hand the barks turned, gently bumped against the longboat, and held fast against the current.

Miles stepped into the longboat and slapped a hand on the burly shoulder of the lone sailor standing at the bow. "Any sign of him, Watts?" Miles asked.

Watts shook his bald head, his gaze never wavering from the water. "Nay, sir."

"Keep looking, Watts. British frigates are rather difficult to hide on a river. Captain Osgood is out there. You can be sure he's seen us. Give him time."

"Could be Osgood won' come, sir. Could 'ave changed 'is mind."

"He'll come," Miles replied with grim certainty. "His men are hungry, tired, and bored with blockade duty. For his coop-eration in our scheme I promised him food and wine to last a fortnight and two hogsheads of my finest tobacco. He'll be here. Just to make sure . . ." From the folds of his cloak he withdrew two large corked bottles and hefted them into the moonlight.

Watts, formerly of Cornwall, England, where the spoils of scuttled ships heavily laden with fine Jamaican rum had long been enjoyed, smacked his lips and gave a swift nod. "Aye, he'll come, sir. If only fer the rum, if he's truly an Englishman he'll surely come. I'd wager ye'll 'ave no trouble with the rest of the lading, sir."

"Not from him. Let's hope Cockburn keeps him patrolling the Elizabeth until we're fully laden. That should take less than a month. How are the men faring?"

Watts jerked his head to the barks. " 'Tis sure to occupy 'em, sir.''

"And the ship?"

"Like ye ordered, sir, we coppered her hull and altered her trim to draw only five feet forward and a little over twelve aft. Had a new suit of sails bent to her. She'll be the fastest brig anyone ever took a wheel to, sir."

"She'll need to be quicker and nimbler than anything British or American afloat. What of her guns?"

"All twenty shotted, sir."

"See that the sweeps are fully operational and the rowlocks well-oiled. Ten miles out the wind could drop to a dead calm. I'd rather not deliver my entire crop and my ship into British hands because I had no sweeps and no one to man them. Five knots is better than nothing, Watts, no matter the toil."

"Aye, sir." The blue-eyed, former British naval-officer-turned-deserter, privateer, and adventurer possessed a remarkably quiet manner and solemn voice given his vocation. Very little about him suggested that shortly after deserting seven years ago he had become the terror of British shipping off the coast of Halifax, Nova Scotia. His most recent close call, over two years before, had been with a British man-of-war in Halifax harbor, an unlikely and dreadful circumstance that resulted in the burning of Watts's ship and the capture, torture, and execution of his crew. He'd evaded capture by hiding out in the burning vessel, jumping ship at the last possible moment only to be rescued by an American frigate and brought back to Baltimore.

The British, forever suspicious, offered a thirty-thousand-dollar reward for the capture of any ship with Watts on her. Their quest had as yet been unsuccessful.

Miles, in search of a crew to man the *Leviathan*, had found Watts in a dockside pub in Norfolk just a year ago, a place known to cater to the riffraff and ne'er-do-wells that typify the daredevilish lot of privateers. Watts, penniless, hungry, and angry as a bantam rooster, was precisely what Miles had been looking for. In return for command of refitting and loading the *Leviathan*, Watts had sworn his allegiance to Miles and had accumulated a crew as hard-bitten and bold as any that manned a British frigate.

"There." Miles pointed into the pitch. "I can hear her."

Watts stood motionless, then shook his head.

"Her longboat just met the water. Hear the oars?" Miles paused. "You can always feel a ship before you see her, Watts. Hell, you know that."

"Aye, sir. 'Tis the same with a woman."

Miles glanced sharply at Watts. It was true, though Miles wouldn't have agreed three weeks ago. He might have thought Watts addled had he not experienced it firsthand—the instinctive, unwitting bodily response, the rousing of all his senses that occurred the split second before Teddie entered a room.

"I see 'er now, sir. What if 'e's got fifteen men with 'im, all armed an' ready to run us through? It could be a trap."

"It's no trap. We've an agreement."

"He's a veteran of Trafalgar, 'e is. Served under Nelson. Not a treasonous bone in 'is body. Damned patriotic."

"And damned thirsty. They're coming fast. Listen to the oars. They're dipping shallow and swift. The longboat rides light. I'd wager he's got only one or two men with him. His most trusted, I'd guess. Get out of the light, Watts. I'll talk to him." Adjusting his hat lower to shadow his face, Miles dimmed the lantern and calmly awaited Captain Osgood of the British frigate *Leopard*.

Less than twenty minutes later, Captain Osgood's longboat returned to his ship with a bark heavily laden with spoils securely roped behind it. While Osgood's men plundered the food and tobacco, and Osgood set himself to the first bottle of Jamaican rum and a thick cigar in the comforts of his cabin, Miles saw his hogsheads safely and without incident from the James and south down the Elizabeth, where the *Leviathan* rode at anchor. His return trip went as uninterrupted, in full view of the *Leopard*'s watch.

Saturday dawned cheerful and unusually clear and bright, with not a breeze to be found to stir the smothering blanket of heat. Despite this, several hundred of the plantation aristocracy throughout Gloucester County dragged themselves from their beds at dawn, donned layers of starched Saturday-afternoon finery, polished their coaches, oiled their mounts, and converged upon the racecourse at Devil's Field with purses bulging and excitement peaking. This was to be no ordinary public test of speed where a field of a dozen or more horses competed through several heats until the slower horses were eliminated. Today there would be only two horses, and two riders, both of whom were gentlemen renowned for sparing neither trouble nor expense in importing the best stock and improving their breeds by proper and judicious crossing. There would be only one race, three times around the mile-long track, a true test of distance, requiring bottom as well as speed in the horses. There would be only one chance to wager.

Devil's Field was no ordinary course. Unlike most racecourses, which resembled narrow, straight paths about a quarter mile in length laid out in an abandoned fields, Devil's Field was a mile-long circular track with a grandstand flanking the long backstretch and a paddock area where the spectators could view the entrants before making their bets.

On this particular day liveried servants offered cool champagne and other refreshments in the shade of an elegant, red-and-white-striped tent. Further along, a four-piece string ensemble warbled delightfully beneath an enormous sycamore tree.

"Reynolds's doing," Aunt Edwina said to Teddie, indicating the violinists and refreshment tent as their curricle pulled to a stop amidst a tangle of horses, carriages, and elegantly attired ladies and their escorts. "Only Jules Reynolds could muster up champagne during a full continental blockade."

"How thoughtful," Teddie said as she stepped from the carriage and narrowly missed being plowed down by a passing buggy.

Behind her, Aunt Edwina huffed and puffed her way out of the buggy, then paused beside Teddie and snapped her parasol open. "Your husband feels no such compulsion."

Teddie felt her backbone draw up stiff. Adjusting her silk-fringed parasol higher over her head against the blasting sun, she kept her gaze steady beneath the feathers and loops of ribbon trimming her bonnet. "Jules Reynolds is a showman. Winchester is not."

"I quite agree. But you must admit Reynolds makes it all such jolly fun. Were it up to Winchester we'd all be left to rot in the heat with no place to put our bums, much less our buggies or our horses."

"I disagree, Aunt Edwina," Teddie replied with a cheeky lift of her chin. "Winchester would make certain your horses were well-tended."

"A true Virginian," Aunt Edwina snorted, pasting on a sweet smile as she nodded to a passing acquaintance. "It is said, Theodora, that the men in this region hold so much value for the saddle that rather than walk to church five miles they'll go eight to catch their horses, then ride there." Linking her arm through Teddie's, she urged, "Come, I believe I smell champagne in the air. If only for that, my wager is with Reynolds. What of you, my dear?"

"I'll know better when I see them in the paddock."

This wasn't easily accomplished, as spectators jammed the area surrounding each of the paddocks. Most were men, wearing tall-crowned felt hats and broad-shouldered frock coats with flaring skirts, all of which only frustrated Teddie's attempts to peer around or over them.

"I would never expect to see anything like this at Newmarket," Aunt Edwina announced in her shrill vibrato, drawing annoyed looks from several men standing directly in their path. To emphasize her point Aunt Edwina seemed determined to put her parasol and the formidable breadth of her hips to use in clearing them a path. In doing so she interrupted a good number of wagers, in amounts so startling Teddie was certain that horse racing alone had been responsible for the economic prosperity that had built the Tidewater mansions and furnished them with imported luxuries. These men wagered fortunes as easily as their wives drained their glasses of champagne. And the majority of them were advanced in years, most of their younger counterparts having enlisted in the militia or the navy.

"Here we are!" Aunt Edwina exclaimed, staking out a

broad territory with clear vantage of the fenced paddock area. With a lift of her powdered chin she directed Teddie's attention to the left paddock. "My dear, Theodora, now *there* is a capital horse. You can be sure Reynolds's Valiant would make no despicable figure at Newmarket. Nor is his speed, bottom, or blood inferior to his appearance."

The inference was clear, though Teddie chose to postpone her judgments for the moment and narrowed her eyes on Reynolds's mount. The ebony stallion Valiant was as sleek, proud, and elegant-limbed as an English racer just imported. He pawed the ground with the conscious dignity of an aristocrat as his groom slapped a saddle onto Valiant's back and cinched it tightly beneath his belly. At his head stood Jules Reynolds, elegantly turned out in a burgundy silk waistcoat jacket, a crisp shirt of brilliant white linen, and close-fitting burgundy riding breeches. At his neck spilled a frothy white cravat held in place by an enormous ruby-and-diamond-headed stickpin. His black knee boots gleamed with high polish. In his burgundy-gloved right hand he gripped the ruby-encrusted handle of an ebony cane. In his left he twirled a riding quirt. His calm manner in the face of the melee surrounding him bespoke centuries of fine breeding for this exact purpose. His voice was a smooth, mellow rumble as he directed the groom tending to Valiant. Reynolds's hair gleamed like molten gold in the sunlight. His eyes were an uncommon shade of azure. And when he lifted his head and his smile dazzled more brilliantly than the sunlight, Teddie was certain that every woman's eyes were upon him.

Aunt Edwina's head snapped around. "I believe he's looking at you, my dear," she murmured, her brows quivering with curiosity.

Teddie fiddled with the handle of her parasol, certain that Reynolds approached them beneath the watchful eyes of all surrounding. In her high-necked ivory silk she felt suddenly, uncomfortably hot. "Who?" she hedged, her gaze slanting nervously to the adjoining paddock. There the plebeian Wildair, as monstrous and shaggy-looking as Valiant was sleek and coiffed, poked the earth with his pillared legs as if ashamed of his presumption to venture into such noble company. Had she been judging with the common eye she would have thought him an outrage to all rules of English stable lore. Having once been on his back, she knew better.

Simon stood at Wildair's head. Winchester, to her relief, was nowhere to be seen.

"My dear Mrs. Winchester," Jules Reynolds said silkily, his eyes twinkling as he bent over her extended hand. He greeted Aunt Edwina and engaged her in conversation with the easy, convivial manner of a host leisurely enjoying his own party. Watching him, Teddie might never have guessed that he was perhaps just minutes away from relinquishing the finest stallion descended from the famed Godolphin Arabian, a crushing blow to any stable. But more than that, Teddie doubted Jules Reynolds, the elegant showman, would suffer defeat as gracefully as he might wish everyone to think.

Some instinct told Teddie that beneath his polished exterior the man was as coolly, shrewdly calculating as Miles Winchester. Perhaps even more so. Yet despite her suspicion that he was up to some sort of mischief, she couldn't help but warm to his charm and harmless banter. Aunt Edwina truly outdid herself in that regard, particularly when Reynolds bent low and murmured something to her. From behind her discreetly angled parasol, Edwina's peals of high-pitched laughter drew more than their share of curious looks before she directed her attention back to the paddock area, leaving Reynolds's intent focus on Teddie.

He inclined his head toward Wildair. "Has your husband come to his senses and suffered a change of heart?" His gaze warmed with appreciation as it flickered over the trim of her bonnet. "He is conspicuously late."

Teddie lifted her chin with conviction. "He'll be here."

"Good." Reynolds leaned nearer, his voice as smooth as warm brandy. "I taste sweet victory today. Might I ask who you intend to put your money on, dear lady? The elegant Valiant perhaps?"

Teddie angled her eyes briefly at Valiant. "In my experience, Jules, one must look beyond the well-oiled coat and braided mane and tail to truly judge a mount's capabilities and, more important, his spirit.''

"Look as deep as you wish," Jules Reynolds murmured, his innuendo not lost on Teddie, particularly when he lightly touched the silk lapel of his coat directly over his heart. "You will not be disappointed."

Teddie took the bait, though some part of her realized the wisdom in treading lightly on uncharted ground, particularly with a master like Jules Reynolds. "He looks abominably fanciful and fickle," she teased, aware that Aunt Edwina suddenly stared at both of them.

"Nevermore," he replied, his voice startlingly hushed. "His loyalty to you and you alone would be everlasting. He would bring you untold pleasures, I can assure you."

"Rogues can't be trusted, Sir Jules," she sniffed.

He leaned a whisper closer, his spicy scent tickling her nostrils. "And what of reformed rogues?"

She angled her parasol at him, drawing him up short. "They're the very worst of the lot."

"I'd relish the opportunity to convince you otherwise."

"I'm afraid I would only disappoint you."

"Never."

"At the very least you would become unbearably frustrated. You see, I'm rather stubbornly set in my thinking at times."

"I can't help but envision the myriad methods I could employ to achieve your change of heart. I'm imagining long, languid afternoons of gentle, sweet coaxing."

Teddie gave a helpless shrug and a dramatic sigh. "Your efforts would be in vain. Call it foolish, but I'll forever put my faith first in some shaggy, scarred beast. Beneath their gruff exteriors they possess the stoutest of hearts and noblest of spirits." Beneath his probing stare she flushed and fiddled with the handle of her parasol, suddenly afraid that she had unwittingly revealed too much. "Truly, Jules. I'm a lost cause in this regard."

"You're not in love with him."

All color drained from her face. Her legs seemed to momentarily wobble beneath her. She blinked up at him, taken completely unawares.

His eyes narrowed, all mischief banished. "No," he muttered. "I don't believe you are. Fool's luck, I suppose."

"Whatever are you talking about, Jules?"

His sudden grin took her breath away. "One thing about reformed rogues, dear lady. They never, ever squander opportunity. On that you can lay all your money. As for your shaggy beasts, however noble they might have once been, they could spend entire lifetimes not knowing what to do with all the opportunity in the world. Perhaps because they're too damned proud and stubborn to recognize it if it fell in their mangy laps . . . until it's too late."

She detected a hint of bitterness chilling his voice, a distant look in his eyes as if some memory haunted him. It seemed Jules Reynolds hid much beneath his elegant veneer, at least more than he would ever let on. Teddie laid a gloved hand on his sleeve. "I suspect even Valiant was mangy once."

His face relaxed with his smile and his voice dropped conspiratorially low. "Don't tell anyone, but beneath it all he's a plebeian. As mangy as they come."

"He puts on a good show."

"He has no choice."

Teddie smiled up at him, her heart warming. "I promise to tell no one, Jules. And you must promise to remain my dear friend."

Jules sighed wistfully. "Dear lady, keep looking at me like that and I'll promise you anything."

A movement out of the corner of Teddie's eye caught her attention. "Winchester," she whispered, half to herself. At first sight of him her blood leapt in her veins and her dress seemed to grip her tight all over, particularly over her breasts. He'd apparently just arrived, but he didn't pause beside Wildair or Simon. Instead, he marched straight toward Teddie and Jules, white shirt sleeves billowing, powerful legs in their black breeches and tall black boots churning up the ground in long, determined strides. His eyes spat black fire and his mouth twisted in a grim, unforgiving line. Teddie pressed a hand over her heart, feeling it hammering beneath the ivory silk.

Jules glanced over his shoulder. "Ah. He arrives. And in an unusually obvious ill humor, the reason for which will undoubtedly present itself momentarily. If instinct serves, I'd wager it has something to do with your conspiring with the enemy."

"We've done nothing untoward," Teddie said as a flush swept to her hairline.

"Try telling him that. Winchester jealous. Imagine that." Reynolds peered closely at her, then added wistfully, "A pity you'll never blush for me like that."

Teddie glanced sharply at him. "Jules—"

He lifted one gloved hand, then leaned slightly nearer, his voice dipping low. "If I'm to emerge the loser in this, which is becoming painfully apparent to me, I say we have a bit of fun with it. Are you game?"

Teddie blinked at him. "I-I don't know what you're up to, but I don't think it would be wise to—"

"Trust me, you'll thank me. In my experience, in dealing with the common, mangy beast it never hurts to tweak his tail a bit." Reynolds arched a confident brow and drew himself up as if squaring his shoulders for a good fight. "Nothing could be more satisfying to me than teaching your husband a well-deserved lesson."

"A lesson? In what, pray?"

"Why, love, of course. What else?" Reynolds spun around to greet Winchester before Teddie could retrieve her voice.

"A smashing good day to you, old boy!" Jules boomed, slapping Winchester on one meaty shoulder, which did nothing to temper his scowl. "You really should try to do something about your mood. Always so damned grim. You're not reconsidering the wager?"

"Never." The resonant rumble of Winchester's voice plunged straight to Teddie's core. She was having a devil of a time keeping her eyes off him, particularly when he pinned her with his gaze and a vagrant breeze ruffled through his ebony hair. Her heart seemed to turn over in her breast. Her throat closed up and went dry, all of which made little sense. She should have disliked the man immensely given his recent behavior.

In the last week since Damian's departure, she'd spoken with Winchester only three times. Each had occurred in passing, usually in the foyer or the wide center hall, their conversations brief and businesslike, all discussions of her progress through the pile on his desk, which as she'd expected was going swimmingly. They'd shared only one meal, that being a formal dinner in the dining room where twenty could have easily joined them at the table. The meal had passed in conspicuous silence, Winchester distracted and cool, and Teddie stubbornly determined to ignore him. She'd thought him an abominable boor, deserving of his misery. When he paid attention to her he treated her like his secretary. He never spoke in anything but a growl. And he hadn't even had the courtesy to offer Aunt Edwina more than a snarled greeting when she arrived unexpectedly one afternoon to visit.

Why, then, did Teddie feel as though a yawning void had been filled the moment she spotted him across the paddock? Surely she hadn't missed the man!

Beneath his unflappable regard Teddie was certain she would burst from her gown with the next breath. There was nothing genteel or gracious in his manner. Nothing gentlemanly in his open perusal. He was quite obviously a man who felt no compulsion to put on airs of any kind. She wondered if he realized his eyes burned like twin flames.

"Ladies," he murmured with a curt nod at both Teddie and her aunt. Yet he offered nothing more to betray the reason for his agitation.

"You know, old boy," Jules interrupted, a thoughtful frown puckering his brows despite the levity in his tone, "I've given some thought to the wager myself. Doesn't seem quite fair that you should lose two horses whereas I place only one in the balance."

Winchester folded his arms over his chest and regarded Jules with a dubious look. "Feeling philanthropic again, Reynolds?"

"Just being gracious. And feeling damned lucky, truth be told. Wouldn't want to deal you a crippling blow."

Winchester's smile was bleak. "You won't be given the opportunity."

"Indeed. But have you considered, even briefly, that you could quite possibly lose?"

"I don't ponder impossibilities."

"Then humor me a moment. Do you deny that losing two Bulle Rock mares would devastate you?"

"If it happened, yes, I suppose it might, but therein lies the challenge. Without it why race at all?"

"Certainly wouldn't want to take the fun out of it for you. Hell, if I'd known you felt that strongly about challenges, I'd have demanded that you put half your stable in the balance. Maybe next time."

"Fine. I'd wager you anything, anytime."

A sudden hush fell over the crowd surrounding the paddocks as all attention riveted shamelessly on the two men. The spectators all understood that once a wager was made there was no acceptable excuse for withdrawing it, unless the stakes were raised significantly. The air crackled with heightened anticipation.

A master of the dramatic moment, Jules paused, obviously as taken aback by Winchester's bold challenge as Teddie. "Anything?" he asked slowly.

"Anything," Winchester replied.

"That certain, are you?"

"Absolutely."

With a mounting dread Teddie glanced between the two men. They stood all but nose to nose, chests jutting, chins outthrust, booted feet braced wide, thighs bunched. What had been a friendly rivalry suddenly simmered with far deeper passions. Winchester's arrogance today bordered on recklessness. Knowing Reynolds as he did, he should have realized the folly in this. Teddie certainly did, particularly since she suspected Reynolds was up to great mischief.

She loosened her grip on her parasol, aware that every muscle in her body tensed in anticipation. Winchester would not take kindly to being taught anything, particularly by Jules Reynolds.

Reynolds squinted into the distance for a moment. "Anything, you say? So be it. I believe your arrogance defies even mine, old boy, and demands that I raise the stakes to new heights. If Valiant wins, I want only the one mare and"—Jules swung his gaze to Teddie—"one afternoon in the charming company of your wife."

Teddie swallowed. From Aunt Edwina's direction came the sound of a great sucking in of air. Gasps swelled all around them.

Winchester barely flinched, the only evidence he'd even heard Reynolds the heightened tic in his jaw. His gaze never wavered from Reynolds. "Done," he said tonelessly. Then, with a cutting glance at Teddie, he turned and strode back to Wildair.

As he swung onto Wildair's back, Teddie felt her stomach fall to her feet. Bitter disappointment welled inside her. Something stung her eyes and the devil if she knew why.

"You are a naughty man, Jules Reynolds," Aunt Edwina sniffed, but the tap she gave his arm seemed more playful than scolding.

Jules regarded Aunt Edwina through hooded eyes. "If only I could agree with you, madam, I would be a profoundly happy man. But just this once I can't. Enjoy the race, ladies." With a polite incline of his head he swung about and made his way back to Valiant.

Teddie spun around as well, bracing herself against the flurry that no doubt itched on her aunt's tongue. But whether the crush of the crowd or the stifling heat was to blame, Edwina offered nothing until they'd found a choice spot to view the race at the center of the grandstand just before the race was to start.

Even then her comment was decidedly brief. "I do so enjoy Jules Reynolds, don't you, dear? Such a delightfully wicked man. Always up to some sort of fun."

To Teddie's way of thinking there was nothing fun about this new wager. But lest her aunt suspect that anything had upset her, she murmured her assent through stiff lips and trained her eyes on the two horses, both black as pitch, rearing and circling in front of the grandstand as they jockeyed for the coveted position at the rail. The starter stood to one side with his pistol pointing skyward.

The crowd instantly grew hushed. Teddie held her breath, gripped her parasol, and fixed her eyes on Winchester as Wildair reared, pawed the air, and gave a piercing scream. A tap of his quirt against Wildair's thick neck brought the stallion's hooves to the ground. He was a masterful rider, his mount unmatched in strength, depth, and heart. His confidence and arrogance were well-grounded. Otherwise, he never would have risked letting her spend an entire afternoon in the company of the most notorious philanderer in all of Virginia. Or had his damnable male ego left him little choice but to agree to any wager Reynolds put forth?

Her insides twisted in knots at the thought of him losing this race. Oddly enough, the reason had very little to do with Reynolds's wager . . . and far more to do with Winchester's wounded pride.

The shot jolted through Teddie. A thunderous roar erupted from the spectators. As if shot from a cannon, both horses bolted away at full speed.

Chapter Eleven

Wildair didn't gallop or spring like the graceful Valiant. All fire
and spirits, he scoured the earth like a demon of pestilence, his
nose erect as if he sniffed a distant field of corn, his mane and
tail floating like a pirate's pennons. On his back Winchester
loomed like the mighty god of storms, thundering over the
ocean to engulf a fleet. Beside him, Jules Reynolds sat his
horse as though he'd been born to do so with unmatched elegance.

"If that bloody Wildair wins it will be to the shame of all
propriety and horse science," Aunt Edwina sniffed, craning
her neck as the horses bent into the first turn, neck and neck.

Noting the grip her aunt maintained on her reticule, which
tinkled as though heavy with coin, Teddie remarked, "Not to
mention what Valiant's loss would do to the weight of your
purse."

"The devil take my purse," Edwina scoffed as the horses
moved stride for stride along the backstretch. "Nothing is half
so satisfying as watching a man eat a plateful of his own
blasted pride. Your Winchester is too smug, and I'm not talking
about bloodlines. It's high time he had his comeuppance.
Damn and blast, but I think Wildair is pulling away. Can you
see, Theodora?"

Teddie rose on tiptoes and leaned over the railing just as the
horses rounded the far turn. As one they barreled toward her,
Valiant at the rail, Wildair directly at his side, their hooves
churning dust in their wake.

"I can't be sure," Teddie replied above the roar of the
crowd. Her voice suddenly caught in her throat. For some reason the image of Winchester and Jules thundering toward her
stirred a memory as disturbing as it was vague. Something

about the way they sat their mounts, the way Winchester's sleeves billowed and Jules's waistcoat flapped in the wind roused a peculiar suspicion in her. She narrowed her eyes, but they swept past in a roar of hoofbeats and a cloud of dust, and the memory eluded her.

"They're running them into the ground," Teddie said, chewing at her lower lip. "At this pace they'll be lucky if they don't break both horses."

Aunt Edwina snorted. "Give a man a chance to prove himself possessing of no more sense than a child and he will exceed your every expectation. Make it a test of his physical abilities—ha! What are two broken horses to the man who emerges victorious in such an arena, with hundreds to witness his triumph? Pride clouds good sense. That's why we're in the midst of this stupid war. Why, if it were left to the women of this country, there would never have been a bloody war. We would have come up with a way out of it that wouldn't have spilled a drop of blood. We are ruled by compassion, not by boastful arrogance and pride just waiting to be avenged." Her soft gray eyes angled at Teddie. "Don't tell George I've been talking like this. Like most men, he can't abide progressive thinking in a female. They don't understand us and therefore label our behavior as conniving and ruthlessly scheming. They can't understand why we don't applaud the ordering of our young men into the jaws of battle. There is nothing proud or noble in war."

"I couldn't agree more," Teddie replied. "But I think Uncle George listens to you more than you think."

"Of course he does! I afford him little choice, poor man. But who wouldn't listen to good sense? After twenty years of marriage even the most stubborn man can't help but come around in his thinking. But if he takes my opinion into consideration he doesn't tell me right off. Good heavens, what would Madison do if he found out I'd given George all of his best strategic ideas?"

Teddie stared at her aunt. "Are you orchestrating naval maneuverings out of your parlor, Aunt Edwina?"

"You give me too much credit, dear."

"No. I believe I'm sorely underestimating you."

"Balderdash. You're too smart for that. Good heavens, here they come."

Teddie snapped her head around. As they rounded the far turn, Wildair, still on the outside, pulled away by a head. In a flash of dust and thunder they swept past the grandstand and into the final lap of the race.

A lump lodged itself in Teddie's throat. She gripped the rail, stood on tiptoes, and gritted her teeth as they swept into the backstretch. She blinked, struggling to differentiate between the two mounts. Their necks pumped vigorously, Wildair a nose ahead, then Valiant a nose ahead, stride after stride. Their ears lay flat against their heads as they stretched themselves flat out and entered the far turn. Miraculously, neither rider had yet applied his quirt.

"Here they come," Teddie whispered as the horses barreled out of the last turn.

"It's Valiant," Aunt Edwina said, her gloved fingers digging into Teddie's arm.

"No, it's not."

"The devil it isn't."

"It's Wildair by a nose."

"You'd better hope it isn't."

"I beg your pardon, Aunt Edwina. I—" Teddie swallowed her words. Closer and closer they came, lumbering down the track with froth spilling from their mighty chests and noble heads pumping.

Amidst a thunderous applause, they swept beneath the string. Aunt Edwina let out a most unladylike whoop and threw her arms around Teddie. Teddie's mouth went bone-dry. Valiant had won by a nose.

The trill of crickets filled the early evening air when Teddie stepped through Miramer's front door. She moved into the foyer, her eyes lifting to Jillie slowly descending the stairs, a silver tray in one hand bearing an empty crystal decanter.

"Has Winchester arrived?" Teddie asked, well aware that the servant had donned her usual cloak of haughty subservience. But Teddie was not about to allow the woman to get under her skin, no matter that she was fairly certain Jillie's duties extended beyond the normal realm of a servant. As if to further impress this on Teddie, Jillie paused one step above her and drew a hand to the gaping neckline of her gray gown, where the row of parted buttons offered easy access to what lay beneath. In spite of herself Teddie felt a knot gather in her belly at the thought of Winchester availing himself of such an opportunity. A sudden urge to pinch the other woman nearly overwhelmed her. She squashed it and instead twisted her fingers into her skirts.

"He has," Jillie replied, then, in a tone that had undoubtedly brooked little argument from her fellow servants, she quickly added, "But he doesn't wish to be disturbed."

"I see." Lifting her skirts, Teddie turned and proceeded into the salon, where she found a full decanter of brandy on the sideboard. With decanter in hand she swept past Jillie and up the stairs with a breezy "I trust he has a glass."

"He doesn't wish to be—"

"Yes, you told me. That will be all for this evening, Jillie."

"But, madam—"

Teddie drew up sharply, her skirts swinging as she glanced over her shoulder and offered Jillie a grim smile. "Thank you, Jillie, but I know the way." She proceeded up the stairs and into the main hall of the east wing, self-satisfaction welling from her belly. She decided this had a great deal to do with the look of utter shock that had emblazoned itself on Jillie's pale face.

And yet when Teddie reached the door to Winchester's chamber and lifted her hand to knock on the wood, she froze, all confidence draining out of her. Memory flooded over her in an unwelcome deluge. Even the flickering wall sconces and the elusive spicy scents here seemed to evoke sensual images better left buried deep.

She swallowed and squared her shoulders. Sometime during the afternoon she'd determined that a clearing of the air was vastly in order. For some blasted reason it mattered very much to her that Winchester understand that she played no hand in

Jules Reynolds's mischief earlier that day. She wasn't about to let a few vagrant memories keep her from her task. After all, she was made of stern stuff. Women of stern stuff didn't fall victim to romantic fantasy, no matter how tempting it might prove.

Again she lifted her hand, then dropped it to the door handle. At her gentle touch the door swung open on well-oiled hinges. She bit her lip. Logic demanded that she turn around now and flee. She was tempting something here . . . something dangerous, something deliciously forbidden.

The lush burgundy-draped chamber glowed with warm golden light from candles lit in every corner. With heart hammering in her breast and her voice clogged in her throat, Teddie took another two steps into the room. And then she saw him— very little of him actually, just the back of his head and the magnificent breadth of his shoulders. The rest of him was immersed in an enormous gilt-edged marble tub set before the windows.

Miles opened his eyes on the glorious sunset beyond his windows. Though the door made no sound as it opened, he instinctively knew it had. The subtle stirring of air over his skin had roused him more than Jillie's hands could have tonight. Guilt stirred somewhere in the distant recesses of his soul. He was surprised that she'd returned, given that he'd shown little interest in her efforts to please him tonight. And for the past four nights.

He might not have been disturbed by this if he wasn't certain his lack of interest in her had everything to do with his preoccupation with his new bride.

He might as well have handed Teddie to Reynolds on a silver platter, with a bow tied under her stubborn little chin and a plump cherry between her teeth. A pity he had no one to blame but himself.

"You can fill this for me, Jillie," he muttered, indicating his empty snifter on the table beside the tub without glancing over his shoulder at her. He wondered how much brandy he would require to numb the emptiness he felt tonight, or if it were even possible. He'd spent the better part of the afternoon attempting it.

Again he closed his eyes. He listened to the rustle of her dress as she moved near. Her step seemed oddly hesitant. Crystal trembled against crystal as she filled his glass. Her breaths came short, as though emitted through softly parted lips.

Strange that he should be so acutely attuned to her of a sudden. . . .

It was then that sweet lilac fragrance spilled over him. White-hot desire shot through him an instant before he opened his eyes, his fingers encircling her wrist before she could even think to turn and flee.

"Good evening, wife," he rumbled, his body coming alive as if from a hundred years' slumber. He was acutely aware that with one tug of his hand she could be in his lap.

She closed her eyes, blushed an uncommonly enchanting shade of pink, and gulped three times before she managed a squeaked, "I-I—"

"You've come to gloat." His voice sounded thick, slightly hoarse. For all the reasons he might have to be angry with her for the part she'd played in Reynolds's little show, at the moment he couldn't recall a single one. His thumb brushed over the inside of her wrist where a pulse fluttered beneath the soft skin. It seemed even a woman of remarkable cheek and intelligence could be struck without words in certain situations. "How brave of you, my dear wife, to think to do it here in my chamber," he said.

She opened her eyes, blinked furiously as though uncertain where she could safely look—the clear depths of the tub being the very last place—before averting her flaming face to the windows. "I-I didn't know that you would be in your bath with no—that is—without any of your—"

"No, you couldn't have known that I bathe without my clothes, odd as it might be. Otherwise, I don't suppose you would have come at all, even were the house burning down. Of course, you could have fled the moment you opened that door. And you didn't."

"I didn't think you would talk to me unless I caught you somewhat unawares."

"That you did," he said softly, narrowing his eyes on her luminous profile. He could still remember the taste of her lips as they trembled open beneath his.

"And I knew you were expecting someone."

"Ah. That." A sudden curious compulsion to explain himself overcame him. "She's my—"

"I know who the devil she is."

He detected a fleeting shrill note in her voice, a faint high-pitched strain, and found himself at once chest-puffingly pleased even as he was possessed of an urge to clarify her obvious misconceptions. "Jillie has been with me since I returned from Tripoli. She's my—"

"Don't explain."

"I want to."

"Please let go of my hand."

"No. You'll leave."

"That would seem the prudent thing to do. You have no clothes on."

"Quite true. But I can still explain myself, especially to clear up a misunderstanding."

Her nose jutted up another inch, her eyes still averted. She looked like a prim and pristine school mistress, high-buttoned and overflowing with self-righteous indignation. To Miles's eye she couldn't have been more appealing at the moment had she tried. "I understand perfectly, Winchester. In my education I became aware that men have what they loosely and frequently refer to as 'needs.' This seems a very natural occurrence, one that was impressed upon me as being beyond a man's control. Denying these needs results in tremendous anguish and discomfort, not to mention the disastrous effects this would have on the mind. Over the course of a few months a man could go mad."

Miles felt his lips twitch upward, his mind filling with the image of a wide-eyed Teddie eavesdropping on her schoolmates. "You're remarkably educated on the subject."

"Thank you, Winchester. So you see, I understand perfectly.

I'm not the least bit angry or upset about something that is beyond your control. I don't care in the least whom you choose to fill this particular need—''

"Of course, you don't."

"—be it Jillie or that blond widow with the shrill voice—''

"That would be Lydia."

"Whoever. I truly haven't given the matter a moment's thought."

"Obviously. Then you wouldn't be interested to know that I've been a faithful husband."

She swallowed, glanced swiftly at him, then just as swiftly turned away. But her chin seemed to quiver. "No. I've not the slightest interest in that. Why should I? We have an understanding."

"Contract bound," he murmured, his thumb rubbing over her wrist. "And what if I go mad, Teddie?"

"Jillie won't allow it."

"Jillie has nothing to do with it. Neither does Lydia, or any other woman for that matter. Save one."

Her breath seemed to catch. Silence hung. Miles loosened his fingers around her wrist, then slipped his thumb beneath the ruffle at the edge of her sleeve and slid it several inches along the inside of her forearm. Through hooded eyes he watched her upthrust bosom expand. His entire body went rigid. "Tell me why you came here, before I reconsider my contractual obligation."

She turned to him, her eyes glowing with unspoken desires, dewy lips parting with her whispered words. "Which obligation would that be?"

He surged up out of the water, on fire with need, his blood raging beyond his control. Her mouth fell open, her eyes flew wide, and she might have stumbled back had he not grabbed her by her upper arms and lifted her flush against him, from breast to hip, fully impressing his burgeoning need upon her.

"There will be no games between us," he bit out, battling a devouring urge to crush his mouth over hers. Every sweet inch of her molded against him as though specifically formed for that purpose. "Rest assured, I will let my need for you drive me mad before I give in to it and play into your uncle's hands. All your efforts will be in vain. You can't tempt me.''

She blinked up at him, her eyes guileless pools of deep purple. ''I didn't come here to tempt you. I-I only meant to explain that I had nothing to do with Reynolds's wager.'' She pressed her palms against his chest, her feather-light touch sending shafts of desire plunging through him. ''I want you to know that I wish you'd won the race. I suppose I also wanted to ease your pain—''

''I don't need your comfort,'' he snarled, his grip on her arms tightening as his most savage desires raged a brutal war on his convictions. Christ, but he would have preferred that she'd confessed to scheming with Reynolds. This would have offered him some solace and would have bolstered his defenses. The more innocent she was, the more pure her offer of comfort, the more sweetly irresistible she became. He'd never known such torture. He couldn't imagine how he'd survive it.

Releasing her, he grabbed a towel from a nearby chair and slung it around his waist, knotting it there, his gaze never once wavering from hers. ''I'm warning you now,'' he rasped, gritting his teeth against his crumbling defenses as he stepped from the tub to tower over her. ''I've conquered temptation far greater than your sweetly whispered words and lush body. I've prevailed over diabolical enemies. I've clawed my way out of an opium-induced madness in the middle of the desert. *I won't be brought to my knees by a woman. . . .*'' He wanted to shake her, throw her from his mind, but he found himself powerless, his hands incapable of anything but a firm tenderness on her skin as he grasped her upper arms and pulled her close. Her eyes swept closed. Her full lips parted with a husky breath that cut through him like a fiery blade. ''I won't, damn you,'' he rasped. One hand caught at the back of her head, his fingers digging into the silken curls, spilling them over her shoulders in a lilac cascade. ''No games,'' he groaned. ''Do you hear me?''

''No games,'' she whispered, her arms sliding around his neck. ''Miles . . .'' Like a supple willow she arched against him, offering her mouth up to his. "I don't know why, but I want to kiss you, Miles, quite desperately."

"You don't know what you're doing, Teddie—"

"I know I don't," she murmured, rising on tiptoes so that her breath played against his lips. "Teach me."

Miles went rigid as stone. "Open your eyes, Teddie. Look at me."

Thick lashes swept upward. "What does *consummate* mean, Miles?"

Miles gritted his teeth. "I don't like where this is going."

"The contract was quite specific regarding consummating, but it said nothing about kissing. We wouldn't be in breach of contract by—"

"You're not listening to me, Teddie."

"Yes, I am. I've heard you state several times quite emphatically that you are beyond temptation. I can't tell you how reassuring that is to me, Miles, since all this tempting you've been accusing me of has been rather incidental on my part." Her soft smile brought a lump to his chest. "I wouldn't know the first thing about seducing a man. But at the moment I have this urge . . ." Her fingertips whispered over his mouth, tracing the firm contours. "We women are compassionate creatures. We have a shameless need to make things better. I want to make you better."

"You can't." He caught her hand in his, his gaze probing deep into hers. "No one can."

One fine brow arched over eyes hooded by passion. She looked like the most accomplished seductress known to man. "You're afraid of something . . . maybe that I'll glimpse what lies beneath all your anger?"

"You won't like what you find."

"I disagree. You're not as adept at hiding it all as you might wish to think. I think you realize it and that scares you. Damian achieved a glimpse the other day, didn't he? And you didn't like that at all. So you stomped and snarled your way through the rest of the week. Far better to let us all think you some arrogant boor, hmm? I suppose anyone could find comfort even in that over time."

"Amazing," he murmured, his eyes narrowing. "It's the challenge, isn't it?"

"I've always been intensely curious, if that's what you mean."

"More curious than anyone should be. But you warm to the challenge. The overcoming of odds. The discovery of the unknown. The lure of secrets. We all have them. Even you, I suspect."

"I suppose we all do," she said quietly.

"We're alike, you and I. Dangle something we can't possess in front of our noses and we become obsessed with possessing it. Like that damned contract. By signing it I made you unattainable to me. As a result I'm obsessed with having you."

The corners of her mouth tipped up. "You are?"

"I've conquered obsessions in the past."

"So you keep telling me." She inclined her head and stared at his mouth. "I still have this urge to kiss you." Her eyes lifted to his. "It's not a test, Miles. Honestly, you're forever on the lookout for enemies, aren't you? Must keep the guard up, I suppose. Well, you should be pleased to know that I think you are the most stubbornly unyielding man I've ever known, possessing of a will of steel."

"I am," he grunted.

"Thank heavens," she murmured, drawing his head to hers as she rose up on tiptoes and pressed her body against his. Her breath played warm and sweet on his mouth and her lashes fluttered closed. "Then one small kiss won't hurt at all, will it?"

"No," he heard himself rumble as he gathered her close in his arms. Some things in life, no matter a man's will, couldn't be denied. And God knew her argument made convoluted sense to him. Why not? It was, after all, just one small kiss. Nothing at all, in truth. Hardly a test of will.

Their lips met in a warm, gentle exploration, a lingering tasting of breaths, a parting, a moment's hesitation. Their chests expanded against each other.

"That was nice," Teddie breathed, lowering her head.

"Yes." Miles pressed his forehead to hers, his desires tightly reined, for the moment.

"Are you all right?"

"Quite. You?"

"Very well. I-I don't suppose another would hurt."

"If it would make you happy, wife. In that regard the contract was rather specific." With one finger beneath her chin, he lifted her lips to his again. They trembled for a moment beneath his, then parted at the first sweep of his tongue, offering up the sweet depths of her mouth. At once all reason fled, and all restraint. He was like a parched soul given his first taste of water. No strength of will could have kept him from drinking his fill.

He wanted to devour her from the inside out, to draw her breath deep into his lungs, to possess the essence of her. If she'd let him he would consume her.

He crushed her in his arms, molding her as close against him as possible, and slanted his mouth over hers. The tempest he'd thought long dead raged with mighty abandon in his blood, breathing life into him. With this woman it seemed he was again wholly a man.

With a cry she twisted her head away and gasped for breath. Her palms pressed against his chest, but he allowed her no retreat or escape.

"What is it?" he whispered, pressing his lips to her temple where the tendrils curled with winsome abundance. He filled his lungs with her scent, his hands with the delicate feel of her, and in his soul an ache swelled so poignantly his chest grew tight.

"Y-you take my breath from me," she whispered.

"You take mine when you enter a room."

Her head dipped. In the soft light her cheeks flushed a deep rosy hue, and Miles was all but overcome with the need to gather her gently in his arms and tenderly rouse her. Given the depths of his unleashed ardor not moments before and the savagery this demanded to fulfill it, he found his thoughtfulness difficult to comprehend.

"I should go," she said, her eyes lifting to his. He detected hesitation in her, a self-consciousness in her touch, in her voice, and in her eyes. He found it captivating and strangely intoxicating.

He nearly asked her to stay with him, then caught himself. What the hell? It wasn't as if he was lonely, dammit, as if he needed her. He'd never needed anyone, least of all anyone's compassion and tenderness. He particularly didn't need a woman who intended to make him the subject of her abundant curiosity. Afforded even a little opportunity, she could indeed probe deep. He'd just experienced it. And he wasn't a man who enjoyed being unsettled.

"Yes, you should go," he said, his thoughts adding a gruff edge to his voice. And yet it was with a certain deeply felt reluctance that he released her and bent to retrieve his brandy. Lifting the glass, he took several deep gulps, hoping to clear his mind. "Reynolds intends to come at noon tomorrow," he said, watching her closely. "For several hours."

She met his abrupt change in manner with chin jutted, nose lifted, and stare unerringly forthright. "Then I must go at once. Otherwise, I'll be up half the night deciding what to wear. Good night, Winchester."

And then, before he could have anticipated such a thing, she rose up and pressed a kiss to his stubbled cheek. In a swirl of lilac-scented ivory skirts, she turned and swept out of the room. Miles stared at the door as it closed softly behind her. Already the chill had descended over his room. In moments it reclaimed his soul.

One good thing about a big house: Slipping out of it undetected in the depths of night was easily accomplished. Silent as the movement of the clouds in the midnight sky, Teddie closed the side door behind her and hurried down the path that led to the stable. Beneath her simple cotton dress she wore a black shirt, breeches, and knee-high boots. In one boot she'd stuffed her pistol. In the other her knife. Over her shoulders she'd slung the black cloak. In her hand she carried the wide-brimmed black hat.

The stable latch lifted easily and she snuck within. Blinking several times, she allowed her eyes to adjust to the dimly lit interior, then hurried to the rear of the stable and peeked into the darkened back room.

"Empty," she breathed with relief. Over the past several nights, as she'd enjoyed her evening stroll around the gardens, she'd noted that Simon left the stable for his quarters somewhere between nine and ten each evening. The idea of explaining her need for a midnight ride to the smiling-eyed overseer didn't sit well with her. Not that she wouldn't do anything to ensure Will's safety, her deception of her aunt and uncle being the very least of it. But Teddie wasn't a born liar. No matter her well-founded reasons for doing it. Guilt still washed over her every time she met her aunt's gaze. It would be the same with Simon if she was forced to lie to him.

Turning to Cleo's stall, she slipped the bridle into the mare's mouth and led her toward the door. With some surprise she noticed that Wildair's stall was empty as she passed. Perhaps Winchester had found the need to take to the saddle this evening.

This stopped her cold. She chewed at her lower lip, envisioning an unexpected midnight encounter with him. Explaining her unusual dress to Simon was one thing. A delicate circumstance, but not beyond her. Knowing Winchester, and with the memory of his kiss still rousing tingles all over her, she doubted she would be capable of composing a logical sentence, much less a believable tale. But explaining herself to him would be the least of her worries.

She still couldn't understand what had come over her in his bedchamber. She'd behaved no better than a wanton, all but struck senseless at the sight of him in his bath, as bold and glorious as a king in his ridiculous, oversize tub. A tub designed to accommodate a man and a woman with ease.

And when he'd surged up out of the water looking like the venerable Neptune himself, and water and candlelight had spilled over his skin . . .

Her cheeks went instantly hot. There was nothing diminutive about the man. Of this she had been made instantly, alarmingly aware.

God help her if the urge to kiss him overcame her ever again. She doubted it would, given the unexpected ferocity of his response. Surely that would hold her for a while . . . although she could imagine that some women—of far looser moral fiber than she, of course—might find being so soundly ravished rather addictive. The idea of a midnight encounter beneath starlit skies would hold tremendous appeal to those women.

Teddie shook herself, banishing such a notion. "That wouldn't do at all. I must meet with *Cockburn* tonight, as planned, not Winchester."

Her mind flew, seeking a more logical, more amenable explanation for Wildair's absence. At a sudden thought her mood brightened considerably. Winchester had left the stallion in a pasture for the night. That was it. After his race that afternoon, what better place for a magnanimous loser to recuperate than an open field of abundant grass?

Dismissing the matter entirely, she mounted Cleo and urged her around the back of the stable and into an open field, where the soft turf was certain to muffle her hoofbeats and the shadow of tall timber flanking the field to the north concealed her movements. She kept her pace frustratingly slow until she reached a low rise some distance from the house and the slaves' quarters. Only then did she dismount and shed her dress, secreting it in the bramble beneath an enormous sycamore. She tucked the knife and pistol into her waistband, donned the wide-brimmed black hat, and remounted Cleo. With a grim set to her mouth and a swift kick of her heels, Teddie turned the mare toward the east, where the waters of the bay loomed on the horizon.

Chapter Twelve

From a thicket atop a sloping dune a half mile north of Lighthouse Point, Miles watched the mammoth British man-of-war ride at anchor not a sixth of a mile out. Every instinct he possessed dictated that a rendezvous between Cockburn and the Night Hawk impostor would occur tonight, precisely one week after the last known rendezvous. Over the past several weeks he had experienced firsthand the difficulty in tracking Cockburn's ship along the coast. Without a prearranged time and location his impostor would have the same trouble.

Watching the ship, Miles couldn't help but sense that it waited there, purposeful in its stealth. The darkened decks seemed deserted, eerily silent, as though Jeremiah Cockburn had ordered all hands below and all lanterns doused. Save for plundering the coast, Miles could think of no reason for Cockburn to anchor his ship so near the shore. And from what Miles had heard of Cockburn, if the British admiral wished to come ashore and wreak havoc and devastation on the Virginians, the deserted region around Lighthouse Point seemed an unlikely choice. Cockburn would choose a highly populated area like Hampton to do his pillaging and looting.

No, Cockburn had come to Lighthouse Point for more covert reasons. That this seemed the most logical and most obvious assumption momentarily concerned Miles. Farrell's men patrolled the coastal areas nightly for signs of impending British land attack and to capture the traitorous Night Hawk. If Miles had spotted the British ship so near shore, then he would be remiss in thinking Farrell's men wouldn't at some point. And when they did they would be certain to come and investigate.

His gloved hands gripped tighter around Wildair's reins. The muted rush of waves on the shore provided a soothing, surreal background. Silver-bellied clouds scudded low in the indigo sky, driven by a restless, hot wind that snapped at Miles's cloak.

Restless . . .

He shifted in his saddle, his gaze intent on the man-of-war's decks. He waited for the telltale flash of swaying lantern light. With an inevitability that was becoming distinctly less disturbing to him, his thoughts strayed to Teddie. His wife: as elusive as a moonbeam, and for that reason as captivating as any woman could ever hope to be. He'd spoken the truth. She'd become an obsession for him, but he now realized the obsession reached far deeper than the simple terms of a mere slip of paper. With each interlude his fascination for her seemed to reach new levels. Not because she had been made forbidden to him in the most primal sense. Not because Reynolds intended to pursue her beneath Miramer's roof. Because of who she was. Because he realized he wanted an entire lifetime of sweet, lingering interludes to peel away all the layers of her. Because for an instant she had brought sunlight into his soul.

And he wanted more of that. So much more.

As he lingered there in the dark thicket with the wind whistling through the grass, he realized the true depths of his loneliness. How could she have sensed it so quickly?

Wildair suddenly went rigid. His ears pricked forward, his nostrils blowing with the scent he'd caught.

"Easy," Miles murmured, leaning over the stallion's neck. His eyes probed the darkness for some shadowy movement. He saw nothing. His ears strained for telltale hoofbeats. This impostor was undoubtedly an experienced horseman and his mount exceptionally surefooted. They'd approached without making a whisper of sound.

Not for the first time, Miles felt a reluctant admiration for the bold fellow, no matter the nature of his business with Cockburn or the threat he represented to Miles's own schemes.

Out of the corner of his eye Miles caught a flicker of movement. There—not twenty feet to his left, a ripple of shadow, a heightened stirring of the tall grasses, and then a lone horse and rider stepped from the thicket. Miles stared as if looking at his own silhouette when a gust of wind spread the impostor's cloak like giant wings.

Anger surged through him. To hell with admiring the fellow's audacity. He'd put Miles's own neck at tremendous risk for his own purposes, not to mention the manner in which he'd impudently flaunted the Night Hawk's reputation. No one did that to a Winchester!

Miles dug his bootheels into Wildair's flanks, and the stallion leapt from the thicket and plunged down the dune directly into the impostor's path. With a growl of rage Miles reined Wildair sharply up the dune toward the impostor. To his credit the fellow, obviously caught unawares, reined his nimble mount about in the sloped dune with an agility unmatched by many horsemen and plunged into the tall grass that flanked the main road for a quarter mile on each side. Unfortunately for the fellow, whatever deftness Miles and Wildair lacked due to their size they more than compensated for through sheer strength and determination.

In three enormous strides Wildair's hooves gobbled up the dune. In another five he'd overtaken the impostor. Miles drew Wildair alongside the slighter mount and leaned well out of his saddle, one hand grasping for the impostor's bridle. His fingertips just brushed the leather strap when the impostor recklessly swung his mount away toward a dense thicket. Miles bit out an oath as he steered Wildair after them and gave the stallion every bit of his head. Only a fool would plunge his horse into that tangle of overgrown thorny brush at full speed on so dark a night with no moon to guide him.

A fool, perhaps. Or someone desperate enough to do almost anything to escape. A part of Miles understood that. Still, as much as he wanted to capture the fellow, he wasn't about to risk injuring Wildair to do it. He had to catch them before they reached the thicket.

This time he leaned from his saddle and reached for the impostor's reins just before Wildair surged alongside. Miles realized the inherent danger in this tactic, considering that both horses extended themselves at breakneck speed toward a looming wall of dense brush. Wresting control of another mount and

its reluctant rider was difficult enough in the best of circumstances.

Just as his fingers wrapped around the bridle strap and the
two horses jostled together, it occurred to Miles that the fellow
was quite possibly armed. Why he hadn't thought to withdraw
his own pistol struck him like an invisible blow. Admiring the
fellow was one thing. Treating him as anything other than a
dangerous foe was quite another. And damned stupid of him.
No Winchester had ever let down his guard, unless he fully
intended to grapple with the consequences.

He expected the white-hot lashing of a blade across his middle or the crack of gunfire as a lead ball ripped into him.
Instead, a booted toe jabbed him squarely in the shin. Another
sharp jab met his knee. And another. The frenzied slash of the
fellow's arm caught Miles on the side of his head. Another
connected soundly beneath his chin. Miles's jaw snapped.
Snarling, he stood straight up in his stirrups to slow Wildair
and maintain his hold on the other horse's reins. A tenuous
position at best, leaving him for one wrenching moment vulnerable to any sudden change in course. He realized his folly
an instant too late.

With a hoarse cry, the impostor slashed his quirt against
Wildair's neck. At once the stallion braced all four legs, nearly
skidding to his rump in the sandy earth before lunging forward
and tearing his reins from Miles's hand. Then with a piercing
scream the stallion rose up on his hind legs, with forelegs pawing the night sky. The impostor's rein jerked from Miles's hand
as well. In a last attempt to keep his seat and maintain hold of
the other horse, Miles caught the fellow's arm just as the quirt
again whistled through the air toward Wildair's neck.

With one flex of his arm he drew the impostor all but out of
his saddle and up against the entire length of his side. At once
Miles went rigid, unexplainably, and his grip for an instant
slackened. As if sensing his momentary advantage and with a
lightning-quick movement, the impostor drove a sharp elbow
into Miles's side and slashed the quirt through the air. The end
of the whip lay a scalding path across Miles's left cheek. Like
water spilling through Miles's fingers, the impostor slipped

from his grasp and somehow managed to regain his seat astride his own skittish mount. The pair tore off into the darkness toward the thicket.

Miles clawed at air for the loose reins, growling incomprehensible commands. The frenzied Wildair lunged, then reared again, and Miles tumbled from his back, landing soundly on his rump in a clump of grass. To Miles's utter amazement, Wildair took off after the impostor with tail streaming and nose lifted, looking nothing like a loser for the second time that day.

Springing to his feet with a vivid curse, Miles watched the impostor disappear at full gallop into the thicket. Wildair had enough sense or, as Miles preferred to think, good training not to follow blindly. With head held proudly, he returned to Miles.

"What the hell happened?" Miles roared, grasping Wildair's reins and mounting swiftly. "Damn. Damn. Damn." He reined Wildair toward the thicket, fairly certain that the impostor hid there and fully intending to follow his foe into hell and back if that's what it took. It was then that he heard the muted thud of hoofbeats on the road directly to the north.

He gritted his teeth. "Christ." Not one set of hoofbeats. Clearly more than one. An entire regiment of hoofbeats. And he stood in an open field of grass with Cockburn anchored not a quarter mile away. They wouldn't pause to ask questions at this point.

It seemed the Fates were determined to get him in Farrell's hands one way or another.

Bitter frustration welled in his throat. Swiftly, he considered his options. As much as he was confident in Wildair's abilities, he wondered how much horse he had left after the race that day and their recent encounter with the impostor. A flat-out race on open road against a well-mounted regiment didn't seem the prudent course, given his close call with a regiment bullet just a few weeks past. Briefly, he considered taking refuge in the thicket. Something about that option did not appeal to him. It seemed the impostor possessed a great deal more patience than he did. Indeed, he could envision waiting hours in that thicket for the regiment to scour the area to their satisfaction, hours of doing nothing but waiting. No, he'd never been good at that.

Besides, the regiment could possibly follow him into the thicket, and he had no intention of leading them to the impostor just yet.

On a sudden thought he reined Wildair left, toward the shore. It was without question the most unlikely course, through sand, surf, and uneven dunes, requiring a certain familiarity with the coastline. The regiment wouldn't think to follow anyone there. Just as they wouldn't think anyone hid in the thicket, quietly awaiting the opportunity to emerge.

Cockburn's ship still rode at anchor when Wildair surged over the dune then plunged toward the smoother sand nearer the water. With rage simmering anew, Miles pointed the stallion south and gave him his head. Only when he was certain that he hadn't been followed did Miles abandon the shoreline for the open roads that would take him back to Miramer.

Teddie held her breath and stared into the pitch of the thicket surrounding her. Her heart pounded in her chest like the regiment of hoofbeats thudding on tamped-down earth. Her hands shook as she twisted Cleo's reins tighter, her palms damp within her leather gloves. Perspiration wove in narrow trails from her temples and down her chest. Irritably, she swatted at the mosquito-infested darkness.

She strained for the sound of the regiment's hoofbeats, fading into the distance to the south. The regiment could just as quickly return to this area, particularly if they'd spotted Cockburn's ship. Undoubtedly they had. To Teddie's way of thinking, then, she had a narrow window of time to make her escape.

Exhaling in a long, trembling breath, she dug her teeth into her lower lip and forced the tears from her eyes.

"Calm," she said half-aloud. Inhaling deeply, she willed the tension from her limbs, the panic from her heart, the terror from her mind. "Think clearly." A difficult prospect, given that she'd nearly been caught. By the mysterious Night Hawk. *He'd been waiting for her.* The thought parched her throat. He could still be out there, lurking in the darkness, enraged beyond reason. He could kill her by sheer brute strength. When he'd lifted her out of her saddle as though she weighed next to nothing, he'd fully impressed upon her the unleashed power in his formless bulk. She wondered why he hadn't killed her then and been done with it.

A shudder tremored through her, followed quickly by a frustration so raw and deep that a sob broke from her lips. What would Cockburn do if she failed to meet him tonight? What would happen to Will?

Somehow she had to signal Cockburn's ship. Concern for her own hide at this juncture seemed inconsequential given that Cockburn held her brother at his fickle mercy.

Gingerly, she urged Cleo from the thicket into the open field and toward the soft rise of the dune. The wind still tossed the grasses. The clouds still scudded low across the sky. She could see no sign of the Night Hawk or any regiments. Yet.

She didn't realize she held her breath until she drew Cleo to a stop atop the dune and her breath released in a rush. Cockburn's ship still rode at anchor a sixth of a mile out. With trembling hands she unhooked her lantern from the side of her saddle and lit it. Slowly, she swung it to and fro, paused, then swung it again, the signal to abort their rendezvous.

Moments later an answering signal flashed from the ship's decks.

In two nights she would try again near this spot. She bit her lips against the tide of frustration engulfing her and watched for several moments as the *Rattlesnake*'s sails were slowly unfurled. Opportunity lost.

Will . . .

Swallowing the lump in her throat, she reined Cleo south and dug her heels into the mare's flanks. Sand sprayed from beneath the horse's hooves, followed by the splash of surf as Cleo lengthened her stride. Wind-whipped tears pooled in Teddie's eyes and she shoved them away.

Two days. She sniffed and dug deep for renewed determination. Logic dictated that the Night Hawk would be expecting her to rendezvous again in precisely one week. Not two days. It didn't matter. She'd evaded him twice. She'd do so again. Even if it took more than a few kicks to his knees and a quirt to do it.

He might have denied her tonight, but she'd be damned if she ever allowed him to again.

Not more than a half hour later Teddie lifted the latch to Miramer's stable and led a soundly cooled Cleo into the dimly lit interior. She took two steps and froze, her heart lurching in her chest when she saw the silhouette of a man standing not two feet in front of her.

"Good gracious, S-Simon," she breathed, trying not to notice the shaking of her voice, trying even harder not to fidget with her hastily donned gown, whose top five buttons had been left conspicuously open when she'd slung it over her head. Thank heavens she'd left the cloak and hat in a pile just outside the stable door. In her present state of mind there would be no explaining her need for those garments.

The gangly overseer stepped from the deeper shadows into the arc of lantern light. His smile was easy, his manner as affable as always, and yet Teddie was distinctly certain that he was a man who made a habit of noticing much. "Ma'am," he drawled in his singsong voice, giving her a nod and hooking long thumbs in his suspenders. Something about his manner, however congenial, prompted her to offer more than she might have given her circumstances.

She swallowed and motioned vaguely to the door. "I-I couldn't sleep. So I-I went . . . riding." Again she swallowed, his silence making her increasingly uncomfortable. She tried her very best to assume the air of a noble mistress of the manor—albeit an insomniac mistress—one who had just returned from a midnight ride about her vast acreage. Forcing levity to her voice, she added, "It was quite lovely. Just what I needed."

"You bes' don' go too far. No tellin' what you gonna find out on the roads aftuh dark . . . thieves . . . deserters . . ."

"Indeed," she said quickly, then bit her lip. Simon watched her so closely, she wanted to squirm. "And I certainly wouldn't want to meet that mysterious Night Hawk fellow everyone is talking about, now, would I? From what I've heard of him he's quite a frightful fellow."

Simon seemed to ponder this, his wide stare unflinching. "Most folks ain' a bit afraid o' him, ma'am. They ain' got no reason to be."

Perhaps not, particularly if he was supplying them all with smuggled goods like fine Jamaican rum. But she surely had reason. He could foil everything for her. The sooner she could get Cockburn after him, the better. "Anyone who rides about in the deep of night is only up to no good, Simon," she said, unaware of the irony of her statement until Simon arched a knowing brow at her as she moved past him toward Cleo's stall. She averted her hot cheeks and tugged especially hard on Cleo's tether when the mare resisted. One glance in Wildair's stall offered the reason for the mare's distraction. The ebony stallion reached his finely tapered nose over his stall and nipped at Cleo's flanks.

"Winchester didn't want him out all night eating his bellyful of grass, I see," Teddie tossed over her shoulder as she led Cleo into her stall then closed the door behind her. Giving the mare a final pat on the neck, she turned to Simon. "Is that why you're here so late, Simon? To tend to Wildair?"

"Yes'm." He nodded at the quirt she still held in one black-gloved hand. "I'll take that to the back room fo' you if you like, ma'am."

"Yes, of course. I certainly don't need it." She handed him the quirt and wondered why the devil she felt so squirmy with him. It wasn't as if he could see into her thoughts and probe the depths of her deception. A quivery smile curved her lips. "Thank you, Simon. Good night."

The black gave her a slow, mellow smile that should have dissipated all her distress. But for some reason it didn't. "Good night, ma'am. I's hope you sleep well."

Though the chances of this were decidedly slim, Teddie found herself longing for the haven of her room as she never had before, and her steps were swift and purposeful as she made her way to the upper west wing. Perhaps there she might find a moment's solitary peace to put her troubled mind to rest. If only for a brief time. Circumstances would allow her nothing more.

Her dilemma loomed clear: She must effectively deal with the Night Hawk before he unmasked her. What he intended to do with her after that she could only guess. Turning her treasonous hide over to George Farrell was the most obvious course. Torturing her for impersonating him was another. Killing her—no, she wouldn't think about that. She wouldn't give him the opportunity.

In a few days' time she would learn all she could of the mysterious Night Hawk from the slaves, from Winchester, even from Jules Reynolds. And then she would hand all her information over to Cockburn. Together they would lay a trap for him, with her as the bait.

The thought of conspiring with Cockburn to trap anyone brought a sour taste to her mouth and a sick feeling to the pit of her belly. The man had proven himself merciless with prisoners. How could she justify purposely delivering anyone to such a fate?

And yet Will's life hung in the balance if she didn't effectively remove the Night Hawk's threat. Besides, Cockburn would feast on such a scheme, perhaps enough to agree to an exchange of sorts. Will for the Night Hawk. She clung to the thought and battled her reservations. There was, it seemed, no other way. It wasn't as if she were betraying a friend.

Still when she finally closed her eyes and restlessly sought sleep, she couldn't shake the fleeting sense of disquiet roused by her plan. And something more troubled her . . . something elusive, lurking in the misty, sleep-shrouded edges of her mind . . . something she couldn't quite grasp. . . .

"Look at him. Arrogant bastard's early." With a snort of disgust Miles all but leapt from Wildair's saddle; he handed the reins to Simon with such force that the leather snapped. Planting his hands on his hips, Miles squinted against the midday sun and glared at the sleek ebony carriage speeding up Miramer's drive behind a pair of superbly matched white horses. The sparkling carriage wheels churned a cloud of dust in their wake, a potent testament to the carriage occupant's impatience. The intricately scrolled *R* emblazoned on the door of the conveyance and the impeccably liveried footman and driver attending it left little doubt that Jules Reynolds had arrived with grand aplomb to reap the rewards of his wager.

"You done it to yo'self," Simon observed with little hesitation in his voice. "An' now you gonna pout."

Miles narrowed his gaze as the carriage swept to a halt at Miramer's entrance. "I've never pouted in my life, dammit. And if I ever did it certainly wasn't over something that wasn't my fault."

"Uh huh," Simon grunted, his disagreement obvious. "I didn' see no one pointin' a gun at yo' head an' makin' you take that bet from Reynolds."

"No one needed to. I had no choice but to take it."

"Had to save face?"

"Precisely."

"Uh huh."

Miles shot the Negro a withering glance. "No Winchester ever backed away from a challenge, Simon."

Simon grunted again. "Yo' gran'pappy would o' bet his whole stable 'fo' he let anothuh man wager time wit' his own wife. An' *he* wouldn' o' cared who knew it neither. Yo' gran'pappy was a grand man. An' proud as a bantam rooster. But it didn' bother him none if everybody knew what he cared 'bout mos' in his life. An' it weren't his horses, his tobaccy, his money, or his own pride, I can tell you that straight off."

"What the hell are you suggesting, Simon?"

"Oh, I weren' suggestin' nothin', *suh*." Simon's carefully placed emphasis belied every trace of subservience. "Uh uh. I ain't suggestin' that maybe you startin' to care more 'bout yo' wife than you rightly think you should."

"That's enough, Simon."

"An' I ain' suggestin'," the Negro continued in his lazy singsong, "that if you could have it any other way you'd give ol' Reynolds Wildair hisself to git him to go on home now. I ain' suggestin' that you 'bout eatin' yo' fists over this. Uh uh. I ain' suggestin' that fo' a man who's got all kinds o' work to do, you's standin' here lookin' fit to kill somebody, an' it ain' over tobaccy prices. I ain' suggestin' none of that, *suh*, 'cause I knows you a smart man. 'Bout as smart as yo' gran'pappy were.''

"Thank you, Simon. My grandfather was a brilliant man."

" 'Course he weren't half so blind-proud as you. He wouldn' waste his time poutin' over his own mistakes. He'd have a plan o' his own to fix it. Uh huh.''

Miles glanced sharply at Simon and felt his chest puff within his billowy white linen shirt. "And what makes you so damned certain I don't have a plan . . . not that I need one?''

"You's out here talkin' to an ol' man like me, an' Reynolds is 'bout to go in there an' git yo' wife.''

"Reynolds hasn't gotten anything, dammit.''

"Not yet, I s'pose.''

They both watched as the footman swept the carriage door open and Reynolds lurched out, walking stick in one hand, a wide-brimmed, plumed hat in the other. "Christ, look at him,'' Miles muttered. "The man's wardrobe exceeds those of the best-dressed women in all of Gloucester County. Have you ever seen a topcoat of that precise shade of crimson, Simon?''

"No, suh. He's a fine-lookin' man. Miss Teddie's sho' to think so.''

Miles shot Simon a sharp glare. "I don't own any crimson topcoats, Simon, or any damned feathered hats, for that matter. I never have and I never will, particularly not to catch a woman's fancy. So don't even think—''

"I ain' suggestin' that you need any o' that. Miss Teddie's not likely to notice.''

Miles stared at his overseer, then scowled at Reynolds as he lumbered toward the front door. "Quite right. She's an unusual woman. Highly unusual. A man has to appeal to her in less than obvious ways. Truth to tell, it's not her that I'm worried about.''

"Oh, I reckon she can handle Reynolds.''

"What makes you so certain?''

"Oh, I s'pect that lady could turn a man aroun' on hisself an' inside out without him even knowin' it.'' Simon met Miles's glare with innocently raised brows. " 'Course I might be wrong.''

"Indeed, you just might," Miles muttered wryly, giving his overseer a dubious frown. "Rare as that is. Quit trying to teach me a lesson and get to work."

Simon gave a brief incline of his head. "I'll tend to Wildair, now."

Miles nodded. "See to his shoes. The left rear seems to have jarred loose after last night." A cloud descended over his features at the first thought of the prior night's events. Thoughtfully, he stroked the stallion's tapered muzzle. "Next time our impostor will be begging me for mercy, eh, boy?"

"Unless he gets lucky and escapes again, eh?" Simon muttered under his breath, his mockery almost palpable.

Miles's heard his teeth click. "It wasn't prowess, dammit. It was luck, a fool's luck. Nothing more."

A rolling chuckle rumbled from Simon's throat as he slowly shook his head. "Yo' gran'pappy weren't half so blind-proud as you. Uh uh. He knowed when he's beaten."

"Beaten?" Miles barked. "I'll have you know the fight hasn't even begun."

"Uh huh. You's the one wit' the sore backside this mornin'. No one else. An' you stand here sayin' *he's* the fool. You wanna know what I's think?"

"I don't suppose it would much matter if I didn't, Simon."

"I's think you like chasin' him. I s'pect you's forgotten why you's aftuh him in the first place. It ain' got nothin' to do wit' him spyin' an' impersonatin' you. You just want him 'cause you can' git him. An' that makes you itch."

"Rubbish. He's a threat to my operation."

Simon snorted. "C'mon, Wildair. 'Tween you an' me, I ain' never seen a man so damned stubborn. Blind, to boot. There ain' no hope fo' him."

Miles stared after the pair, wondering why the hell he suddenly felt entirely out of his element at every turn this morning, particularly when he had more than ample reason to be content. His crop flourished. His ship was nearly ready to sail for the West Indies directly beneath the bribed noses of a British fleet. Success seemed imminent. Miramer would continue to prosper. All his efforts had proven fruitful. Even the memories of Tripoli seemed to have lost their brutal edges and merciless, almost constant tormenting.

So why the hell did all that, which had meant so much to him for so long, and still did—why did it seem of secondary importance suddenly? Why was his mind so easily distracted? It was as though some other force possessed control over the turn of his thoughts . . . as though his senses were under perpetual bombardment, his desires under constant siege, his will under grueling test. And amidst it all, reason and logic, and level-headed thinking had abandoned him.

He was not normally a jealous or violent man. And yet he could taste the satisfaction he would get from pummeling Reynolds into the ground.

He was not normally a man given to daydreaming. And yet his mind was perpetually flooded with visions of his wife, day and night. The nightmares of the past had fled.

His torment had taken new form.

As if at his silent bidding Teddie emerged from the house and into the sun-dappled brilliance of the day, like a delicate butterfly unfolding its gossamer wings to take flight. And like that butterfly she would flutter, radiant and elusive, forever just beyond anyone's grasp. Even in her acquiescence last evening in his chamber, she'd retained her aura of mystery. If Reynolds hadn't already realized this, he would soon give up the chase.

Enchanting. Captivating. Winsomely seductive. She was all of these with such guileless ease, Miles was struck with the realization that she was his.

Yet not his.

Possessing her physically was forbidden to him. But possessing her soul as he suddenly yearned to do . . .

Slowly, he started toward them, his strides growing longer, his step lighter, his world a touch brighter when she suddenly glanced away from Reynolds and their gazes locked. The smile lighting her eyes faded, then trembled on her full lips. He knew precisely when memory plunged through her mind and the startling images of last evening blossomed anew. A magnetic charge seemed to pass between them. And her cheeks blushed so enchanting a shade of pink the roses lining the veranda should have bowed their heads in shame.

The smile that burst upon his lips seemed to well from the aching pit of his soul. Warmth, and wave upon wave of satisfaction, flooded over him.

Hell if he knew why. His wife was all but in the arms of another man. And he'd put her there. But in doing so he hadn't promised not to make a nuisance of himself.

Indeed, with what Miles had in mind, Reynolds would wish he'd never stepped foot on Miramer today.

Chapter Thirteen

❖

Teddie wasn't easily scared. She also wasn't prone to dramatics. Unlike many of her female contemporaries she had never made a habit of courting high drama for the sake of feeding an overblown sense of self-worth. Even in the most dire situations she tried to maintain a level head, and had succeeded on many occasions to such a degree that her stalwart good sense rivaled that of the most unemotional of men. A Herculean feat, or so her father had often proclaimed, given that she was descended of a line of females notorious for their lack of good sense and frequent bouts with the vapors. In all her twenty years Teddie had yet to crumple to the floor in a faint.

It was, then, with some distress and confusion that she felt her knees wobble and a peculiar liquid sensation wash over her when she realized that Winchester strode directly toward them. Given that she had anticipated some sort of grand male brouhaha to erupt once Reynolds arrived, and being confident in her ability to deal with Winchester's black moods, her marked reaction to his approach bewildered her. What the devil had come over her? Dealing with male confrontation was typically not a daunting prospect. She'd done it all her life, at school, with her father and Will, and more particularly with Cockburn. So why did she feel so blasted weak all of a sudden?

The closer he came, the more peculiar she felt. And then she realized. His brow lay smooth and unfurrowed. His eyes sparkled with vitality, as though lit by the deep creases around them. Those creases around his eyes . . . she'd never seen them before. Her heart lurched. Within her pale-yellow cotton bodice her bosom swelled as her breath trapped in her lungs. She stared at him, at the half-smile flirting with his lips and all but obliterating the scar on his cheek. Astonishingly, he looked years younger. He looked marvelously happy.

He looked nothing like a man intent on a grand brouhaha.

What the devil had happened to him? With a growling, scowling, grumbling boor, she was willing and able to deal. But with this . . . this . . .

His transformation paralyzed her.

She gulped as a breeze ruffled through his hair and billowed in his sleeves. His shoulders seemed miles wide, his hips impossibly narrow, his legs thick, the musculature superbly displayed by his dove-gray breeches. If only she could catch her breath.

"A smashing good day to you, Reynolds, *old boy!*" His hearty slap on Reynolds's shoulder would have toppled any man less stalwart. Before Reynolds could respond with more than a dumbfounded stare, Winchester dismissed him with a turn of his shoulders and swung his disarming smile on Teddie.

The world pitched, then righted itself. Or perhaps his firm grip on her fingers was all that saved her from dissolving in a heap. "My dear," he murmured, his voice hushed, his breath warm upon the back of her hand as he pressed his lips to her skin. His gaze lifted quite obviously to her mouth, then drifted over her high-buttoned collar and along the row of tiny pearl buttons adorning her bodice as though he memorized the shape and texture of each button. Or sought to commit to memory the shape of what lay beneath.

"Beautiful," he murmured, his eyes flaming, betraying a passion so startling in its intensity that Teddie had to gasp for a breath. She yanked her hand from his and immediately squelched an urge to draw it to her lips.

"Jules," she breathed, blinking up at Reynolds as though seeing him for the first time. Odd that she should feel so grateful for his presence. Had he not been standing there, she would have felt entirely at Winchester's whim and mercy.

"Yes, I'm here," Reynolds replied with his typical charming smile. Yet his gaze deepened and narrowed on her briefly before angling at Winchester. "Whatever it is you ate this morning, I'd like to try some of it. Even cut yourself shaving with all that exuberance, I see. Such a rare good humor I find you in."

"I am," Winchester rumbled in a voice so evocative of sensual images, so simmering with implications, Teddie's every nerve tingled with an odd anticipation. She could barely keep her eyes from straying to his, knowing he watched her with an intensity that would have rivaled a wolf on the hunt. "You expected otherwise, old man?"

"You're not a magnanimous sort of loser."

"On the contrary. I'm a splendid loser when the occasion presents itself. Ah, but you wouldn't have known that, would you, Reynolds? I haven't lost to you before. And I don't intend to ever again." His bravado was palpable, his arrogance expected, but beneath that simmered an undertone of mischief that couldn't help but fascinate Teddie. Winchester, mischievous? Ridiculous.

"You're up to something," Reynolds mused, folding both gloved hands on his walking stick and giving Winchester a dubious look that matched Teddie's.

Winchester smiled at Jules, his lips parting so easily, his eyes twinkling so devilishly, Teddie wondered how she could have thought him incapable of feeling mirth or warmth. Or mischief.

She stared at him, aware of a fluttering sensation gathering deep in her belly.

"Ah, hell," he muttered, planting his hands on his hips. "I suppose you'd like to know if I'm feeling well, eh? Or if I overindulged in spirits this morning? I'll save you both some breath. I feel fine. Fit as ever. Can't a man walk around with a damned smile on his face without rousing suspicions that he's up to something devious?" He glanced between the two of them, one black brow arched, his lips compressing. "I see. I'll have to do something about your more pressing misconceptions."

His gaze lingered obviously on Teddie, prompting another blush that she averted by turning to Jules Reynolds. Unfortunately, it wouldn't have mattered where she put her eyes. She sensed that Winchester's regard had settled with a disturbing permanence on her. Something told her she would have to grow accustomed to it today. It also mattered very little that Jules Reynolds was quite possibly the most handsome, dashing, and charming man in all of England and Virginia, a man any woman would find difficult to ignore. A man not typically used to being upstaged or outwitted by another man.

As much as she wished otherwise, her senses were under continuous, riotous assault from only one man, a man who required no brilliant-colored topcoats, jewel-studded accessories, or eloquent speeches to capture her fascination or enhance his darkly mysterious allure. He only had to smile.

So much for tweaking the beast's tail and teaching him a lesson or two. Winchester seemed to have turned the tables on them both.

If Teddie betrayed any of her thoughts, Jules was gentleman enough to ignore it. "I'm distressingly aware of what little time we have together, my dear lady," he said. "Shall we embark on our day? A stroll in the gardens first, followed by a display of my rather limited talents on the pianoforte? I might even be persuaded to give you a rare turn around a dance floor."

Teddie instantly fell under his charm. "I'd love it. And we'll enjoy a midafternoon luncheon in a charming spot I've discovered near a stream. I've much to discuss with you, Jules. I've stumbled upon a curiosity and was hoping that you can help me with it."

Setting his plumed hat jauntily on his head, Jules offered a brief bow. "I'm in your service, particularly if there's a mystery to be solved." From beneath the broad brim he slanted Winchester a cool look. With arms folded across his chest and boots braced wide, Winchester looked as immovable as a fortress. "Judging by that glint in your eye," Jules muttered, "I suppose it would be too much to hope that you've mountains of work to accomplish today, eh?"

"Far too much to hope," Winchester replied with an abominably satisfied grin. "I've the entire afternoon free."

"Imagine that," Jules replied. "Something tells me I've only myself to blame."

"Underestimating the enemy, I'd say. A beginner's mistake.

That's not usually like you, Reynolds. Getting sloppy in your old age, perhaps?"

"It's a mistake I won't be making with you ever again," Reynolds replied, his tone plunging ominously low, simmering with almost threatening undertones despite his outwardly affable air. "On that you can be sure."

Winchester met his gaze with eyes gone instantly steely. "You can take both mares and leave now. We can call it even. No one need ever know the difference."

The air suddenly sizzled between the two men. They faced each other squarely, chins jutting, chests straining together, stares battle-locked. Teddie bit her lip and wondered why men were forever allowing their pride and competitive natures to get the better of them. To her way of thinking, somewhere along the way these two had deprived themselves of a rare friendship.

After several tense moments Reynolds shrugged and slapped Winchester on the shoulder with a great deal more fervor than he would have displayed with a good friend. "And deprive you of your fun? No, I think I'll keep to our wager, even if you intend to spoil it for me by coming along."

"You'll be joining us?" Teddie heard herself say to Winchester, certain that the idea caused her heart to trip along at a heightened rate.

Winchester's gaze hooded on her. "I can't think of anything I'd rather do. Besides, I'm sure Reynolds would enjoy a tour of the plantation, wouldn't you?"

"The thought hadn't occurred to me."

"So you say. Not the least bit curious about your nearest competition for tobacco buyers?"

"Not half so curious as I am about Mrs. Winchester's bit of mystery. Touring your plantation sounds suspiciously like business to me. And you know I have an aversion to anything businesslike. Besides, I grow tired of seeking new ways to plant the damned tobacco. I tell you it will soon become inadequate support for the scale on which I wish to live. It's a dreary business, in all truth. I've an inkling the future of this area lies elsewhere. At least my future does. I'll spare you the trouble of a grand tour."

"It's no trouble. Unless you're not physically up to it . . ." Winchester arched a brow.

Reynolds's cane shot out toward the lawn, his shoulders thrown back wide. "Lead on, old boy. I'll meet you stride for stride."

"I never doubted it. Come, Theodora." Winchester left her little choice or moment's hesitation, tucking her hand in his.

Warmth spilled through her as he drew her close against his side. With a jaunty "Come along, Reynolds," Winchester turned to lead her across the veranda and out onto the lawns that flanked the house. As he swept her past Reynolds, she hooked her free arm with his and the three proceeded abreast down the front steps.

Teddie filled her lungs with the fragrant warmth of the day, drank in the sunshine, and surrendered to the heady feelings for the first rare moment in her life. For these two short hours the war, the death, the injustices of the world would all cease to exist beyond Miramer's brick-walled perimeter. She would grasp her moment of happiness with eager hands, embrace it and hold it dear. One misstep in the depths of night a few days from now and it could all be snatched away from her. Forever.

Through heavily hooded eyes Miles watched Teddie lean back against the thick trunk of a boxwood, which angled out of the stream bank as though purposely offering itself up as the one spot she might think to find rest against. To Miles's discerning eye the angle of the tree was perfect, and Teddie draped sinuously on it with her head turned in profile toward the stream and her back slightly arched, a visual feast. The early-afternoon sunlight set her aflame in her golden dress, offering up the dramatic fullness of her breasts and sleek limbs for his leisurely perusal. She looked like a long, lush plate of overripe fruit.

Either she had no idea what she looked like or she thought him asleep. Maybe both. There was no careful orchestration to her gestures, no outward sign that she was aware that he watched her from his spot sprawled on the grassy stream bank. With Teddie, seduction flowed effortlessly through her movements like prudently applied spice: never overwhelming, yet undeniable and impossible for him to ignore. That she remained unaware of her effect on men—on him in particular—only compounded her allure. That and his certainty that her thoughts were miles away.

With something close to pain, he watched as she drew a deep breath and the cotton bodice gripped around the swells of her breasts in perfect, full-circle outline. If he looked close enough he could see the thrust of her nipples against the smooth cotton, as though those pink buds ached to be free.

Desire shot through him like cannon fire. Shifting uncomfortably in his breeches, he imagined no prison more torturous than a lifetime of denying himself such a woman. Much more of this and he'd be on Farrell's doorstep begging for a privateer commission in his navy.

The irony of his circumstances struck him. For the first time in years he wanted a woman with a singularity of purpose that blinded him to all else. With a subtlety that astounded him, she'd freed him of the shackles he'd borne since Tripoli. And yet here he lay—in a spot that seemed designed by nature specifically for long, leisurely afternoons of lovemaking—a prisoner of his desires, with Reynolds hovering over his wife with a fastidiousness that would have made her Aunt Edwina proud.

Bound by contract. The words repeated in his mind like a mantra. Winchester men were bound by their word, known for their noble, upstanding code of honor. Yet somehow he couldn't imagine his grandfather Maximilian allowing a hastily signed contract to keep him from his wife's bed. After all, the entire British monarchy hadn't been able to do it. Why should a damned contract?

Of course, his grandfather Maximilian would never have signed the damned thing to begin with. His grandfather Maximilian wouldn't have set himself to an impossible task simply to prove himself worthy of the Winchester name. Guilt, it seemed, made men do incredibly stupid things.

"Enough of this," Reynolds said, heaving himself from the spread blanket, upon which he had been indulging himself in a feast of fruit, cheese, and wine. He stood for a moment massaging his right thigh as though he suffered a deep ache there. "My curiosity overcomes me, my dear Mrs. Winchester. For the past two hours I've entertained you with my singing, piano playing, and idle chatter." Reynolds's walking stick poked Miles in the thigh. "The old boy here tried his best to bore us with a tour of his vast and impressive holdings. Luncheon was delightful. This spot, a slice of heaven itself. And you, dear lady, are a rare gem to behold."

Miles stifled his snort of disgust in his wineglass. Teddie beamed.

"And yet you haven't broached the subject of your curiosity," Reynolds continued, clearly puzzled. "Your distraction is obvious. I don't easily suffer this from my female companions. I can't speak for Winchester here. No doubt he would prefer to sleep his afternoon away than ponder a woman's thoughts. I say we leave him to his slumber."

"And deny me the pleasure of your company?" Miles chimed in, levering up on one arm and slanting Reynolds an arched brow. Bracing one bent leg against the grass, he offered Teddie a look through half-hooded eyes. "Besides, nothing could be more captivating than a beautiful woman with a secret."

She drew up stiff, chin inching up. "I have no secrets," she said so quickly that Miles's first inclination was not to believe her. "I'm simply curious."

"Yes," Miles murmured. "I know."

"About the Night Hawk."

"Ah." Miles reached for a handful of grapes. One by one he lifted them to his mouth, his eyes never once straying from Teddie.

"The Night Hawk, eh? Now there's a mystery worth solving," Reynolds put in. "Damned elusive fellow. Some highly placed military men would prefer to believe he's the product of overactive imaginations. They can scarcely function thinking a spy lurks in their midst, especially since no one can seem to catch the slippery chap. For quite some time he kept to the southern shores of the James, near the Elizabeth, and farther south near Albemarle.''

"And his purpose there?'' Teddie asked.

Reynolds shrugged. ''If I were to speculate I'd say he's refitting a ship down there.''

"To run the blockade,'' Teddie said.

Both men glanced sharply at her, Miles, for one, taken aback by her quick deduction and her obvious curiosity about the Night Hawk in particular. He watched her brows knit, a sure sign that her thoughts flew, and found himself wishing she weren't so damned clever.

"But does he intend to engage the British,'' she went on, her voice thoughtful, ''or is he purely a smuggler?''

"My money is on the smuggling,'' Reynolds replied, then glanced at Miles. ''Old boy?''

Miles looked bored and forced a shrug through his shoulders. "Then I say he's going after the British, ship by ship.''

"The devil you believe that,'' Reynolds scoffed. ''You know as well as I that would be suicide, no matter how swiftly a ship is fitted or how heavy her guns. It's just beyond you to agree with me. Admit it.''

"The hell I will,'' Miles countered crisply. ''I say he's after the British, dammit. Care to make a wager on it?'' Miles's gaze locked with Reynolds's. For several moments the air grew strangely quiet.

"Good grief, listen to yourselves,'' Teddie huffed, hands on her hips, eyes blazing with contempt. ''Stop your childish fighting at once and help me with this. It doesn't matter what his intent is. How the devil does he intend to break through a British fleet?''

"With great care,'' Reynolds replied. ''He's outgunned and outmanned even by the lightest British frigate.''

Teddie nodded. "Their ships scour the coastline for privateers. And if he's doing all this refitting, wouldn't they become aware of it at some point?''

"Not if he's carefully hidden his ship somewhere in the sound.''

She seemed to ponder this a moment, then shook her head.

"Too difficult. Ships are rather large objects to attempt to conceal. And the British can smell a privateer. They would almost have to make a concerted effort *not* to notice his ship. And they'd almost have to be looking the other way the precise moment he decides to make a run—'' She stopped, blinked several times, then looked at both of them as if seeing them for the first time. "He's in league with them."

Reynolds stared at her. "He's in league with who?"

"The British." Her smile momentarily dazzled even Miles, who was rather grimly cursing the Fates for saddling him with a curious and meddling—albeit brilliant—wife. She'd make one hell of a military strategist. His only piece of luck in the matter was that Farrell was in Baltimore and at present unable to pursue her little theory. But for how long, Miles couldn't guess. Nor could he afford to push his luck in the matter. The sooner he made Watts and the *Leviathan* ready to sail, the better.

"Doesn't make sense," he put in, despite knowing full well there would be no swaying Teddie's opinion at this point.

True to form, she grimaced at him for attempting to rain on her little show, then showered the obliging Reynolds with the full force of her radiant smile. "That's it, Jules! The British know precisely what he's up to in the Albemarle Sound."

"There's a twist on the theory," Reynolds boomed. "He's a wily chap, spying in exchange for free passage through the blockade."

"Or he's bribing them."

"With what?"

"Food. Liquor. They're all but starving on those ships. And their prisoners fare much worse."

Something stirred in Miles, a distinct unease for some reason. Something in the way she spoke of the British, as though she knew precisely what went on in a warship. But how could she possibly?

"Exceedingly well done, my dear," Reynolds said. "They should send you to Washington."

She beamed, clearly pleased with herself, much to Miles's

chagrin. "Thank you, Jules. I couldn't have done it without you."

"I doubt that. But one mystery still remains: Why has the Night Hawk suddenly appeared farther north, precisely where Cockburn's ship is anchored, if not to spy? I can tell you top brass is in fits and frets over this. According to my delicately placed sources, rumor has it that all officers have been ordered to refrain from discussing military maneuverings with their own wives."

"Why would they—" Teddie blinked furiously for several moments, then pursed her lips and slanted Reynolds a teasing glance that captivated Miles. "The reason for this should have been obvious to me, Jules, knowing your notorious reputation with women. I can't imagine you'll allow marriage vows to get in the way of your inclinations."

"In some cases the husbands pose the greatest difficulty," Reynolds replied, his azure stare fixing pointedly on Miles. "However, in this instance I believe these military gentlemen suffer from an altogether different supposition, one that, as luck would have it, does not involve me."

"And what supposition is that, Jules?"

"The Night Hawk could be a woman."

Miles glanced up sharply, gripped by a sudden cold, grim realization. *His impostor was a woman.* Not a boy as he'd suspected. Chagrin flooded over him as he pondered this and half-hoped it wasn't so. Outwitted, outmaneuvered, outdone— by a woman? The idea was enough to gall him. Unfortunately, as much as he would have preferred to dismiss the notion out of hand, he couldn't. Indeed, the impostor's slight weight, lack of bulk, even his choice of mount could easily be attributed to a female. It certainly explained several things that had been troubling him since their encounter last night.

To his way of thinking, a male youth wouldn't have resorted to kicking and frenzied arm slapping to achieve his escape. He would have immediately drawn his weapon to prove himself. After all, men—even young men—fell victim to pride. Nobly defending oneself was far more instinctive and important to a man than achieving escape. Women, on the other hand, cared very little for putting on a good show, so long as they saved their hides.

A woman. A bold, reckless woman of the night, more brave and audacious than many men he'd known. A reluctant admiration stirred in him . . . and something more. He recognized it as interest fully, impatiently roused.

A woman.

It certainly would explain the bothersome matter of the unwitting and unexpected jolt of physical pleasure that had shot through him when he'd lifted the impostor out of his saddle. The ferocity of his bodily response had momentarily stunned him, perhaps because he hadn't expected it. His body, it seemed, had understood what he had refused to consider despite the clues.

A woman was making a fool of him. It was ludicrous. Almost incomprehensible. Enough to make him itch to crawl out of his skin. Little wonder he hadn't thought of it himself.

A scowl descended over his brows at another sudden thought. No one suspected that an impostor was on the loose. They all believed the Night Hawk had been a woman all along. Christ.

He should feel exonerated. Instead, he felt soundly outdone at his own damned game.

"A woman?" Teddie laughed, husky and full-bodied. She pushed away from the tree, her lissome movements drawing Miles's full interest and touching the spark to his smoldering desires once again. Beneath the yoke of their arranged marriage she had blossomed like a plump, ripe rosebud unfolding beneath the warmth of the sun. Her cheeks flushed as rosy as her soft lips, her eyes glowed an enchanting shade of violet, and she strolled slowly through the wildflowers as though she were one of them. Miles's fingers itched to pluck her, to make her his on this grassy bank, to lay her sweet skin open to the heat of his own bare flesh.

"Don't say that too loudly, or too often," Reynolds advised. "There are some very highly placed men in our government who can't eat or sleep for fear that word will leak out that a female spy has made a laughingstock of their best mounted regiments. National security is at stake here. Their very jobs hang in the balance over this."

Teddie drew a long-stemmed daisy to her nose. "They're that convinced the Night Hawk is a woman?"

"They are," Reynolds replied. "The notion mystifies and intrigues as much as it embarrasses them. I suspect their suspicions have something to do with the ease with which she has eluded them, as though she slinks through the night. Men on horseback don't know how to slink. They can outrun and outshoot, and they much prefer to prove this."

"You're suggesting that slinking is beyond them?" Teddie asked, one brow arching provocatively.

"Precisely. A man would never succumb to slinking."

"And a woman would? There's something fundamentally wrong with your thinking, Jules," Teddie said a touch crisply, her eyes raking over Reynolds. "But I'll let it pass."

"Ah. Could it be you've taken a liking to me?" Reynolds probed with his most dashing grin.

"Oh, I like you, Jules," she replied, her smile warming the furthest recesses of Miles's soul. "You're vastly helpful as a sleuth. It's your confounded male arrogance that I could do without."

That her violet gaze slid past Reynolds and riveted almost at once on Miles told him much. "A woman's arrogance can match a man's," Miles offered, his blood firing when she took the bait and her eyes flashed in warning. "Take our Night Hawk. Spying for the British requires extreme insolence and an almost instinctive bent for duplicity."

"Which is another trait reserved solely for women, I presume?" she said, her hands finding her narrow waist, her prim nose lifting with full-blown, self-righteous indignation.

"Convince me otherwise," Miles countered, rising to his feet and facing her squarely, a rather unwise move given the immediacy of his physical response to her. "Give it your best, Teddie. We men have centuries of experience with females. Ask any of us if we've ever met one who wasn't traitorous and duplicitous. Reynolds? Care to comment?"

"I'll leave this to you," Reynolds replied, his tone light with relief as he directed his attention to their abandoned luncheon. "I'm looking for more wine. Yes, here it is. Nearly empty. Blast. I don't suppose I could interest either of you in coming along to fetch some more?"

"No thank you, Jules," Teddie shot at him. "And if the Americans lose the war," she surged on, her eyes spitting violet fire up at Miles, "the men will blame it all on this one woman, I presume?"

"Sounds damned convenient to me," Miles replied, feasting on her glorious indignation. Her hair had begun a riotous descent from the knot atop her head and fell in abandon over her shouders. She blew at one wayward curl dangling over her forehead and moved a step nearer to further impress her glare on him. It was all Miles could do to keep his hands glued to his sides.

"Ha!" she spat. "I can almost hear them all concocting this ridiculous theory simply to avoid blame. 'Indeed, Mr. President, we did all we could, but, alas, the country fell to the British due to one woman's duplicitous nature. You understand, of course. It was her slinking about that inevitably did us in.' That they think no man capable of such deception proves to me why they haven't caught the fellow yet." She frowned up at him, her lashes sweeping clear to the fine arch of her brows. "They can't catch the Night Hawk, so to justify this they'll make her something she isn't and lay the entire war in her hands! She doesn't deserve that."

"No," Miles replied bitterly. "She deserves to be hanged. She's a spy, betraying military secrets to the enemy. And she will hang, once Farrell gets his hands on her. Someone is bound to catch her."

This seemed to stop her cold. "And what makes you so certain of that?"

"Her luck is running dangerously low," Miles replied, aware that his voice had grown thick and deep with his own vehemence and frustration, and with something more: the crumbling of his control, the roaring release of his basest desires. Grimly, he realized he had his limits with Teddie and at the moment, standing so near him, she tempted him beyond those limits. He should be considering what he said to her very carefully, treading very lightly in discussing the Night Hawk, trying his damnedest to get her on an altogether different subject. But careful consideration and the subtle maneuvering of a stubborn female suddenly seemed beyond him. At the moment his mind was possessed of only one consuming thought, which, oddly enough, would accomplish all that for him. A vision blossomed of Teddie sleekly laid out upon the soft grass, her mouth opened in a soundless gasp as he descended upon her.

"Luck?" She tossed back her head, inadvertently moving nearer to him. Only a whisper of air dared to pass between the melding heat of their bodies. "A woman is duplicitous, certainly not clever. Lucky, but never skillful. It would kill you men to admit that any woman had fairly outwitted you."

"It would, particularly with national security in the balance."

"How odd that sounds coming from you, Winchester. Do I detect a trace of patriotic fervor in your voice?" She arched a brow, her manner coy, as though she sought the perfect spot to burrow beneath his skin. He had half a mind to tell her she already had. "You, a man with loyalties to no one but himself, what should you care if a spy betrays this country, female or otherwise?"

"I believe we were discussing duplicitous females and the havoc they inevitably wreak on men's lives."

She stared up at him, the slight narrowing of her eyes betraying the turn of her thoughts. "Not all the tragedies and failures in men's lives are the fault of a traitorous woman."

"I prefer to believe some of them are." His chest expanded with his breath, testing the confines of his shirt, pushing into the softness of her breasts. "But the truth of it in my case is that the weakness was entirely mine. I failed to see through the beautiful facade once. It nearly got me killed."

"In Tripoli?" she said, her voice plunging intimately low, cajoling a response he should have kept tightly concealed had he possessed an ounce of sense or will to resist her.

"Yes." He lifted his hands along the slender length of her upper arms despite the warnings clanging in his mind. "No man in his right mind will allow himself to fall victim to a beautiful woman's wiles more than once. After the hell I went through I vowed I wouldn't.''

Her palms pressed feather-light against the upper planes of his chest, yet he felt the warmth of her touch reaching deep into the cold, lifeless pit of his soul. ''Have you kept to your vow?'' she whispered, her eyes dilating, her lips glistening dewy soft, just inches below his.

''Yes, damn you,'' he growled, resisting her with his mind, with his last vestiges of reason. His fingers dug into her upper arms, yet she didn't cry out or resist, even when he lifted her full against him and sparks seemed to shower between them. ''Winchesters keep their word. And their contracts, no matter the temptations.''

She stared up at him in silence for several moments. ''You have Jillie.''

He swallowed deeply, aware of a fierce need to lay her fears to rest. ''Yes. For base, physical release. Even I have those needs.''

''I see.''

''No.'' When she would have averted her face he grasped her chin and lifted her gaze again to his. ''Look at me. For some damned reason you have to know this. I haven't taken her to my bed since I found you there. In fact, it would be physically impossible for me to bed another woman at this point.''

Her lips parted, but nothing more than a soft breath escaped. Relief glowed in her eyes. She believed him. Simple as that. Somehow, while everyone else assumed the very worst of him, he'd managed to inspire faith in this woman. Warmth flooded over him, and a need so poignant he ached with it.

''Close your eyes, Teddie,'' he said, his voice suddenly hoarse. Sliding his fingers around her neck, he tilted her face fully up to his.

''Why?''

''I'm going to kiss you.''

''What about Jules?''

''To hell with Jules.''

''But—''

"Lesson one," he murmured, pressing his lips to her fluttering eyelids. "Don't think about another man when you're being kissed."

"But I'm thinking about him, I'm just wondering what *he* could possibly be thinking we're doing."

"Lesson two." He pressed the pad of his thumb to her lips, silencing her. "Stop talking. Jules had the good sense to wander off some time ago, looking for more wine."

"We ignored him, Winchester. You must be certain to send him a long letter of apology and invite him back."

"If it would make you happy he can visit daily. Now stop talking and close your eyes again. You're beginning to frustrate me."

"What about your vow?" Her arms slid around his neck as her lush young body arched with a wondrous abandon against him. "I wouldn't want you to fall victim to my wiles. It might cause you undue distress."

"I'll deal with that later," he growled, desire consuming him like flame leaping through dry tinder. "At the moment I've a far more pressing need." Slowly, he brushed his thumb over the fullness of her lips, back and forth, nudging them apart and laying open the soft warmth of her mouth. Gently, he traced the smooth inner curves of her lips until her breath came deep and fast, then slid his thumb over her teeth. "Open for me, Teddie," he rasped. Her pink tongue slipped between her teeth, flicked tentatively against his thumb, then retreated, inviting him deeper. He could almost hear the great crash as the last of the defenses crumbled between them.

He tasted her, lifted his head, then leisurely tasted the sweetness again, startlingly aware of a desire to pleasure her at all costs, to tenderly initiate her into the art of lovemaking, which required he keep his more savage desires tightly reined lest he scare her off. She trembled, stiffened, then melted in his arms with a groan of supplication.

Restraint was instantly but a memory, an impossible task for any man with so magnificent a woman. In all her innocence she'd never learned to suppress her desires, to ignore her base instincts, to preserve all chaste and pure notions of womanhood by resisting again and again, forcing a man to play along though both realized she would inevitably surrender. She knew none of that. She wanted precisely what he wanted, with a fervor that matched his.

Her gasps were desperate, pleading, full of mysterious yearnings that had lain undiscovered for far too long. Her hands quivered, smoothed, clutched as they molded his shoulders, gripped his biceps, then twisted into his linen shirt as though seeking the flesh beneath. With an abandon unlike anything he'd ever imagined in a woman, she met the full measure of his passions with her own primal, audaciously elemental need.

There was no retreat from the fury of his kisses, the plunging of his tongue deep into her mouth, the claiming of her hips and buttocks with his hands. There was no scandalized exclamation or fumbling resistance when he lifted her pelvis and rocked her against the bulge filling his breeches. As in all other aspects she matched his desires, her every sinuous movement challenging him for more, yet he'd never felt so supremely male and so spectacularly aware that she was female.

He was enflamed beyond reason, beyond hope. Nothing mattered but finding surcease within this enchanting woman. Not even his Winchester pride. Not even Miramer. He would gladly spend the rest of his life in noble servitude to Farrell with a foolish smile on his face as penance for one blissful afternoon with Teddie on this bed of grass.

He would consume her.

With a soft cry she twisted her mouth from his, gasping for breaths against the back of one trembling hand, then whimpering softly when his mouth plunged over the length of her throat to the lace-edged collar.

"No," he rumbled, sweeping her fingertips from the highest buttons. "It's too late for that."

"Oh, Miles," she breathed, her fingers threading deep into his hair, cradling his head closer to her breasts. She trembled like a sparrow in his arms. "We can't do this."

"We have to." Willing patience to his movements, he laid the row of tiny buttons open to the uppermost curve of her breasts. Slowly, reverently, he drew the cotton back, exposing the pearly mounds swelling above her cotton chemise. "I have to taste you," he rasped, lowering his mouth to the luminous swells and filling his lungs with the scent that was hers alone. Her name fell raggedly from his lips against her skin like the plea of a dying man. His mind swam with the staggering depths of his passion for her. His body quivered and ached with it.

Slowly, he lifted his gaze to hers, his mouth slack with desire, his soul laid bare, gaping open and raw. "I need you, Teddie. You can't deny me."

"I can't deny myself," she whispered, her eyes sweeping closed when his lips claimed the tender spot beneath her ear. "How could I possibly deny you? Please . . ." She caught his hand and pressed it to her breast. "Please, Miles . . . I promise to tell no one that we didn't abide by the contract."

A satisfied purr rumbled through his chest as he worked the last of the buttons free, then tugged the thin satin ribbon binding her chemise. "I've never found duplicity more appealing." His words caught as the sheer linen drifted open. "Sweet Jesus—" Gently, he eased the linen over one breast, then the other. Cupping one in each hand, he lowered his head and took one pink nipple deep into his mouth in one slow, languorous pull.

Her nails bit into his shoulders and she arched her back, offering herself up for much more. *"Miles."*

He lifted his head and feasted on the sight of her unbound, unrestrained, tousled, pink, and passion-swollen. "I want to watch the sun warm your bare skin . . . everywhere."

"Yes . . ." she breathed, her eyes limpid with desire, her fingers flying over the buttons of his shirt. As her palms spread the linen wide over his chest and shoulders, her tongue slipped over her parted lips as though she savored some delicious taste.

Fiercely, he crushed her to him. Softness melted into steely sinew. His mouth plundered hers, drawing her breath from her lungs. He was a man starved and she the one woman who could fulfill all his needs.

The heavens could have crashed to earth and Miles wouldn't have noticed. Little wonder then that he reared up like a lion caught unawares when Simon's raised voice finally penetrated his consciousness.

And like that protective lion, he swept Teddie behind his back as he spun around with eyes blazing and mouth set grimly.

"You'd best have a damned good reason, Simon."

"Yessuh. Indeed, suh." With his typical lack of regard for Miles's rage and sporting an abominably sly grin, Simon peeked over Miles's shoulder. "Aftuhnoon, Miss Teddie."

"Good afternoon, Simon," she replied, her forehead pressed to Miles's back.

"Out with it, Simon," Miles growled, his impatience and frustration reaching new heights when the overseer's face fell with his obvious concern. It seemed their streamside interlude would have to wait. Simon wouldn't have interrupted him without ample reason.

"It's Lizzy," Simon said, referring to his pregnant daughter. "The baby's comin'."

Miles jerked his shirt up over his shoulder, his brows meeting. "Lizzy? It's not her time. Not for at least another two months."

"I know. The womenfolk tol' me to come git you. They says the baby's gonna come today."

"I'll be right there, Simon. Fetch the medical bag from the house and meet me at Lizzy's."

"Yessuh." On winged feet, the overseer turned and raced back toward the house.

Miles turned to Teddie and found her fumbling with the buttons of her gown. "Let me." He swept her fingers aside and quickly tended to the buttons, aware that she seemed determined not to meet his gaze.

"I'm coming with you," she said, her tone brusque and businesslike.

Catching her chin, he lifted her gaze to his. Uncertainty lurked in her eyes and he ached to banish it. "Fine," he said. "I'll need your help." His lips curved with seductive promise, bringing another flush to her cheeks. "We've some unfinished business between us, wife."

"I suppose we do. But in the meantime one of us might change our minds about—"

"Not likely." His words drifted off as he yanked her against him and lowered his mouth to hers in a slow, languorous, savoring kiss that held far too much promise to be denied. Gripping her upper arms, he lifted his head then crushed her against the tightness gripping his chest. "There's so much I want to tell you—so much you should know—"

"I'm not afraid of you, Winchester. I never will be."

"I know."

She eased away from him and smoothed his shirt over his chest with trembling hands that betrayed her light tone. "Go. Lizzy needs you. They all need you."

"Yes, but do you?"

Her eyes lifted, shining bright with tears that cleaved through Miles like a blade. "I need you so much I ache with it. What's happened to me, Miles?"

Sweeping a curl from her forehead, he pressed his mouth to her temple and gathered her closer in his arms. "Nothing that I can't cure in one lifetime. Now go to the stable. In the back room you'll find some blankets and extra bandages. Bring them down to the slaves' quarters. I'll meet you there."

He left her then and raced across the field toward the slaves' quarters. His heart pounded in his chest. And his soul swelled with a joy that shone as bright, deep, and glorious as the sun in the heavens.

Chapter Fourteen

"Blankets. Blankets." Slamming the cupboard door closed, Teddie glanced around the small tack room. "Where could they be?" Laying her armful of bandages on the cot, she peeked under the cot, rummaged in an overhead shelf, then spied a battered sea chest shoved into one corner. It looked deep enough to hold many blankets.

Dropping to one knee, she flicked up the latches and lifted the lid. A musty scent tickled at her nose, a salty, mildew scent reminiscent of her months spent aboard the *Rattlesnake*. Those days seemed so distant to her now.

Guilt washed over her. While she'd been gaily shedding her clothes and her reservations on a stream bank, her brother chafed at his irons in the bowels of Cockburn's ship, a whim away from death.

And Winchester thought he had much to tell. A cold panic suddenly gripped her. She stared into the dark depths of the trunk, knowing that she'd been all but overcome with a desire to unburden her soul to him as completely as he'd laid her bosom bare on that stream bank. But here reality and consequences intruded with arresting finality. How could she confide everything to him and lay her trust, her deception, her life and Will's completely in his hands?

The realization that she would have done so without the slightest hesitation paralyzed her.

The uncontrollable yearnings of her body were one thing and would forever remain beyond her comprehension. She was fairly certain her physical need for him was instinctive, as natural and elemental as the changing of the seasons and not subject to reason, careful scrutiny, or control. But did the effortless surrendering of her body to him necessarily require that she surrender all her secrets as freely? Could she do one without the other? Where was the wisdom in this, particularly when it involved a great deal of deception?

More precisely, treason. Reasons mattered very little when national security was at stake.

She nearly winced, then chewed at her lip when she remembered Winchester's words. . . .

She deserves to be hanged.

Could he make glorious love to her, then hand her over to the authorities and watch with bitter satisfaction as they sentenced her to hang? Could a man so infinitely tender, so wondrously passionate, coldly turn his back on her?

Yes. Winchester could if he believed he'd been deceived again by a duplicitous woman. He would be mercilessly unforgiving.

He'd never allow her the opportunity to convince him otherwise.

Tears leapt to her eyes. "Damn," she croaked, plunging her hands into the sea chest. She withdrew some sort of broadbrimmed hat and quickly tossed it aside as the tears spilled to her cheeks. Hats, she assumed, were frightfully inept at wiping away tears. Shoving her hands deeper into the chest, she pulled out a blanket and buried her face in it.

She'd made a mess of things, tangling herself all up in emotion. But how could she have known she would come to this? How could she have imagined that her heart could be so tragically torn between her obligation to her brother and her love for—

Her heart lurched in her chest. No.

She buried her face in the blanket, a blanket made, oddly enough, of a fine worsted wool and smelling not of salt and mildew, but of spice, of sandalwood. Of Winchester. She clutched the cloth to the ache swelling in her heart, and for the first time in her life let her tears flow freely.

There was, she realized, only one course in this. No matter the increasing risk of being captured, she couldn't abandon Will. She would masquerade again as the Night Hawk and secure Will's release by delivering the real Night Hawk into

Cockburn's hands. Until then, she'd remain dedicated to her task, confident in her abilities, justified in her deception, well beyond the temptation to surrender her secrets along with her body, which she knew she would do if given the opportunity. She'd never done anything with only half her heart.

Which meant she had to stay out of Winchester's bed. Not an altogether impossible feat. She simply had to keep her wits about her, perhaps remind him of their contract.

She'd been reckless and careless enough to fall in love with him, knowing the stakes. Surely she would only be compounding the tragedy by venturing deeper into the unknown in his bed.

Her masquerade, which she'd somehow managed to keep up with only a snatch of guilt, now weighed like a gravestone upon her. And when the game was up and Will was free, what then? Was she capable of looking into Winchester's eyes every day and living a lie for the rest of her life? Could she face him with the truth, knowing she would surely lose him? Or should she flee him?

She'd never run from anything in her life. She'd never loved a man either. And he needed her. . . .

He needed the blankets.

Shoving all thoughts aside, she reached into the chest and scooped up the pile of blankets. Clutching them to her belly, she jerked to her feet, only to pause when the woolen blanket she'd cried all over slipped from her arms and pooled at her feet. Levering the pile of blankets on one hip, she bent to scoop the wool blanket from the floor, pausing when her fingers met with a small clasp sewn into the wool.

Odd. Most blankets didn't have clasps. It must have been a garment of some sort, though why Winchester would keep any garments—particularly one made of so fine a cloth—in an old sea chest in the back of the stable escaped her at the moment. Dismissing her curiosity, she tossed the garment into the chest, then as an afterthought scooped the hat from the floor and replaced it in the chest as well.

Without another thought she spun around, grabbed a handful

of bandages from the cot, and hurried from the stable toward the slaves' quarters.

Miles wiped the last of the blood from his hands on a clean cloth and allowed his muscles to finally relax into the stiffbacked chair. At his back a fire blazed, filling the small room with a near suffocating heat. His blood-soaked shirt clung to his chest and arms. Perspiration dotted his bare forearms and trickled over his brow. Every muscle he possessed ached from hours of tension. Fatigue settled deep in his bones. Yet the feeling was a welcome one, and he couldn't have felt more content, or more at peace with himself and his lot.

An odd feeling for him. He hardly recognized it.

Following the afternoon's hell, darkness hovered like a comforting cocoon beyond the one small window. And in the bed at Mike's side, young Lizzy slept with her tiny babe nestled at her breast.

An invisible hand wrapped around his heart and gently squeezed as he watched the young mother and her son. From her laudanum-induced haze, she'd wept when he'd finally laid her swaddled baby in her arms. They'd all wept, even sourpussed old Winnie, who stoutly refused to accustom herself to his presence during births, especially the difficult ones. The grizzled midwife forever scoffed at his argument that modern medical techniques could go hand in hand with her centuries old method of bringing babies into the world. He wondered if she'd adjusted her thinking at all when he'd decided to cut the baby out.

Had he not he almost certainly would have lost them both.

A glass was pressed into his hand. He glanced up, expecting Teddie for some reason. The last he'd seen of her, she was standing by Lizzy's head, eyes wide and unblinking in a face pale as death when he made the incision. He wanted her here with him now, listening to the baby's first breaths.

"Simon," he said.

"Winnie says drink this up." Simon hunkered down beside the bed, his long fingers tentative as they barely lifted the coverlet from the baby's head. "Lord Jesus, but you saved my girl

Lizzy. You's a damned fine man. Yo' gran'pappy sho' woulda been proud o' you.''

"I did my job, just as he would have." Miles was vaguely uncomfortable with the notion of being thought of as a damned fine man, particularly by an overseer who considered himself an expert on several generations of Winchesters, and no doubt was. Miles buried his nose in his glass, at once recognizing the drink. The brew, a potent concoction of Winnie's, supposedly possessed the power to free a man of his demons. He vividly remembered the last time Winnie had offered him the drink, several years before, when the memories of Tripoli had haunted him with a merciless zeal through days, nights, and into weeks and years, a time when he did nothing but cloister himself within Miramer for days with only his rum for company. A time when he'd cursed his heritage and the plantation. A time when he cared very little if Miramer and its people crumbled into dust or if everyone who knew him thought him half-mad.

Winnie's brew had driven him first to Jillie's bed, then onto Wildair's back for a suicidal ride through a blinding thunderstorm to his Williamsburg club and a high-stakes game of faro, all frustrating and ineffectual attempts to sate the fever raging in his blood. He'd awakened the next morning in his bed, his clothes soaked with rum and river water, his purse inside out and empty, his mind numb.

Yet that very morning he'd first become possessed of his scheme to save Miramer from ruin. Winnie's brew hadn't slaked every memory. Nothing could. But somehow it had managed to free him of their constant torment.

With this clearly in mind, he prudently drank only two sips, set the glass on the floor, then met Simon's probing gaze.

"Jest doin' yo' job, eh?" Simon asked. "Then why you still here? It ain' jest a job to you, bein' 'massa.' You don' even wanna be called massa. It don' matter what you say neither. Jest like it don' matter that you say you don' care 'bout Miss Teddie. From what I seen today by the stream—"

"That's enough, Simon." Miles rose from his chair, chagrin bombarding him as Simon's singsong chuckles echoed from every corner of the small room.

"Jest in case you's wonderin,' she's on the south veranda, lookin' out at the river. I s'pect she's waitin' fo' you to come on home."

Turning to duck beneath the low-hanging doorjamb, Miles hesitated, then clasped a hand on Simon's shoulder. It was an uncommon gesture for Miles, hesitant, slightly awkward, and drew Simon's swift and curious look. "Congratulations on your grandson, Simon."

A smile untainted by sarcasm or goading spread wide over Simon's face. "Thank you, suh."

Muttering a good night, Miles turned and stepped into the cool night air. The stars hung low from a cloudless, moonless sky, glittering like fine diamonds just beyond reach of his fingertips, dancing over the swaying heads of the tobacco plants. A cooling breeze knifed through his hair, prompting him to shed his soiled shirt and lay his fevered skin bare. Already he could feel the effects of Winnie's brew working its languid magic on his muscles. His blood fired and leapt in his veins. His mind surrendered to a gentle numbing, freeing him from all thoughts but one.

Damned poison was an aphrodisiac.

He paused beside a barrel of fresh water, lifted the lid, and plunged his face and head into the cool depths. He surfaced, and the air exploded from his lungs with a lusty, guttural growl of satisfaction. Shoving his hands through his hair, he blinked the water from his eyes, left the rest to wash over his bare chest and arms, then headed for the house with long, loping strides.

Beneath his damp skin, desires smoldered to life the closer he moved to the house. The windows were all dark, and those of the kitchen were as well. It must be well past midnight.

He didn't realize he held his breath until he came around the west side of the house to the southern veranda and a great weight seemed to press into his chest. Beneath that weight, his breath slowly left him as he moved deeper into the shadows surrounding the house. His eyes probed the darkness, intent on the slightest shifting of shadow amidst the cluster of Windsor chairs strategically positioned along the veranda to offer the most advantageous views of the river.

He paused, the male beast on the hunt for his mate, nostrils flaring to catch his female's scent on the wind. And like the beast, his muscles coiled, flexed in anticipation. Blood pumped through him in rhythmic surges, settling heavy and full in his loins. He felt the raw ache pulsing there, the tautness pulling his breeches snug over his hips as he mounted the steps, his eyes glittering with passions fully roused.

He stopped, tensed, his every fiber under sensory bombardment, then turned and found her curled in a chair at the far end of the veranda.

He thought her asleep, so motionlessly did she sit there. But as he drew nearer he realized she stared out over the river with a faraway look, as though she wished herself miles from here. From him. A need above all those physical gripped him, an urgency to capture and make his all that was elusive and mysterious about her. If only bodily strength and determination could achieve that, she would be his now. He wondered if, like the gossamer butterfly, she would forever elude him, and if any power existed to banish the sadness that seemed so much a part of her now.

She looked up at him, sadness and longing piercing through him like a handful of daggers expertly thrown. "Miles," she murmured, her voice slurring as though her tongue was heavy with thick honey. Limpid dark-violet pools beseeched him, drew him out of himself, inside out.

He reached for the empty glass she held and lifted it to his nose. Dropping to one knee beside her, concern etched on his brow, he softly asked, "How much did you drink?"

Her head lifted, then lolled as though heavily weighted. "All of it. Winnie told me the stuff would cure anything that ails me. So I thought I'd try some."

"She gave it to you?"

"No. She told me not to touch it."

"You should have listened to her."

A frown puckered her brows. "I-I don't think it's working yet."

"What ails you, sweetheart?"

Slowly, she shook her head, evading him even in her semi-somnolence. Her tongue passed over her parted lips, then lingered to peek between her teeth. Beneath a surge of desire, Miles watched her heavily lidded eyes slide from his down to his chest, then sweep closed. Like firebrands her hands spread over his chest, splayed fingers threading up through the damp fur, then along both sides of his neck and curving around his jaw as though she wished to memorize the shape and feel of him. His mouth opened to the brush of her thumbs on his lips. Gently, he drew one thumb against his tongue, laving it, caressing it. A purr rumbled from his throat as he rubbed his teeth against it.

"Miles . . ." she pleaded, arching up with a deep gasp for breath, her eyes fluttering open, then widening with the first hints of desperation. The drug was taking slow, certain possession of her.

Regret sliced through him. His ingenuous Teddie was bewitched. This willful, curious chit would taste madness for the first time in her life. She hooked her fingers in the high lace collar of her dress and tugged at the fabric. Several pearl buttons popped from the fabric and spilled to the floor. Several more hit Miles in the chest as she rent the cotton.

He caught both her hands and pressed them to his lips, feeling the fevered pulse emanating from her fingertips. "You're on fire," he rasped, grasping her narrow waist as she swayed. Beneath his hands she quivered with an all-consuming, savage need he remembered all too well. He imagined the drug roaring through her veins, pulling every nerve painfully taut, leaving her skin exquisitely sensitive to touch, even to the barest whisper of air.

Her fingernails bit into his shoulders as she arched herself up and against him in a sweet, sinuous undulation that tested his greatest powers of restraint. Against his neck her breath fanned with an extraordinary heat, and her voice rasped from the tortured depths of her. "Help me, Miles. I feel like I'm going to die or explode. It's the drink, isn't it?"

"It was made to free the mind, to liberate you of your inhibitions."

"I-it makes me want with a deep, dark need."

"It's an aphrodisiac."

Her breath choked out of her. "No. I-I can't. I need to . . . need to keep control . . . always."

"Never with me." He sank his fingers into her hair, freeing the heavy mass from its pins, stirring the lilac scent buried there. Curls spilled over his bare chest and arms like warm, fragrant silk. He closed his eyes, drowning in the feel of all of her. His voice tremored, hoarse and heavy with passion. "Never hold anything from me, Teddie."

Quivering fingertips moved featherlike over his lips, then the heat of her mouth. "I must." She breathed life and fire into his mouth, her lips brushing his with hesitant, delicate, whisperlike strokes. "So much I can't say. Promise me—"

"I'll give you anything."

"Please," she whispered, "don't let me lose control. Promise me you won't—"

"I promise, sweet wife."

Her mouth moved over his chin, his beard-stubbled cheek, her tongue laving like a healing balm against the length of his scar to his temple. "Make it stop burning, Miles. I need ice—bowls of ice chunks to cover me. Let me swim in a river of ice. With you. . . ."

He gathered her into his arms and rose to his feet, his need for her consuming him. "I didn't want it like this," he muttered, moving purposefully to the door and yanking it wide. The door thwacked against the outside wall, then banged shut behind him, but he was already to the stairs. "I want you to remember everything, not just the fever. Next time you will."

With arms clutched around his neck, she lifted her face against his throat. "No . . . we can't. I won't let you . . . again. It's not . . . what I want. Take me to my room. Just leave me there. Please . . ."

A vision took full shape in his mind of Teddie trapped in the fiery talons of the drug, naked and tangled in sweat-dampened sheets, crying out with her insatiable need for release, just as he'd once cried out with the agony of freeing himself of opium. No one had heard his cries out in the desert. No one could have eased his pain. The sun had finally baked all traces of the drug from his skin.

"I won't do that to you," he said, taking the steps two at a time. His movements brought the tops of his thighs against the softness of her buttocks. The contact elicited whimpers from her, agonized whimpers that faded into deep, open-mouthed moans of sensual delight. Her teeth grazed his throat.

When he bared her skin she would burst into flame, from the inside out.

"There's a lesson in this somewhere," he said through his teeth as he turned and moved into the dimly lit upper hall of the east wing. He had a disturbing feeling the lesson would be one of restraint, for him. For the first time in months he almost damned his noble and upstanding Winchester heritage, a heritage that demanded he keep his own needs tightly reined, his own passions at bay. For her sake.

He would have to keep well in mind that she hadn't any idea what she was doing. She was acting out of instinct alone, pure, untainted, primal instinct.

At the end of the hall he paused, shouldered open his chamber door, stepped inside, then kicked the door closed behind him.

Darkness engulfed them, the kind of all-consuming, heavy darkness of a room draped and closed to the world beyond it. The heat here would be unbearable in another minute if he didn't throw the drapes and windows wide.

"Easy," he murmured, gently lowering her to the bed. Her sigh whispered over his face as she dipped into the downy ticking, trailing her fingertips down his chest to the taut ridges of his belly. Then, with a fervor that caught him slightly unawares, she pulled his head to hers, her mouth hot and eager to receive him. Her tongue darted over her lips, flicked impatiently over his mouth. Her teeth grazed his, she gave a frustrated groan, then arched her head back and thrust her body against him in slow, fevered undulations.

It was all Miles could do to stay rigid and unmoving above her, taking each sweet thrust of her breasts and pelvis against his torso like the sting of a cat-o'-nine.

"Miles . . ." She gripped his biceps and pulled herself up flush against him. Her pelvis rocked gently, in smooth, sweet ripples against the rock-hard length of his manhood. "It burns between my legs."

"I know." With one arm braced along her spine, he cradled her close, knowing there was only one escape from her prison. Release . . . the kind that only a man can bring a woman. It was what her body yearned for, though she was as yet unaware or else fought it with the last vestiges of reason she possessed. Teddie was not a woman who would relinquish control of herself without a fierce battle, even if she was doomed to defeat, even if surrender meant staggering pleasure.

"I'll cool you," he whispered, his arm flexing as he lowered her to the bed. Intertwining his fingers with hers, he spread her arms wide on either side of her, feeling the resistance in her. She would fight his every attempt to ease this for her. He paused above her, his bare chest pushing into the soft thrust of her breasts, pinning her there. "My sweet bewitched wife, lie still."

"Don't leave me."

"Never. I'm going to open a window."

He left her then to sweep the heavy drapes wide and throw open all the windows. Against his damp skin the whisper of breeze was a godsend and he filled his lungs with the night air, willing his carnal appetites cooled, denying the effects of the drug on his own crumbling inhibitions.

Turning, he lit a candle, then moved slowly around the foot of the bed. In his deepest imaginings he'd seen her there upon his bed, passing into and out of his vision as he rounded one thick, draped bedpost and moved nearer. But in those dreams— and there had been hundreds—she lay serene in her sensuality, accepting of their consuming mutual need, eager to explore it. Her eyes in those dreams glowed deep and dark, boundless and limitless, all-knowing yet innocent. And when she opened herself up and gave herself to him, she was the rose gently unfurling to the warmth of the sun.

In those imaginings no fever possessed her, no drug bewitched her. There was nothing frantic or desperate about her. Nothing of the lust-driven she-animal he now had in his bed.

Were he possessing of any less of this damned noble purpose, if he were any less a husband to her, he would give her what she so desperately wanted, punishingly hard, violent, and fast, as many times as he was physically able. She'd remember little come morning, when her mind would thicken with fuzz as the drug finally left. The lingering soreness between her thighs would be her only reminder of her madness.

If he was given to lust, to madness, he would. If he didn't love her so completely, he would. . . .

The candleholder clattered to the bedside table. Her eyes glowed like a she-wolf's, devouring him in swift, short order. He stood above her, arms hanging loosely at his sides, the ache in his loins swelling to excruciating limits, pulsing with need, tempting him beyond himself, demanding that he find surcease within her. The obvious magnitude of his desire drew her fevered gaze. He watched the flames begin to devour her as the gasps fell from her lips and her hips began a languorous writhing, lifting from the bed in lustful offering.

Bracing one knee on the bed and one arm alongside her, he curved his hand around her head into the thickness of her hair and stared into the fiery depths of her eyes. "Trust me, Teddie," he murmured, lowering his mouth over hers in a slow, gentle kiss intended to calm her. She tasted like a plump, dewkissed rosebud about to burst open. "Relax, sweet," he breathed. "Close your beautiful eyes and let me help you." Beneath the tender brush of his mouth her lips throbbed, quivered, parted. The velvety softness of her tongue met his in a frenzied dance.

A strangled cry shuddered through her, then she hooked her fingers in the banded waist of his breeches and arched her pelvis up against him. "Not like that," he crooned, grasping both her wrists in one hand and drawing her hands over her head.

"Miles . . . take off your clothes. I need to see you . . . to touch all of you. . . ."

"Easy, love. You will." Keeping her hands anchored above

her head, he worked the remaining buttons of her gown free until the gown lay open past her waist. A moist, fragrant heat wafted up from her chemise as he spread the gaping dress wide. The linen undergarment, damp and all but transparent, clung to her breasts and ribs. His throat went dry and his every muscle rigid. The blush-pink nubs of her nipples distended into the fabric from the luminous ivory mounds.

"Easy—" He lay his palm at the base of her throat, battling desires no man could tame. Beneath his fingertips a riotous pulse leapt through her skin, matching his. Her chest quivered with her quick breaths. "Breathe, my sweet wife, deep and even—like me," he rasped, his own breath wheezing through his teeth.

"I c-can't. Hurry, Miles. . . . or I'll go mad."

"Not unless I go with you." Slipping his arm around her waist, he arched her up, curving her back over his arm and pulling her high against him until the lace edge of the chemise poised upon her nipples. His mind clouded with desire, restraint fast losing the battle, he lowered his face to the fullness swelling above the chemise and drank of her skin's lilac essence with mouth and tongue. Releasing her hands, he peeled the damp linen from her skin with trembling fingers as hers dug into his back and shoulders and faint spasms shuddered through her body. Chemise ribbons loosened, sagged, and the garment dissolved with a sound not unlike the catching of a man's breath in his throat.

"Oh, Miles . . ." With arms clutching around him and head thrown back, she met every stroke of his tongue on her soft flesh with a husky gasp of pleasure, every caress of his hands with a sinuous molding of her body deeper into his palms and the longing lift of her hips against him. Like a long, tapered candle held between his hands, she flared vibrant and hot, her inner flame leaping and dancing as he caressed her velvet skin and branded each sweet inch of her breasts with his mouth.

When he first brushed his lips over one turgid peak, she cried out, the pressure leaping to an excruciating pitch within her. Her breath came in tortured gasps. The hands that had clutched at him now clawed at his skin as she reared up against him, her eyes wild, vacant, devoid of their enchanting, curious, bedeviling glitter.

His heart turned over in his chest. "Christ, I'm sorry," he rasped, knowing that she barely heard him over the roar of blood in her ears. Knowing that, at the moment, she didn't care. "Sweet wife, let me take the burn from you."

With features set hard and unforgiving, he pulled her into his lap, settling the softness of her buttocks against the hardness of his loins. Then, with no seductive prelude, no tender initiation, he reached beneath the tangle of skirts and chemise, slid his hand up the inner length of one silk-stockinged leg, past the lace-trimmed garters, over a silken expanse of bare thigh to the core of her torment. Gently, reverently, he cupped his palm over the molten heat seeping from her and brushed his thumb once—just once was all she would need—over the exquisitely sensitive bud nestled deep within the soft petals.

He silenced her startled outcry with the force of his mouth on hers, shuddering with his own unassuaged need when the spasms thundered over her in wave after consuming wave and a river of warmth flowed into his palm. With each crescendo she cried out against his mouth, her pleasure so intense it had become agony, every sensation merciless torture, the pressure of his hand between her slick thighs suddenly like the brand of a red-hot iron. Miles kissed the tears from her cheeks and crushed her protectively against him, taking her convulsions deep into himself. And when the spasms gave way to breathless shudders and long, deep sighs, still the fever burned, ravenous in its need.

"Yes," she breathed, her fingertips beginning to scratch plaintively at his chest like the paws of a mewling kitten, her hips rocking against his loins. "Love me, Miles . . . again. You just have to touch me."

"I know." He lowered his mouth to hers in a kiss meant to be savored, given with a tenderness meant to ease the onslaught on nerves already laid open and raw. And for a moment of heaven she surrendered to the gentle pressure of his lips on hers and the warmth of his hand on her womanhood with nothing but a blissful sigh of contentment. His desires leapt and he crushed her bare breasts to his chest, feeling the plump softness of her buttocks against the swollen length of him.

"Sweet Teddie, you feel like heaven . . ." Her thighs quivered and parted, bidding him entrance no man could have denied any longer. His fingers slipped within the honeyed depths, so slick and impossibly tight he nearly lost himself. He barely moved.

"Miles . . ." In a torrent her climax roared over her, pulling hoarse cries from the depths of her soul.

Some time later, when the last shudder quivered through her body and the fever left its final damp sheen on her cooling skin, when her breath came slow and even and she perched on the edge of slumber, Miles gathered her in his arms and carried her through the long, dark halls to the comfort of her bed. There, as she slept with an almost enviable peace, he stripped away her damp clothes, loosed the lace garters, and peeled the stockings from her long legs.

He didn't know how long he stayed there on the bed beside her, feasting on the serene beauty of her laid out in all her womanly splendor upon the sheets. With something like wonder, something beyond the callings of lust and passion left unsated, he smoothed the tangled curls from her brow and with his fingertips traced the delicate contours of her cheekbones and jaw. His fingers hovered over her parted lips, felt the play of her breath, then swept over the graceful curve of her neck. In the darkness she seemed to glow with an inner luminescence. Her skin was cool, creamy silk beneath his hands as he slowly smoothed them over her shoulders, down the lengths of her arms and back again. Lowering his head, he touched his lips to hers and felt a tug in the pit of his being.

"Love," he whispered, hoarse with emotion. "I never thought to find you. Now I can never let you go. And you will be mine. . . ." As if to reassure himself of this, and to be certain that his hard-won restraint had not been for nothing, he cupped her breasts, then traced the full, firm contours lifting toward him with each of her breaths. He was not driven by lust or passion, but by something far deeper, something that brought a reverence to his touch and a wonder to his cynic's soul. Beneath his palms she was as if made of the finest, most fragile porcelain, her belly quivering taut and warm and womanly in its subtle curve, her hips flaring and full as if fashioned by angels. And in the soft tangle of dark curls at the apex of her thighs, he cupped and claimed the lingering heat once more.

"Sleep, my delight." He drew the sheet over her with a sudden profound sense of regret and a fleeting sense of loss. He knew he should leave her to her sleep and allow her to awaken alone, haunted only by wisps of a dusky dream and not by guilt or conscience or a husband's needs.

And yet instinct, not lust, goaded him to shed his clothes and climb into the bed beside her, to gather her warmth close against him, to listen to her soft breathing the night through and to await the dawn. His contentment would be astonishingly simple with her sleeping in his arms, his peace complete.

Peace and contentment. He'd never thought to find either of them, especially with a woman. Perhaps because he truly believed he didn't deserve either. As penance for surviving as long as he had on sheer fool's luck, he had to face the demons with each dawn and lose the daily grapple with the guilt, didn't he? He had no right to embrace hope, did he? Besides, guilty fools—even the most diabolical—didn't bungle their way into happiness and a future untainted by memory. Guilt-ridden men faced the prospect of contentment with a cynical, twisted eye. To them, opportunity didn't just happen along by chance.

And if it did, that happiness would surely vanish by the next sunrise. After all, how could he be deserving?

Then he should grasp it with both hands and make it his now. . . .

Again, regret and the instinct to deny what was happening to him swept through him as he closed the bedchamber door behind him. He'd been without feeling for so long, purposely distanced from people, that he'd found far more comfort in loneliness than in the careful peeling open and laying bare of his soul by a woman.

The farther he moved down the hall away from her, the emptier he became, as though with each step his lifeblood seeped bit by bit out of him. By the time he reached his own chamber the familiar lonely chill had crept over him, wiping everything from his heart but one almost insignificant spot of hope that flickered like a waning fire. By morning it would die if left untended.

Shedding his breeches and boots, he lay on the sheets that still smelled of her, listened to the night creeping beyond his open windows, and wondered how she'd wriggled into his heart without him knowing.

"You look dreadful, my dear."

With a blink, Teddie jerked from her thoughts and lifted a wan, unconvincing smile. "Thank you, Aunt Edwina. More tea?"

Aunt Edwina's fair brows quivered beneath her trademark sweep of snowy-white hair. She sat on the settee, cushy and plump in reams of satin and lace like a pale-pink cream puff, and yet the subtle purse of her lips and the take-no-prisoners directness of her stare would have done the strictest schoolmaster proud. "I've had four cups already and it's only ten in the morning. What are you trying to do to me, my dear? Look at you. The color has all but vanished from your cheeks. Your mouth has that pinched look so common to distressed women. You've kept your hands twisted in your lap since you sat down, no doubt for fear that I will notice their trembling. What the devil has Winchester done to you?"

Teddie closed her eyes and swallowed deeply. A faint wooziness drifted over her, leaving her momentarily light-headed. No doubt the lingering effects of that blasted drink she'd so recklessly swallowed, despite Winnie's warning. Her curiosity, it seemed, had led her far afield with that. Or perhaps witnessing Winchester bring a child into the world had filled her with a joyous need for celebration. The spectacle itself had lifted her beyond herself.

Forcing her eyes open, she blinked against the midmorning sunlight blazing into Miramer's parlor. "H-he's done nothing." Vaguely, she waved a hand before her face. "I suppose it's the heat."

This was a lie, of course, and her aunt damned well knew it. Winchester had done everything—well, *almost* everything a man could do to a woman. At least she thought he had. Memory slammed around in her muddled mind, eluding her, fantasy melding with reality. She'd awakened certain that the blush-inspiring images bombarding her were fragments of some drug-induced dream, and that she alone had somehow managed to get herself naked and abed last evening and had simply forgotten the particulars—like where Winchester fit into it all. At least this was the preferred version of the evening's events. She refused to greet the day believing she'd done anything worse last evening than fall prey to her curiosity and her elation and drink too much of something she shouldn't have touched. A woman of her own resilient, unbending will didn't abandon her principles and good logic to some blasted witches' brew! She was made of much sterner stuff.

And yet as she dressed, the brush of her linen undergarments over her sensitive skin roused disturbingly vivid images of Winchester's mouth and hands on her breasts. His scent didn't only linger on her skin, it seemed to have invaded her. Could a dream be so vivid? Or could it actually be more than a dream?

And then there was the tiny matter of the faint rawness between her thighs.

A cold, clammy sheen at once bathed her skin. Had the drug—which freed her of every bit of resistance and allowed him such liberties with her body—also done the unthinkable and freed her tongue? In such a state could she have confessed everything to him: the deception, Will's imprisonment, her masquerade as the Night Hawk?

Why the devil couldn't she remember? She trembled with her frustration and had another sudden thought. If she couldn't remember any of it, was Winchester the sort that would take full and swift advantage of a woman in such a mindless state?

Her most pressing difficulty at the moment, however, was her Aunt Edwina's dubious expression which was fixed grimly on Teddie. There would be no escaping without some sort of explanation, something that would satisfy a worldly-wise woman like her aunt.

Then there was the inevitability of running into Winchester at some point. Would it be there, written all over his face, plain to see? Surely he would have trussed and gagged her and delivered her to some diabolical fate befitting of spies if she'd confessed everything, wouldn't he? Or would he stalk her like a wolf in the night, betraying nothing of their encounter last evening, pushing her to the brink of madness?

He would be merciless, even though he was the same man who had worked a miracle in that hut last evening. She would never forget the happiness in his eyes when he'd laid the baby in Lizzy's arms.

"Winchester's on his morning tour of the plantation," she blurted, the relief weighing heavy in her tone, striking a deep concern on her aunt's face. "A baby was born last night, Aunt Edwina."

"He's bound to return any moment, my dear."

For the first time in her life Teddie felt pure, mind-staggering terror clutch at her heart. She blinked up at her aunt. "Yes, I suppose he is."

"Good heavens, you're shaking." In the next instant Aunt Edwina's eyes flew wide. "Aha! The monster! I knew it! I told George that contract would never work, and as usual I was right!" With an imperious jut of her chin, she raised one pink-gloved finger skyward. "The devil take Winchester but he will be on the next frigate out of Baltimore."

"No—" Teddie surged forward in her seat then bit her lip, surprised by the depth of her reaction to Winchester being forced into servitude. Not a moment ago the man had been a cad for taking advantage of her when he shouldn't have. That sort of man deserved such a punishment, even if he did birth babies. "It's not that. He . . . he hasn't . . . that is, I'm rather certain we haven't done anything to breach the contract."

" 'Rather certain'? My dear, there is nothing vague about it. You either have or you haven't. Now, which is it?"

Teddie flushed to her hairline and contemplated her tightly clasped hands. "We have not."

"Ah," Aunt Edwina murmured. "Temptation is a wicked thing, my dear."

Teddie's eyes fluttered closed as wanton memory flooded her mind. Oddly enough, the thought was quite timely. Best that her aunt believe she'd merely fallen under some sort of seductive spell. Which she hadn't, of course. "Very wicked," she murmured.

"Especially when something is made forbidden, as you are to your husband. Indeed, it would test the stoutest man's character to have so lovely and charming a wife in his house and yet beyond his grasp. Perhaps your uncle was right after all, hmm?" A door slammed somewhere with such force the house seemed to tremble. "Ah, that must be Winchester now. Nothing subtle about him, is there?"

The mischievous twinkle in Aunt Edwina's eye was not lost on Teddie, though she wished she felt a small fraction of her aunt's usually infectious gaiety. But how could she when the hairs on the back of her neck stood on end and her heart slammed against her lungs as his determined footfalls drew closer and closer?

She all but sprang from the settee, never one to take anything sitting down, particularly if she was to be delivered to her doom. Chin high and shoulders back, she told herself. A watery feeling plunged into her legs and her breasts began to tingle as if in anticipation of something wonderful.

"Take my hand, dear," Aunt Edwina whispered close to her ear, materializing at her side, "before you crumple onto this lovely carpet you can't seem to take your eyes from. That's it. Here he is now, and looking in desperate need of conquering something. Nothing is half so breathtaking as the male animal in his virile prime. Do play along, my dear."

Teddie drew a deep breath and lifted her eyes.

Chapter Fifteen

Miles barely favored Edwina Farrell with a brisk greeting and a nod before he swung his full attention to Teddie. The instant their eyes met she blushed—a bewitching shade of crimson that perfectly matched the red roses embroidered on her white cotton dress—then immediately looked away.

No doubt about it, the girl was haunted. Still. He'd purposely given her the morning alone to recover and had forced himself into the fields, where he'd spent the last four hours harvesting leaves and transporting the bulging scaffolds to the river warehouse, not only to keep himself from disturbing her. After last evening he had his own physical demons to conquer. Four hours of the toughest labor on the plantation had left his arm, back, and thigh muscles burning with a welcome fatigue, the kind that should have vanquished his more lascivious thoughts.

He should have known better. His reaction to Teddie would always be the same combustive burst of physical, mental, and spiritual awareness that no fatigue, no amount of cynicism, and no strength of will could possibly refute. If anything, the exertions of physical labor had left his body aching with a mind-staggering need for surcease only she could give him.

He could hardly wait to get her alone, to pull the pins from her upswept hair and peel the dress from her ripe young body. To love her as she was meant to be loved. And he didn't give a damn if it showed all over him or if at the moment, it was the source of Edwina Farrell's smug little smile and bubbling, non-sensical chitchat. Damned old woman all but wriggled with glee, knowing his torment. She must truly despise him to deny her niece fulfillment in her marriage. Or to think she could. Hell, let her gloat at his expense. It was small price to pay knowing his reward dangled within reach of his hot hands, blushingly beautiful in her sinuous sheath of rose-sprigged white cotton.

"Good," Edwina Farrell chirped. "That's settled. Get your shawl, Theodora. We must be off."

"What?" Miles was caught so off guard that he could only stare after Teddie as she slipped past him in a whisper of air. He was painfully aware that in doing so she purposely maintained a healthy distance, a good arm's reach or more, as though she knew he ached to reach out and grab her.

As though she didn't want him to.

He swung on Edwina Farrell. "Where the hell do you think you're taking her?"

Edwina Farrell gave him a mildly befuddled look. "I just told you, Winchester. My niece and I are going calling. Haven't you been listening? Or are you perhaps preoccupied with something?"

Miles set his jaw, male ire leaping to life in the face of this ridiculous woman's twinkly-eyed self-satisfaction. "She's not going."

Edwina Farrell laughed and patted his dirt-smudged forearm with her plump, pink-gloved hand as though she were about to scold him for something he should have known years ago. "Oh, but she must. It's custom that every new bride pay courtesy calls on her wedding guests during the first few months following the nuptials. You know, display one's marital bliss for all to see lest they begin to talk."

"We can't have that," Miles muttered with unbridled derision. He'd never cared one whit if he'd been grist for the gossip mill over the years, and Edwina Farrell knew it. He returned her smile with one of his own, though his was so forced it seemed to crack the weathered creases in his skin. "Very well. Just to ensure that no one is left disappointed or disenchanted, I'll accompany you."

"You can't do that," Edwina replied quickly. "Good heavens, man, didn't you realize the custom specifically excludes the groom?"

"What version of custom is this?" Miles asked, eyes narrowing on the ever-duplicitous Edwina Farrell. "It smacks of a scheme, if you'll forgive my saying."

Edwina Farrell blinked. "A scheme? For heaven's sake to accomplish what, pray?"

Miles folded his arms over his chest. "You know damned well what you're doing."

With what Miles decided was a much practiced, vague little smile, Edwina sniffed, "No, I won't forgive you for that, sir. I've never stooped to scheming in all my life. I'll have you know this Farrell custom dates back *centuries*. And I simply will not be accused of being the first in generations of Virginia Farrells to snub or besmirch it by dragging around the county a superfluous, tagalong groom. Can you imagine what George would say?"

At the moment Miles had the distinct feeling that George Farrell would be soundly on his side of the argument. *Superfluous*? That any woman would use that word to describe any man, especially in his own damned house . . .

"Besides," Edwina added, almost as an afterthought, "my niece looks in dire need of a change of scenery and I thought I'd provide it. I'll have her back by evening."

There it was. The real reason: Teddie was fleeing for the day, voluntarily it seemed, and damned quickly. He had to wonder if she'd intended to slip away without telling him. Damn. What reason had she given Edwina Farrell for her distress? Nothing too heinous or he'd be dancing to George Farrell's orders by now. His breath left him in a hiss as he momentarily gave serious consideration to trying to stop her. The notion evaporated in the next instant. He'd never be able to force Teddie not to do anything. Neither could her aunt.

His wife wanted to get the hell away from him and nothing short of bodily restraint was going to stop her.

"Ah, there she is." Edwina peered over his shoulder into the foyer. "She's an absolute vision. I'm coming, Theodora dear."

Setting his jaw and soundly determined not to allow the meddlesome Edwina Farrell to get the better of him today, Miles turned only to find Edwina's pink parasol jabbing into his ribs. She lurched in front of him with elbows flying and arms poking and tucking and arranging her various feathers and plumes and ruffles and bows, a truly godawful combination of every imaginable feminine adornment, designed specifically to thwart a man's progress around any woman wearing such an abomination. Her ambling pace around the closely placed furniture only frustrated him further, forcing him to shuffle along behind her or take to leaping over furniture. If he didn't know better, he'd think she was purposely trying to keep him from reaching Teddie. Over the bobbing pink feather at the very top of her wide-brimmed bonnet, he glimpsed only the wispy end of the crimson sash trailing from Teddie's gown as she hurried out the front door to the Farrells' waiting coach.

His teeth met and ground with frustration. The next instant Edwina Farrell paused directly in the middle of the doorway, the breadth of her hips augmented by yards of ruffles and lace, making passage around her impossible.

She fiddled with something in her hands. "Now where did I put my handkerchief?"

"Mrs. Farrell."

"Yes?" With eyes wide and blank, she turned and peered up at him, then dangled a pink satin reticule before his nose as though he would find this or her lost handkerchief of any damned interest at the moment. "I believe I've lost my—oh! There it is. How forgetful of me. I left it on the settee. If you would excuse me, Winchester, I'll just—"

"Allow me," he muttered. In two great bounds he returned to the settee, retrieved her adroitly lost handkerchief, then returned it to her in as few strides. "Mrs. Farrell, one day you will push me to my limit."

"Indeed." She plucked the handkerchief from his hand, her soft gray eyes glittering with keen amusement as she stared up at him a moment. "I haven't a notion what you're grumbling about, Winchester. So like a man."

With that she turned and proceeded into the foyer, which was precisely where he left her when he bounded past her and through the front door, across the wide veranda, and down the front steps two at a time. With nothing more than a grunt to the footman, he yanked the coach door wide and thrust his head inside the plush gold-velvet interior.

There, nestled upon one tufted seat like a priceless diamond, he found Teddie.

His voice caught in his throat. Words, explanations, demands to know what the hell she was doing momentarily fled him. A peculiar heat worked its way up from his open collar. In his chest his heart leapt. "We . . . that is . . . I have to talk to you." God knew what possessed him, but he grabbed the white-gloved hands clenched in her lap in one massive fist as if that alone would keep her there. He stared into eyes gone wide and wary and whispered, "Are you coming back?"

She blinked once, seemed to exhale deeply, then looked out the opposite window. The words seemed to tremble from her lips. "Yes, of course."

"Good." He swallowed over the clog in his throat and wondered why the hell he couldn't think of anything better to say. On impulse he drew her hands to his mouth, pressed his lips to the fingers quivering beneath the soft white leather and murmured, "I'll be here."

Lifting his head, he found her staring at him with such unabashed longing that he felt a strange tightening in his chest which blossomed into a poignant ache.

"Out of my way, Winchester," Edwina yodeled with a stomp of her parasol on the cobblestones behind him.

Teddie at once redirected herself to the opposite window, but the faint upward curve of her lips betrayed her. "Enjoy yourself, sweetheart," Miles said huskily, turning one hand palm up against his open mouth. With deep satisfaction he felt the tension leap through her, heard her swift intake of breath. His blood fired.

Yes, the reward would be worth waiting for another day.

He turned, ducked out of the coach, then assisted Edwina Farrell into the thing, which earned him a breathless "Thank you ever so much, Winchester" from the busybody.

"Anything to keep from being superfluous," he muttered with a gallant incline of his head.

He watched the coach until it had disappeared from view down his drive.

It was just after dusk when she returned. Teddie stepped from the coach and faced the manor house's imposing door with resolve duly bolstered, mind clear, and shoulders pinched back. She was a new woman. Her day of "customary calling" had been nothing more than a long, leisurely exercise in self-indulgence at Timberneck Manor. At her aunt's command she'd spent an hour soaking in a tub. Then, wrapped only in a wispy white linen robe, she had lunched on ripe fruit and scones swimming in rich cream. A three hour nap had been her only course after this, and she'd found peaceful slumber in a room shaded by an enormous sycamore and swept cool by crisscrossing breezes. The remainder of the afternoon she'd spent with her aunt on the south veranda overlooking the York River. She'd watched the sun dapple the water as she slowly sipped iced lemonade and listened to her aunt recall her youth in England in her comforting, lilting froth of never-ending chatter.

Neither spoke of Winchester all day. Teddie tried her best not to think about him and how he'd made her feel when he kissed the palm of her hand in the coach. Given his mood, she felt safe in assuming he wasn't the least bit enraged with her. Her secrets, it seemed, were safe, for now.

What remained of her virtue, however, seemed infinitely more imperiled, even more so as she approached the house. Winchester's house. According to English law, at least, she was his property, to do with what he wanted, when he wanted, where he wanted. . . .

Rather than rousing the goodly amount of female indignation expected of an educated, logical, feet-grounded-in-reality sort of woman, the thought only quickened Teddie's pulse and made her knees wobble momentarily.

The front door opened just as she climbed the steps to the veranda. Jillie stepped into the glow of the twin gas lamps suspended on either side of the double doors. With hands clasped before her and lips pinched the servant watched Teddie approach, much like a lioness guarding her den. Lifting her chin a notch, Teddie quickened her step and met Jillie's stare with her own, but the closer she came her initial burst of indignation gave rise to a much more troubling sensation in the pit of her belly. Something was wrong. She could tell by the tightening of Jillie's mouth and something in her eyes, a trace of desperation for once ineptly masked beneath the starched gray dress and emotionless veneer.

"There you are, madam," the servant bit out, her typical sublime servitude falling victim to a much more potent antagonism at the moment and tainting her voice with acerbic bite. "Quick. He needs you."

Teddie felt the bottom fall from her stomach. "Miles," she whispered.

Jillie glanced sharply at her. "*He* will never need any woman. You would do well to remember that. It's Captain Coyle. He's asking for you."

"Damian?" Teddie drew up short. "But he's in Baltimore, preparing the fleet—"

Jillie shook her head and briskly turned to hold the door wide. "He's been injured. They sent him home. He arrived early this afternoon. He's in his chamber in the east wing. You'd best go to him now. I . . . he doesn't want me there anymore."

"Is the doctor with him?" Teddie asked as she swept past Jillie into the foyer and toward the stairs.

"No. The doctors can do nothing more for him."

Teddie froze at the foot of the stairs, one hand clutching the banister. She could feel the blood drain from her face. An ache swelled in her chest, the same hard knot of frustration she felt each time she thought of Will, a powerless victim of men's games of war. How many women grappled with this same frustration each day? And how did they live with it when their husbands and sons came home not to be tended but to be buried?

No. Not Damian, so proud and young and bursting with patriotic fervor. "Where's Winchester?" she asked.

"Gone, madam."

Teddie looked over her shoulder at Jillie. "Gone where?"

"I don't know, madam. Not long after Captain Coyle arrived he rode out on Wildair. That was several hours ago."

"Where do you think he went, Jillie? You know him."

Jillie's upper lip twitched faintly. "No, madam, he is as much a stranger to me now as he was eight years ago when he stepped through these very doors. Indeed, you know him far better than I ever will."

Teddie supposed there was some comfort to be found in the servant's admission, a concession to Teddie's victory. Oddly enough she felt no victorious elation, perhaps because Jillie suddenly seemed deflated of life, as if the past eight years had ruthlessly sapped her of all joy. Another victim of the ravages of war. She'd lost her heart and wasted her youth loving a war-scarred man and hadn't realized until now that she would never possess the ability to reach him.

"If I were to guess, madam," Jillie said softly, "he might have gone to his club in Williamsburg. Shall I send Simon after him?"

"No. He'll come back." Lifting her skirts in one hand, Teddie proceeded up the stairs at a pace that would have better suited a militiaman. "When he's ready to stop running from his family, he'll come back."

Teddie moved briskly down the east wing's upper hall, past Winchester's darkened chamber and into a short hall that housed Damian's quarters. She found his door slightly ajar. With two short raps she announced herself, then pushed the door open.

At first she thought her eyes deceived her. Damian sat half-hidden in a deep upholstered chair facing a blazing fire, clad in a dark-burgundy silk dressing gown. A blanket covered his legs. A clean white bandage shielded his brow and disappeared into the shaggy fall of his usually meticulously combed golden hair. Teddie stared at his drawn profile and swallowed the lump that had lodged in her throat the moment she'd learned he'd been injured. For some reason she'd thought him on death's door. Relief washed over her in great heaping bucketfuls.

"Damian, thank God," she breathed, bursting into the room with arms outstretched.

He glanced at her, eyes glassy, his face registering nothing, then slowly rose to his feet and turned toward her, allowing the blanket to slide to the floor. One arm lifted to greet her, then braced against the back of his chair as he seemed to sway on unsteady legs. The other arm—

Teddie froze, instantly rooted to the floor with horror. The dressing gown hung limp from Damian's left shoulder. Where there had been a strong young arm there was nothing.

Her sob tore from her before she could muffle it against her hand. "Oh, God . . ." she whispered. She felt the hot promise of tears, that well of despair that threatened to overflow every day until she beat it down, never allowing it to get the better of her. But this . . . the suddenness, the injustice of it . . .

The tears would surely defy her now.

She bit them back, knowing that Damian would hate a raw display of sympathy as much as she hated losing her composure. Still, she moved toward him, then threw her arms around him, burying her face against his right shoulder. "Thank God, you're alive," she whispered.

He remained stiff, unmoved, as though beyond anyone's reach, consumed by a fever that made him hot to her touch. "A mistake, that," he said tonelessly. "I was supposed to die." He moved out of her embrace, turned, and stared at the fire.

"You should be in bed. The fever will consume you. Or infection."

"Is that what Jillie said? She's wrong, you know. She keeps giving me that laudanum to ease the pain. The doctors all said I could have rum, as much as I need, for as long as I need. Years. It will take me years to recover." He looked over at her, his eyes dim beneath lowered brows, his skin colorless, like pale wax. Knowing him as she did, she found his uncharacteristic lack of emotion more eerie than any raw display. "Please get me some rum, Theodora."

"Come lie down. For a short time. I'll get a cool cloth for your head."

"You sound like Jillie. Damned woman won't leave me alone."

"You don't need to be left alone."

"The hell I don't."

"You sound just like Winchester."

His mouth fell open and his chest heaved with his sudden deep breaths. A spark of indignation flared, then died in his eyes. Teddie knew some men were born with an instinct to refuse pampering or a woman's care when they most needed it. Damian and his cousin Winchester were these sorts of men. With them the key to achieving cooperation was digging deep enough to rouse their ire and get their blood flowing in their veins over something other than their malady. With something better to occupy their energies, they'd be less likely to balk at suggestion . . . or think they needed to.

"Come," she said, moving to the side of the bed where a tall-backed wooden chair lay upended against the wall, no doubt a lingering testament to Winchester's encounter with Damian earlier. Righting the chair, she scooted it close to the bed and sat down.

"You didn't strike me as a martyr," Damian muttered, jaw thrust impudently as he made his way to the bed, his empty sleeve flapping like a limp flag. "Even martyrs don't waste their time with cowards."

"You're no coward, Damian. I don't care what happened."

"Ask your husband if he feels the same, *Mrs. Winchester*," he spat, falling heavily onto the bed. He stared at the ceiling a moment, then covered his eyes with his arm. Teddie watched his Adam's apple jerk in his throat. "Just ask him what I've done to his precious family name."

"Every day great, brave men are injured in battle, Damian, and manage to hold their heads high in the name of the liberty and the country they were fighting for. Family heritage has nothing to do with it. You've nothing to be ashamed of."

His laugh pierced through her like the swipe of a jagged piece of glass. Levering himself on his arm, he glared at her with eyes bloodshot and seething. "Battle? What is battle? I never saw an instant of battle. I never even saw a glimpse of British sail on the distant horizon. Our ship never got out of Baltimore's harbor. The other two frigates sailed on out into the bay without us. And you want to know why? I lost my arm during a routine exercise, shotting a carronade. In all my exuberance to prove myself worthy of my reputation as a sure shot, in all my blind stupidity, I used too much powder. The fuse was short, my arm somehow got in the way . . . it fired. . . .'' His lips spread wide over bared teeth and his words sizzled like venom on his tongue. "If that had happened during battle I would have died somewhere far out at sea, with fire and bloodshed all around me. No city doctor would have been waiting onshore to drug me and cut my shredded limb clean and tar my stump. And I would have been content to bleed to death knowing that my ineptitude would go forever unknown by anyone but me, knowing I deserved my fate for shaming myself so. Instead, I'm condemned to wearing my badge of dishonor for all to see. And I will have to recount my foolish tale and relive my humiliation countless times until I die. It's what I deserve, you know. A true Winchester would have died out there, a hero. I will never be one of them.''

"Yes, you are one of them. Painfully so.'' Anguish uncoiled deep in Teddie's belly, writhing like a living thing, infusing her voice with a hoarse, impassioned tone. "Is it some Winchester legacy for the men to torture themselves so? To revere their forefathers with such high regard? To expect the impossible of themselves? These men you hold up as your ideal—and God knows I wish one of them were here now to talk some much-needed sense into you—they were as human as you, just as fallible, just as exuberant. The only difference between them and you is that they died before their time. Whereas you and Winchester have been given a greater opportunity and a greater gift through survival. And yet you both refuse to see it.''

"Because it's not there.''

"You both hide behind your scars.''

"I wish I could.''

"Oh, but you are. Just as Winchester has. You will deny yourself life to pay your penance for beating the odds, is that it? Your forefathers would not pity you for your lost limb, Damian, but for your despair, because that is by far the greater loss. Little wonder Winchester couldn't bear to come face to face with it.''

Damian collapsed against his pillows, a wince shooting across his brow, his voice strained. "He's gone to drown himself in drink, lucky bastard."

"It won't help. It will only make the pain worse."

"A man can't be blamed for trying."

Teddie placed a soothing hand on Damian's brow. His eyes fluttered closed at her touch. For some time she stroked his damp brow and listened to the faint tick of a clock in the outside hall. Every now and then he jerked, his eyes flying wide, staring up at her, then slowly drifting closed.

"Even now you fight the laudanum and sleep and anything that will make you feel better," she murmured. "Give up this fight at least."

"Sing to me, Theodora," Damian murmured drowsily.

"I . . . I don't sing. My mother could warble like a sparrow, I've been told. I can't carry even a hint of a tune. I'm sorry." She watched the even rise and fall of his chest for several moments and thought he'd finally drifted off.

"Jillie sings," he rasped from the edges of sleep. "I've heard her in the kitchen when she thinks she's alone and no one is listening. She sings when she's sad, I think. She sings often. It's his fault. Damned bastard never loved her no matter what she did. He doesn't even know she sings. . . ." A long breath escaped Damian's lips. ". . . Like an angel would sing."

"I'll get her."

She left him and found Jillie in the hall, pale, pinched, worrying her white hands. "He asked for you," Teddie said.

Jillie blinked. "You must be mistaken, madam. He threw me from the room not a half hour past in a rage."

"Perhaps if you sing to him."

Color bloomed in Jillie's pale cheeks. "Sing? I . . . I don't . . . " She seemed to swallow with some difficulty, then pinched her narrow shoulders back and pursed her lips. "I suppose I could try, madam, if you think it might help Captain Coyle."

"Yes, I believe it would. Thank you, Jillie. I'll return after midnight to relieve you. I don't think he should be left alone."

Teddie laid a lingering hand on Jillie's shoulder and their eyes met for a brief instant before Jillie drew herself up stiff and turned away.

Teddie continued down the hall toward the west wing, weariness flooding into her limbs and a heaviness settling around her heart. The hall clock struck nine. In the distance thunder grumbled an ominous warning and intermittent gusts of wind rattled the panes in the windows.

She prayed the storm would keep well at sea. In three hours she was to rendezvous with Cockburn and set her scheme to trap the Night Hawk in motion. If she couldn't free Winchester or Damian of their demons, she'd certainly free Will of his prison and herself of her masquerade. And nothing, not even a force of nature, would stop her this time.

"Will looks weak," Teddie said the moment she and Cockburn had moved out of earshot of the longboat. A sudden burst of dry wind snatched at her breath and set her cloak snapping like a ship's pennant. Lightning flashed farther out over the bay, throwing Will's broad-shouldered silhouette into stark relief against the storm-tossed skies. Even at this distance Teddie could tell that his head lolled heavily to one side. When he'd spoken to her just moments before, his voice had barely lifted above a hoarse whisper. "You're not feeding him."

Cockburn snorted. "With what? We'll be lucky if our rations last the week."

Teddie masked her apprehension behind a level glare. "What about additional provisions?"

"I'm inclined to believe, Theodora, that the rest of the British fleet, including supply ships, is otherwise occupied farther north, where the action is. Where is Farrell?"

The lie leapt to her tongue with remarkable ease. "With the rest of the fleet, of course, near the St. Lawrence."

Cockburn looked supremely pleased. "Too damned scared to mount an offensive anywhere near here, eh?"

Teddie fed his self-satisfaction, absolutely determined not to betray that Farrell was indeed mounting a three-frigate fleet near Baltimore, intent on surprise attack. "Perhaps Farrell knows England is mistress of the seas just as Napoléon is master of the continent.''

He glanced sharply at her. ''Napoléon fell, my dear, not four months past. You'd best hope our end doesn't come with the same crushing finality. I wouldn't spare your brother for the American savages.'' He paused. ''No, it's becoming increasingly apparent to me that we may have to come ashore near Hampton and raid for food.''

Teddie knew what raiding meant: pillaging, burning, murdering, and raping. Food would suddenly be secondary. Cockburn and his crew itched for action, of any sort. From what she'd overheard, Hampton was well fortified with militia against just such a raid. And Will would be caught between both sides. ''I can get you food,'' she said quickly, eager to squelch Cockburn's plan. ''Plenty of it. Along with the Night Hawk.''

Cockburn's twisted grin flashed spasmodically with the bursts of lightning. ''Do go on.''

''In exchange for Will.''

''That certain, are you?''

''Of the Night Hawk's worth to you? Yes, I am. I'm also certain that he'll successfully run your blockade if you don't catch him. I assume you don't suffer humiliation well.''

Cockburn stared at her. ''You don't believe I could catch him myself, even with the aid of my frigates near Albemarle Sound?''

''Not without my help you won't.''

''Your arrogance this evening intrigues me. Or is it recklessness, Theodora?''

''I'm offering you a deal. Suddenly you don't trust me?''

''Oh, I trust you, not that I didn't have my doubts initially in your ability to carry this masquerade off. At first, it was a source of some amusement for me, something to occupy my nights. I had nothing to lose, whereas you . . . you had everything to lose, on both sides of the coin. No, I trust you. You're too smart to play both sides with your brother's life in the balance. And now you're dangling the Night Hawk in front of me, using yourself as bait to catch him, if I assume correctly, thinking to bribe me for your brother's return." The wind tossed his laugh skyward and sent a chill creeping down Teddie's spine. Cockburn stepped close to her and pushed his nose at hers, yet she didn't flinch or retreat a pace despite the apprehension gnawing a raw hole in her belly. "Have you once considered, my clever little spy, that by giving me precisely what I want most you will make yourself indispensable to me? That I will never release you of your role, or your brother of his prison, so long as the war rages?"

Teddie's throat went bone-dry. No, she hadn't considered that, perhaps because the thought was too horrifying. She gritted her teeth against the dread that swept over her. "Then I won't give you the Night Hawk."

Cockburn's eyes glowed with such malicious satisfaction that Teddie's heart plummeted. She could almost hear the click of the invisible shackles binding her. "Ah, but you will, and until you do, your brother won't get more than a few sips of water."

Teddie nearly choked on her frustration. She should have known! How could she have been so foolish to think she could dictate terms to a man like Cockburn? Why hadn't she foreseen this? Had she been thinking clearly, without distraction, she might have. Then she could have mounted some sort of defense. At least then she wouldn't have left herself so vulnerable, so soundly trapped.

It seemed she had no choice but to play along with his game. Again.

"Five days," she ground out, nearly wincing with physical pain when Cockburn's fleshy lips peeled back over his teeth in a grin that was pure malice.

"Where?"

"Lighthouse Point. At midnight."

"I'll have my men concealed in the thicket. Heavily armed," he added with pronounced emphasis, no doubt to defuse any ideas she might have to attempt to double-cross him at that point.

"I'll want reassurance that Will is all right."

"Or else?" Again he snorted. "My dear Theodora, your

cheek at the moment surprises even me, and I more than anyone know the limitless depth of your gall. Like most of my
fellow British commanders, I admire boldness in an adversary.
Indeed, I think no man in your circumstances would expect
anything of me in the way of reassurance. And yet you, the
female, do. Why is it I must forever remind you that it is I, not
you, who wields complete control here?''

She lifted her chin into the wind, feeling the first splashes of
rain on her face. ''If Will dies you will realize who has the
control here, Cockburn. Nothing is more reckless than a
woman with nothing left to lose. Not even a man.'' With that
she turned and strode toward Cleo, leaving Cockburn to stare
after her until she disappeared between flashes of lightning.

The barn was as dark and silent when Teddie returned to
Miramer as when she'd left it. Muttering a silent prayer of
thanks, she bedded the cooled Cleo down for the night and,
with her cloak and hat rolled in a ball and tucked under her
arm, hurried toward the house and the side door she'd left
unlocked. The wind roared through the trees overhead, carrying with it the pungent scent of approaching rain. By driving
Cleo at a merciless pace she'd managed to outrun the roiling
front edge of the storm. Just barely. Lightning flickered almost
constantly now, lighting her way along the cobbled path. Thunder shook the earth beneath her feet like the roar of an advancing demon.

The first huge splashes of rain began to fall when she tugged
open the door and slipped into the house. She paused, drew a
deep shuddering breath of relief, and took one step into the
shadowy hall.

''Wife.''

Teddie froze. From the deepest shadows Winchester stepped
into the arc of a flickering wall sconce. His shirt hung open and
loose past his hips, laying a breadth of bronzed skin bare from
his neck to the low-riding waist of his black breeches. His hair
was a riotous fall of wind-tossed waves. From one hand dangled an empty lead-crystal glass. He reeked of liquor and
smoke all mixed up with his spicy cologne.

He was everything that was wicked.

The breadth of his shoulders filled the hall. His height dwarfed her. Even in his liquored state he'd easily catch her if she tried to escape, with one swipe of his thick arm.

Escape. . . .

Beneath her hastily donned dress she wore her black breeches and shirt. On her feet, tall black boots. And under her arm, she carried the bundled cloak and hat.

No explanation would suffice. If she'd erred in underestimating Cockburn tonight, she'd surely fall into her own trap trying to outwit Winchester.

Escape. . . .

Her heart thundered in her breast. Lightning sizzled through the air. And he advanced on her, more dangerous than the storm. She took a step back, then another, and bumped into the closed door. Pressing herself into the wood, she sucked in her breath and felt it trap in her chest when he levered one elbow against the door alongside her head and slowly leaned close. The jut of his chest brushed like hot flame against the curve of her tingling breasts, his hips rested in bold, seductive promise against hers, but the heat of him. . . .

She swam in it, feeling it flow through her until her veins swelled and throbbed to life and every inch of her skin burned. When he lowered his head, her eyes swept closed and her lips parted beneath the brandied heat of his breath.

"And now, sweet wife," he whispered against her lips, "you can tell me where you've been for the past three hours."

Chapter Sixteen

❖

"You're drunk."

Miles curved his lips against hers. "You're right." Sliding his hand around her head, he filled his fist with the loose curls and pressed them to his face. His head swam with the feel and the scent of her wrapping around him, filling all the emptiness, gently wiping away the pain. "You smell like the sea."

"It's the storm coming in," she murmured. "The rain tastes of salt."

"So do you." He lowered his mouth over hers, but she turned her head away, evading him. Pressing his forehead to hers, he sensed the trembling in her beneath a stiff resistance that he couldn't quite understand. A rasp burst from his throat. "Teddie, why are you keeping yourself from me?"

"I needed air. I couldn't sleep."

"You were gone all day . . . all night. You're running from me because of last night."

She stiffened. "I'm not . . . I . . . I've never run from anything. I . . . to be perfectly honest I can't seem to remember much of last evening that's all. . . . Not that this is causing me any distress, of course."

"Of course. You've suffered memory lapses in the past, I presume."

She stared up at him. He could hear her noisy swallow. "It's not what I would call customary for me, no. I don't think I'll ever drink anything that Winnie brews again."

"Ah. You should know I rose above myself and the limits of my restraint last evening. I did the noble Winchester legacy proud."

He could almost feel the sigh of relief whispering through

her, followed quickly by a renewed strength. "Thank you, Winchester. I feel reassured. How very thoughtful of you."

"It wasn't easy," he murmured, dipping his head to nuzzle the soft side of her neck. "You were bewitching."

A shock seemed to jolt through her, and again he sensed the innate resistance in her. "Did you find what you were looking for in your drink?"

He closed his eyes against the intermittent spinning in his head. A red fog had descended over his mind. He hadn't expected her to be pleased with him and his state at the moment. He also hadn't expected to feel so soundly contrite about it. "I didn't."

"I thought so. You were at your club in Williamsburg?"

"As far as I can remember."

"Did you accomplish anything besides drinking yourself silly?"

"Yes, as a matter of fact." He lifted his head and regarded her through bleary eyes, forcing a levity he didn't feel into his tone. "I lost my entire purse to a jolly man from Williamsburg, and I believe I won several horses of exceedingly muddled and undetermined blood from another man from Kentucky. All in all a draw." He curved his hand around her head and forced her gaze up to his. "I don't want to have a conversation with you, Teddie," he rumbled, lowering his mouth to hers.

She shoved one palm into the middle of his chest, for the moment keeping him at bay. "I couldn't agree more. You're in no condition to talk. It's a wonder you can walk aright."

His sigh wheezed through his teeth. "You sound like a schoolmistress I once had. A Miss Maplethorpe. I remember at the time I thought her quite old, but now that I think about it she must have been obscenely young, very blond, with a crisp command in everything she said. I also remember she had breasts of the most astonishing shape and size. I spent the entire sixth grade in complete distraction." His lopsided grin faded as he hooded his gaze again on the dewy fullness of her mouth.

Every instinct he possessed screamed out for the comfort and solace only she could bring him. He ached for it: the intimacy and warmth of her bare skin against his, the gentle play of her hands stroking over him, the quiet strength that was so much a part of her, empowering him, soothing him, making him whole. He didn't know how to do it without her. So he'd tried in vain elsewhere. He'd been a fool to think he'd find it at his club, making reckless wagers with men he didn't know, men who wouldn't ever understand why he'd felt such a need to tempt fate and lose. All they'd cared about was reaping the reward of his folly.

He looked deep into her eyes and for several moments the pain there mirrored that writhing in the pit of his belly. He swallowed past the thickness in his throat. "I've been an ass."

"Yes, I can believe that." Her features softened slightly, but her tone held the same crispness, the same astonishing lack of intimacy given their close, overwhelming physical proximity. Outwardly, she appeared unaffected. And yet *he* could feel every pulse of her blood as it flowed through her veins. Their breaths mingled, hers coming shallow and swift, betraying her cool facade.

"I blame myself," he muttered, drawing back slightly. He lifted his glass to his lips and found it empty. He glanced at her. She watched him, clutching whatever was in that bundle to her chest and waiting patiently. Unlike so many women who couldn't abide a moment of contemplative silence in their conversations, Teddie didn't make any attempts to put words in his mouth or fill the void with idle chitchat. It was almost as if she heard the muddle of his thoughts and somehow made sense of it all where he couldn't.

Thunder shook the planks beneath his feet. He shoved a hand through his hair. "Damned fool Damian thinks I'm angry with him."

"I don't suppose you told him otherwise."

"Not in so many words." Their gazes met, and a profound weariness and ineptitude consumed him. He allowed his head to fall back and briefly watched the lightning flash on the carved moldings crowning the ten-foot ceilings overhead. "Ah, hell, Teddie, I don't know. Maybe I'm angry at him for charging after a fool's dream of glory in a war that makes no sense to me.'' He felt the rage building again in the center of his chest, the tightening that refused his every effort to dispel it. His gaze sought hers, the shred of solace amidst the turmoil. ''Teddie, England has been bled white by Napoléon. This country is weakened by sectional dissension between the greedy businessmen of the north and the hate-filled war hawks of the south. Neither side has enough strength or manpower to sustain an effective invasion, the Americans into Canada, or the British into America, by land or sea.

''All that has come of three years of fighting is scattered skirmishes, needless loss of life, and a virtual guarantee of an inconclusive outcome. Men like Damian allow themselves to be consumed with their lust for glory. They understand nothing of the implications. They refuse to see that neutrality has brought this country prosperity. All they see is the humiliations suffered by our country when our merchants' ships are seized and our sailors impressed onto British ships. All they know is that this is to be a second war of independence. And most of them will die in it, just like their fathers and grandfathers did in the first war for independence. Damned legacy.'' He swallowed deeply. ''He thinks I believe him a coward.''

''Do you?''

''No.'' The tightening in his chest twisted around itself, infusing his voice with hoarse emotion. ''He may be all kinds of a fool, but he's no coward. I just should have stopped him when I could. Instead, I shoved him out that door with my damned pride and ignorance, my lack of responsibility toward anyone but myself. I was blinded, Teddie. Blinded by my need to teach him a lesson in life, but even more by my need to justify my own private hell. I succeeded.''

''You couldn't have stopped him, Winchester. You're not responsible for all the madness.''

''Only my own.''

''Not even for that.''

''Christ, Teddie, I'm his only family. And I've spent the last eight years in hell preparing him for this. We'll be lucky if he doesn't kill himself.''

''*You* didn't. You crawled through a desert to save yourself.

The unspeakable horrors you witnessed and endured didn't matter. You simply didn't want to die.''

He glanced sharply at her. ''I thought about it. You can bet he is.''

''Is Jillie with him?''

''She's been with him all night. Keeping him drugged. She sings to him.'' His lids drooped over his eyes. ''Would you sing to me, if I asked?''

''You would ask only once,'' she murmured, laying a hand on his chest, which he at once covered with his own, afraid that if he didn't she would remove hers. ''You're relieved he's home,'' she said.

He hesitated. ''I'm relieved he's alive, in any form.''

''Then tell him.''

He snorted. ''He needs me for the one thing I can't give him, and that's to validate him as a soldier and a Winchester.''

''Maybe. But until you can see your way to that, you can give him your understanding instead of your contempt.''

His brows descended, chest puffing, as he sharply drew himself up. The floor instantly tilted beneath his feet. ''I'm not—''

''You see yourself laying there with no arm.''

''The hell I do.''

''Just as you saw yourself in the proud and noble young man charging off to battle to find glory in yet another war that made no sense. The Barbary pirates still rule their waters despite all the bloodshed, don't they?''

He set his teeth. ''They do. But that was altogether different, and I was never so—''

''Foolhardy? Maybe impassioned is a better word, all but bursting with golden dreams of liberty? These dreams die painfully, and often too swiftly. Winchester, Damian doesn't need validation any more than you do. He needs compassion. He needs understanding. He needs love. Or like you he'll condemn himself to his own private hell, where no one will be able to reach him. And that's the greatest tragedy. A sad legacy, don't you agree?''

He swallowed, unable to compose a hint of response or argument. He felt pinned to the wall, soundly lambasted, and laid open. And he didn't like it in the least. When she brushed past him and headed down the hall with strong, sure strides, he could only watch her.

"Where are you going?" he finally bellowed after her.

"To relieve Jillie. Goodnight, Winchester."

She didn't even look back.

Over the next several days Teddie and Jillie kept round-the-clock, four-hour watches over Damian. When not at his side Teddie either closeted herself in her chamber to catch snatches of sleep or buried herself in Winchester's study with medical books. Somehow she had to feel useful in this time of great need. The energetic Jillie achieved this by cooking enormous pots of chicken soup, washing bed linen every day, changing wound dressings, and singing at Damian's bedside, all of which helped to bring his fever gradually down but did nothing for his black mood. After two days he refused any more laudanum for either the pain or his mental anguish, and for hours at a time he sat in silence, staring blankly into the fire that Jillie kept ablaze. He didn't speak. He barely touched his food. Melancholy wrapped around him, consuming him more surely than any fever or infection ever could.

And the specter of suicide hung as palpably as the heavy curtains draping the windows.

Teddie, through her endless research into every medical book Winchester owned, could find nothing to aid her in helping rid Damian of his anguish. She penned desperate missives to several Richmond doctors Winchester had noted in his writings and anxiously awaited their replies, knowing she could wait weeks. Her talk with Winchester had served her just as poorly, and she couldn't contain her frustration and helplessness over his obvious though unspoken refusal to face his own torment and attempt a reconciliation with Damian. From her window each morning, before dawn had chased away the last smudges of darkness, she watched him leave the house and take to the fields. He worked as tirelessly as the stoutest of the slaves, cutting leaves and stacking them on scaffolds. One afternoon she sat at the window for some time watching him, memorizing the fluid motion of his swinging arms, drinking of the almost pagan strength he displayed.

Hoping that with one more vicious swipe of his blade, or one more trip to the warehouse with the bulging scaffold levered in his arms, he would finally see his way through the pain of forgiving himself of his own failings and come to Damian.

Yet each day ended the same, with him returning long after dark, long after the windows throughout the house had been closed, the drapes drawn, the candles dimmed, and the last of the evening meal cleared. With an increasingly heavy heart Teddie listened from Damian's room for Winchester's tread. He never came. Nor did he seek her out in the days following their midnight encounter in the lower hall, when she'd managed to avoid betraying herself solely because of his liquored state.

She was beginning to think she'd been wrong in leaving him to find his way alone. He might never. As surely as Damian had descended into his melancholy, Winchester had retreated beyond anyone's reach. And she couldn't shake the feeling that she was somehow to blame. She was nearly convinced that he'd become entirely uncaring, bereft of all feeling and compassion, and that she'd simply imagined the depth of feeling she'd seen in him, the untapped well of emotion that seemed at times on the verge of spilling out of him. But then on the third night, after she'd left Damian's room and was walking toward the west wing past Winchester's room, she noticed his door slightly ajar. Unable to resist, goaded on by her mounting frustration with him, she paused to peek into the darkened bedchamber. She found him standing at the windows, staring out over the milky, moon-washed fields of flowering tobacco. As lonely as a man could be, as troubled as she'd ever seen him, seeking something out there in the darkness, something she knew he would only find within himself.

Forgiveness. Why was it so difficult a thing for a man, especially when he needed most to forgive himself? Why did that span of carpeted hall between his room and Damian's suddenly loom like some unbridgeable chasm to him, a man who had risen above some of the greatest physical challenges that could ever confront a human being?

As silently as she'd come, she retreated to her room and her precious four hours of sleep. She knew why she'd left him, difficult as it was. The trouble was, she didn't know why he didn't come to her.

Miles roared awake, heaving up in his bed with eyes wide and glazed and a scream dying in his throat. He stared into the darkness and listened to his labored breathing as the last red-hazed vestiges of the nightmare finally drifted out of his consciousness. Licking perspiration from his lips, he released his white-fisted grip on the sheets and swung his legs over the side of the bed. With elbows braced on his knees and feet spread wide on the carpet, he stared at the floor.

The nightmares had returned with a vengeance, a ghastly landscape of horror and torture, of losing his mind to a drug and his will to a lascivious Tripolitan ruler incapable of functioning as a man for all his wives. Tonight, as always, the dream had been bathed in a bright, bloodied crimson, just as he last remembered the waters in the Bay of Tripoli. But tonight the dream had ended much differently. The woman lying beneath him on the dey's red velvet sofa had not been a dusky-skinned, black-haired, black-eyed Tripolitan gone slack with the effects of the same opium that clouded his mind and purposely prolonged his sexual function, the better to pleasure the dey who watched from behind a filmy screen. Nor was she the sly young virgin-bride Manal, whose traitorous affections for Miles cost her her life and condemned him to the dey's opium-laced salon.

No, tonight the woman's skin glowed an unearthly shade of pearled pink. Tonight, she didn't lie unresponsive beneath him until hours of cajoling roused a halfhearted response. Tonight she writhed and bucked at the whisper of his fingertips on her heated flesh, on the high mounds of her breasts, and in that dark nest of curls between her slick thighs. Tonight she stoked and matched his savagery and never once shrank from it. She only begged for more.

Tonight the lady wore a black mask and nothing else.

Tonight his manhood distended full and heavy against his belly.

The nightmare had indeed ended differently.

That he had dreamed of his lady impostor didn't surprise him. Intent on keeping his thoughts from Damian, he'd been thinking a great deal about her over the last several days while he worked in the fields with the sun slapping the back of his neck and his arm and back muscles screaming for some respite from his labor. It was then, at the very heights of his physical stress, that he most keenly remembered the supple curve of her body rising up against his as they'd both surged out of their saddles. He knew now what he'd refused to acknowledge then: She was without question a woman, bold and audacious, elusive, mysterious, and too reckless.

And she was on the verge of being captured.

One more night, precisely a week to the day after the last rendezvous. Then the mystery would be up. The game played to the final hand. She would taunt him no more. At least in this arena he would prevail with his due amount of Winchester bravado.

Then he would be able to face his duty here, Damian's madness, and Teddie's silence, which spoke with far more eloquence and conviction than any waspish harping ever composed by a frustrated and embittered wife.

He reached for his silk robe, shrugged into it, and left his room. Just beyond his door he paused, listening for the muted humming coming from Damian's room, the reassurance that Damian fared well. Still, as he moved down the dark hall toward the stairs and silence swelled around him, he couldn't shake the unease taking deep root within him. That he quite obviously desired his lady impostor didn't disturb him nearly as much as the blinding magnitude of this desire. In his dream he had been the hunter, she the prey he would stalk, capture, and tame. In his dream he had prevailed. Was it the challenge met and the success achieved that had set him aflame, or was it the elusive woman of mystery, as elusive as Teddie had become for him?

Why was he consumed with a need to possess them both, to prove himself worthy and able of conquering at least one foe?

He paused at the top of the stairs and stared into the long length of hall leading deep into the west wing. Behind the very last door Teddie slumbered, laid out long and lush against cool sheets, with only some filmy thing upon her skin. The image blossomed through his mind, and his nostrils flared as if he could catch her scent in the air. Desire leapt through him with renewed urgency and he gripped the mahogany banister. He was a man tortured tonight, by the achingly beautiful wife he'd vowed not to touch and by the bewitching and bold lady of the night he couldn't catch. Two women.

Tomorrow night he would capture one—the mysterious foe—and in so doing, he told himself, he would conquer his lust for her as well. Only then would he face the other—his wife—and together they would conquer the last of the demons that haunted him.

"Miss Teddie, you's left Cleo in her stall. She sho' would enjoy spendin' the aftuhnoon in the meadow."

Teddie shook her head, as much to clear it of its distraction as in reply to Simon, who stood in the open stable door watching her. "No . . . thank you, Simon. I'd like her left here for the day."

A horse allowed to eat her bellyful of clover and grass wouldn't race across the fields and the sand at midnight with lightning in her hooves.

Teddie glanced at the feed trough half-filled with oats, satisfied that Cleo would be in top form this evening. She had kept their morning exercise purposely brief in the hope that the mare would lunge into her bit tonight, when her speed and heart would be put to a mountainous test. For the hundredth time that morning since she'd risen and seen to Damian, apprehension gnawed at Teddie's belly. She'd done everything she could to banish it, to keep her thoughts on Damian, not on her rendezvous this evening with Cockburn and the trap they'd laid for the Night Hawk. And she'd failed miserably. Her limbs seemed possessed of a peculiar jittering and her thoughts all tumbled together in an incoherent mess. Her ride had done her little good.

Perhaps because she realized she simply couldn't fail tonight. Opportunity dangled before her, waiting for her to grasp it with both hands. And her plan was crystal clear: In order to have the leverage needed to convince Cockburn to release Will, she had to capture the Night Hawk herself, *before* Cockburn's men did. Only then would she have the power to negotiate for her brother's release.

Accomplishing this, she suspected, would be far more difficult than simply conceiving of it.

Smoothing her palm over Cleo's muzzle one last time, she turned to brush past Simon. "See there," she said, indicating Wildair as he poked his nose at her over the top edge of his stall. "Winchester has him cooped up as well. Perhaps like Cleo, Wildair can't abide the clover."

"It ain' the clovuh, Miss Teddie," Simon replied, giving her a broad smile that revealed no trace of suspicion, and yet guilt threatened to flood over her, just as the heat climbed ominously into her cheeks. "The clovuh nevuh bothuhed Wildair or Cleo befo', ma'am."

"It might today," she said quickly, forcing a smile, then dropping her eyes from his. "She doesn't quite seem herself."

Simon nodded slowly. "Yes'm. 'Course, Wildair's gonna race tomorrow, ma'am. He cain't run wit' the wind if he gots a bellyful o' clovuh. But you's a fine horsewoman. You knows that, don't you, ma'am?" His singsong chuckle set her frayed nerves on edge. "Maybe you's gonna race Cleo, ma'am. You sho' treatin' her like she gonna race real soon."

Surely she was imagining the subtle taunt in Simon's voice, the knowing glitter in his twinkly gaze. She clung to reason. How the devil could he suspect that she was the Night Hawk impostor simply because she refused to set Cleo free in a field full of clover? Preposterous. She'd never even heard Simon mention the Night Hawk. The subject had yet to come up among any of the people here at Miramer.

Shrugging off her unease, she gave Wildair's muzzle a fond pat. "Now that would be something, pitting Wildair against

Cleo. I would attempt it, Simon, if I wasn't certain Wildair would easily win.'' She brushed past the overseer with a cheery good day and had just stepped into the midmorning sunlight when Simon's voice stopped her cold.

''Oh, I 'spect if the race was run on sand, ma'am, Cleo could git away from any stallion.''

Slowly, Teddie turned and stared at Simon. Her pulse suddenly thundered in her ears. A lump lodged in the middle of her chest, and her voice rasped from a throat suddenly gone dry as bone. ''What did you say, Simon?''

The overseer merely smiled. ''Sand, ma'am. Wildair's too strong an' big to move on sand like a sprightly mare. That's all I's sayin'. I's more 'n anyone would love to see the massa's horse beat. Uh huh. An' by a mare. Yes'm. When you race, do it on sand.'' His eyes narrowed slightly as he paused then added, ''I's bettuh git back to work. Good day, Miss Teddie.''

''Good day, Simon.'' She watched him lumber to the back of the stable. ''Coincidence,'' she muttered half-aloud as she turned and strode briskly along the cobbled path that led to the house. With eyes on the cobblestones, she worried her lower lip and continued muttering. ''Simply coincidence. He suspects nothing. Nothing at all. If he did he would tell Winchester, wouldn't he? Of course, he would. He'd have no reason not to. And Winchester would throw me in irons immediately for spying.'' Three more strides and she'd all but convinced herself. ''Coincidence, that's it. Nothing to worry about. Nothing at all. . . .''

By the time she reached the kitchen, set back a good twenty paces from the main house, she'd put the better part of her apprehension to rest. One glance inside the kitchen building, however, and the familiar acrid bite of dread threatened to choke her again, but this time for an altogether different reason.

''Jillie—'' She pushed the wooden door wide, her voice catching when Jillie didn't look up from the potatoes she was peeling with swift, vicious strokes of her knife. Even in the splash of midday sunlight streaming through the nearby window, the servant's face was tightly drawn, expressionless, her pale pink mouth pursed with its typical sourness. Somehow,

even with kettles spewing more unnecessary steam into the air
and fires burning in the massive twin hearths set at opposite
ends of the room, Jillie managed to look cool and crisp, not a
hair wilting beneath her ruffled cap or a dot of perspiration
marring her luminescent skin. And yet something inside Teddie
went cold at the sight of her. "What is it, Jillie? Why aren't
you with Damian?"

The knife flashed in the sunlight as Jillie looked up and
turned her stare from the window. Only then did Teddie see the
twin paths her tears had woven over her cheeks. "Jillie," she
gasped, moving to the servant's side and laying a tentative hand
on her shoulder. At her touch Jillie seemed to shrink into herself before swaying against Teddie.

"I'm so sorry, madam," Jillie whispered, "but I can't sit
beside him anymore. I can't bear it. Winnie's with him now."
She swallowed and returned to her peeling, her tears splashing
onto the potatoes. "He's no worse. Perhaps even better. It's
just . . . is it my fate to love men who can't love in return? I
want so desperately to help them and I can't."

Shuddering with relief, Teddie replied, "You may not see it,
but I know you've helped Damian."

Jillie shook her head and dumped potatoes into a large pot of
water. "He rages at me. He tells me to leave him alone."

"It's his helplessness that makes him rage, not you. He
wants you at his side, singing to him."

Jillie shoved the back of her hand over her cheeks. "He
doesn't even hear me."

"I believe he does. He told me he thinks you sing like an
angel. Before all this he used to come to hear you sing while
you worked here in the kitchen."

Jillie lifted eyes brimming with tears, with hope, and with
pain.

And somewhere in the other woman's stricken face, as her
carefully tended thick outer shell crumbled, Teddie saw herself
struggling to keep her own walls intact. "Sometimes it's the
small things we do, Jillie, the tenderness and the caring we
show through almost insignificant acts that bear the most fruit.
Every day it's as if a single fragile crocus struggles from the

ground and up to the sun. One fragile crocus, followed by another, and then another, until you've sown a field of them, and they sweep from horizon to horizon like a blanket that can't be breached."

"I believe some men are beyond all hope, madam."

"Perhaps some are. But none lives in this house."

"I don't believe that."

"If you don't believe it then why are you peeling enough potatoes to fill these two enormous pots? Is it soup he wants today?"

"Potato soup," Jillie replied quietly.

"Specifically requested, I presume. He must have smelled it bubbling on this stove while he listened to you sing all those days."

Jillie looked up, her eyes clouding with suspicion. "Why are you telling me this? You should hate me. I believe I hated you when you first came here to be mistress of Miramer. From what I'd heard I thought you had trapped him into marriage and had purposely set Damian against him. I thought you were a selfish, spoiled woman who cared about nothing but herself. More than that I thought you would never love Miles as I believed I did. I was terribly wrong, about all of it, even about the feelings I had for Miles. You love him, madam, far more than I ever could have, don't you?"

Teddie felt her breath catch. To hear the words spoken jarred her. "Quite desperately."

"That is but a shadow of the love he feels for you."

A heat unmatched by the elements swept through Teddie. Quickly, she riveted her attention on one pot of potatoes, blinking the sudden mist from her eyes. "I . . . I don't believe that—at the moment. Here, let me help you with this."

"You've sowed meadow upon meadow of flowers for Miles. How can you not see it, madam, when you can see it in others?"

With an agitated sniff, Teddie curled both her trembling hands around the pot handle and attempted to hoist it from the table. "I—I don't know what you're talking about. Perhaps your powers of perception would serve you better if you focused them entirely on Damian. He would benefit a great deal from realizing that you love him yourself.''

''We all would benefit knowing we were loved.''

Teddie paused. ''Yes, we would, Jillie, immensely.''

''Then you must tell Miles that you're in love with him.''

''That's entirely out of the question.''

''Why shouldn't you?''

''I . . . I—'' Teddie snapped her teeth and summoned a frown she thought well-suited to a high-handed mistress of the manor. ''I don't suppose it would matter much at the moment if I reminded you of your place.''

Jillie looked far too smug to suit. ''No, madam, it wouldn't.''

''Well, I'm not going to tell Winchester anything. Now move out of the way so I can get this pot on the table—'' She lifted the pot, turned toward the table strewn with vegetables, when a voice ringing with the familiar rich, mellow tones that would forever warm her soul suddenly stopped her in her tracks.

''What is it you're not going to tell me, wife?''

Pot gripped in both hands, Teddie spun around so quickly the water sloshed out of the pot all over her blue serge gown. Winchester stood silhouetted in the kitchen doorway, taller, broader, more imposing than memory had served. His features were undefined, thrown into deep shadow, impossible to identify. But she knew he stared at her. *Like a predator.* A breeze ruffled through his shirt, setting his sleeves billowing like great wings just moments from spreading wide to catch the full thrust of the wind.

Like a hawk.

The pot slipped from Teddie's fingers and crashed to the floor. Potatoes flew out of the pot and water splashed all over Teddie's shoes and the hem of her gown. At once she bent to retrieve the pot, battling an almost unconscionable desire to flee, to seek safe haven somewhere, anywhere, *away from him.* Away from the suspicion flaring in some dark recesses of her mind.

''Teddie.'' He seemed to loom around and over her, trapping

her there with the force of his bodily presence and the hushed intimacy lacing his voice.

Her lungs compressed. She could scarcely draw a clean breath.

"Christ, Teddie, you're pale as death. What is it?"

She nearly shrank back when his hands cupped her upper arms and he gently shook her. "The heat . . ." she managed, avoiding looking at him by trying to scoop the potatoes back into the pot. "I . . . I told you I've never accomplished the womanly arts. How can anyone work in such heat?"

Yes, the heat. Hallucination and all manner of odd, suspicious thoughts could be prompted by this suffocating heat. That's all it was. Mere hallucination.

She knew he wasn't convinced, simply by the increasing pressure of his hands on her arms, drawing her closer against him, offering himself as solace, as comfort, as protection.

She jerked to her feet, bracing one hand on the table. "I'm fine. See. Standing aright." She paused, glancing up at him through a fringe of tendrils plucked loose by the steam. A mistake, that. When had she ever been able to look up at him and not feel something inside her twist around itself and cry out with need?

"What is it that you can't tell me?" he asked, brows lowering slightly, his tone suddenly brooking little argument. "And if you don't tell me, Jillie will."

"No, she won't," Teddie said quickly. "I can tell you myself, if you'd like."

"I would."

"Fine."

He stared at her for several long moments, then leaned slightly closer. "Well?"

Teddie swallowed, then thrust up her chin. "Your cousin Damian is improving."

From over her shoulder Teddie could hear Jillie's swift, frustrated exhale, as though she'd held her breath for some time. Seconds later the side door to the kitchen thwacked closed as Jillie made a hasty retreat, leaving them very much alone in the sun-dappled kitchen with the bubbling steam and the blazing hearths and the two sleeping cats in the corner chair.

Teddie felt her heart skip a beat.

Winchester blinked once, twice, then his frown deepened. "Thank you for telling me. You considered keeping this from me?"

"I wasn't aware that you cared."

"That's not fair."

"And what is?" Teddie tossed her head and flung an arm toward the house. "Allowing him to wallow in despair without even attempting to help, instead pretending that he isn't even there? Or that perhaps his anguish will simply go away with his fever? I can tell you no drug, no amount of care or potato soup will wrest that out of him."

His features tightened into deep, unforgiving lines. "Dammit, I can't solve that for him."

"No, you simply refuse to try. Now, let me pass, you stubborn oaf."

His hand shot out and caught her upper arm. "Not so fast, sweetheart," he growled. Then, with one easy flex of his arm, he yanked her flush against him.

Teddie's first thought jarred her: Three days of toil in the fields had honed him from head to toe into one solid length of tempered steel. And her body reacted to him as it always had and always would, with an instantaneous, almost blinding sensory awareness along every inch of her that was pressed against him. No matter the blatherings of the mind, however logical and solidly based in reason. She couldn't deny it.

But she could damned well try.

With fists braced against the jut of his biceps, she shoved her chin up and glared at him. "You've never resorted to barbaric attempts to restrain me, Winchester."

"True. But you've never resorted to childish name-calling either. Why so angry, love?"

Teddie pressed her lips together. "Don't call me that."

"Do you want to know what Jules Reynolds would advise at the moment, wife?" he purred, his lids sliding low over smoldering black eyes. "You do have a look about you, Teddie."

"Quite right. I'm angry."

"Without question. Your anger—it simmers just below your skin. You look heated by some inner source. I've never seen you strung so tightly with it. You need release, Teddie, swift and savage."

She stiffened, trying her damnedest to ignore the seductive honeyed tone in his voice and its resulting effect on her. Even now she could feel her resistance slipping precariously, the slow, inevitable melting of her body into his. "Indeed. I rode this morning."

"This morning." One black brow arched with purely wicked intent. "It did nothing for you, did it, sweet?" He stared at her mouth, his own parting, revealing his white teeth, the tip of his tongue sliding along the lower edge. "I can't find it either," he murmured, "no matter how hard I try to convince myself that I have. On this alone I concede to Reynolds. There is only one cure for what ails us, wife. And you know what that is."

Teddie felt her lips part as if at his will, heard the rumble in his chest when her breasts swelled against him with her agitated breaths. "Winchester—"

His fingers pressed to her lips. "No, don't tell me. Show me."

Chapter Seventeen

The rough edge of the table dug into Teddie's lower back as she pressed herself deeper against it, groping at it with both hands. But Winchester granted her no quarter. No whisper of air dared to pass between them to offer a hint of cooling solace as he bent her back over the table strewn with vegetables, with the inescapable force of an advancing storm.

"Show me," he rumbled again, his mouth lowering over hers, the pressure of his chest forcing the breath from her lungs.

Her fingers wrapped around a bunch of carrots and she clutched at them as if to the last vestiges of her resistance. "We're in the kitchen," she reminded him delicately.

"I don't give a damn where we are." With one swipe of his arm he cleared the tabletop. Vegetables scattered. A pot clanged to the floor and rolled against one wall.

"But the door is open—" What remained of Teddie's voice left her in a sudden rush of air when he cupped her buttocks and lifted her pelvis up and against his, then laid her flat on the table.

"I've had more than enough of talking," he rasped, "and more than enough of doors, closed or open." His voice was taut and full, betraying the depths of a reckless passion loosely and tenuously reined. The savage intensity darkened his eyes as they raked over her breasts and probed the serge bunched at her hips. She could feel the impatience in his hands, the singularity of purpose as he shoved her skirts up to her thighs. And yet instead of rousing fear or ire or a desire to flee him, this only roused the hunger in her to new, staggering heights. Her fingers clutched at the edges of the table as a wild, liquid heat spilled through her veins.

Shudders rippled through her at the first brush of his finger-tips along the lace edging at the tops of her stockings. Swallowing a moan of complete helplessness, she surrendered herself as those long fingers slipped beneath the lace edges at the tops of her thighs and traced a torturous path inward along the delicate skin of her thighs, then back to the fragile garters. With palms flat he slowly molded the contours of her thighs through the silken stocking, then slowly caressed lower over her knees, fingers delving into the indentation behind, then encircling her calves and her ankles. Eyes hooded, chest testing the confines of white linen with each deep breath he drew, he curved his fingers around and over every silken, tingling inch of her legs. Without encountering a whisper of resistance, he laid his palms on her inner thighs and parted them, his murmur of satisfaction rumbling from his throat when the heat of his loins probed against hers.

"I'm going to drive your anger from you, Theodora," he murmured, his chest and stomach like hot irons against the length of her as he leaned close and brushed his lips over hers. "Again and again, through days and into weeks. But even that won't ease the need I have in my blood for you."

Teddie sank her fingers into the lustrous thickness of his hair, her breaths coming short and swift from lips parted and eager. Her eyes lifted to his and somehow she sensed he hesitated, still, despite the desire threatening to devour them both. Even now she could feel the pressure hot and full in her loins, the ache building there, the intense, almost painful need to be filled by the thickness of him.

"Please, Miles," she whispered, drawing his mouth to hers, surrendering with the most elemental part of herself.

With punishing force his mouth crushed over hers, his tongue pushing deep with masterful strokes. She met the savagery of his passion with her own wanton, reckless, and glorious release of innocence. With no misgivings, reluctance, or mistrust, she plunged with him into the unknown, a place of darkly mysterious desires and primal need, of the basest lust, a swollen river of physical pleasure.

And yet, as the buttons popped from their moors beneath

impatient fingers, laces tugged free, and linen, serge, and thin batiste jerked aside to lay seams open and flesh to flesh from breast to hip, Teddie knew her need of him went well beyond the basest of physical desires. When he drank of her flesh, in one long, open-mouthed plundering of her breasts and beyond the lower curve of her belly, she was the dove set free of a lifetime of bonds, for the first time spreading her wings to the warmth of the sun. And when he loomed over her, whispering love words to her, then lifted her up, into, and against him so that he poised at the pulsing entrance to her, she clung to him, not out of desperation or fear, but out of her boundless love for him.

In one long fluid stroke he filled her, driving so deeply she bit out a cry. For several moments he didn't move.

"My honeyed, sweet Theodora," he rasped against her lips. "Burn for me, love. Let me make you cry with the sweetness of it. . . ."

At first his hips moved in a gentle undulating rhythm, and she met each thrust with a lifting of her hips as the pressure crescendoed, like waves building on waves, each peak surpassing the last. With a hoarse plea for release she flung her head back, arching up against him, and he lifted her with one hand curved around her back. She swam in the heat of his mouth on her breasts, the wildly possessive breadth of his hand cupping them, lifting the nipples to his mouth. He possessed her, inside and out, and she drank of him as he drank of her and lifted her up into the clouds, the dove set free by him alone.

Her climax thundered over her in cataclysmic waves, one after another, in relentless succession. With hoarse cries she clutched at the muscle popping in his shoulders, and he went at once entirely rigid, arching up like some magnificent lion and spilling himself into her with long, slow, shuddering spasms. Then with a groan he sagged over her, arms braced on the table on either side of her, head hanging.

Only the sound of their breath could be heard for several moments. Teddie opened her eyes and blinked at the low-beamed ceiling overhead. Reality crept over her, inch by inch, dousing all the flames. Consequences—she lay on the table as vulnerable as a peeled vegetable, her heart open, gaping. That she loved him beyond reason was becoming painfully obvious to her. But what did that mean?

Through a thickness in her throat she managed, "Th-that was quite—"

"I know." He lifted his head and smiled at her, a smooth, lazy smile that set stars twinkling in his eyes and turned Teddie's heart over in her breast. "Quite magnificent. Quite beyond compare or expectation. Let's do it again."

Teddie shoved her palms into his bare chest the instant he began to lower himself over her. No, a repeat of their . . . no, that wouldn't be wise considering that guilt and deception suddenly loomed like an invisible fortress between them. There was, however, little escaping the fact that they were still joined in the most intimate manner and that she could feel him swelling again within her the instant his loins rocked gently against hers. "I don't think—"

"No, don't think," he murmured, lowering his head over her breasts and cupping one in his large hand. "And don't talk." His tongue flicked over one nipple, drawing it painfully taut and fully distended.

Teddie squirmed, which only seemed to have the opposite of its intended effect, particularly on her. Every tingly, heat-dampened inch of her bare skin rubbed against his, slick and sleek and deliciously wanton. "Oh, God," she whispered. "Please, Winchester, there are things you must know."

"Like what?" His breath came hotter on her breasts, one long sigh escaping him as he slowly withdrew then buried himself deep within her. "Like what you want me to do to you, Theodora?"

"No—y-you've got a marvelous grasp on that." Her breath caught as he slid himself up against the length of her. Every inch of her flesh burned into his.

"No, my sweet honey-love," he rasped against her mouth, his lips curving wickedly. "It is you who has the grasp, and it's tighter, warmer, wetter—"

"Stop." Deeply chagrined, she pressed trembling fingertips to his lips. She swallowed deeply, unable to keep from tracing the sensual curve of his mouth. Mush, that's what she was, complete mush. "I have no will with you."

He nipped at her fingers, his eyes holding her mesmerized. "You don't need will with me."

"I feel lost without it. I've never been so without control over myself. And yet . . ." She breathed a sigh, her eyes fluttering closed as she surrendered to the sensations building deep within her again.

"Yet?" He rose above her, features drawing taut and shadowed with his rising passions. "You were saying?" he said huskily. "Have I somehow driven all words from you? Or have you found that there can be unspeakable pleasure in losing all control?"

"Oh, Miles," she breathed, pulling his head to hers.

"I thought so," he muttered, before he claimed her mouth as easily as he'd claimed her body and her soul.

Sometime later, with a good deal of reluctance, Miles drew Teddie up from the table and set himself to recreating some sense of feminine propriety out of the tangle of underclothes and laces and bows and hooks and garters that he had lain to complete disorder with remarkable speed and agility. He'd been so consumed he hadn't even shed his breeches. A man could accomplish great feats if given the proper motivation. And he was not lacking for that.

The blue serge gown lay open past her waist, the batiste shift as well, offering up as lush and ripe a visual feast as Miles had ever imagined. Every inch of her glowed rosy, from her love-swollen lips to the dewy tips of her breasts.

He was bewitched. Entirely. Gloriously out of his mind with the joy of it. And her sudden blushing self-consciousness and inability to look him square in the eye only made him itch to tumble her back on that table.

He paused as he drew the chemise together, curving one hand around her throat and jaw and lowering his mouth to hers. "If I didn't know you better I'd think you were a shy, retiring maiden." Her lips trembled beneath his, then parted at the gentle thrust of his tongue. Even now she tasted of unspoiled innocence. He curved his hand around her breast. Beneath the flimsy linen one nipple swelled like a flower bursting open into his palm. Desire poured through him. Christ, but at this rate he'd accomplish nothing for the rest of his life, Miramer would crumble into dust, and he'd still die a supremely happy man.

He lifted his head, drawing a ragged breath. "This may sound banal, but I've got to leave now. I've appointments today in Williamsburg with several men who are looking to sell or trade some of their horses. I'm always looking for fresh stock."

"Then you should go," she said softly, tugging her dress closed, her eyes low, shielded.

He swallowed, at a loss with her shyness, even more with his own tight-throated inability to find the right words at the moment. And then there was the persistent ache in the center of his chest, like a woman's fist squeezing. "I don't want to leave you . . . ever. Especially now that we've—"

"Yes, we have, haven't we?"

Indeed they had. In their zeal they'd managed to shove the kitchen table several feet across the planked floor.

He rubbed the pad of his thumb over her cheek. "I may be quite late." Depending on how handily he bagged his impostor. He opened his mouth, then caught himself. No sense in telling her the whole scheme now. As it was, he'd have to run Zeus into the ground to reach Williamsburg in time for his appointments. After he returned tonight, after he'd caught his impostor and unmasked her, then he'd lay it all out for Teddie, when he had the time to explain. "We'll talk tonight then," he said.

Finally, she lifted her eyes to his, and he glimpsed a haunted look there that momentarily chilled him. "Yes, we must. I'll wait up for you."

"The talk may have to wait, you know," he murmured, drawing her close against him. "At least for a short time." With a wicked half-smile, he lowered his mouth over hers.

"Or longer," she whispered, arching up against him with an eagerness that belied every bit of her shyness.

But though she melted supple in his arms and bloomed vibrantly responsive beneath his kiss, he couldn't shake a plaguing unease that all was not as it should be. Something was troubling her, something far deeper than an innocent's self-consciousness with her first wanton taste of lust, something that had put that haunting sadness in her eyes. But that would have to wait as well.

What was one more day when he'd waited for her, for this, an entire lifetime, thinking he'd never find it?

She twisted her head away then leaned her forehead against his bare chest. Their breaths came deep, matched. "Go," she whispered, "before I change my mind about letting you go."

He grinned, a joyous eruption that was but a mere fraction of the warmth swelling his soul near to bursting. "Ah. A possessive wife."

"No, merely a lusty one." She tugged his shirt together and swiftly tended to the buttons. He let her, content for the moment to watch her eyes follow the work of her hands on the buttons, lower and lower until her fingers brushed the hem of his shirt directly over the bulge pulling his breeches taut across his loins. Her lips parted slightly. Slowly, her eyes slanted up at him.

He deepened his gaze.

Boldly, her fingers slipped beneath the shirt and traced the contours of his manhood swelling against his breeches. "You are impressive, Winchester," she murmured, slightly breathless, "in every way."

"Then we are evenly matched, wife." Wrapping her hand in his, he lifted it to his lips, his eyes full of unspoken promises. "Yes, I believe you'll agree we should save the talking for the morning. In the meantime, I'll see that your things are moved into my chamber today." His voice grew husky with burgeoning anticipation. "I want you waiting for me there tonight."

"I might not be able to stay awake," she said coyly, rubbing her fingertips against his lips.

"I'll wake you," he rumbled. "Wear nothing. And leave a low candle burning. I've seen you in my dreams laid out naked for me on those sheets. I'm not going to deny myself of it another night."

Her eyes went limpid. "As you wish, my lord."

A growl vibrated in his throat. "You tempt me even in your acquiescence."

"That's as it should be." She laid her palms on his chest and gently pushed. "Go."

"I'm leaving." He didn't move. "Come with me."

"You know I can't."

"The hell I do. I know of several inns along the way. We could stop for food . . . a bed. . . ." He paused, arching a wicked brow. "Surely you're game, my lusty wench?"

"Soft grass would do," she murmured, her eyes darkening with desire before she veiled them with her lashes.

He filled his hands with the plump curves of her buttocks, his voice growing husky with promise as he nuzzled the side of her neck. "The softer the better, wife, for the next ride we take together will be a hard one."

She dipped her head, avoiding his mouth. "They might not wait for you."

"If they knew what I was leaving behind they'd forgive me anything." He nudged her chin up. "I'll carry a sweet memory with me. This was no dream, Teddie."

"To me it is. Now go."

He left her then before another moment passed, before bloodlines, tobacco prices, yield, family honor, or impostors meant positively nothing to him.

Just after dark the clouds descended and the mist rolled in off the bay. By midnight not even a faint breeze stirred the air to offer the slightest respite from the smothering heat. The closer Teddie came to shore, the thicker the mantle of fog became and the heavier the air, making her cloak, shirt, and breeches cling to her damp skin. Vaporous images swam in the low-slung mass overhead, seeming just beyond reach of her fingertips. Somewhere above the murk the moon shone, but here beneath it only an eerie pale blue haze filtered through. Beyond ten yards Teddie could see nothing, particularly out over the bay, where the *Rattlesnake* undoubtedly rode at anchor just to the north.

A quarter mile south of their rendezvous point she pulled

Cleo up short in the concealment of thicket and strained for any sound that the fog hadn't muffled. She felt trapped in a thick cocoon. Blast the mist, but she would have to rely on instinct tonight more than she would have preferred, particularly in outfoxing the Night Hawk. She'd escaped him before through agility and a good deal of fool's luck, but if she couldn't see or hear him approach, if he managed to take her unawares, agility wouldn't do her any good. Her scheme—her life and Will's—would be doomed.

A tightness gripped her throat. She was grimly aware that she wasn't only the hunter this evening but the prey. That being true, the fog could work in her favor. Still, she found it difficult to imagine that the mysterious Night Hawk had ever allowed the mere whims of nature to hinder him. If any man could bend Mother Nature to his will, it would be him, just as easily as he would bend her.

She squirmed, itching everywhere. How did men stay comfortable in the heat without the benefit of a soft layer of undergarments? Even her head was hot, with her hair all stuffed under her hat and the brim tugged low to shield her face. Her hands were damp beneath the leather gloves, and she looped the reins tight several times around them. Against her bare calf her knife lay cool, concealed inside her boot, but oddly enough she drew no comfort from either it or the pistol she'd stuffed into the back of her waistband. Nor did the cutlass in its scabbard at her hip provide its typical bolstering of her spirits. She'd used her weapons once to achieve her escape from an overzealous American regiment, but never had she taken them up with the intent to do anyone harm.

She blinked out into the gloom and felt a cold dread seeping through her. To save herself, to save Will, she'd kill a man, if it came to that.

She desperately prayed it wouldn't. Peculiar as it seemed, she'd come to feel a camaraderie of sorts with the Night Hawk who, like she, required the cloak of darkness to achieve his ends. Neither of them belonged here, to either the British or the Americans. They had somehow found themselves—perhaps unwittingly and certainly precariously—balanced between two warring factions, for their own interests. His bribery of the British could well be viewed as just as treasonous as her spying for Cockburn. But she had come to understand how easily righteous, moral ethics could be forsaken in the face of far greater losses. The realization of this might be painful, but the alternative was unthinkable.

She wondered if he merely sought adventure or if, as she suspected, his reasons ran deep.

Even now, in the muted silence with only a whisper of waves to suggest that the bay loomed not twenty yards farther into the murk, she knew he was out there, very near, listening, watching, just as she did. His presence was palpable, yet as subtle as the curling of the mist through the air.

A formidable foe.

He would have made a formidable ally as well, and she might have considered seeking his aid in this were she not certain that Cockburn thirsted for his blood too much to leave his capture to chance. The inlet at Lighthouse Point, just a quarter mile to the north, would be a virtual death trap, swarming with the hundred-odd heavily armed, bloodthirsty crewmen from the *Rattlesnake*. Even the Night Hawk couldn't foil all of them.

But did Cockburn want him alive enough to bargain with her? On this she was laying every hope, so much so that she could use herself as bait.

Plump, willing bait. The Night Hawk wanted to capture her almost as much as she needed to capture him. But would he sense a trap?

Drawing a deep breath against the swarm of doubts, she abandoned her cover and eased Cleo from the thicket onto the narrow dirt path that bordered the dunes. Cleo tossed her head, eager to take the bit completely. Leather strap snapped with each toss. The bridle jangled like a church bell tolling midnight in the utter quiet of a sleeping town. Each clop of Cleo's hooves on the tamped path was like the thunder of an approaching regiment. The bait was laid.

Every fine hair on Teddie's neck stood on end. Her back jarred stiff and brittle as an ancient oak against the saddle as she eased Cleo into a trot, absolutely unable to keep the mare to a docile walk. Low branches caught at her arms. Her eyes darted from side to side into the thicket. He could be anywhere, watching her.

The force came from out of the thicket behind her, a silent explosion of power that threw her from the saddle. The reins sliced into her wrists, yanked her shoulders from their sockets, and ripped her gloves from her hands. She landed in the dirt, her left shoulder and arm taking the brunt of her fall. Jagged pain tore through her, and she sank her teeth into her upper lip to bite back her cry. Feverishly, she glanced over her shoulder. From out of the mist-shrouded thicket stepped a lone black horse and rider.

Teddie scrambled to her feet. A raw ache spread from the center of her back, the size of a man's fist where it had plunged between her shoulder blades. He'd toppled her from Cleo's back with a terrifying ease. And now . . .

Her eyes darted about for Cleo. The mare had ambled off some distance farther up the path to graze.

With a horrifying surety of purpose the Night Hawk descended on her, a mammoth black specter. For the first time in her life Teddie froze with utter terror. There was no escaping him. She couldn't outrun his horse. And God knew she wouldn't die fleeing, shot in the back like a coward.

Gritting her teeth against the sting of tears, she braced her boots in the dirt and drew her cutlass from its scabbard. The clang of metal sliding against metal snapped his mount's head up. Not ten yards from her, the horse drew to a halt. In the murk they were one broad silhouette, the massive horse indistinguishable from his equally massive rider, and both enveloped in pale-blue mist.

Teddie's throat closed up entirely. The hopelessness of her scheme crashed over her. How had she ever thought to entrap this man? Her foolish confidence had never led her so far afield, with such grave consequences. She fully expected he would kill her now, with one simple shot. The unmistakable acrid bite of imminent death filled her nostrils, burned on her tongue.

She braced herself and whispered a prayer. And then in one fluid movement of his cloak—startling because of the sheer grace and agility he displayed for a man his size—he slipped from his saddle. He took three strides toward her, paused, and drew his own sword, hefting the weighty blade as though it weighed next to nothing.

A chill swept over Teddie. A fight to the death.

Beneath the low sweep of his hat she could see nothing but shadow. Not even a glint of satisfaction at the game handily won. Death had come in a faceless form.

Her cutlass seemed suddenly weighted with stone, her limbs as well. She hadn't a prayer of a chance.

Despair washed over her in huge, consuming waves. Tears stung hot and unwelcome at her eyes. And still pride brought her chin up, shoved one forearm across her cheeks, hoisted her sword. Will would never cower, and he'd endured far worse. She'd spent the last four days preaching to Damian about the pitfalls of succumbing to despair. She certainly couldn't now, now when things seemed their most bleak.

He was too strong.

True, but she had agility. And she had Will waiting for her, as powerful a motivation as anyone needed.

She wouldn't cower and plead for mercy. She would fight him, outsmart him, turn his strengths against him, exploit her own and somehow prevail. And by God she wouldn't let him know she was a woman until she'd done just that.

Warily, they circled, blades poised, tips wavering as they judged each other. Sweat dripped down Teddie's neck and ran in rivulets down her chest and back. Her breaths came swift and short. This pleased her. If she was laboring beneath the heat, so too would a man twice her size, perhaps even more. His cloak was heavy, voluminous, draping over his massive shoulders and falling clear to the tops of his boots where it swung as he moved. His build remained indistinguishable beneath his cloak, but his movements were lithe, graceful, yet powerful, his strides long, sure, seasoned. She rather doubted his girth came anywhere near to matching the breadth of his shoulders.

He was waiting for her to launch the first offensive. A gentleman despite it all. She almost shook her head to banish the thought. No gentleman had ever so embodied a beast on the prowl, out for blood. He made no sound as he stalked her, just like the panther on his nightly hunt. Despite the shadow of his hat she felt the intensity of his stare and experienced an odd sense of being consumed.

She lunged, blade thrusting then slicing upward at the last moment, a rather unconventional move she had honed to perfection during her weaponry lessons at school. He sidestepped the thrust and deflected her blade as if he'd anticipated that precise move. She gulped. Lightning-quick he lunged, forcing her back a pace, then another. She skidded in the dirt, nearly fell to one knee then surged up without a break in her parrying. Planting her left foot, she deflected one deep thrust with a swift parry and launched a blistering offensive, her sword slicing through the air in a brilliant display of her fencing prowess. She drove him deep into the shadow of the thicket. He retreated, held, sidestepped, and parried, leading her on, then with a staggering deftness forced her back. Neither gained a foothold, and the clang of the swords rose up eerily into the mist.

Every muscle Teddie possessed burned. Her breaths came ragged, struggling past a parched throat. Perspiration blurred her vision. Her blood thundered ominously in her ears. And yet instinct took hold and she lunged, dodged, then deflected his countering thrusts with a skill she'd never known she possessed. Perhaps because in the courtyard at her school the stakes had never been so high and the opponent so worthy. She had never been so surely tested.

He was, quite simply, superb. As she launched offensive after offensive she grew disturbingly certain that he merely toyed with her, gradually sapping her strength by forcing her to attack.

The blades met in a harsh scrape, locked, and Teddie was yanked so hard against him that her wind was knocked from her, as if she'd run smack into a brick wall.

"My lady impostor," he rasped, just inches above her, "surrender to me now."

Teddie went entirely numb. Her sword slipped from her fingers and clanged to the ground. The earth tipped on its axis. *No!*

She heard his sword fall to the ground as well, felt the brute strength in his hands gripping her upper arms, the familiar steel-thewed length of him braced against her from chest to hip. Even now her body responded to his of its own will, arching, swelling, pulsing alive with wanton, reckless need. She bit back a cry as her nipples swelled then distended painfully against damp cotton, pushing into his chest. God help her, but her loins nestled provocatively against his, rocking once, twice, gently, undeniably.

He seemed to suck in a breath. "I'll know who you are, wanton," he growled, "and then I'll do with you as you deserve."

The absolute chill in his voice turned Teddie to stone. He would be merciless with her, ruthless and uncompromising, perhaps even more so because she'd deceived him so flagrantly. It mattered very little that he desired her, that she was indeed his wife. Tonight she barely recognized him as the tender lover she'd known that afternoon. Men could easily separate themselves from their lust when they most needed to and remain emotionally detached. Perhaps even now he was doing that in battling the elemental attraction between them.

As for their marriage, he'd never once professed any kind of affection for her. He might desire her, but he didn't love her. She would know if he did. How could he possibly understand or forgive her this when he'd vowed never to lay his trust in a woman? He wouldn't.

Then he must never know.

In another moment he would tug the hat from her head. Then it would be too late for explanations. The dream of happiness with him would remain just that, a fantasy.

Escape.

The knife slid from the top of her boot and into her palm. In a flash she shoved it beneath his chin. He went entirely rigid.

An invisible fist seemed to plunge between her ribs. Her heart ached as if it would burst. Words poised on her tongue and died. Tears sprang into her eyes.

"Be sure," he murmured. "Because I will catch you."

She swallowed and gently increased the pressure on the blade until she felt it pierce his skin. She jolted, horrified, and for one agonizing moment he stared at her so intensely that she was certain she had betrayed herself. The instant his hands fell from her arms she spun around and lunged for his horse.

Wildair.

How could she not have known him?

From behind her came Winchester's shouted command to the stallion. Teddie tripped on her cloak, nearly fell to her knees, and dove for the reins. She didn't dare look back. He was at her heels, grabbing at her cloak flapping behind her.

He caught it in one massive fist. The cloth stretched taut, he tugged, she lunged, and the frayed wool split at a low seam, freeing Teddie and leaving Winchester with nothing but a handful of cloth. He snarled an expletive and lunged for her, but she'd leapt aboard Wildair's back with an agility he would never match. His roar of frustration startled Wildair, and the stallion shied then rose up on his hind legs, pawing the air. Terrified, Teddie struggled to keep hold of the reins and retain her seat, a feat made all but impossible when the stallion leapt forward with a staggering burst of speed. The force yanked the reins from Teddie's hands and she fell heavily against Wildair's neck. It was then that she realized Winchester had made one last diving leap for the saddle and now clung to it with both hands, inch by inch pulling himself onto Wildair's back behind her while his legs dragged along the ground, inches from Wildair's thrashing hooves.

Perilously, she leaned over the stallion's pumping neck, fingertips outstretched, straining to reach the reins dangling between Wildair's pumping forelegs. The stallion plunged at breakneck speed down the path, oblivious to his master's commands to stop or to Teddie's murmured pleas. Between his flattened ears Teddie could see Cleo running just ahead, her tail streaming like a plume behind her, an irresistible lure to

Wildair. With the weight of two people on his back, despite his depth and speed, Wildair would never catch the riderless, energetic Cleo.

With a sinking heart Teddie realized the stallion would follow wherever she led, for as long as she ran. And she looked eager to keep to this road, where less than a quarter mile further along Cockburn and his men awaited.

Reality crashed over Teddie with the force of a tidal wave. She was about to deliver Winchester into Cockburn's hands!

Gritting her teeth, she stretched herself entirely over the stallion's neck, fingertips outstretched. The reins slapped against her hands, but she could barely see through wind-whipped tears to catch them. She choked on a sob, a new despair threatening with each ground-gobbling stride Wildair took.

No, she couldn't give up yet.

They emerged from the thicket-fringed path onto an open stretch, flanked only by down-sloping dunes. Suddenly, Wildair veered right and plunged down the dune. Teddie fell heavily against his neck and would have fallen beneath his hooves had Winchester not yanked her roughly back against him at that moment.

He was sturdy as an oak, his breath in her ear warm, hoarse. . . .

At his touch something inside her shattered irreparably. A helplessness like nothing she could have imagined engulfed her. All she could do was cling to Wildair's neck and hope beyond hope that Cockburn's men failed to stop Cleo. Despair convulsed from the untouched depths of her soul. Above the roar of the wind in her ears, she thought she heard a gun's report, then another, coming from just ahead.

But Wildair only lengthened his stride, cleaving through the shallow surf and splashing spray up over them.

"What the hell?" Winchester growled, drawing up stiff against her.

Without looking, Teddie knew what awaited them.

"Christ."

A gun exploded directly ahead. Wildair locked his forelegs and all but slid onto his rump in the sand. Before Teddie could scramble from his back, a dozen seamen swarmed around them, wielding swords, knives, and pistols. They hauled her from Wildair's back and shoved her aside so roughly that she fell to her knees in the sand beside a man who held Cleo's reins. From behind her came the sound of meaty fists meeting flesh, accompanied by the wicked cackles of the seamen and an odd silence from Winchester. Teddie lurched to her feet and spun around, her cries dying on her lips when a hand gripped her shoulder from behind. She went rigid.

"Hold there!" Cockburn's shout rang out. "Bring him here, men, into the lantern light. Let me have a look at my booty."

A lantern was hoisted. Into the arc of its dim light two seamen hauled Winchester between them. They paused not two paces from her, yanked his hat from his head, and thrust him forward.

His head lifted and his eyes at once locked on Teddie's, still shielded beneath her hat. A knife slicing through her would surely have hurt less than the cutting hatred he displayed there. Unconsciously, she shrank a step back, deeper into the shadows, as hot bile rose up into her throat. Blood dripped from his nose and his swollen upper lip. One eye seemed to swell with each passing second. In the center of his throat, a thin trickle of blood marked the spot where she had pushed the tip of her knife into his skin.

Cockburn stepped forward, shoulders thrust back with pompous self-importance. "The venerable Night Hawk, I presume?"

Beneath ominously low black brows Winchester's eyes shifted to Cockburn, but he said nothing.

Cockburn gave a mocking incline of his head. "I am Admiral Sir Jeremiah Cockburn. And you, bold sir, are my prisoner of war, charged with the crime of conspiring to run my blockade. Your name?"

Winchester didn't reply.

Cockburn shifted beneath the uncompromising stare, finally muttering, "I see. Reckless and stubborn. I will take that from you, sir, have no doubt." His plumed hat angled at Teddie. "I applaud you, Teddie, on a scheme well done."

For an instant the air crackled between them. And then Winchester moved so quickly no one had a prayer's chance of stopping him. With lightning speed he stepped past Cockburn and flicked Teddie's hat from her head. God help her, but she averted her face from the lamplight, from him, as her hair spilled over her shoulders. Another swipe of his hand and her scrap of cloak fell to the sand, the curves filling the dark shirt and breeches leaving little doubt in any man's mind that she was a woman. Above the chorus of surprised gasps and ribald comments from Cockburn's crew, she thought she heard Winchester's biting epithet.

"You know this man?" Cockburn asked her, his attention fastened on her.

Lifting her chin, Teddie shook her head.

Winchester growled something truly scathing before he was again swarmed, dragged back, shoved to the sand and pummeled heavily in his belly and ribs for his efforts.

"Hold there, men!" Cockburn shouted as several of the more lascivious of his crew all but leapt at Teddie. "She's mine."

Whatever gratitude Teddie felt toward Cockburn for calling off his dogs and sparing her fled for the moment beneath Winchester's hoarse grunts of pain. Teddie winced with each punch, all but doubling over with the grievous ache swelling between her ribs. She felt Cockburn's eyes on her. He watched her closely—too closely. Could he possibly suspect that the Night Hawk was her husband? No, but in her distress she could unwittingly betray that she loved him with a desperation that she now realized transcended all else. If she was to afford herself any opportunity to right this horrible wrong, this scathing betrayal, Cockburn must not know she felt anything for his prisoner. If he even suspected, he would exploit the weakness, use it against her and Winchester, indeed never set her free to spy for him again. And she needed her freedom if she was going to mount some kind of rescue effort.

She bit her lips and shoved a hand over her cheeks, dashing away the last of the tears and the salt spray and all her despair.

Winchester. To save him she would have to betray him, renounce him, again.

He would never forgive her. In one brilliant bit of foolish recklessness she'd lain complete waste to the fragile trust between them. The field of crocuses was trampled. To him she had become what he despised most, yet another deceitful, duplicitous woman.

So be it. She could live with his contempt, even his hatred, for the rest of her life, but she would not be able to draw another breath if he died.

Slowly, painfully, she drew her cool reserve over the gaping emotion. Shoving up her chin, she fixed a blank stare on Cockburn. "Where's Will?"

"In good time, my dear Teddie." Cockburn cocked a brow at her, watching her as if he sought something he knew she refused to give him. Winchester grunted as punch after punch was delivered. And Cockburn watched her.

She barely breathed, yet managed to keep her tone flat, emotionless, trying her best not to betray her deepest fear. "You're going to let them kill him for you?"

"Perhaps I should."

The unmistakable talons of dread clawed at Teddie's insides. "He'd be far more useful to you alive," she forced out, hoping Cockburn didn't detect the tremor in her voice, the absolute terror threatening to engulf her. She knew how randomly and at mere whim Cockburn murdered. "See how it takes three men to restrain him."

Cockburn's red mouth curved into a wicked, toothless smile and he eyed Winchester with a rekindled interest that turned Teddie's stomach. "Indeed," Cockburn observed, "he's a magnificent specimen. Just chock full of brute strength. Of quite imposing proportions, I must say."

"He knows much," Teddie said quickly. "Much that could be useful to you."

"Indeed, he most probably does. It's the getting it out of him that will prove a test of both our wills, eh? How long do you think a man like him can hold out under torture?"

Hopefully as long as it would take for her to rescue him.

He'd endured a Tripolitan desert, hadn't he? "He's worth nothing to you dead," she pointed out.

"So true. But revenge can be strange, Teddie. Killing him might deny me all he knows, true, but it would certainly avenge the honor he so pompously thought to trounce." Cockburn lifted a hand and glanced at the men. "Enough. Take him to the longboat. My lovely Theodora, come with me."

Chapter Eighteen

They threw him into the bilge-filled bowels of the ship. He landed face and chest first in the rancid water, then arched up out of the stench with a roar that was forced back with the bile into his throat by the foul-tasting gag they'd shoved in his mouth. With every movement coarse hemp bit into his wrists, bound taut at his back. The balled chain joining his ankles allowed only the smallest steps, the weight of the ball no doubt fashioned to sink him to the bottom of the bay like a rock. At Cockburn's whim. He'd be there now if Cockburn didn't want something from him.

He lurched to his feet, eyes probing into the pitch blackness. No light and certainly no air crept through the ceiling door nine feet overhead. He took a step, stumbled over something beneath the water, and fell up to his thighs in water. Pain stabbed through his legs and sliced up his back, carving deep into his spine. The salty bilge ate at every piece of flesh Cockburn's men had laid open with their fists. The stench rising around him convinced him that Cockburn's men used this hole much like a common chamber pot, left to simmer and stew in the heat.

Again he struggled to his feet, then fell back against the side of the ship and closed his eyes against the pain that radiated through his ribs with each breath he drew. Perspiration bathed his face and chest. He tasted it on his cracked lips, and the blood, as well, and a fleeting taste of lilac.

With every ounce of will he forced the thoughts from his mind, searching, retreating inside himself . . . reaching. . . .

He knew there was a place inside every man's mind well beyond his daily reach or imagination. He knew because he'd found it out on the desert in Tripoli after he'd escaped from the dey's palace. It was a place many layers deep, a precarious place that for him bordered on madness. Eight years ago it was the only place where he had found solace. It had taken him eight years to crawl out of that place, but finding it had kept him alive out in that twenty-mile desert expanse of hell. A different kind of hell than this, a hell where the sun had blistered every inch of his exposed skin, then blistered it again when it oozed open, a hell where the opium withdrawal had eaten him alive from the inside out and nearly taken his mind.

In that place in his mind he knew he could find retreat from the worst hell. There was no anger there, no feeling, no weakness for thought or memory. Only there could he ultimately triumph.

But tonight the thoughts, the memories, and the images bombarded him relentlessly, allowing him no respite and no opportunity for retreat within himself. And he knew why. The anger was different now than it had been in Tripoli. There the pain had obliterated the rage. Here the red haze of rage was like a tempest roaring up out of him, obliterating all else. He was possessed by it. It permeated every breath, oozed from every pore. He was as imprisoned by it as he was by the shackles he wore. Next to it the physical pain seemed almost inconsequential.

And it was. All the horrors of Tripoli couldn't compare to what Teddie had done to him.

Before Cockburn's men had shoved him into the bottom of the longboat, he'd watched her mount Cleo. In an instant she'd disappeared into the mist, with Wildair at her heels and her hair streaming behind her.

Even now, despite it all, he could still feel the lushness of her arching up against him as she pressed that knife to his throat. Even now he couldn't wipe his mind free of the image of her standing in the lantern light, her face shielded by the tangled curtain of her hair, every dramatic proportion of her body displayed by the clinging shirt and breeches.

At that moment, when Miles had stripped her of her voluminous cloak, he had been possessed of an overpowering need to protect her from all those men.

But she had the rooster Cockburn for that. Her cocon-spirator. If he was any sort of man he no doubt demanded much more of her than information. What privileges had she granted the strutting British admiral while Miles had kept him-self to his own bed out of some misbegotten sense of duty and honor? She'd certainly been a virgin most pure when he'd first bedded her, but since then . . . ?

Even the most virtuous of deflowered virgins had been known to spread their legs after the fact without a hint of their former reluctance, shame, or deep contemplation of the man or the consequences.

Certainly his wanton wife could. After all, she'd displayed a lustful nature beyond the reaches of most men just that after-noon when she'd clasped him against her breasts and drawn him deep between her sleek thighs.

The red haze squashed the faint voice in his mind whisper-ing that it couldn't be so.

He reveled in the feel of the rope carving into his wrists as he strained with all his might against the bonds. Muscle popped, stretched, burned, and burned some more for a release he refused to give. The rope slid blood-slick into his skin. His lungs exploded with a roar of the deepest frustration and anger, of humiliation and self-contempt, all tightly twisted up and around itself until it throbbed and ached like a festering wound in the center of his chest.

She should have killed him when she had the chance, instead of just pricking his skin. She should have driven that blade deep, because when he got the hell out of here he was going to make her wish that she had.

Even before Cleo skidded to a halt just outside Miramer's sta-ble, Teddie slipped from her back. Beneath her fist the stable door thwacked open, startling the horses in their stalls. She hurried to the back tack room, just as Simon stepped from the room.

"You're waiting for him," she said, her voice cracking, her chest heaving with desperation.

"I's waitin' on both o' you, Miss Teddie."

Teddie's heart constricted. Simon had known she was the impostor and he hadn't betrayed her, not even to Winchester. "Dear Simon, why didn't you tell me? If I had known that Winchester was the Night Hawk—"

"I's loyal, Miss Teddie, to you an' the massa. I always has been. 'Sides, it weren't my place to tell yo' secrets. It was yours, an' you would have, in yo' own time."

"Oh, Simon." She closed her eyes. "I-I've done a terrible thing. I thought I could outsmart him."

"You sho' did, Miss Teddie. You done tied him all up 'round hisself. Someone sho' had to. I's damned glad it was you."

"Stop—" She laid both hands on his arms. "Please, listen to me."

Simon smiled, a warm, comforting smile that tore at the last bit of Teddie's resolve. "He loves you, Miss Teddie."

Teddie shuddered and her will crumbled in a heap. Tears leapt into her eyes. "No, he doesn't. Please—"

"He's jest like his gran'pappy. An' you's his Mira. I seen it all along. An' I knows. Don' cry, Miss Teddie. The massa— he'd give his life fo' you."

"Oh, God—" The tears came then, in great spasms that welled up from the pit of her being. They plunged down her cheeks and into her mouth in an endless cascade. Weeks and months of tears denied finally defied her. And when Simon drew her into his comforting embrace, she felt the last of her strength slip away. "They've got him," she bit out against his shoulder, her fingers twisting into his shirt. "I gave him to them and they've got him."

"The massa?" Simon gripped her arms and held her slightly away. His voice plunged low, severe, sending a chill through Teddie. "Farrell caught him?"

Teddie shook her head, her gaze unwavering. "No, Cockburn. The British admiral. Simon, if I had known—"

"Now hold on, Miss Teddie. Stop cryin' now." He drew a handkerchief from his pocket and pressed it into her hand. "I shoulda known it was sompin' bad fo' you to cry. You nevuh cry, Miss Teddie. You love the massa more n' you thinked you did."

Teddie swiped the handkerchief over her eyes with brisk strokes. "I betrayed him, Simon."

"If you did you gots good reason."

Teddie stared at the overseer. "I thought I did, but now—"

"Then you did what you thought you had to do, Miss Teddie."

"Oh, Simon, you're too forgiving."

Simon cocked his head. "Maybe I is. But I's seen much in my life. An' I knows from the start you's no spy for nobody 'less you thought you had damned good reason. 'Course it all looks different now. We all thinks we has good reason fo' what we do. The massa too."

"Cockburn has my brother," she whispered.

"That's good reason for doin' jest 'bout anythin'."

She stared at the handkerchief twisted in her fingers. "And now he has Winchester as well. All because of my ridiculous confidence in myself to carry out schemes even the bravest of men would find impossible."

"Even the bravest men couldn't choose 'tween two people they love, Miss Teddie. Nobody could. Not even the bravest woman."

"I'm not brave, Simon. I'm only reckless."

"Now that depends on the outcome, don' it?"

Teddie set her jaw.

"You didn' come here to cry. You's gonna fix what you did."

"There's no fixing what I did to him inside, Simon. But I can certainly try my best to save his life. And Will's. It's what I should have done all along."

"What's that?"

"If I've learned anything in this, Simon, it's that the greatest tragedy of war is the hope it kills between men. And the trust. It makes cynics out of the most naive. Look at Damian. Look at me. I couldn't trust anyone with my scheme, not my aunt, not even Winchester, thinking that the callings of war, the threat to men's liberty muddles all compassion. In many it does. But not all. As for a cynic like Winchester, after Tripoli he thinks everyone is his enemy. And they're not."

"You's sho' 'bout that?"

"I'm hoping. Call me naive. And I'm surely reckless. But I still believe in the inherent goodness in people, a fairness that goes beyond the cause they're fighting for to the heart and soul of the men. I hope I'm not wrong."

"You gots yo'self a plan?"

"I do."

"You wan' me to git Farrell's men?"

Teddie shook her head. "We haven't the time for you to ride all the way to Baltimore. Besides, we're not going by land."

"You could use a fleet o' ships to back you, Miss Teddie. Massa Damian says Farrell's got a fleet o' three ships all ready to go in Baltimore harbor."

"Even if we had the time to send them word I wouldn't, because confrontation is precisely what Cockburn wants. And the bloodier the better. Besides, at the first sign of enemy sail he'll kill my brother and he'll kill Winchester. We'll surprise him, and it must be tonight when he least suspects it." Teddie thought a moment. "You've gone with Winchester to his ship, haven't you?"

"Yes'm, many times."

"And it's in the Albemarle Sound?"

"You's a smart lady, Miss Teddie."

"Thank you, Simon. I assume you could get us there. And to Mount Airy."

Simon's eyes narrowed. "You's goin' to Reynolds's plantation now?"

"Indeed, I am. And you're going with me." Teddie stuffed her hair up under her hat, then checked the pistol still tucked into her waistband. "Get a pistol, Simon. Several. Are Winchester's men armed?"

"Yes'm. But there's only thirty-odd men 'board the *Leviathan*."

Teddie's heart sank. Thirty. Cockburn's men numbered in excess of a hundred, give or take a few deserters and those too disheartened to muster up much of a fight. The odds, it seemed, weighed heavily against them. "Surprise can prove more potent than a hundred-man army," she said.

"You's sho' 'bout that?"

"No, but I'm hoping. We'll need fresh mounts. We've got to hurry, Simon." Teddie spun around, took two steps toward the stall of one particularly frisky horse, then drew up short.

Damian stood in the open stable door wearing his silk dressing gown over boots and breeches. His skin was drawn tight over his cheekbones, his color pale, but Teddie glimpsed a flicker of something in his eyes, something that gave life to a hope that had long died inside of her.

"Where are you going?" he asked, concern lacing his voice.

She looked him square in the eye. "To save Winchester from Admiral Cockburn. If you're coming you'd best get your pistol and a mount. We could use you."

His Adam's apple jerked in his throat. One golden brow cocked, his lips twisted snidely, and for an instant Teddie knew a despair so complete, she had to bite her lips to keep from crying out.

And then Damian's eyes flickered to Simon. "Saddle up Bel Air for me, Simon." Again his gaze met Teddie's. "Are you certain you want—?"

"Absolutely certain," Teddie said quickly.

Damian blinked. "I . . . I never wanted to kill him . . . at the wedding. It's just—"

"I know, Damian. You owe me no explanations."

"Teddie, a woman doesn't belong—?"

"Damian Coyle, you ought to know better than to tell me where I belong. If you feel you must, you and Simon can both tie me up and throw me into the back room. But I'd escape and then I'd never forgive you. Besides, of any of us, Cockburn trusts me. If our scheme is to succeed I have to be part of it."

He seemed to consider this a moment, then said, "Give me five minutes to change."

"No longer."

"I'll hurry."

As Teddie watched him dash from the stable, the tears misting her eyes were not born of despair and betrayal, but of hope. The kind of everlasting hope and faith she intended to prove to Winchester. Tonight.

She turned to saddle another mount and prayed that she had not guessed wrong about Jules Reynolds. All the compassion in the world for his fellow man might not stand a chance against the bounteous charms of the woman who no doubt slumbered beside him in his bed.

"I want you to know that your damnable husband has absolutely nothing to do with my agreeing to your scheme," Jules Reynolds grumbled, shifting his shoulders within his voluminous black cloak as though the idea of doing anything on Winchester's behalf made him exceedingly uncomfortable. From beneath the sweep of his broad-brimmed black hat, he slanted Teddie a piercing look that seemed to cut through the haze of their lantern light. Had it not been for the mischief Teddie glimpsed in his eyes she might have believed him entirely put upon. "Were it not for my unwavering devotion to you and you alone, Theodora, I would still be comfortably abed, most decidedly warm, and certain to be kept that way by my companion. I can't help but marvel at the boundless capacity of friendship that would have a man eagerly forsaking such heaven for this."

Teddie stared out into the fog hanging low over the James River. Night pressed in all around them, the air still beneath its blanket of heat. Behind her she could hear the dips of the oars as Simon expertly navigated the bark south toward the mouth of the Elizabeth. The vessel rode low beneath the weight of three tobacco-stuffed hogsheads strapped onto it. Despite the palpable tension Teddie couldn't suppress the softening of her lips. "And what did your evening companion have to say about your loyalties to me, Jules?"

"Not a word, of course, because I didn't tell her. And with damned good reason. You women are insanely jealous creatures. By dint of your natures you are given to drama of such excessive proportion a man can scarcely breathe for fear of doing it wrong."

"And yet you're out here with me—a drama-riddled female—in the middle of the night, looking very much like the Night Hawk, at certain risk to your life. Could it be, Jules, that your loyalties, just like Damian's here, lie not so much with me but elsewhere? Could you bear some warm feeling for Winchester after all?''

Jules snorted with a bit too much vehemence and waved a black-gloved hand. ''Bah. If I do bear any feeling for the man, at the moment it's supreme annoyance, both for so flagrantly practicing his deceit on me with this simple black cloak and hat and for getting himself caught by Cockburn. Say what you will—and you're a most honorable woman, fearless as any man I've known—but you didn't betray him tonight as much as he lost his sense of self-preservation. The old boy should have been more careful.''

The concern edging his voice was not lost on Teddie. Nor was his tight-lipped contemplation of the gloom hovering around them. ''Fog's too damned thick,'' he muttered. ''No man in his right mind would sail a tobacco-weighted frigate into it. I suppose that's why you asked me to do it, eh, Theodora?''

''Of course. Men like you and Winchester relish impossible odds.''

Jules gave a grunt. ''I should have known better than to expect reassurance from you. Simon, I hope you know where the hell you're going.''

''I do, suh,'' Simon replied just as the belly of the bark scraped ominously against the river bottom. Low-hanging branches snagged at Teddie's sleeve, yet the bark slipped unimpeded through the shallows. ''It's jest a bit farthuh, suh. Osgood's ship is usually right at the mouth o' the Elizabeth, jest waitin', jest lazy an' waitin'. He gonna see us 'fore we see him. We give him his 'baccy then, an' he give us what we want.''

''Tonight we want more than safe passage for the *Leviathan* out of Albemarle Sound,'' Jules grunted in reply. ''Even a bribed British captain doesn't easily part with his colors.''

''The rum should help with that,'' Damian offered, patting one of the hogsheads. ''All but emptied the cellar of every drop of smuggled Jamaican finest. I believe a great deal of it was originally brought in by Grandfather Maximilian. I wonder what the old fellow would have said if he knew his brew would eventually be used to buy a British flag?''

"He would say one can't put a price on a man's freedom,"
Teddie said. "And I think Winchester would agree."

For several moments only the slice of the oars penetrated the
silence. "Damned fool's luck," Jules finally said.

Teddie glanced up at him. Dressed as he was, his face
thrown into deep shadow, he cut a silhouette as imposing as
Winchester's. Had she not known better she wouldn't have
known the difference between the two were they standing side
by side. Their movements were eerily similar, every gesture
laced with the same fluid grace and physical awareness uncommon to men of their size. Even now she remembered the peculiar feeling she'd gotten when she watched them barreling
toward her, side by side, down the track at Devil's Field. Now
she knew the reason for that odd feeling: On horseback, both
had reminded her of the Night Hawk. Perhaps even then she'd
innately sensed something she refused to acknowledge as possibility.

"You're doubting in the goodness of friendship?" she
asked.

"No. It's your husband I'm talking about. You've forgiven
him, haven't you?"

"I don't believe I ever had a choice in that."

"Good God. The man doesn't deserve you."

"Because I forgive him his inability to trust me or anyone
but Simon with his deepest secrets? I more than anyone understand the burden and the guilt of shouldering such responsibility. Deception is not taken on lightly, or without just reason. I
had mine in Will. Winchester has his. No one can judge him
harshly for that."

"No one can judge *you* harshly, Theodora, for doing anything you could to save your brother. For so clever a woman it's
a wonder you didn't realize that sooner."

"I was taught to be self-reliant. It's not in my nature to seek
help if I think I can accomplish something. It's the damned
odds that confound me."

"Particularly when they're so neatly stacked against you."

"I don't suppose I realized the rules of war can be bent."

"And that some of us could forgive you? The old boy, however, is another matter altogether. At first glance his motives look disturbingly self-serving."

"Miramer is home to many. Not just Winchester. Many there depend on him for their livelihood and their freedom. He's their protector, though he would tell you otherwise because he prefers to believe otherwise. I think his reasons go far deeper than filling Miramer's coffers."

"He's got all the riches he needs in you, Theodora. I hope he damned well knows it."

Teddie had to avert her eyes for fear the tears would spring up again. But Jules was a man well-attuned to women and their devices, frustratingly so.

Grasping her chin, he lifted her shining eyes to his. "Rest assured, dear lady, if he doesn't know your value, he will. Or by God I'll slay him with my own sword. On that you have my vow."

"Stop it, Jules. You mean no such thing."

"Then you don't know me. For reasons that loom beyond my comprehension at the moment, I may be willing to risk my life to save his worthless hide, but our friendship won't withstand his contempt of you. For that, no man has good reason."

Though his words offered some comfort, the dread looming deep within Teddie seemed to uncoil and spread with each dip of the oars. A dread that had nothing to do with their scheme to free Will and Winchester.

"If it weren't for the blasted fog," Cockburn said, waving a gloved hand at the murk hovering above the lantern-lit deck, "I would sail down the coast and confront Captain Osgood for his side of this. At which point you would stand accused and be tried for your crime. It seems, sir, that you will be granted several more hours." Cockburn's strangely red lips curved upward in a sinister smile that embedded itself in his powdered cheeks. "I, of course, am left with no alternative but to take advantage of the opportunity nature has provided me. Before I do, perhaps you finally wish to say something to alter your fate, hmm? Perhaps agree to cast your lot with me? We could come to a mutually beneficial arrangement." He paused beside the mainmast, where Miles stood with hands trussed behind him to the mast. Cockburn's eyes traveled a slow path up Miles's shirt where the crisscross tracks of the cat-o'-nine had laid open cotton and carved into flesh.

Miles met the admiral's gaze with his own cold, blood-crusted stare. At the mere flick of one of Cockburn's limp wrists, the mammoth, bare-chested seaman Griggs would again send the cat-o'-nine slicing through the night's eerie silence. Another twenty lashes. And yet despite this, something in Cockburn's demeanor sent a fleeting suspicion through Miles, something about the way his eyes moved over every inch of Miles's exposed flesh. Something that made Miles suddenly want to crawl from his skin with revulsion.

And then he knew. Teddie and this man had not been lovers. He squelched his surge of elation with a quick turn of his thoughts. So what hold did the admiral have over her, a hold so unshakable she had forsaken her aunt and uncle and turned traitor on her own husband? It had to be something of tremendous worth to her. A woman like Teddie would not easily be subservient to anyone, most especially to a popinjay like Cockburn.

Moments passed in silence. The ship creaked and swayed with the incoming tide.

Obviously impatient, Cockburn pursed his lips and heaved a sigh. "No turning coat, eh? I see." Sniffing, he drew a gloved hand to his nose and turned slightly away. "The stench of the bilge oozes from you, sir. Your back and chest have been laid raw and open to the bite of salt water. Your clothes are in tatters, and you are unarmed. And yet you stand before me, trussed like prime livestock, as would the proudest of English noblemen. Does your arrogance know no bounds, man? Have you no sense of self-preservation?"

As he'd done in Tripoli with the dey's prison guards, Miles stared through Cockburn, refusing to give the man the slightest satisfaction of a response.

The admiral gave a brutal snort and continued with his goading. "So stoic. Perhaps you can't bear the idea that you were trapped by a mere woman, eh? Bitter medicine for a man, especially a man used to taking what he wants. Life comes easily to men like you. Ah, but then to be undone by a woman. I can tell you she would have made a better lad. You remind me of her, you know. Like you, she stood before me, my prisoner, at my whim, and had the audacity to shove her chin up at me. Then she attempted to bargain with me for the dullard. Ha! Of course, she finally came around to cooperating. She's a clever girl and yet she knows her bounds. She wants quite desperately to keep her brother alive. That kind of desperation can be exploited. But you, sir, seem blithely unaware of your circumstances, or else you don't give a damn about yourself or anyone else. You purposely give me nothing to use against you except your life. You won't even give me the benefit of knowing you're in pain. Not even a grunt.''

Miles stared out into the gloom, teeth clenched, wishing to God he'd seen it all sooner, that he'd had a trace of intuition with her and had pressed her for all her deeply held secrets. He'd sensed her melancholy, all right, and damn that part of him that had thought it born of some inconsequential matter. All the melancholy women he'd ever known had usually gotten that way over a broken fingernail and insufficient attention from their male admirers.

Those women would never have conceived of risking their lives for their brother. They would throw themselves helpless upon someone else, laying the difficulty entirely in their laps.

But Teddie wasn't that kind of woman. The strength of will required of her to harbor such a secret for so long staggered him. He could only imagine how she'd come to be on Cockburn's ship, instinctively knowing the scheme had been recklessly conceived and no doubt boldly executed. Something must have gone terribly wrong, something that had forced her into a role she would never willingly play.

And yet some deeply cynical part of him rejected any explanation for her deceit. The reasons, he told himself, mattered little. She'd still found it necessary to keep it all from him. She hadn't trusted him enough.

But who's damned fault was that?

Still, she'd betrayed him.

But she'd denied knowing him to Cockburn, perhaps sparing him.

Sparing herself.

The woman he'd held in his arms just that afternoon had glowed with a joy and warmth and love no one could deny was real.

"Say something, man!" Cockburn whined, feigning a look of utter dismay. "God knows all this whipping is becoming a dreadful bore. Besides, you're dripping blood all over the deck. Hold for a moment, Griggs. You there, ah, the dullard, Will. That's a good lad, swabbing decks, while the rest of them sleep below. Fetch a pail of seawater. Our prisoner here needs to feel the salt cutting into his wounds."

Miles's gaze flicked to Cockburn, then probed the gloom beyond. The dullard. Will. Teddie's brother, from what he could surmise. He heard the thump and roll of the ball scraping across the deck an instant before the Goliath emerged from the mist into the glow of the mast lantern. Miles felt an invisible knife twist in his gut. Not because of the man's size, which dwarfed the burly, whip-wielding Griggs, or his obvious strength, attested to by the two-foot length of iron chain binding his ankles and the huge ball he dragged behind him. Not even because of his youth or the telltale marks of torture and starvation wracking his mammoth frame.

Because he was, without question, Teddie's brother. The hair was the same shade of blue-black, the features eerily similar to Teddie's, only a cruder, masculine version, the eyes dusky purple. Only Will's were flat, devoid of any sparkle of life, youth, and vitality, as dull as Teddie's were vibrant, as impenetrable as hers were the window to her soul.

With a certain unwelcome wrenching in his gut Miles watched Will glance first at Cockburn for his nod. Then without hesitation or any indication of thought or conscience, Will hefted his pail and doused Miles in salt water. Miles bit back his roar as the salt carved deep into his open flesh with fiery talons. Bucket in hand, Will watched him silently, his face a broad, expressionless mask.

"Ah," Cockburn crooned, "could it be our venerable Night Hawk winces? Another bucket, Will."

Will blinked for several moments at Cockburn, as though comprehending his order.

"Now, ox!" Cockburn raged, eyes bulging. "Don't look at me like that, boy, or I'll truss you up next to him and let Griggs have a go at both of you. Better yet, why don't we test the sturdiness of your thick neck? Griggs, I say the yardarm will give before the oxen's neck snaps. What say you?"

The movement was involuntary, instinctive, beyond the limits of Miles's control. It surprised him probably more than it did Cockburn. A simple movement—a reflexive jerk of his hands, the resultant shudder that passed through him—but it betrayed far too much to a man like Cockburn intent on exploiting vulnerabilities.

Damn. The rage simmered now, bubbling low and deep and hot when Cockburn glanced sharply at him and instantly seemed to grow several inches up out of his boots.

"Well, now, look at this!" Cockburn crooned, strolling closer. His bootheels clicked imperiously on the wood, his eyes glittering with purely evil intent. "Something distresses you, sir. It's not the thought of a hanging. I'd wager you've seen much of that sort of thing. No." Cockburn tapped an index finger to his lips in contemplative silence. "Could it be . . . ?" He paused, glanced at Will. A slow, feral smile spread his lips over long teeth and smoothed the furrow between his brows. "The dullard, why, of course. Griggs, it seems we've a man of some conscience and tender sensibilities on our hands. I can't help but find this rather odd, Sir Night Hawk. No man endures torture like you do unless he's been through hell. I presume that's where you got this." Cockburn flicked a finger over Miles's scarred cheek. "How you stare at me, like an animal with no feeling. And yet . . ." Cockburn narrowed his eyes. "Indeed, there is more here."

Frustration and a hatred he'd thought himself incapable of feeling ever again roared to life within Miles. Over Cockburn's shoulder, Will watched Miles with eyes gone blank. He looked as if he registered nothing. Or perhaps he simply didn't care. Miles had worn that look once.

"Hang the dullard," Cockburn said tonelessly.

"No—" It was a plea, hoarse and low, but a plea nonetheless. Miles had no choice. He might have eight years ago when the only life in the balance was his own. But he didn't now.

Cockburn arched a brow and began to circle Miles with the deliberate strides of a victorious commander. "Ah, you've reconsidered, Sir Night Hawk. In exchange for his life you will give me—what? Something of tremendous value, I hope."

"Anything," Miles replied.

Cockburn paused and his colorless brows shot up. "Anything? Did you hear that, Griggs? This man would turn traitor on his own country to save this dumb ox, a man he shares no blood with and has never met before. These Americans are more foolish than I'd thought. And what makes you think, Sir Night Hawk, that you won't give me anything regardless? I am a man who enjoys making other men squirm because of their weakness. Perhaps more than I should. But who can blame me? I've wallowed for far too long in inactivity here, while many miles north others secure their niche in British naval history. Some form of distraction is required. I'd wager Teddie knows that. And so should you."

Miles tensed, anticipating the very worst from this maniac.

Cockburn jerked his head at Will and angled his eyes at Griggs. "Hang him."

Miles surged against his bonds, feet braced wide on the blood-slicked deck, his bellow of frustration echoing into the murk overhead, mingling with Will's lone wail of despair. "Take me instead!" he raged.

"In good time," Cockburn preened.

Miles barely felt the hemp carving into his wrists, barely heard Cockburn's gleeful cackle as Griggs hauled Will across the deck toward the yardarm.

With a gut-wrenching frustration, Miles realized he'd betrayed Will and delivered him to his fate because of his inability to keep from feeling . . . feeling for Teddie, the kind of pervasive, consuming emotion he'd never realized existed. The kind that extended beyond her to all the people she loved.

The kind that made a man feel like his soul was being torn from him bit by bit.

This would destroy her, no matter how strong she was.

Something stung his eyes and he blinked it away. Will was silent now, stumbling beside Griggs as he was led to his death. The noose hung limp from the yardarm, waiting, as Griggs stooped and freed the heavy ball and chain from Will's ankles.

Miles stared hard at Will. *Now.*

Cockburn watched Miles with the cool shrewdness of a maniac. The ship creaked gently. A slight breeze stirred the air but didn't even register in the furled canvas. Miles watched Will, so docile standing there, so accepting of his fate. They'd beaten the life out of the boy. He'd never even think to try to escape.

It was entirely up to him. Somehow.

Above the stillness Miles could almost hear the rhythmic *clop* of oars dipping into the water.

Clop . . . swish . . . clop . . .

He hadn't heard that sound since the *Leviathan* had found herself in the middle of the Atlantic in fog, with no wind, conditions precisely like this. A damned ridiculous time for memory to intrude.

Clop . . . swish . . . clop . . .

If a man knew these waters or was an expert sailor, the sweeps in their oiled rowlocks would be the way to maneuver with scant wind, particularly if surprise was in order.

Clop . . . swish . . . clop . . .

There was no denying it. He could almost feel the presence of another ship slipping silently through the bay. Or was he only wishing it, knowing how damned futile escape would be without help?

And then, just off the starboard side, he saw a pinpoint of fuzzy gold light filtering out of the fog, as though a lone lantern swayed at a still-invisible mainmast. Moments later the *Leviathan*'s bow poked through the mist, its figurehead the carved alligator whose jaws had grinned in horrible defiance of all enemies. High above her bow, a British flag hung above the limp Stars and Stripes.

Cockburn spun about and froze as the frigate took startling shape. "What the devil—?" He hesitated and took several steps then stopped. "It would seem Captain Osgood has captured himself an American frigate. Damned fool, maneuvering in such fog and at such an hour. Her hold must be bulging with goods of great worth else he'd have burned her as I ordered. Odd, but I don't see Osgood—or anyone else for that matter—on the decks."

Like a ghost ship beneath the guidance of a divine hand, the *Leviathan* fully emerged out of the fog. Her decks were eerily vacant, the sweeps in their rowlocks now still. Her canvas hung loose, not tightly furled for the night, but as if in ready wait of the slightest breeze to draw them full.

Cockburn made a strangled sound. *"Griggs! Summon all hands!"*

At the precise moment Cockburn turned his back and drew his sword from its sheath, Miles braced himself against the mast, lifted his legs, and swung them with all his might at Cockburn. The admiral, caught unawares, fell flat on his face, his sword clattering to the deck beside him and spiraling at Miles's feet. Just then the *Leviathan* bumped gently against the *Rattlesnake*'s side. Not a moment later thirty-odd men, armed with all manner of pistol, cutlass, and knife, swarmed over her bulwarks. And leading the charge was Jules Reynolds, with Damian at his side.

Chapter Nineteen

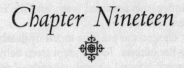

The trouble with being female, Teddie decided, was the burden of conscience in the thick of battle. While men could turn a blind eye to the horrors going on around them and hoist their weaponry with not the slightest misgiving, women saw no sides to the battle and no opportunity for glory, only the senseless killing, the disfigurement, and the dismemberment. How could victory possibly be savored if the memories remained of the dead and dying, of the wild-eyed stare a man got the moment before a cutlass sliced through his shoulder and tore into his chest, all but severing his torso in two?

Beneath one swipe of Watts's blade, a British seaman she knew only as Bowens toppled to the deck like a felled oak, precisely in that fashion. Long after Watts surged past her over the *Rattlesnake*'s bulwarks, she stared at Bowens's lifeless body, at the pistol resting in his palm, still cocked. Had Watts not followed closely at her heels, Bowens would have emptied his pistol into Teddie before she could have hefted her own cutlass in vain defense. She would undoubtedly be lying precisely where Bowens had fallen had Watts not responded with such swift savagery, before Bowens could squeeze off his shot. And yet gratitude proved elusive. Why was there such guilt in surviving, particularly on a mere whim of fate?

Sporadic gunfire jolted her from her thoughts. Swallowing bile, she slipped over the bulwarks and stepped past Bowens's body. Crouching behind a row of barrels, she glanced around the deck in search of Winchester and Will. At the stern of the ship the *Leviathan*'s crew swarmed down the companionway to the gun deck, blades raised, pistols cocked, eager to claim their victory over the *Rattlesnake*'s sleeping crew. From below came the roar of gunfire, the agonized cries, and the clang of sword scraping against sword.

Gunpowder choked the air. The smell of death lurked in the mist. Gripping her cutlass, Teddie crept from behind the barrels and picked her way around several tall coils of rope toward the fog-enshrouded center of the ship. The roar of battle grew stronger as the British in greater numbers roused and began to drive their attackers from below onto the upper deck. Soon the decks would be a writhing mass of dueling men, its floorboards rivers of blood, littered with the dead.

Jules had ordered her to remain aboard the *Leviathan* in what had been Winchester's cabin. She rather doubted he expected her to obey, though the murderous glower he had given her just moments before they'd reached the *Rattlesnake* had squelched her more rebellious thoughts. For only a moment.

She wasn't about to let them go into the thick of things without her. Besides, she'd witnessed battle and pillaging before, when Cockburn had first arrived to stake his claim off the Virginia shore. She'd spent several months aboard ship with these very men, privy not only to their daily lives, but also to their tales of battle. She also knew how to use her sword better than most.

She was not a sniveling female. Indeed, she could take care of herself—at least for as long as it took for her to find Will and Winchester.

Cockburn typically preferred the forecastle to carry out his tortures. It was just a bit farther, around another mast.

The mists seemed to lift as she crept along then snuck behind several barrels that offered cover from all sides. Crouched low, she attempted to ignore the stench of rotten fish seeping from the barrels as she peeped between them. Nausea gripped her belly and she gulped for air. Sweat dripped into her eyes and plunged down her chest. She was certain she was going to be violently ill all over the decks. And then, through the lifting mist, she saw Winchester, not fifteen feet farther, tied to the mainmast. Standing before him, wild-eyed with rage, was Cockburn, the tip of his cutlass pressed at Winchester's throat. She went cold to the bone.

"No!" she shrieked, surging up from behind her cover. Both turned at the sound of her voice. At once her gaze locked with Winchester's and she saw it then in his eyes—a void as fathomless as it was foreign. Her heart wrenched. Leaping over a barrel, she took two steps only to be struck from behind, as if a mammoth fist drove into the center of her back. She fell to the deck and for a moment, until the wind returned to her lungs, could only lay there wondering bleakly if she'd been shot. With lightning swiftness she rolled to her back, hoisting her cutlass at her attacker. Above her stood the gap-toothed bosun Griggs, a man made remarkable to her on the voyage from England only because of his astonishing abundance of body hair. With tree-trunk legs spread wide on both sides of her, he leered at her down the balloon of his bare chest and belly, a cutlass in one paw.

"Look what I find waitin' fer me," he sneered, licking the spittle from his lips as his eyes roamed eagerly over her chest. "I ain't goin' to tell the cap'n what I found, lassie. He ain't got the proper use fer ye. But I do. Ye jest be nice to ol' Griggs an' ye won' get 'urt. Put down yer sword. It ain't that kind o' fight I want out o' ye, lass."

"Go to hell," Teddie growled, then with all her might she drove her boot up into his exposed groin. With a yowl Griggs doubled over long enough to allow her to scramble to her feet, but just as she spun around to escape she tripped on a coil of rope and nearly fell to her knees. Booming a curse, Griggs lunged after her with meaty fists swiping. She clawed at rope, halyards, and rigging, struggling to regain her footing just as Griggs tore her hat from her head. Seconds later his fist clamped in her hair and hauled her to her feet. Roughly, he yanked her back against him, pinioning her sword arm beneath his.

He stunk of stale sweat and the vermin that no doubt inhabited his mammoth, furred body. Teddie was certain she would retch.

His growl was pure evil. "Now, lassie, I ain' goin' to be nice no more. I can promise ye that."

* * *

Over the length of his blade Cockburn sneered at Miles. "I'll see your pettifogging little schooner into my noose, brigand, and you at your proper depth, of fifty fathoms, in hell."

The tip of the blade pierced Miles's skin. In another moment Cockburn might decide to put his weight behind his sword and sever Miles's head from his body. Involuntarily, Miles tensed but kept absolutely still, knowing Cockburn fed off the drama of the moment and that he perhaps had mere seconds to plan his escape. Escape . . . he had to. Who the hell would save Teddie from Griggs?

His voice rumbled from his throat and he looked Cockburn square in the eye, his contempt oozing from him. "Hell? I look forward to it, sir. I can't imagine what you're waiting for."

An evil light flared in Cockburn's eyes, and a flicker of doubt, perhaps even fear of the unexpected. His lips twisted as though he savored this last bit of high drama. Lifting his arm, he steadied his sword, eyes narrowing as though he took sure aim. Miles felt his thigh muscles bunch in preparation for attack, and in that split second he weighed the odds of Cockburn falling forward and plunging his blade into Miles's throat in a final act of murderous revenge if caught off balance. And then from nowhere came a blindsiding blow to Cockburn's head, of such force it knocked him from his feet. With a crashing thud Cockburn hit the deck, blood spouting from his nose and mouth.

Miles blinked at the sprawled admiral, then looked up to find Will watching him, enormous fists clenching and unclenching against his thighs as if he itched to put them to good use again.

"You knocked him unconscious," Miles said with no small measure of disbelief.

"He's not dead," Will said, his voice flat and unemotional. "I should kill him, shouldn't I?"

"Leave that to me," Miles replied, jerking his head first at Cockburn's sword laying on the deck, then indicating the mast behind him. "Cut me loose me, Will. We've little time. We're outnumbered over two to one. Fast, man! We have to make the ship and get the hell out of here before they man their cannon."

Will scooped up Cockburn's sword, then slashed the ropes binding Miles's wrists. "The ship," he said, frowning at Miles.

"My ship, the *Leviathan*." Miles untangled the last of the rope from his wrists and tossed it aside. "Listen, Will, you've got to trust me. These men have come to rescue us. Your sister's with them."

Will blinked, and a faint spark of life lit his face. "Teddie?"

"I know you don't know who the hell I am. You've no reason to trust me—"

"No. I do. You were willing to die for me. I won't ever forget that."

Chagrin swept over Miles. For some reason the notion of being noble and heroic—or perhaps simply the idea of being noticed for it—didn't sit at all well with him. "Quick, to the ship there. Round up the rest of the men with you. Fast!"

Will hesitated before he turned and leapt over the ship's rail to safety. "Where are you going?"

"To find your sister."

Big, hairy seamen could be strong. Horrifyingly so. But they were nothing short of clumsy, particularly if caught unawares by a nimble foe. Sometimes force was better left unused, particularly if you were grossly outdone in that regard.

With precise aim and all her might, Teddie brought her foot down on Griggs's bare toes. The seaman roared with pain. Though he didn't release her entirely, his grip slackened for an instant. That was all Teddie needed. Like a slippery fox she broke free of him, spinning around with cutlass arcing through the air. He was waiting for her. Their blades met with a *clang*, slid, parted, arced, and met again. The grin embedded in Griggs's jowls faded at once, replaced by a gap-toothed snarl that momentarily chilled Teddie's blood and made her doubt for the hundredth time the wisdom of deciding to come aboard. The blades scraped and they parted, Teddie keeping good distance, her cutlass poised. But Griggs was not Winchester, a man whose grace and finesse were so deeply ingrained they had become instinctive, even in the throes of a sword fight. Griggs, by contrast, had long ago sacrificed finesse and agility

for bone-crushing bulk and matchless strength. What little un-
polished skill or speed he possessed with a sword was augmented threefold by the power behind each swipe of his blade.
If his sword did meet flesh it wouldn't merely graze the skin, it
would sever limbs.

Though his parries were sluggish, Teddie doubted she possessed the strength required to fend them off for any length of
time. When she attempted to circle him he charged, again and
again, allowing her no respite from his feverish attack. Skill
suddenly didn't seem nearly as valuable as endurance and
power—and knowing precisely where each coil of rope lay on
the deck. Despite her best efforts to deflect his thrusts, her
trickiest sidestepping, her most agile deflections, he still advanced, forcing her to retreat, undaunted by any defense or
attack she could launch. When she spun away he surged after
her, forcing her into another furious exchange of parries. The
burn in her arm muscles seeped into her back and down the
front of her thighs. Imminent victory gleamed in his eyes and
he pressed down on her, driving her back step after step around
the foremast until she bumped against the bulwarks and could
retreat no more. Then with a dizzying swipe of his blade he
locked his sword with hers, and with a sharp yank of his arm
that seemed to tear her shoulder from its socket, he wrested her
cutlass from her grasp. She spun left and his sword sliced into
her path, cleaving a gash into the bulwark. Frantic, she spun
right, only to be met with one hairy forearm. She attempted to
duck under his arm, but he caught a fistful of her hair, yanked
her head up, then thrust her back against the bulwarks, anchor-
ing her thrashing legs with the pressure of his thick thighs.
Pudgy fingers wriggled under the banded neck of her shirt,
then tore the garment to her waist.

Bile surged up into her throat and she had to close her eyes
to Griggs's lecherous leer, the animalistic sagging of his
mouth.

His cackle reeked of decaying teeth. "Gor, but ye got the
titties of a whore, lassie. I'll use ye fine, then I'll tie ye to the
mainmast an' let the rest o' me maties take what's due 'em. It's
'bout time we 'ad our fill of a 'oney pot." His sword clanged to

the deck and he groped at her breasts then between her legs, tearing at the laces binding her breeches.

Teddie went rigid. If only she could distance herself from the violation, free her mind of the horror he would inflict on her body . . .

Tears slipped from her closed eyes. His strength in a battle had been formidable. In lust he was like a steel-thewed wall. Inescapable. All the recklessness and bravery in the world couldn't possibly help her now. She needed a miracle.

Like the basest of animals he grunted, fumbling frantically at his breeches. Then suddenly he went rigid and collapsed full against her, driving the breath from her lungs beneath his gross weight. Teddie opened her eyes just as someone heaved Griggs's lifeless body off her and tossed him to the decks. For several moments Teddie stared at the sword deeply embedded in Griggs's side, then at his eyes staring blankly into the mist.

Her cutlass slipped from her fingers, clattering to the deck, just as her legs wobbled ominously beneath her and the blood seemed to leave her limbs. A strange haze filtered over her eyes. The blood rushed in her ears.

Strong hands gripped her upper arms and shook her. "Don't faint now, dammit. Look at me, Teddie."

Winchester. His voice sounded as if she were deep in a hole and he far above her. She blinked up into his face, drinking of the sight of him, clinging to the thread of concern edging his voice. The bleak lines of his face hardened when his gaze lowered to the tattered remains of her shirt and the sagging laces of her breeches. "He didn't—"

"No," she whispered, tears again pooling in her eyes when her fingers pressed against the raw slices of flesh beneath his bloodied shirt, where the cat-o'-nine had left its telltale mark. "Miles, please—"

He jerked his shirt over his head, then shoved it over hers. With eyes lowered, she poked her arms through the sleeves, shoving one across her tearstained cheeks. Gathering up the long hem, she tied it at her waist. She could feel his anger, his impatience, his utter contempt. It stood like an unconquerable fortress between them. No doubt he'd saved her life so that he could torture her for what she'd done to him. Her fingers fumbled with the laces of her breeches, tripping all over themselves beneath his scrutiny.

"Christ, woman—"

"I'm not used to breeches," she murmured, blinking through a new surge of tears.

"You damned well ought to be by now." Shoving her hands aside, he yanked the laces tight, his long fingers brushing over the low curve of her belly as they nimbly wove the laces. "How many times did you don your disguise?" he snarled, yanking tighter and tighter. "At least a half dozen. You needed little help then, with any of it." He yanked one last time. "There. Where's your hat?"

She stared at his booted feet. "I don't know."

He gripped her chin and shoved her face up. His stare was cold, unforgiving. "Humility doesn't suit you. Nor do tears." He brushed the pad of his thumb over her damp cheek then pressed the tear to his parted lips. His eyes burned into hers with a savage intensity that weakened her. "Bolster those defenses, Teddie. You're going to need them. We've some unfinished business between us."

He scooped her cutlass from the deck, grabbed her hand, and charged off across the deck toward the *Leviathan*. The *Rattlesnake*'s decks teemed with men engaged in battle. Bodies lay twisted and limp, strewn about as if by a careless hand. Teddie tripped over several as Winchester yanked her along behind him. He paused only once, exchanging a scathing round of swordplay with a British seaman before plunging his sword deep into the man's belly, then just as swiftly withdrawing it. Without glancing at Teddie, he stepped over the crumpled man, tugging her behind him.

"Abandon ship, men!" he shouted. An instant later he turned, grasped her by the waist, and lifted her over the ship's rail, then clambered after her onto the *Leviathan*'s deck.

Again he grabbed her hand and yanked her along behind him. "Watts! Damian! Reynolds!" he barked, striding to the *Leviathan*'s stern as his men began to swarm back over the ship's side. "Heave off! Man the sweeps! Will! Dammit, where is everyone? Ah, Watts." He barely glanced at the bald-pated first mate as he strode past, tossing over his shoulder, "Take the wheel. Are the cannon shotted?"

"Indeed they are, cap'n, all twenty o' them," Watts replied, giving Teddie a lingering look as she lurched past. "With twelve-pound cannon. No grapeshot."

"Good. Then open the ports and man the falls with as many men as you can spare of the sweeps," Winchester ordered. "When they've run the guns through the ports, prime them. Fire when ready."

Two at a time Winchester took to the companionway steps, Teddie stumbling behind him. Her last glimpse of the *Rattlesnake* was through a clammy white curtain of mist. Already the *Leviathan* seemed to be edging away from the other ship as her crew strained at the sweeps.

Beneath Winchester's fist his cabin door slammed open against the opposite wall, and he ducked inside, dragging her behind him.

"I want to see my brother," she demanded.

"You've acquired that shrewish tone so typical to wives of twenty years," he muttered. "And now you're making demands like a spoiled brat."

"Demands?" she said shrilly, her voice catching when he turned suddenly and loomed over her.

"Don't push me just yet," he said with deceptive softness. He glanced around, then yanked open several wall cupboards. He muttered something and slammed the cupboards closed, then moved to the deep chest shoved against one wall. Throwing up the lid, he rummaged inside, tossing garments out as he delved deeper. Teddie watched one particularly filmy garment float to the floor. It looked suspiciously like a woman's chemise, made of a lace far too delicate to be of any use save for whetting a man's more carnal appetites. Heat climbed into Teddie's cheeks as she stared at the garment and envisioned the ivory-skinned, amply proportioned temptress who had last worn the thing. Several more garments sailed from the trunk, one a woman's dress of the most shocking fuchsia satin. Teddie pursed her lips and debated the wisdom of launching into a jealous tirade at the moment. Something told her Winchester would not be amenable to any scolding at the moment, particularly regarding his vices prior to taking her as his wife. Her suspicions were confirmed when he straightened with a grunt, turned, and with a look of devilish satisfaction clamped an iron shackle around her ankle.

"No—" she choked out, stumbling as he dragged her across the floor toward the berth. There he clamped the other end of the chained shackle to the sturdy wooden leg of the bed, which looked to be nailed to the floor.

She yanked on the heavy chain, fury roaring to life. "You can't—" she spat, her eyes blazing fire up at him.

He loomed over her like some magnificent, scarred pirate, muscled legs braced wide, bare chest gleaming, a savage glitter lighting his eyes. "I can, wife, and I will. It's what I should have done long ago to keep you where you belong."

"I want to see Will."

"I've seen him. As far as I know he's fine."

"As far as you know? I demand to see him! Release me—"

The boom of cannon fire rocked the ship, throwing Teddie off balance. She fell back against the side of the ship and would have fallen to the floor had Winchester not caught her by the arms and drawn her full against him. His heat wrapped around her like invisible bonds, more powerful than all his strength, and she had to avert her face lest she bleat up at him like a lamb.

"It's for your own good," he rasped, his tone harsh, brooking little argument. She felt the heat of his breath in her hair, the tightly coiled strength in his limbs, and couldn't suppress a shudder. "I have good reason not to trust you to stay where I put you."

"You're treating me no better than your prisoner," she ground out.

"Precisely. And that's the way it's going to remain between us until I say otherwise. Wish me luck, Theodora. Even I will be gentler with you than Cockburn's men."

She must have imagined it, must have wished something from him so desperately. No, he wouldn't brush his knuckles up the length of her throat and under her chin. The gesture was much too tender, too intimate. And he far too consumed with his demons to summon an ounce of tenderness. He would do with her what he wished, of this she was certain.

Before she could glance up he turned and left the cabin. The door slammed behind him just as another boom of the cannon tipped the deck beneath her feet. She slid down against the wall and began to whisper a prayer.

Miles glanced up at the canvas hanging limp from the spars then probed the soupy gray gloom that smudged the outline of the *Leviathan*'s noble bow. From out of the gloom to the west came a flash of fire, then the boom of a cannon. Seconds later shot whistled through the mist, splashing into the bay some twenty yards off port.

For a moment only the splash of the sweeps cleaved the silence, then the thunder of cannon fired from below. Like elephants roused from slumber by the thrust of a spear, the great guns reared back in recoil as a concussion quivered through the ship. Smoke blown inboard from the gun ports eddied through the gun deck, making the air acrid and sulfurous.

Already the gun crews scurried into action. "Watts," Miles muttered. "Hold fire. Only the shots that hit count, and we won't be hitting much but fog. And neither will Cockburn. Call off the sweeps for now. We don't want to run aground. Hold her steady to the north."

Watts shouted the order to the bosun.

"How long to Halifax Harbor?" Miles asked.

As Miles expected, Watts didn't answer directly. The British had heavily fortified Nova Scotia, particularly the harbor. But both Miles and Watts knew the area well, especially Mahone Bay. It was said that there was an island for every day of the year in the bay. Once inside they could play hide-and-seek among the isles and inlets while preying upon British shipping for supplies.

"Five days," Watts replied at length. "An' that's with fresh trades, pleasant weather, a smooth sea, and all drawing sails set. Likely longer. If yer thinkin' o' makin' Mahone Bay, cap'n, you'll be puttin' the ship under the very muzzles o' the shore battery to get there.''

"True. But they won't fire if we hoist British colors. Only Cockburn knows the ship on sight. Besides, the American fleet is cruising near the mouth of the St. Lawrence should we need them. And we will. Our ship's too heavily laden with tobacco to outrun even a clumsy ship of the line, anywhere.''

"No ship's faster than the *Leviathan* since we refitted her, sir, tobacco lading and all.''

Miles considered this. ''That's a theory I'd rather not test on a hell bent run for the Indies, in waters swarming with British ships. Besides, that's where Cockburn thinks I'm running. He's sure to follow.'' He paused, rolling the word over his tongue. *Running.* It left a sour taste. But no wise man ever took on a ship of the line with half the crew and a third less guns, no matter how much he might wish to believe he could. When he spoke, even he heard the regret lacing his voice. ''By the time Cockburn suspects we've made a run for Nova Scotia, we'll have several days on him.''

"I was wondering, old boy,'' Jules Reynolds interrupted, limping up to Miles and squinting into the murk, ''Have you any spirits aboard? Perhaps in your cabin?''

Miles slanted Jules a hooded look. Gone was the polished man of leisure. In his place, a smudged and sweaty warrior of the sea, his dark shirt blood-splattered, his jaw stubbled with a day's growth of beard. His hands were blistered from manning the sweeps, and the lines embedded around his eyes by the sun seemed more pronounced. He looked as if he hadn't slept in days. Idly, he rubbed his right thigh as though massaging a deep ache there.

Miles felt something squirm in his gut, something that made him avert his gaze from Reynolds's. ''My wife is in my cabin,'' he said, having some difficulty summoning his typical low growl. Oddly enough he felt compelled to shake Reynolds's hand—hell, pump it furiously—and shout out his thanks.

Instead, he set his jaw and reminded himself that adversaries did not grovel with thanks, no matter how appropriate the sentiment. He shoved up his chin and stared out over the ship's bow from beneath low-slung brows. "You'll find some in the lower hold. The barrel labeled SUGAR, I believe. You're welcome to it."

Reynolds gripped his shoulder. "It's good to see you, old boy," he said softly. "Damned good."

Something crumpled inside Miles. He turned to his friend. "Not half so good as it was to see you come over the side of that ship." Their gazes locked briefly, and for several moments there were no barriers between them, no grievances or pitting of abilities against each other. For those moments they shared a mutual respect and admiration for each other that spoke more eloquently than any words ever could.

Miles glanced away as Damian lurched up from the gun deck and strode toward them, the empty sleeve of his dark-blue jacket flapping uselessly at his side. A tightness gripped Miles's chest.

"I say, cousin, I should shoot you now for being so damned reckless," Damian barked, brows meeting in a furious scowl that brought Miles a peculiar relief.

Folding his arms over his chest, Miles glowered mightily at his young cousin and summoned an appropriately commanding tone. "You're looking fit, Damian. All goes well below decks?"

Damian blinked, then drew himself up and lifted his chin as he'd no doubt done before George Farrell himself. "Yes, indeed. Well, indeed. I . . . I was gun captain, sir. I don't believe I hit anything though."

Their eyes met. "Neither did they. Well done then, Damian," Miles said, noting the exuberant flush coloring Damian's cheeks. "And you will remain gun captain. We will need your expertise very soon, I suspect, and that much-bally-hooed aim of yours."

"Can we outrun them?" Damian asked.

"Possibly. But I'd prefer trickery over jeopardizing lives on a gross miscalculation of our swiftness. I say we make for Nova Scotia."

Damian's eyes narrowed on Miles. "You'd rather not run anywhere?"

Miles glanced sharply at him, wondering how he'd betrayed his deepest thoughts.

"Winchesters don't run, cousin."

Jules Reynolds smothered a cough in his fist. "Any man who can masquerade about the whole of Tidewater as some ridiculous winged night creature does not easily turn tail, eh?"

Miles shot Reynolds a blistering look. "Men do what they must in times of war, Jules. You know that."

"Indeed, old boy. I will never again underestimate your gumption when you go after something you want."

"Whereas Cockburn might," Damian added thoughtfully. All eyes trained on him. He stared at Miles, a slow smile curving his lips. "You don't want to run, cousin. So don't. Stay here in the Chesapeake."

Reynolds grunted. "The pup's every bit a Winchester. Don't mind him, old boy. Listen to me. I say we make a swift run."

Miles's eyes narrowed on Damian. "Go on."

"If I judge correctly," Damian surged on, his eyes glittering with excitement, "Farrell's three-frigate squadron still sits somewhere south of Baltimore's harbor, each mounted with forty heavy guns and twice as many men."

"What the devil is he waiting for?" Reynolds muttered.

"Surprise," Miles replied. "He wants to catch Cockburn unawares. It's his only chance."

"Precisely," Damian said. "Farrell knows his ships are outgunned and outmanned, especially against Cockburn and two other British ships of the line with a hundred men and sixty guns each. But we know that Osgood and his sister ship are sitting in fog near the Elizabeth with enough rum to keep them into their cups for days. They'll be no use to anyone."

"And Cockburn is chasing his tail in fog to find the *Leviathan*," Miles added, fingering his chin thoughtfully. He glanced at Reynolds, noting the black shirt and breeches and the cape slung over his shoulders. "Ridiculous winged night creature, eh?"

Reynolds puffed up his formidable chest. "Old boy, men do

what they must in dire times, particularly if it involves bribing the enemy. Even I will don a disguise if it helps the common cause. I must say I've newfound respect for the power of a draught of rum and a good smoke of tobacco. I thought the Brits beyond turning coat and a blind eye. Thankfully, I was wrong."

Miles arched a brow. "As far as Osgood is concerned. Cockburn is an altogether different animal. His inactivity eats at him like a rodent buried deep in his bones. Farrell was wise to await the proper time. If he struck too soon Cockburn could have launched a land offensive." He directed his gaze again out over the bow. "He's like a badly broken horse. Entirely too unpredictable."

Damian moved close to Miles's side, his voice low yet trembling with an excitement that Miles himself was hard-pressed to deny another moment. "Sail north, cousin," Damian said, "straight up the bay to Baltimore. Deliver him straight to Farrell."

An odd anticipation bubbled up inside Miles. Eight years was a hell of a long time to deny oneself this feeling. And yet he had, stubborn fool that he'd been, thinking he didn't deserve any of the glory, but all of the heartache. "We'll have to wait until the fog lifts," he said. "Cockburn has to see us first to follow us."

"Not too closely, old boy," Reynolds put in quickly. "I wouldn't want to break a promise I made to a certain comely companion. I'll have you know she awaits me as we speak."

"A most noble sacrifice, Reynolds," Miles said with a curious arch of one brow. "A bit much, isn't it, for a man you barely call friend?"

Reynolds shrugged. "In dire times, old boy, even we men make incredible sacrifices." He leaned nearer, his voice dipping meaningfully. "It's not just the women."

Miles set his jaw, knowing precisely where this was leading and wanting nothing of it at the moment. "Not now, Reynolds."

"Ah, but now seems all too appropriate to discuss the matter of your wife. It might not be my business to say this—"

"Then don't."

"—but I can't help but miss the girl. Such infectious spirit, such wondrous innocence. Such bravery. Ah, you're scowling again, old boy. I don't suppose you wish to hear that from me."

"Oddly enough, no. Did I mention the barrel of rum in the hold, Reynolds?"

"Of course, who am I to elaborate on your wife's boundless charms. You would be a blind fool not to know them well. A man would do everything he could to keep a woman like that. Hold her dear and all. Still, I can't help but wonder how you kept her below all this time while none of us could convince her to stay put. Did you perhaps chain her to the bed or some such barbarism?"

Though Miles kept his face hooded in bored indifference, he could do nothing about the flush of chagrin creeping up his neck. Reynolds's boisterous "Ha ha!" and sound slap on his back did nothing to temper his mood or his sudden overwhelming desire to go below into his cabin.

"Perhaps I spoke out of turn, eh?" Reynolds drawled, amusement lighting his eyes. "You don't seem to need my help at the moment. Indeed, you're a better man than I, old boy. Restraint and all that. Can't help but wonder what's keeping you above decks."

"Not your company," Miles muttered, brushing past a grinning Jules Reynolds. "Has anyone checked on Will?"

"He's below, sir," Watts replied. "We managed to cut the chain off 'is ankle. Now 'e's eating 'is bellyful of fine Virginia ham and turnips. Shall I send 'im to ye?"

Miles shook his head. "Let him rest. Stay on course, Watts. Man the sweeps once an hour for fifteen minutes until the breeze stirs the canvas. If the fog begins to lift, let me know. Damian, take the watch in four hours. I'd suggest you get some sleep until then. I suggest we all do. If you need me I'll be in my cabin. Preferably until morning."

Chapter Twenty

❖

Teddie opened her eyes. Winchester stood in the cabin's doorway, in bold relief against a silvery backdrop of mist. His features were deeply shadowed, yet until she died she would know his silhouette simply by the way her heart hammered riotously in her breast at the sight of him. Even in her restless sleep she had sensed his presence, her body rousing, sensing what she could not in slumber. When he wished, he could move as silently as the curling of the fog through the air.

He stepped into the arc of lamplight emitted by a lantern set upon an overturned barrel in the far corner. The coldness in his eyes offered her no reassurances as they rested on her for several moments. She swallowed, attempting to ignore the blood-encrusted slashes marring the bronzed expanse of his chest, wounds that needed tending, a loving hand. . . .

With a swipe of his hand he scooped something from the floor, then took another step toward her. She straightened her legs, inching up the side of the cabin, her back flat against the wood. The chain binding her ankle clanked. She watched his thick fingers work the flimsy white linen between them, felt the uncompromising savagery of his stare. Not a handbreadth from her he paused, towering over her with a primal, beastly magnificence that heated her blood to a feverish pitch.

"By the time I return," he rumbled, "I want you wearing this."

She caught the linen against her belly. "Where is Will?" she threw at his back.

He paused, one hand on the door handle. "Resting comfortably below decks, with the rest of the crew, so long as the fog stays. Battened down until morning, I suspect." His eyes flickered over the linen she clutched. "We've got hours until then, Theodora."

She opened her mouth, but he'd already turned and left the cabin, slamming the door behind him.

"Brute," she tossed at the thick door, achieving little satisfaction. With a scowl she held up the filmy white linen, knowing what it was simply by the fine transparency of the weave and the scalloped lace edging along the scooped neckline. A lovely garment. French made. Under different circumstances she might be inclined to see how it felt next to her skin, particularly with the heat so damned unbearable.

Under different circumstances, indeed. She ground her teeth and felt every rebellious fiber within her leap to life. If he thought for one minute that she would agree to this sort of humiliation, simply to feed his abominable ego . . . if he thought to teach her a lesson in humility. . . . By God, she'd never been anyone's docile prisoner!

He obviously wasn't intending to deliver her to her Uncle George any time soon. A sobering thought. She glowered at the door and wondered where he'd gone and what the devil he would do if she disobeyed him. He looked capable of just about anything. She'd watched him kill without hesitation or an ounce of regret. And he'd never admitted to having a conscience about anything. Loyalties to no one but himself.

The devil take her, but she hated being told what to do.

Setting her teeth, she jerked the knot at her waist loose and yanked his shirt over her head. Her own torn shirt landed beside it on the floor. Despite the smothering heat her flesh quivered with each movement as if touched by a chill. Beneath several yanks on the laces her breeches pooled at her ankles. Kicking off one boot, she slid one bare foot free. Leaving the breeches crumpled around her shackled ankle, she reached for the chemise and slipped it over her head.

Like a whisper of gossamer it spilled over her body, its delicate lace hem falling to just above her ankles. She pursed her lips, taking reluctant notice that the garment had been designed for a woman perhaps several inches shorter, of narrower proportions, and a good deal less bosom.

"Damned pirate knew that," she muttered, cursing Winchester's discerning eye and every narrow-hipped, willowy young maiden on the planet. It was either that or scolding herself for overindulging in Jillie's tea cakes, which she preferred not to even consider. Whatever the reason, the fit was all wrong. Where the linen should have draped, it clung, most especially over her breasts and buttocks and along the length of her thighs. As for the transparency, she might well have been wearing nothing at all for all the protection it provided.

Protection. Yes, she would surely need some of that when Winchester pounced through that door.

A shiver whispered through her as she set her fingers to lacing the ridiculously fragile white ribbon that was supposed to hold the panels of the bodice closed over her ribs and bosom. A futile task at best. There was simply too much of her for the garment to contain.

Biting off a groan of frustration, she jerked the tie into a knot, closed her eyes, and pressed her palm to the base of her throat. Against her skin her fingers were like ice. Beneath her feet the decks gently idled against the tide, and yet her belly roiled as if the ship plunged into the teeth of a gale and mountainous green seas crashed over her bow.

The door thudded open. Teddie jerked and her eyes snapped open, instantly meeting Winchester's. With a wariness better suited to tigers on a hunt, she watched him watch her from the doorway for what seemed an eternity. In one hand he carried a bottle full of amber liquid. In the other an ivory-handled knife with a blade of such length and breadth that's Teddie's chest compressed. He wore nothing but close-fitting black breeches and boots.

Her mouth tasted acrid and dry. A pulse thundered in her ears, and she had to look away when his eyes hooded and with a savage insolence moved over the length of her. She didn't know if she could bear to see contempt there, yet on her skin his gaze felt like the brush of warm fingertips. Heat coursed through her, and a reckless, wanton need poured liquid down her legs and drew her nipples taut against the linen. What little modesty she'd retained by standing in profile to him was instantly shattered.

The door creaked closed behind him. All the air suddenly seemed to suck out of the cabin and the temperature soared another twenty degrees.

"Turn around. Face me."

Teddie thrust her chin up at him. "Why are you doing this? I will not be humiliated. If you have anything to say to me, just say it and be done with it. Care to measure my neck for your noose?"

His eyes bored into hers. "Turn around," he rumbled, ominous as an advancing storm.

So that's how he wanted it. No doubt it would please him if she cowered at the sight of his knife, at the mere rumble of his voice. Surely he knew the very rafters trembled when he entered a room. So should she, eh?

Nose lifted, shoulders pinched back, she turned to face him and felt all her fury crumble when the flames of passion flared in his eyes. No, this was not humiliation. This was ravagement, the agonizing sort, where the body responded beyond will and reason, beyond the callings of logic. Where a reckless spirit prevailed over levelheadedness. If he wished to probe the core of her for weakness, he was doing so with an expert hand.

If he wished to torture her by exploiting her lust for him, he most certainly would.

As would she, if given the merest opportunity.

Her skin was dewy moist, the linen damp where it clung to her breasts and belly, drawing taut across her hips, pressing against the dark curls between her thighs. She swayed when his gaze lowered there and his chest expanded beneath a breath swiftly drawn and held. Silently, she gave deep thanks for all those sweet tea cakes she'd indulged in.

Somehow she got the distinct feeling he was fast losing his battle with his anger at her.

"Take off this chain," she said softly.

He lifted the bottle to his lips and drank deeply, the thick column of his throat working as he swallowed. He lowered the bottle, his gaze still at the juncture of her thighs. A throbbing fullness settled there in her loins, an ache that swelled as the moments passed and he didn't lift his eyes. He wore his need with a boldness that should have daunted her. Two months ago it would have sent her running for her life. Now it emboldened her, fired her desires, allowing her gaze free roam over him until it settled on the formidable bulge clearly outlined by his taut breeches. Her breath caught.

She lifted her eyes. He was staring at her mouth. He took a step closer. In the lamplight the blade flashed as he flexed his wrist. There was no forgiveness on his face, only desire. A wild, consuming desire.

"Take your hair down," he said tonelessly, his jaw flexing.

Slowly, she lifted her arms and began to pull what was left of the pins from her hair. Reaching up for several high pins, she felt the chemise slip dangerously low over her breasts with the movement. Primal satisfaction filled her when his eyes lowered to her breasts and his face at once turned to stone. Every magnificent inch of his body seemed to tense and pull taut. Teddie dug her nails into her scalp to keep from reaching out to touch him.

One long curl fell over her shoulder, then another, both coiling against her breast. His eyes followed each as they cascaded over her skin. There was something of the animal in him tonight. She could see the mammalian hunger in his eyes, as though he drank of her every movement and thirsted for more. Seduction, she realized with a shiver of anticipation, was indeed a double-edged sword. Her anger would not be the only casualty of this game.

Very subtly she arched her back and reached for the last of the pins. Her lips parted as the movement brought her breasts arching entirely out of the shallow bodice. She pressed her fingers to the ribbon between them and shook her head, loosening her hair until it fell in lustrous waves over her shoulders and nearly to her waist. One shrug of her shoulders and one narrow lace strap slid to her elbow.

Through the tousled curtain of her hair, she slanted her eyes up at him. Slowly she traced one finger up the lace panel from her waist, then gently pulled on the dainty ribbon binding the chemise. The knot slipped free. From beneath a heavy shadow of dark brows, he watched her.

Her lips trembled open. She knew she played with fire here, a reckless, wanton game she could only pray she would win. If she'd guessed his intent. If she hadn't misjudged him. If he was the man she loved, the man she knew him to be. . . .

The blade was like a flash of flame as it swiped up, cleaving through the laces. Again, with another snap of his wrist, the blade swiped down through the hem of the chemise. Teddie felt as if she burst through the garment as it rent, laying her entirely bare to his devouring gaze.

She held her breath, her eyes never leaving his as he lifted the blade and laid it against her throat. The metal was like ice against her skin. Those deep, dark, turbulent pools probed to her soul.

"You're not afraid," he murmured.

"Not with you."

"I could kill you for what you did to me." A breath left him in a hiss and the knife pressed deeper into her skin. She could imagine many men had trembled with terror beneath that blade. "I will be merciless with you."

"I still won't fear you."

A spark lit his eyes. "I don't want your fear, woman." Their breaths heated the scant space between them, lacing the air with the scent of brandy. Slowly, he drew the tip of the knife down her throat and across her collarbone, then beneath the strap at her shoulder. With one flick of his wrist the blade slipped through the linen. She barely breathed, and what was left of the garment drifted to the floor.

"Unlace my breeches," he said.

She reached to his waist, fingers brushing the taut ridge of his belly just above the breeches. His skin seared her fingertips. Lowering her eyes, she tugged at the laces, her fingers fumbling when he spilled cool brandy over her breasts.

"Keep going," he murmured, lowering his head when she lifted hers. They both froze. His mouth hovered over hers, tautly held, still unforgiving. Their eyes met. The ship seemed to rock.

"I love you, Miles," she whispered. "You must forgive me."

"There was never a question of that," he growled beneath his breath, lowering his head to her breasts. The knife clattered to the floor, the bottle as well, and yet she heard nothing above the joy singing in her heart. Sagging into his arms, she clasped him close as the tears welled up from deep in her throat. Wood dug into her back as he pressed her deep against the side of the ship. His tongue was like a firebrand as he drank her breasts clean of the spilled brandy then delved lower over her belly, and lower still where the brandy had trickled deep between her thighs. Rough hands grasped her hips, cupped the fullness of her buttocks, then lifted her pelvis to his mouth. He drank deeply of her, ravaging all her senses with the unleashed savagery of his desires and lifting her up, up into that delicious realm of pleasure.

Teddie cried out her delight in long, torturous spasms, and when he rose up before her and flicked his breeches open, releasing the instrument of his pleasure, she reveled in the artless magnificence of him. Clasping him close, she spread her thighs and welcomed his first thrust, taking him fully, wholly, without reservation.

He silenced her outcries with the force of his mouth on hers and the deep thrust of his tongue. He was not gentle or tender. But he was magnificent, savage, and lustful, as no other could ever be, fulfilling Teddie's every need. Like a beast in need of taming he drove himself into her with hard, fast undulations of his hips, lifting her high against the side of the ship and drawing her legs around his waist. Only when she again cried out with her own glorious release did he arch against her, rigid and beautiful, before he spilled himself inside her with long, fluid spasms.

He collapsed heavily against her, his body slick and sleek and too wonderful. With eyes closed Teddie felt the pumping of his heart beneath his chest, heard the rasping of his breaths, and could imagine no greater happiness.

And then he cupped his hands around her face and lifted it to his. "Say it again," he rasped, brushing his lips over hers with a tenderness that brought the tears flowing from her eyes.

"I love you, Miles Winchester," she whispered, half-choking.

He kissed the tears from her cheeks, one by one, then crushed her head to his chest and wrapped himself around her. Cradling her in his arms, he sank onto the bed. "Sweet love . . . these tears . . . you're breaking my heart."

"Say you forgive me, Miles."

"If you'll stop the damned crying. This isn't like you."

She pushed against him, blinking the tears from her eyes. "You're still angry with me. Surely after this you're not going to hang me."

A corner of his mouth lifted, the first subtle softening. "In another fifty years maybe. Reckless girl, why didn't you trust me enough to tell me about Will? I would have done everything in my power to help you. Why the hell didn't you realize that?"

"Cockburn would have killed Will at the slightest hint of any enemy attack. I couldn't risk telling anyone, especially you, knowing how strongly you felt about the Night Hawk, how deeply averted you were to the war. I was certain that you would hang me, or worse."

"A man doesn't hang the woman he loves. Even if she's the most scheming, reckless, duplicitous woman on the planet."

Teddie felt her heart soar. "At the risk of playing my hand too far, Miles, please say that again."

He arched a sly brow. "You more than anyone know how utterly duplicitous you are. And reckless. You play your hand too far at least once daily."

"It's a wonder any man would have me."

"I couldn't agree more. Only a fool would love you." He nipped at her lips, her chin, then lifted one breast to his mouth. His tongue flicked over the nipple. "Or desire you . . . or need you like he needs the air he breathes."

She pressed her nails into his shoulders. "Say it again, my husband."

"I love you," he breathed against her breasts. "Beyond reason. Beyond the limits of the earth and the seas and the sky and the stars." He lifted his head, and for the first time she saw it all there in his eyes, all the pain, the longing, the need he'd denied for too long. "Teddie, you brought hope into my life when there was none, joy where there had only been pain and sorrow and guilt—so much damned guilt simply for living to see another sunrise when so many didn't. When all those who had gone before me had died so needlessly. I didn't know why the hell I was spared."

"I do," she murmured, smoothing her palm over his chest then laying her head against his heart. "There's no guilt in finding happiness, Miles."

"So it was luck. The odds of surviving the blast of a ship's entire magazine are insurmountable. And yet somehow, by some stroke of fate, I did. And part of me was glad I did, glad that I washed ashore and woke up in irons. I deserved some kind of punishment for ordering that damned fuse lit when I did. Had I not, had the fuse been the proper length—" He swallowed deeply. "They threw me in the dey's prison with the rest of the *Philadelphia*'s crew, the men I'd been sent to save." He gave a caustic grunt, his face growing shadowed, the lines more pronounced as memory encroached. "Instead, I watched half of them die."

"You were not responsible—"

"No? Then who the hell was?"

"Perhaps the men who threw them in there. Miles, you were not spared to save them all. No one man could have."

"We'll never know that. But I could have done more. Teddie, I was stronger than all of them together. They'd been in Tripoli for months, serving as beasts of burden for the dey. The fortunate prisoners—the young and the weak—drew jobs along the harbor, careening vessels to clean their hulls and fitting out the pirate ships for the next cruise. Some were even trusted to unload the spoils of the returning corsairs. The strongest and freshest prisoners, like me, were used to haul rock on wooden sleds from the pits to the harbor to fortify it against attack. The city alleyways were too narrow for wagons, but not for men or sleds. The loads were hoisted at the ends of long poles slung over our shoulders. We were the sled gangs."

Teddie shuddered. "Miles—"

"You have to hear this, Teddie. The overseers drove us unmercifully. Those overseers whose men could haul the largest loads were rewarded by the dey. Anyone who stumbled or faltered was beaten. I remember a father watched his own son stagger and fall in front of a sled that crushed his legs. Another prisoner was bitten by a tarantula on his cheek while carrying timber. His complaint went ignored and his head swelled to twice its normal size." He swallowed deeply, his voice tremoring. "I had a plan, Teddie. I was going to free them all or die trying."

Teddie stared at him, her heart pounding, hope squashing beneath the sardonic twist of his lips, the bleak chill in his eyes.

"But I didn't. I was, as they say, weak of flesh."

An invisible weight pressed on Teddie's chest. "There was a woman."

His features hardened. "Yes, there was one woman I remember more than the others. Manal. She used to stand with all the other women at the palace balcony when our sled gang passed by every day. She was young, quite beautiful, an innocent to the ways of love. I saw only that, nothing deeper, and I wanted her. She told me she was a servant, that she'd chosen me. She began to sneak into the prison at night when the guards slept. I never suspected that she was using me. Like all young, deflowered innocents, she professed deep, passionate love for me. Only after, when she stopped coming, did I learn that she was promised to the dey's brother, a vile, diabolical man no woman would want to marry. She obviously didn't and needed a way out. Sullied virtue was her method. But when he discovered her secret, she rather quickly forgot her deep and abiding affection for me and tried to trade her life for mine while still escaping marriage to him. For her efforts she was taken to sea, tied in a weighted sack, and thrown overboard. On the evening that I was to be beheaded, the dey decided I would prove far more entertaining in his salon."

"His salon." Teddie swallowed. "Doing what?"

"Smoking opium. Servicing his concubines. While he and his brother watched."

"Oh, Miles, please don't—"

"I remember very little of it save for the rage. No man should be slave to another man, or to a drug. It's a hell I wouldn't wish on my enemies. As for the women—the dey made certain that my seed wouldn't take root where it shouldn't, in the form of a sheath made of a goat's udder. The only children of my loins will be born of you . . ." His mouth brushed against the corner of her lips. ". . . If you will have me."

Fresh tears flooded Teddie's eyes and spilled to her cheeks. She grasped his hand and pressed it against her belly. "Scarred and guilt-ridden, tortured with memory, I will have you in any form, Miles, and proudly bear you a brood of children to fill all of Miramer's bedrooms. Believe this, fate might have saved you once, but your own will to live saw you through that desert and here, to Miramer, and to me. You deserve every ounce of happiness you can squeeze from this life. There is no guilt in that. Only honor."

He brushed his thumb over her lips, his eyes hooding. "It's no doubt what my grandfather Maximilian would have done, eh? A pity it took me so long to realize forgiveness is a virtue, not a weakness. Just like love." Gathering her close, he kissed her deeply, lingeringly, his tongue gently thrusting, full of promise she intended to allow him to keep. She arched up against him, pressing deeply against his skin.

Their mouths parted with a gasp.

Teddie averted her eyes. "I know now it was foolish not to tell you everything, Miles. I . . . I wanted to, quite desperately."

"So." He nuzzled her neck and slid one hand up the length of her leg, molding his palm around the top of her thigh. "You were tempted."

"More than tempted. I thought I'd told you everything after I drank Winnie's brew and—." Heat swept to her hairline. "You have a way about you, Miles."

His fingers brushed the damp curls between her thighs. "What way is that, love?"

Teddie's breath left her.

"Such innocence still waiting to be plundered," he murmured, stroking whisper-soft against her womanhood. "You were magnificent that night, my love. A veritable lioness. You pushed me to the very limits of my restraint. As for you spilling your secrets, all that left those rosy lips were several desperate pleas for more."

"More?" she breathed, slanting hooded eyes up at him and running her tongue slowly over her lips. "Surely you will have to unchain me to demonstrate."

"I will beat you if you flee me," he rumbled, withdrawing a key from his pocket. He fit it into the shackle and the irons slid to the floor.

"Give me good reason to stay, and I won't flee," she murmured coyly, trailing her palms down his chest and belly and lower to where his manhood lay full and heavy against his thigh. "Ah, Miles, what's this?"

In one fluid motion he turned with her, pressing her flat beneath his weight on the bed. "Have you reason now?" he said huskily, rising from her long enough to shed his boots and breeches in swift, jerky movements. With an audacity that shot fiery desire through her, he grasped his manhood and slid his hand once, twice along the turgid length. His eyes glowed with wanton desire. "Have you, wife?"

"Yes," she whispered, arching up to him as he fell upon her.

And she did. All the reason she would ever need.

Teddie jerked awake, sitting up in the berth with a jumble of unformed words spilling from her tongue. She glanced around the cabin. Winchester was gone, the sheets beside her cool beneath her fingertips. Outside the tiny porthole the world shone a mottled gray. From just above her a shout rang out. And then the ship rocked beneath the thunder of cannon fire.

She leapt from the bed, took one step toward her clothes and her cutlass, only to fall to her knees as her ankle was all but yanked from her leg.

She stared at the shackle binding her ankle just as another fire of cannon quivered through the rafters.

Chapter Twenty-One

❖

Miles leveled a long glass on the northern horizon beneath a low ceiling of scudding clouds. "Crowd on all sail, Watts."

"We're piling canvas to run, mates!" Watts bellowed. At his order the topmen scuttled aloft like monkeys to set the studding sails.

"Set the yards athwartship," Miles snapped. "She'll make her best speed though she's heavy. We're running dead before the wind. And so is Cockburn."

Watts shouted the order, then turned to Miles. "Sail ho, cap'n?"

Miles snapped the long glass closed. "Not yet. The fog's still lifting. Farrell's got to be close. I can sense it." He glanced over his shoulder at the *Rattlesnake*, not an eighth of a mile off port and slightly behind, her sails billowing full with the wind. "Can we outrun her, Watts, without dumping some lading?"

"Aye, cap'n. We can out run her as we are. I'd hate to see the bay full o' hogsheads."

Miles considered this. Sacrificing Miramer's tobacco for the lives of his crew, his wife . . . hardly a sacrifice at this juncture. "Not yet. We want to lead her on a merry chase, Watts. Right into the mouth of the lion. Let's hope her cannon range is poor."

At that, a puff of smoke lifted off the *Rattlesnake*'s decks, followed by the *boom* of her heavy cannon. The shot plunged into the *Leviathan*'s foamy wake.

"She's got distance, cap'n. But no aim."

"That time. If she hits with her heavy cannon we'll feel it. Fire again when ready. Is Damian at the twelve pounder?"

"Aye, sir. Ye want him there?"

"Absolutely. There's no better aim aboard ship. The lad will make a fine captain of his own vessel."

Watts relayed the order. Not a moment later a concussion rocked the ship. The shot whistled through space, then plowed into the *Rattlesnake* broadside.

A cheer rose from the gun deck.

"Didn't break her stride," Miles muttered, scowling at the mammoth British man-of-war plowing along under full press of sail despite the smoke billowing from the yawning gap in her deck. "Again, Watts. We need to hit her rigging to shorten her sail—"

"Sail ho!" The shout came from the tops, where a wiry sailor clung with one hand to the rigging. With the other he pointed to the north. "A half mile off the bow, cap'n."

Miles stepped up and snapped open his long glass, leveling it north.

"What's her rig?" Watts asked.

"Frigate. Three of them, hoisting the Stars and Stripes."

"Cockburn's sure to see 'em."

"Indeed. He won't turn tail. It's a fight he wants, and he'll sure as hell get it. Let's hope Farrell gets here quick."

"He surely won't, tacking into the wind, sir."

"True, but I can't afford to change course now."

A boom came from off port. The shot whistled ominously, the certain sound a lead ball made just before impact. The explosion threw Miles and Watts to the decks. Smoke billowed over them, choking the air. Flames leapt from the center of the ship, the heat searing. Sweeping debris off his legs, Miles struggled to his feet, a chunk of wooden beam in his hand. One quick glance upward confirmed what he suspected: The shot had split the mainmast. Above him, canvas flapped uselessly from the broken spars.

"Men aloft!" he shouted, already feeling the ship's diminishing speed. Through the smoke he could see the *Rattlesnake* bearing down upon them. Fury congealed in his chest. "Damn, we should have dumped the tobacco. Watts! Bring her around. I'd rather have them come on board than fall smashing broadsides and lose the ship entirely. Besides, I'd prefer to distract Cockburn until Farrell gets here."

"Are ye sure, cap'n? We could still outmaneuver her."

Miles glanced sharply at Watts. The last time anyone had asked him that was when he'd ordered their commando ship set afire in Tripoli's harbor, seconds before the magazine blew, killing all but him. If he'd misjudged Farrell's speed or underestimated Cockburn's zeal for a quick and bloody fight, he would again be delivering his crew to certain death. Indeed, they still could quite possibly outmaneuver the man-of-war—or be pummeled into shards by two broadsides.

He drew up rigid, his thoughts freezing. A chill crept into his blood as realization flooded over him. Guilt and vicious memory hadn't condemned him to his reclusive life at Miramer. They'd been mere shadows of the real reason for his withdrawal. He'd been hiding, driven into hiding for eight damned years for one reason above all others: Only then could he closet himself against decisions that involved other men's lives. The decisions of war. *Afraid*. Even the idea that he was lord and master of his plantation had yet to sit well with him, because of the responsibility the title implied. Even his own wife hadn't been able to lay her trust in his hands.

And yet all his slaves had. This crew as well. If he was wrong about Cockburn's lust for a long, played-out drama of a fight, by God—

"Cap'n, sir?"

If he was wrong—

He should have made a run for Nova Scotia when he'd had the chance.

He swallowed deeply, Damian's words ringing clear and true in his mind. No Winchester had ever turned tail. And they'd never doubted in instinct before, dammit, no matter what mistakes they'd made in the past.

"Cap'n—"

"Bring her around," Miles snapped. "And fast, before the *Rattlesnake* can fire all sixty of her guns."

Another ball plunged through the rigging, toppling the foremast. Flaming canvas plunged to the decks.

"Get the men above decks," Miles shouted as he leapt over a shattered spar. "Get this damned fire out!" Just off the port side the *Rattlesnake*'s black hull loomed, her crew straining over the bulwarks with pistols and cutlasses at the ready. At the helm stood a leering Jeremiah Cockburn. In seconds his men would swarm over the sides like ravenous ants.

"Dammit, Farrell, hurry," Miles snarled, shoving debris from his path as he clambered toward the companionway. Toward Teddie. He'd left her at daybreak, rosy and warm, slumbering peacefully in his berth, accomplishing this only because he knew he'd never again have to leave her. He was glad he'd heeded instinct and shackled her. Else he'd surely be scouring the decks for her now.

He had to free her now, arm her, and defend her. To his death if need be, like his forefathers would have.

Shots rang out all around him and blades locked in battle clanged. The cabin door crashed open beneath his fist. She surged up from the bed, clutching the sheet to her breasts, eyes red-rimmed.

"Damn you!" she growled.

He took two steps and felt something hit his shoulder, like the pound of a huge fist. Only harder. The force propelled him through the air into the cabin. He hit the side of the ship, spun, and the world instantly went black.

Teddie's scream died in her throat when Jeremiah Cockburn swaggered into the cabin, his smoking pistol dangling from one hand.

"Ah, the traitoress," he sneered, sweeping her with his heavy-lidded eyes. He arched a brow, taking obvious note of her shackled ankle. With an ominous finality the door thudded closed behind him. "I see the brigand used you well. A pity he won't any longer. Or anyone else for that matter. Treason carries a high price, Theodora. Ah, but you know that. Makes the neck twitch just thinking about it, doesn't it? Although . . . the sight of you thus fires the imagination, even one as warped as mine. You just may find my methods—how shall I say it?— refreshing. Preferable to the noose, perhaps?"

His sword slid from its sheath and he advanced, forcing her up onto the bed and deep into the corner. "You betrayed me," he spat, slashing the sword over the sheet she clutched. The blade sliced through the cotton and swiped a bloody path over her bare shoulder. She bit out a cry of pain. Cockburn's lips twisted into a grotesque version of a smile. His eyes glowed with a lascivious, demented kind of lust. "Where is the arrogant wench I know? The woman who thought to bargain with an admiral in His Majesty's fleet? You, who once thought yourself better than me, now chained like a dog to this bed, eh? Has your lover sucked you dry of fight, my dear? Worry not, for I intend to put it back in you."

Teddie knew an altogether different horror when Cockburn unhooked his belt and his scabbard slid to the floor. His hand fumbled with the laces of his breeches. Her belly heaved bile into her throat, and the shackle seemed to burn around her ankle. From just above came an almost constant boom of pistols and swordplay. A massacre.

She, too, would not surrender without a fight.

Teddie lunged from the bed, but Cockburn caught her arm, twisting it behind her. With surprising strength he yanked her arm high, spun her, and shoved her to the floor. One blood-splattered boot clamped over her neck and ground the side of her face into the floorboards.

Gritting her teeth, Teddie fought against him, arching her back and letting loose with a vicious scream when he yanked the sheet up over her hips and forced her legs apart.

"I should have tamed you long ago, wench," Cockburn snarled. "Damned women should never be trusted, no matter how clever—"

Through the mist covering her eyes, Teddie imagined she saw Winchester's leg move slightly. Before she could blink, or hope, he leapt from the floor and at Cockburn like a lion springing for a kill, teeth bared in a growl that set the walls trembling.

With an enraged bellow Cockburn crashed to the floor, Miles on top of him. Scrambling to her feet and dragging the sheet with her, Teddie spun around and found Miles hauling Cockburn from the floor by the brass-buttoned front of his uniform. Despite the blood streaming from a gaping shoulder wound, Miles shoved Cockburn against the wall as though he weighed next to nothing. In a flash he pressed the ivory-handled blade up under Cockburn's chin.

The admiral froze. "Do it, savage!" Cockburn shrieked, eyes bulging with terror. "I see it in your eyes. You would carve out my heart and have it for supper. What's keeping you, devil's spawn?"

Teddie dug her fingernails into her palms to keep from crying out. Half of her wished to see Cockburn crumple lifeless to the floor, a miserly recompense for all the innocent lives he'd taken. The other half, the part of her beyond the bloodlust of war and revenge, desperately hoped that Miles would realize the futility of killing. Her chest compressed beneath a breath tightly held. Miles turned the blade until the tip poised against Cockburn's skin. A moment later a drop of blood oozed onto the tip.

No. . . . More bloodshed would solve nothing, no matter that men would forever think it would.

"I've no thirst for your blood," Miles said tonelessly. "I'd rather leave that to Commander Farrell." One hand delved into his pocket, then tossed Teddie the key to the shackles. Quickly, she bent and unlocked the chain at her ankle and the shackle at the bedpost, then moved to his side.

"Farrell?" Cockburn sneered. "He's getting his ass bloodied with the rest of his fleet up near the St. Lawrence, or so I've been told—" He paused. The color drained from his face as he glanced from Miles to Teddie and back again.

"He suspects he's been played afoul, wife," Miles said silkily, angling Teddie a cool look.

"*Wife?*" Cockburn spat. "Good God, to you?"

"Have you any idea what the penalty is in Virginia for attempting to sodomize a man's wife?" Miles said with deceptive softness, his blade gleaming in the dim light. "Far more vile than anything you can muster, I'd wager."

Teddie pressed a hand on his arm. "Miles."

Beneath her hand he was rigid as a mighty oak. Another drop of blood dripped from the tip of the blade.

"Please, Miles, let it be."

His eyes darted to her, then back to Cockburn. The tension seemed to seep out of him. "You're right. Better to let the bastard live out his days knowing his end came at the hand of a clever female. The Admiralty will have no use for him when the war is over. A fate worse than death for a man like you, eh, Cockburn?"

Cockburn's face flushed scarlet with rage.

Miles felt his lips curve. "Ah, there is indeed satisfaction in being merciful."

The cabin door burst open and Commander George Farrell surged into the cabin brandishing a cutlass in one hand and a pistol in the other. At his heels came Damian and several American officers similarly armed. All took precisely three steps into the cabin, then froze.

"Good God, Theodora!" Farrell boomed. "What the devil are you doing here?"

"Good morning, Uncle George," Teddie beamed, then slipped one arm through Miles's. "Oh, Winchester, you did it. You truly did it! He did it, Uncle George!"

"What?" Farrell growled. "What did he do?"

"He saved us all, that's what," Teddie gushed. "Quit scowling at him, Uncle George. He's injured."

"Nothing more than a flesh wound, sir," Miles muttered, oddly chagrined. He tore off a bit of sheet and wrapped it over his shoulder and under his arm several times to staunch the blood flow.

"Don't think I haven't heard that before," Farrell snarled, eyeing Winchester's slashed chest and arms. "I'll have my ship physician take a look at you."

"That's not necessary, sir," Miles said.

"Balderdash. You're just like your damned father was. Fool would have bled to death several times over if I'd let him." Bushy brows plummeted over his nose as he took in Teddie's dishabille. His eyes darted to Cockburn. "Captain Coyle, shackle this one up. Rouse, McAllister, take him above decks and to my ship's hold.''

With chin jutting proudly, Damian stepped past them and grasped Cockburn's arm, then handed him to the two other men who quickly led him from the cabin. Before Damian turned to leave the cabin he paused beside Farrell. ''Perhaps I should mention that two British frigates await us in the Albemarle Sound, sir, once we secure the *Rattlesnake*.''

Farrell's scowl deepened. ''Await us? What the devil are you saying, Coyle?''

Damian's grin lit his eyes. ''Rum soused and unsuspecting, sir, crews and captains both.''

Farrell arched a brow. ''Rum, you say. Whose rum?''

''Fine Winchester rum, sir. My grandfather Maximilian's choicest Jamaican. Enough for two frigates of thirsty men, sir.''

Farrell's gaze grew dubious. ''You have firsthand knowledge of this, Coyle?''

''Indeed, sir. I spoke with Captain Osgood myself, just before he handed us his colors, sir.''

Farrell blinked, clearly astonished. ''His colors, you say?''

''So we could sail the *Leviathan* out of the sound undisturbed, sir.'' Damian's chest puffed.

''Who the devil concocted such a scheme?'' Farrell growled.

''Why, your niece, sir.''

Farrell shot Teddie a look of astonishment.

Teddie lifted her chin despite the flush creeping up her neck. ''We had no choice, Uncle George.''

''*No choice?* You, the niece of the commanding officer of the American fleet, had no choice, you say? Dare I say it, you bribed them, Theodora! Two damned ships of the line!''

''Indeed, we did,'' Teddie chirped, ''Quite smashingly. With a little help from the Night Hawk.''

''Stop!'' Farrell held up a gloved hand, clearly befuddled by the entire affair. ''I will hear no more of this preposterous tale until I've a drink in hand. Indeed, I can only wonder where you fit into all this, Winchester. Something tells me only a Winchester would lead a sixty-gun British man-of-war on a merry chase.''

''Indeed,'' Miles replied, his eyes resting proudly on Damian. ''It was a joint decision, sir, between Captain Coyle and me.''

Farrell's eyes narrowed on Damian. ''Once you get Cockburn secured in the hold, Coyle, I'd like you to assume command of my frigate. Hoist Osgood's damned colors over her, then get the devil down to Albemarle and have another chat with Osgood, eh?''

Damian seemed to grow two inches out of his boots. ''It will be my pleasure, sir. I doubt we'll have to draw a gun.'' He turned to the door then paused, hesitating with uncertainty before grasping Miles's hand. ''Thank you, cousin,'' he said, his voice cracking. ''I understand now. All of it. I was wrong to think you cared nothing for family. I see now that it was the reason behind everything that you did. I ask only that you forgive me.''

''There's nothing to forgive,'' Miles replied, clasping Damian's shoulder. ''When you return from Albemarle with your two British ships in tow, you'll have your own ship awaiting your command.''

Damian swallowed deeply. ''Cousin?''

''Once she's refitted, of course.''

''But the *Leviathan*'s your ship.''

''Indeed. And as owner and captain I can bequeath her to whomever I feel is most deserving of her.''

Damian blinked, his cheeks flushing. ''Bequeath her, you say? I . . . I don't know what to say, cousin.''

''A simple yes would do. No Winchester ever balked at opportunity.''

Damian glanced at his empty sleeve. ''You think me able-bodied?''

''What you lack in limb you more than make up for with spirit and bravery. She could be in no better hands.''

''A privateer captain,'' Damian breathed. ''And once the war is over I'll ship all the tobacco you can harvest—''

''Not after this crop.''

"But what of Miramer? What of Grandfather Maximilian's legacy?"

"Maximilian Winchester wouldn't cling to a crop if he didn't think it wise. Tobacco exhausts the soil rapidly. It requires careful, constant attention. Few have a good word to say about it, especially with cotton growing farther south. I've decided I need to rotate growing tobacco with other crops to adequately house and feed myself and my slaves. Don't fret, Damian, I'll keep you busy enough shipping all my wheat."

"Wheat?"

"And corn. Acres of it. We're going to build mills at Miramer, with huge grinding stones. Blame it on my wife if you don't like the notion. It was her idea."

Farrell grunted at Teddie, then scowled at Damian, who nodded vigorously and quickly left the cabin.

Farrell swept a hand at Teddie, his voice ringing sternly. "Theodora, dress yourself." He glared at Miles. "Five minutes, Winchester. Have her on deck, preferably with a story I can believe."

Even before the door slammed behind Farrell's swinging coattails, Teddie was in Miles's arms.

"Tell me it's over," she choked against his shoulder, feeling the last of her defenses slipping, the tears spilling in bucketfuls down her cheeks. "All of the deception, the secrets. . . . Tell me we will live in peace."

"It's over," he murmured, gathering her into the wonder of his embrace. "My love, my reckless bride, by afternoon the entire British presence in the bay will be destroyed. The American fleet will rule these waters once again. And all because of one duplicitous, scheming female."

"And what of Will?"

"He will have a home at Miramer, of course. With us and the brood of children you promised me." His hands roamed over her hips, pressing her loins deep against his. "Remember, wife?"

Teddie suppressed a smile, pressing her advantage. "But Will loves the sea, Winchester. He always has."

"Fine. Damian will need a strong first mate."

"Thank you, Winchester."

"He saved my life, Teddie. And he's the brother of the woman I love." He nuzzled her neck. "There's nothing more to say. Do stop talking and kiss me."

"Oh, but there is," she whispered, cupping his beloved face between her hands. "Say it again. The part about—"

His mouth brushed hers. "I love you, duplicitous wife."

Her lips parted beneath his in a soul-stirring kiss that lifted her toes from the planks. The sheet rustled to the floor.

"I will miss our midnight rendezvous," Teddie murmured as he laid her back upon the sheets.

He loomed over her, magnificent, emboldened, with love shining in his dark eyes. "Give the Night Hawk reason, my love, and he will ride deep and long into the night, every night if need be."

"Indeed. It may take more than once to get me with child. We will have to pursue it as we do everything else, Winchester."

"And how is that, wife?" he murmured, pressing between her thighs and lifting her up against him.

"Why, with boldness, recklessness . . . at midnight on the shores of the bay with the tide washing over us. . . ."

He drove the breath from her. "And what would your dear Aunt Edwina say of us, my love?"

"I believe she would approve," Teddie breathed. "And congratulate herself on a game brilliantly conceived. And well-played."

"A delightful woman."

"Stop talking, Winchester. We've only five minutes."

"As you wish, my love."

Commander George Farrell banged on the cabin's thick door for the fourth time. Receiving no reply, he again tested the handle. Finding it locked, he swung a scowl on Jules Reynolds and snapped, "What the devil are they doing in there?"

"A pity you must ask, sir."

Farrell flushed and drew himself up. "The devil take Winchester, he's bound by contract not to—'' The commander bit off his words.

Reynolds lifted a brow, a half-smile curving his generous mouth. "Indeed. Bound not to do what, if I may ask, sir? In my experience, Commander, contracts have never stood in the way of true love, particularly those contracts that forbid certain intimacies. In fact, forbidding an act usually hastens its occurrence. In Winchester's case I'd say it virtually guaranteed it. Fool is the fellow who would attempt to thwart it, I say.''

"A bold fellow, aren't you?''

"So the women say, sir.''

"Friend of Winchester's, I take it.''

"Yes, sir. A very good friend. Reynolds is the name. Jules Reynolds.''

Farrell's eyes narrowed. "Ah, yes, I know your story well. Still carrying that lead ball in your thigh, I see. A damned shame. You were a brilliant captain, Reynolds. I'm not the sort to punish a man for a bit of reckless thinking with regard to a woman, and a fickle one at that. Indeed, I could use your expertise on board my ship. Think about it.''

"I will, sir.''

"Winchester should be at the wheel of a ship as well.''

"I believe he has all the reason any man needs to take an extended liberty, sir. For the rest of his life. I'd say he earned it.''

"That may be.'' Farrell scowled at the door for several moments. "Damned woman was right.''

"Sir?''

Farrell slashed a hand through the air. "My wife. She's always so damned right about these things.''

"Women usually are, sir.''

Farrell slanted Reynolds a curious look. "I suppose that sort of thinking is what makes you so appealing to them, eh?''

"It helps, sir.''

"And God knows we men need all the help we can get, particularly when a woman knows she's right.'' Heaving a war-weary sigh, Farrell glanced at the flask Reynolds carried. "I don't suppose that's rum you've got there?''

"Indeed, it is, sir. Fine Jamaican."

"What say you show me where the devil Winchester stows it. And while you're at it, tell me what you know about the Night Hawk."

"The Night Hawk?" Reynolds turned toward the hold, a secretive smile curving his lips. "Merely legend, sir. And I believe that's the way he'll remain."

Dear Reader,

I've heard it said that writers feel a natural affinity for a particular geographic area, a place where their soul feels more "at home" than any other. I have two special places. When I was in London several years ago, I cried my way onto the plane to come home. It felt so wrong to be leaving England. Closer to home, that special place is the area of southeastern Virginia that extends from Charles County to Norfolk and south to the Albemarle Sound and the Outer Banks of North Carolina. This is a bit unfortunate, because my husband works for a company that's headquartered in a western suburb of Chicago. Still, that doesn't keep me from packing up the van and the three kids every June and driving for two days to the Outer Banks. I love the shore there, especially when the ocean churns gunmetal gray and the sky hovers low. I stare out over those waters and feel a hundred stories bubbling inside of me. The beaches there are largely unspoiled. The horses run wild, the bramble creeps at its whim. It's very easy to imagine that a British man-of-war's sails will suddenly appear on the horizon, much as they did in 1812 when England thought to conquer America a second time. This story was born on that beach, while the boys made sand castles at my feet and my husband kayaked and Grandma sat under the beach umbrella slathering sun screen on the baby. I'd love to hear from readers, and I promise to answer every letter. Please write to me at P.O. Box 510, Plainfield, Ill. 60544.

Sincerely,

Kit Garland